BETTER OFF
~~DEAD~~WED
IN DEADWOOD

W0008021

ANN CHARLES

ILLUSTRATED BY C.S. KUNKLE

Cover Art by C.S. Kunkle
Cover Design by Sharon Benton
Editing by Mimi (The Grammar Chick)

Printed in the United States of America

Print book ISBN: 978-1-940364-20-9
Published by: Ann Charles

Ann Charles

BETTER OFF
DEAD~~WED~~
IN DEADWOOD

"Flirty, Frisky, Frantic and Frightening … *Better Off Dead* is just plain Fun!!!!"
~**Terri Reid**, Bestselling Author of the Mary O'Reilly Paranormal Mystery Series

"If you like your amateur sleuths smart and smart-mouthed, your action fast, and your characters the type of people you'd love to meet in real life, you couldn't be happier than picking up *Better Off Dead in Deadwood*!"
~**Mary Buckham**, Award-winning Author of the Invisible Recruit Series

"Sassy, edge of the seat suspenseful, and laugh out loud funny. I couldn't turn the pages fast enough!"
~**Wendy Delaney**, Author of *Trudy, Madly, Deeply* (Working Stiffs Mystery Series)

"A sexy, fast-paced mystery! Another must-read that only makes me hungry for book five."
~**Jacquie Rogers**, Author of the Hearts of Owyhee Series

"Once again, Ann Charles grabs you by the goosebumps and never lets go."
~**Amber Scott**, Bestselling Kindle Author of *Stealing Dusk*

"Fantastic and amazing five-star read! Ann will have you pleading for more of her famous cliffhangers."
~**Kriss Mo**rton

Also by Ann Charles

Deadwood Mystery Series
Nearly Departed in Deadwood (Book 1)
Optical Delusions in Deadwood (Book 2)
Dead Case in Deadwood (Book 3)
Better Off Dead in Deadwood (Book 4)
An Ex to Grind in Deadwood (Book 5)

Short Stories from the Deadwood Mystery Series
Deadwood Shorts: Seeing Trouble
Deadwood Shorts: Boot Points

Jackrabbit Junction Mystery Series
Dance of the Winnebagos (Book 1)
Jackrabbit Junction Jitters (Book 2)
The Great Jackalope Stampede (Book 3)

Goldwash Mystery Series (a future series)
The Old Man's Back in Town (Short Story)

Coming Next from Ann Charles

Dig Site Mystery Series
Look What the Wind Blew In (Book 1)
(Starring Quint Parker, the brother of Violet Parker from the Deadwood
Mystery Series)

Deadwood Mystery Series
Meanwhile Back in Deadwood (Book 6)

Jackrabbit Junction Mystery Series
The Rowdy Coyote Rumble (Book 4)

Dear Reader,

I'm often asked, "How many Deadwood books do you plan on writing?" With this fourth book in front of you, I thought you might be wondering the same thing.

An organized author would have all the books planned out with a high-level outline that indicated how she was going to weave the series plotline through each book, and how everything was going to end and when. Fortunately for you, Violet Parker had other plans.

When I started writing this series, I put together a high-level plot plan for multiple books. I really did! I was going to go about this whole business of writing a series as planned. By the time I'd finished writing the first book, NEARLY DEPARTED IN DEADWOOD, I was already "off" plan and had to pretty much scrap the rest of what I'd written down. At that point, I threw my hands up in the air and told Violet, "Fine, you tell the dang story; I'll just keep notes."

She took over and ever since, I've tried to keep up on the keyboard. The last time I asked Violet how many books she thought it might take to tell this story, she looked at me like I was wearing a red rubber nose and rainbow-colored wig and said, "As many as it takes to reach 'happily ever after.'"

Do I know how it's all going to end? Yes. Well, sort of. I think I do, anyway. But maybe not. With every book, I keep digging and realizing that this adventure goes much much deeper than I ever expected. Like in the mines now filled with water beneath Deadwood and Lead, there are story veins leading in many directions that are rich with fun-filled chambers yet to be explored. New characters arrive on scene with each book, adding more laughs and nail-biting anxieties to the world we're discovering with every page.

Will Violet always leave you hanging at the end of the books in this series? Let's ask my Magic 8 Ball ... It says, "As I see it, yes." There you go. Seriously, this is going to be a long tale, and I need to divide it into books to give everyone a break—the characters, me, and you. I've always enjoyed shows on television that have season finales which leave me excited and anxious for the next installment. My goal is similar; however, I often receive emails in the middle of the night full of cursing because someone couldn't put the book down and now must wait until I finish writing the next. While I don't like to frustrate people, those emails do make me chuckle. I've learned some very colorful language thanks to these folks.

Will the real residents in Deadwood and Lead grow tired of me sitting on benches along their Main Street and daydreaming about Violet's world? I hope not. Judging from their entertaining, exciting histories, they are pretty tolerant of quirky characters.

I hope you enjoy this most recent slice of Violet Parker's life. I sure did a lot of chuckling and wincing and grinning and holding my breath as she told it to me.

Hold on tight, because the ride is getting a little bumpy now.

Welcome back to Deadwood ... and Lead.

Ann Charles

www.anncharles.com

This one is for Mom.

*You've been so wonderful with all of your love and support.
I hope you can still walk through the grocery store in Lead without
having to hide your face after this book is published*

Acknowledgments

This fourth book in the Deadwood Mystery series took a lot of help. In addition to my usual critique partners, advance readers, and editors, I had over two hundred fantastic beta readers who volunteered their time and knowledge to help polish this book to its final shine. In addition to all of these generous readers I want to mention:

My husband and kids and mouthy cat

Mimi "The Grammar Chick" (editor)

My brother, Charles (C.S) Kunkle (cover artist and illustrator) and Sharon Benton (cover graphic artist)

My publicists and sales help—Margo Taylor (and Dave), Janelle Andis, Judy Routt, and Wendy Gildersleeve

First and second draft crew: Beth Harris, Wendy Delaney, Marcia Britton, Mary Ida Kunkle, Paul Franklin, Jody Sherin, Renelle Wilson, Sue Stone-Douglas, Marguerite Phipps, Sharon Benton, Margo Taylor, and Cammie Hall

Terri Reid, Mary Buckham, and Kriss Morton

Jacquie Rogers, Amber Scott, Gerri Russell, and Joleen James

My coworkers at my day job

Neil McNeill

My family

Dr. Steven Fox

The fun and amazingly supportive people of the Black Hills of South Dakota and the surrounding towns and cities, including Kim Rupp from Executive Lodging of the Black Hills, Sarah Carlson from the Historic Homestake Opera House, the Adams Bros. Bookstore, the Homestake Visitor Center, the Lead Chamber of Commerce, Karen Everett from the Lead-Deadwood Arts Council, the Deadwood Chamber of Commerce, the Pack Horse Liquor & Convenience Store and crew, the congregation of the Nemo Church, Janelle Andis from Custer Crossing Store and Campground, and Mary Abell.

Finally, my brother, Clint Taylor (For the Black Hills dirt-bike memories—nobody crashes and burns on those dirt roads like you.)

BETTER OFF DEAD WED IN DEADWOOD

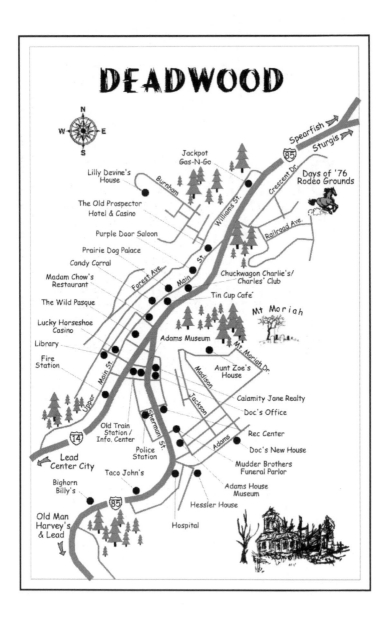

DEADWOOD

Jackpot
Gas-N-Go

Lilly Devine's
House

The Old Prospector
Hotel & Casino

Purple Door Saloon

Prairie Dog Palace

Candy Corral

Madam Chow's
Restaurant

The Wild Pasque

Lucky Horseshoe
Casino

Library

Fire
Station

Spearfish

Sturgis

Days of '76
Rodeo Grounds

Burnham

Williams St.

Crescent Dr.

Railroad Ave.

Forest Ave.

Main St.

Chuckwagon Charlie's/
Charles' Club

Tin Cup Cafe

Mt Moriah

Adams Museum

Mt. Moriah Dr.

Aunt Zoe's
House

Madison

Calamity Jane Realty

Doc's Office

Jackson

Rec Center

Adams

Doc's New House

Upper Main St.

Sherman St.

Old Train
Station /
Info. Center

Lead
Center City

Police
Station

Taco John's

Bighorn
Billy's

Old Man
Harvey's
& Lead

Mudder Brothers
Funeral Parlor

Adams House
Museum

Hessler House

Hospital

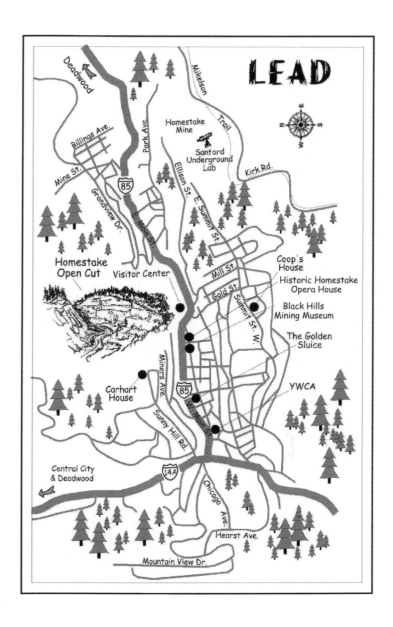

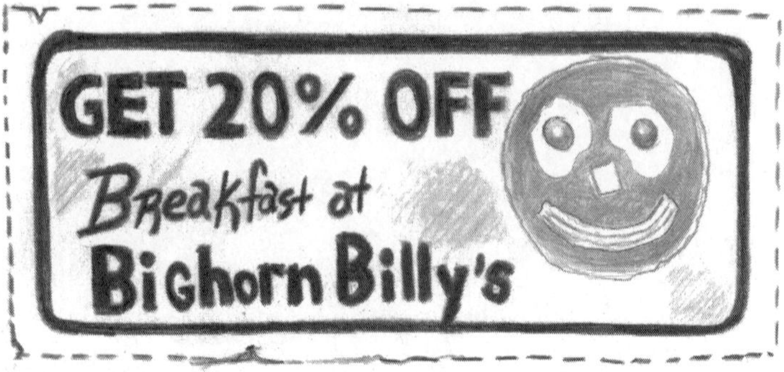
GET 20% OFF
Breakfast at
Bighorn Billy's

Chapter One

Deadwood, South Dakota
Saturday, September 1st

Y ou need to get your ass back in gear, Violet," Old Man Harvey told me. "The world's still spinnin'."

"I just can't believe Jane's dead," I said over the din of conversation surrounding us in Bighorn Billy's Diner, a local favorite here in Deadwood.

I picked at my lunch salad, pushing the lettuce around on my plate, looking for life's answers in between the leaves.

"Death will hornswoggle you like that," Harvey said. "It's like losing a molar; you're gonna keep jabbin' your tongue in that hole for a bit, but you'll get used to it. We all do."

A week had passed since Detective Cooper and his boys in blue had hauled my boss's body up from the bottom of the cavernous pit of Lead's Open Cut mining area, but I still hadn't been able to digest the fact that she was gone. Not even after spending the last two hours teary-eyed at her memorial service.

Gone.

Forever.

Damn.

I sighed, glancing across the table at Harvey.

He flashed me a grin. "Look on the bright side—I'm still around to keep you out of trouble."

That made me smile. "Lucky me."

Willis Harvey was known in Deadwood and in Lead—heck, in all of the northern Black Hills—for three things: chasing skirts, ruffling feathers, and sleeping with Bessie, his double-barreled shotgun.

Back in July when I'd agreed to be his real estate agent and sell his ranch south of town, he'd finagled an arrangement for a weekly meal, on me. Desperate Realtors called for desperate deals, and all that jive. Several meals and murder victims later, the ornery codger had glued himself to my side as my bodyguard and partner in crime … and crime solving.

Taking a sip of steaming coffee, I peered around the dining room at all of the folks dressed in dark colors, just like Harvey and me, fresh from Mudder Brothers Funeral Parlor. The murmurs of grief were muffled now by greasy burgers, drowned out by the clanking of silverware on plates and the scraping of chairs on linoleum.

Life was moving on without Jane.

It was time for me to get moving again, too. There were houses to sell, dollars to make, kids to clothe and feed—namely my two almost-ten-year-olds who both seemed to be hollow from the neck down these days.

"Have you heard any more rumors about what happened to Jane?" Harvey asked, shoving a bite of strawberry-rhubarb pie in his pie-hole.

"No. Cooper's being extremely closemouthed."

Maddeningly so.

Detective Cooper had no problem rattling off his list of questions, but when it came to supplying answers, he kept repeating, "That's police business, Ms. Parker."

I had daydreams of shoving the pen he kept clicking during his interrogations some place where the sun didn't shine, starting with his broken nose.

Harvey shook his head. "I can't believe Jane's ex-husband had the *cojones* to show up at her service with that sweet young piece of candy on his arm."

Months ago, Jane had caught her husband in the act of burning up the sheets on her own bed with a much younger firecracker.

"You mean Jane's *almost* ex," I clarified, stabbing at my salad. "Now I guess he's officially Jane's widower."

"You know, I could swear I saw his filly wrestlin' in a mud-covered bikini last year over in Sturgis during the biker rally."

After seeing the skimpy, black lace dress she'd been popping out of at the service, that wouldn't surprise me. "You think he'll be my boss now?"

For the last couple of months, Jane had been in the process of divorcing his no-good, cheating ass. She'd been trying her damnedest to keep Calamity Jane Realty, along with me and the other two agents who worked there, out of the jerk's greedy mitts.

Shrugging, Harvey said around a mouthful of pie, "Depends if Jane had her will up to snuff."

I swallowed more coffee, contemplating a suspicion that had been festering in my head since hearing Jane was gone. "There's no way I could work for the man who killed her."

Harvey's bushy eyebrows wrinkled. "Did you dump some hooch in your coffee when I wasn't lookin'?"

"No," I put my cup down. "I'm just saying he certainly pushed her to the edge."

A flurry of movement at the door caught my attention.

I watched as a handsome, square-jawed, dark-haired man in a sleek suit paused on his way over the threshold. I'd seen him earlier at Mudder Brothers and guessed him to be in his early forties.

He shook the hands of several lunch patrons who'd swarmed him upon entry. Then he held the door for a petite blonde in a dark blue jersey dress, touching her lower back as they made their way toward an open table. Several members of the funeral crowd greeted him with smiles and nods as he passed.

"Who's that?" I asked, jutting my chin at Mr. Popularity. "The guy in the suit."

"There are a lot of suits in here, girl. We just came from a funeral, remember?"

"The one with that busty blonde in blue on his arm."

I figured that would make Harvey sit up and take notice. I was right. His gaze zeroed in on the woman.

"That's Dominick Masterson and his wife, Ginny. She's purty, but not busty."

"Why did he get to sit in the front row at Jane's service? Is he related to her?"

"Nah, not that I've ever heard, anyway."

Harvey would know; after spending his whole life in the northern Black Hills, he could tell the story of pretty much anyone with a Deadwood or a Lead zip code.

"Is he in real estate, too?" I asked.

"Politics. Right now he's runnin' for mayor up in Lead."

A politician—and a handsome one at that. That made him doubly suspect in my book. Suspect of what, I had no idea, but my history with politicians involved dinners, drinks, and psychotic girlfriends who tied me to a chair, sliced open my thumb, and offered my womb for rent to a demon.

"Pull in your horns, girl," Harvey said under his breath.

"What?"

"Dominick is a good kid. I've known him ever since he was just knee high to a coyote. He worked hard to support his momma when his daddy up and left town."

"Left?"

"Yep, just disappeared one day, leavin' Dominick and his momma alone to fend for themselves. The boy was still wet behind the ears. Years later, someone said they saw his old man at a bar over in Yankton, but they were probably three sheets to the wind."

I assumed that meant "drunk" in Harvey speak.

Hmmm. Dominick and my kids had something in common—no father.

"Masterson's daddy had to be a few clowns short of a rodeo, though," Harvey continued. "That boy's momma was as fine as cream gravy. Stacked clear to here," he held his hand up to his chin, "with hips that just begged to be saddled."

I wrinkled my nose at him.

"Ginny reminds me a lot of her, only not as curvy."

"Is his mom dead?"

Harvey frowned. "You have death on the brain. No, she moved down South years ago, tired of the snow."

As hot as today had been, it was hard to believe the Black Hills would ever cool off, let alone be buried under several feet of snow anytime soon.

"How come I've never seen this Dominick guy before

now?" I asked.

"Probably because you've been livin', eatin', and breathin' Doc for the past month. Hell, heifers in heat moan less."

My cheeks warmed. "I have not."

"How do you spell 'obsessed'?"

"Zip it, old man." My fascination with Doc Nyce wasn't an obsession. It was more of an all-encompassing crush.

Back in July, I'd fallen flat on my face for Doc. By that, I meant I'd walked out Calamity Jane's front door one day, tripped over some boxes stacked in my path, and landed face-down on the sidewalk. When I'd looked up, Doc had been standing over me with his dark hair and even darker eyes. Days later, he'd crossed my threshold looking to buy a house. His animal magnetism had pretty much leapt over my desk and pounced on me, startling the pheromones right out of me.

It'd been amazing that I'd been able to keep our agent-client relationship platonic for three weeks, considering that I'd gone without sex for years. Supporting and raising two kids on my own had left little time for dinner and dancing. I'd spent too many long, lonely nights watching Elvis, Gregory Peck, and young Captain Kirk on the television.

For three weeks I'd held out, but after one touch from Doc in a dark stairwell, my knees had gone weak. That one touch led to more, of course, which led to nakedness, and then to betraying my best friend, Natalie Beals.

My stomach knotted as it often did this last week when I thought of Natalie and the hurt pinching her face when she'd caught Doc and me K-I-S-S-I-N-G.

Damn her for falling for the one guy to whom I might be willing to offer my heart and soul for the first time since getting knocked up with twins. Damn me for being such a chicken shit and waiting too long to tell her the truth about Doc and me.

Natalie still wasn't returning my phone calls or text messages, not that I could blame her. But I had to keep trying. I wasn't willing to lose decades of sharing clothes, beers, and laughs over one guy.

Albeit one charming guy.

One very charming guy who could do things with his tongue

that … I was digressing.

"I'm not obsessed with Doc."

Harvey snorted. "Right, and Mount Rushmore is chiseled out of marshmallows. Where is Doc, anyway? Why didn't he show up at Jane's service?"

Because Doc had a secret that only I knew—he could smell dead people, as in the already buried kind that returned in the wispy form to haunt the living. I figured him for some kind of medium, but he had yet to use a label and cringed every time I referred to his ability as "smelling" ghosts.

I shoved more salad around on my plate.

The sniffing out ghosts sounded a little off-rocker, but I *think* I pretty much believed him. Not that I'd ever witnessed anything wispy myself, but after going on enough tours of ghostly haunts with Doc, watching him react, and hearing him spill secrets that he couldn't have figured out without a party-line to the past, my inner skeptic was courting belief.

Attending Jane's service would have risked Doc having a public display of reaction to the possible ectoplasmic crowd in the funeral parlor. We'd both agreed it was better for him to pay his respects at Jane's grave alone later.

"Doc woke up with a migraine," I lied while hiding behind my coffee cup. My nose often twitched when I fibbed, and Harvey knew my tell. "I told him to stay home."

Harvey seemed to accept this without a second thought. "I need to see him about a mule."

That made me lower my cup a little. "Isn't that code for having to go to the bathroom?"

"Yup. It's also code for I got some money from an uncle who died last month but can't collect it on account of a damned mule."

I didn't even try to make sense of that. "It sounds like you need a vet, not a financial planner."

Doc played with people's money as a day job. With clients like Harvey, who talked him up all over town, and Detective Cooper, who shared his name around the police station, Doc's business had been booming lately. Unfortunately, that meant I got to see even less of him.

Speaking of the detective, I asked Harvey, "Do you think you could ask Cooper what's going on behind the scenes with Jane's case? Maybe get him a little liquored up first to oil his lips."

"Liquor doesn't work on my nephew, only bullets and babes do." He pointed his fork at my chest. "Why don't you pop some buttons, shove a Colt .45 Peacemaker down your pants, and ask him yourself?"

I knocked his fork away. "No way. I don't relish seeing Cooper anytime soon."

Truth be told, I'd been a little surprised *not* to see the detective at Jane's funeral. But then I figured that maybe he didn't want to be bombarded by questions. It wasn't every day a body ended up in the Open Cut. In fact, I didn't know if one ever had before Jane's.

"What makes you think it's an actual *case* and not just a suicide like the paper suggested?" Harvey asked.

"I can't see Jane walking down to the bottom of the pit and slitting her wrists."

"There's no way she could have jumped and made it to the bottom," Harvey said, "not with the way those walls are staggered."

I shoved my salad remains away. "If it's not suicide, then someone left her there. But who'd do that? And why?"

"Let's ask Coop."

"I told you, I don't want to see him again for a while."

"Well, you'd better make tracks then, because he's headin' our way."

What? I looked around and ran smack dab into Detective Cooper's steely glare. Where had he come from? The back door?

He weaved through the tables, never taking his eyes off of me. The Terminator had taken tough-guy lessons from Cooper, who looked like a pissed-off version of Daniel Craig with his two black-and-blue eyes and steri-strip-covered, broken nose.

I didn't waste calories trying to smile when he loomed over me.

"I need you to come down to the station, Ms. Parker."

"Am I under arrest?"

"Not yet."

"What does that mean?"

"It means I need you to come down to the station to answer some questions."

"You can ask them right now."

He frowned at his uncle and said in a low voice for our ears only, "No, I can't."

"Is this about George or Jane?" I mouthed.

"I'll disclose my purpose for your visit when we are in my office."

"Nod once for George," Harvey whispered, "twice for Jane."

Cooper's rugged face hardened even more.

I raised one eyebrow. "You heard your uncle."

Growling in his throat, he nodded twice.

What about Jane?

"You can't arrest me just to get me to answer questions about my boss."

"Yes, I can." He leaned over and spoke next to my ear. "I'm opening a murder investigation, and you're on my list of usual suspects."

I could feel my eyes bulge.

Murder?

Jane?

Me?

"Now are you coming with me," Cooper continued, his tone quiet, yet menacing. "Or do I have to arrest you first?"

Chapter Two

After some foot dragging on my part, and a couple of minutes full of me whining about not being emotionally ready to talk about Jane so soon after her service, Detective Cooper backed off.

Well, sort of.

He gave me exactly one hour to get my hiney down to his office before he came looking for me with a pair of handcuffs.

I got the distinct feeling he wasn't in the mood to play cat and mouse with me this time. Maybe it was the way he'd white-knuckled the table while I sat there sipping my coffee in front of him; or it might have been his parting comment of "Don't fuck with me on this, Parker."

Harvey drove me back to work, where I'd parked my current ride—his ancient, green, dilapidated pickup, aka the Picklemobile.

As soon as I landed my commission check from my pending sale of The Old Prospector Hotel, I would head down to Rapid City to buy a new family truckster. This time I'd make sure I had fire insurance on the sucker. I'd learned my lesson after the last psycho had taken her jealousy out on my poor Bronco with matches.

"Drop me off by the back door," I told Harvey as he pulled into the parking lot behind Calamity Jane Realty.

"You ain't gonna work today, are you? We should be double-fistin' beers up in Lead at The Golden Sluice over this mess."

I'd been drowning in my sorrow for a week now. It was time to dog-paddle back to shore.

"Jane would be happy that I'm working on the day of her funeral and you know it. Besides, I can't get drunk now. I need to be on my toes when I go to see your nephew."

Interrogations by Cooper always made me squirm. It'd be less painful if he'd just jam a truth-telling bug up my nose to tap directly into my brain and be done with it.

Harvey braked next to the back door. "So you're actually gonna go see Coop, eh?"

The codger knew me too well. I'd already run through several escape scenarios involving me, my kids, and the General Lee from *The Dukes of Hazzard*. I had a feeling, though, that Cooper wouldn't just stop the car chase at the county line and shake his fist at me like the cop in the old TV show.

"The detective isn't really giving me much of a choice this time."

"Are you plannin' to honeyfuggle him?" he asked.

Honeyfuggle? What the heck did that mean? Was that what Harvey and his old flame did with that homemade love goop?

My mind flashed a bawdy image of Cooper dripping with honey, making me cringe and blush at the same time. "I'm not honeyfuggling with anyone, you dirty bird."

Although, I wouldn't have a problem licking the sticky stuff off Doc.

Harvey's loud hoot of laughter made me wince. "You're the one with a gutter mind. Honeyfuggle means you're gonna sweet-talk Coop while you pull the wool over his eyes."

"Oh, *that* kind of honeyfuggling."

"What did you think I meant, girl?" The twinkle in his eyes told me he knew exactly what I'd thought he meant.

"Never mind. You could have just asked if I were going to deceive Cooper."

"And miss watching you spit and sputter? Where's the fun in that?"

"Shut up, old man." I grabbed my tote and purse, hopped out, and slammed the pickup door behind me.

"Call me as soon as you're done with Coop," Harvey hollered through the open window. "I want to know all the details, especially the honeyfuggling ones."

With another hoot of laughter, he drove off.

I'd taken a couple of steps toward the back door of Calamity

Jane Realty when I heard Doc call my name.

I turned around and scanned the parking lot.

He stood next to his car, a sexy 1969 black Camaro SS with rally stripes, parked about ten stalls down from his usual spot.

I had several fantasies involving Doc's car—some of them even included him.

Crossing the lot, I let my gaze drift down over Doc's navy blue shirt and khakis. Very professional—creases and all today. His dark hair was combed back, the shallow cleft visible on his smooth-shaven chin. But I preferred his ensemble the last time I'd stood in his bedroom. Even better, skip the towel, finger muss his hair, and add a day or two's worth of beard. Then I'd bring out the honey jar.

"You coming or going?" I asked, leaning against the back quarter panel of his car, keeping some space between us in case anyone was watching.

While we weren't going out of our way to hide that I was showing him a lot more these days than just empty houses, my kids were still clueless about his being anything other than a good friend, and I wasn't in a hurry to change that. Not to mention I wanted to avoid a chance sighting by Natalie, who probably had a voodoo doll of me and was just waiting for another reason to hold it over a gas burner.

"Going," he answered, his sunglasses hiding his brown eyes and whatever was going on behind them. "I like that black dress."

"You've seen me wear it before."

I'd come from a funeral then, too, only that one had ended in my hiding in a crate from one of the lurking Mudder brothers.

"I know. I remember removing it with my teeth."

So did I.

So did my libido, which rolled over and purred at the idea of getting Doc alone and repeating the experience.

"That's right," I said, "but I think I was wearing panties *that* time."

His Adam's apple bobbed. "You were. I remember those, too."

"Black and lacy, weren't they?"

"Satin, not lace, with a little red bow at the top," he said, his voice a tad gravelly.

"Oh, yeah, I forgot about the bow."

"I didn't. Twenty bucks says you're lying about not wearing any now."

He'd win that bet. I was wearing panties, and a slip, too. Who didn't wear underwear to a funeral, especially a friend's service? Well, besides Jane's sleazy widower's tramp? Or Harvey, who claimed going commando in polyester kept heat rashes at bay.

But I was willing to gamble and lose on this with Doc. I had a feeling he wouldn't stop at calling my bluff, and due to life's most recent curveball, I hadn't had the chance to be alone with him since before Jane had died. After a week of wallowing in death, I was ready to get back to living and all of the fun that came with it—especially the kind of fun Doc offered.

I took a step toward him and pulled the hem of my dress up an inch or two, pretending I was adjusting it in case we had any onlookers.

"Care to step into your office and peek for yourself?" I asked.

Doc's focus raked down to my legs, his chin lowering. He whistled low. "Damn."

Leaning closer, I breathed in the subtle aroma of his woodsy cologne, letting his scent fill me. It wasn't enough.

I slid my hem a little higher up my right thigh. "Or you could just frisk me ... against your desk."

He sucked air in between his teeth.

"Is that a 'Yes'?" I asked.

"It's a 'Yes, but I can't.'"

"Oh." I let my hem fall. "They have pills for that now, you know." I couldn't hold in my chuckle.

His attention shifted back to my face. "You're going to pay, vixen, when I get back from Keystone tonight."

"Going to see the men on the mountain, are you?" Mount Rushmore was a hop and a skip down the road from there.

"One man and according to the map, he lives in a valley. A new client."

I licked my lips, aiming for the seductive siren look, wishing I hadn't eaten off my lip gloss at lunch. "You sure you can't slip inside for a moment?"

"Nice pun, but I only have a couple of minutes to spare right now. The next time I have you naked, I want to take my time and explore every inch of your soft skin."

Hmmm. There were a couple of inches here and there on my body that I'd rather he never found. After having the twins, I'd roped off a couple of areas and labeled them as no man's land.

A half-smile lifted one corner of his mouth. "Although that desk frisking idea is now on my to-do list."

He rested his arm on his door, his keys dangling from his fingers, looking for all the world like we were discussing the benefits of diversifying my portfolio, not back-arching, sweaty sex on his desk.

I, on the other hand, could have used a bag of ice to dump down my underwear.

He reached out and brushed something off my shoulder, his fingers lingering, teasing. "How was Jane's service?"

My tongue found that missing molar hole once again that Harvey had talked about during lunch.

"Heart wrenching." Then I thought about some of the attendees. "But interesting."

His hand caught mine, squeezing it gently before letting go. "I'm sorry I wasn't there with you."

I shrugged. "It was for the best. Harvey let me sniffle on his shoulder."

"So why was it 'interesting'? Was Detective Cooper there keeping an eye on the scene?"

"No, thank God. But everyone else in town was."

Harvey had whispered a play-by-play of many of those who came through, helping to keep my mind off the reason we were there.

Lowering my tote to the asphalt, I said, "I had no idea Jane had such a wide circle of friends."

"Nothing draws people like funerals."

"Harvey figured it was because of the whole Open Cut mine mystery. People wanted to see Jane's body."

Unfortunately for them, there was no body to view. No urn either. Just a big, happy picture of her in a white sweater with a red scarf. My eyes got misty behind my sunglasses. I was going to miss her perky smile and those damned lists she loved to write and post.

Doc cocked his head to the side. "Did I hear Harvey say something about Cooper before he drove off?"

"Yeah," I blinked away my tears. "Cooper stopped by Bighorn Billy's after the service. I have to go see him shortly."

"Why?"

"He's opening a murder investigation."

Doc's jaw tightened. "What's that got to do with you?"

"He used the words 'usual suspect.'"

"What? No." He scrubbed his fingers through his hair. "Christ."

"My reaction was similar. Only there were more swear words involved."

"He's got to be messing with you."

"Or not. I didn't get any practical joke vibes off of him." And he certainly wasn't wearing a daisy that squirted water nor did he ask me to pull his finger.

Truth be told, the cold fury in Cooper's eyes had made part of me want to crawl under the table and cling to Harvey's leg. The other part of me was too stubborn—or stupid—to realize that standing up to Cooper like I had was just asking for him to throw me in jail and swallow the key.

As much as I'd rather hide behind Doc than go see Cooper, I was curious to find out what it was that had him breathing fire all over me.

"Maybe you should talk to a lawyer," Doc said.

"No time for that. I told Cooper I'd be there in …" I grabbed Doc's wrist and looked at his watch, "… forty-five minutes."

Doc caught my hand when I let go of his wrist. His thumb rubbed circles in the center of my palm, tickling, sending ripples of pleasure up my arm.

"This doesn't make sense," he said. "How could you be a suspect in Jane's murder? You were mixed up in the Mudder

Brothers' mess at the time and he knows it."

"Maybe he forgot about my whereabouts with this Jane business."

Doc's lips twitched. "His broken nose should remind him every time he looks in the mirror."

I grimaced. "Well, there is that."

Cooper had made the mistake of sneaking up behind me in the basement of Mudder Brothers Funeral Parlor when a killer was on the loose. And then he got grabby. That broken nose was the result of pure fear and adrenaline—mine. Knocking him out cold and then borrowing his gun to shoot at someone hadn't helped our bonding any, either.

Shaking all thoughts of Cooper and his anger-management issue from my head, I pulled my hand away from Doc's teasing touch. It was that or hit him over the head with my purse, drag him by the leg into his office, and have my wicked way with him.

"Speaking of Mudder Brothers," I said, "I need you to take care of something for me." I reached inside my bag.

"What now?" His tone sounded suspicious.

I glanced around, then pulled out a black bottle with a cork in it and handed it to him. "This."

Doc took it after a moment's hesitation. "What is it?"

I pushed his hand holding the bottle lower, shielding it from the rest of the parking lot with my body.

"Hide it under that blanket in your backseat and then I'll tell you."

"How come I get the feeling I'm not going to like where this is heading?" he asked, but hid it anyway. "Okay, what is it?"

I leaned closer and mouthed, "A black bottle."

"I can see that, Nancy Drew. Where did you get it?"

"Mudder Brothers."

"Oh, hell."

"I found it in the crate in the back room last week before the shit hit the fan."

Doc had arrived on the funeral parlor scene after I'd knocked out Cooper and was trying to use his gun to take out the albino chasing after me. I shivered just thinking about the freaky, white-haired guy and his creepy snake-like eyes.

"I stashed it under the front porch before Cooper's men took me to the station for more questioning."

Doc seemed to digest this without too many wrinkles on his forehead. "Violet, please tell me you didn't retrieve that bottle today during Jane's service."

"Of course not."

"Good. Because if someone saw you …"

"I did it before anyone got there. Harvey ran interference for me. Then I stashed it in Mudder Brothers' records closet until the service was over."

Doc cursed under his breath. "Any idea what's in the bottle?"

"No, and Cooper confiscated the rest of the crate so if we break it, we're shit-out-of-luck."

"Did Cooper tell you he confiscated the crate's goods?"

"No, the crate was gone when I peeked in the back room today."

That's where George Mudder had been storing the crates he used to ship God-knew-what back and forth between God-knew-where. Those same crates were where I'd hidden in my black dress. They were also the cause of my coworker almost being filleted on an autopsy table after he'd gotten too nosey about their contents.

"Cooper would have hauled you off to jail if he'd caught you back there again," Doc said. "And I doubt he'd set bail."

"That's why I need you to hide the bottle for me, especially if I end up actually being a suspect in Jane's murder. I'd ask Harvey, but Cooper's out to his house practically every week examining more body parts."

Harvey's ranch had been the scene of the crime for more things than I wanted to think about as his friend and real estate agent.

"Okay," Doc said. "I'll keep the bottle for now. But I'm a little concerned about somebody missing it and coming for you. And if I end up in jail for aiding and abetting, I can't bail you out."

"It's just one bottle."

"It was just one albino, too, and yet a clip full of bullets didn't seem to faze him. Don't you think the safer choice would be to wash your hands of all of George Mudder's mess and let Cooper do the crime solving?"

"Sure, but there's one problem with that. Cooper doesn't believe me about the albino disappearing."

"That's not what he told me."

Say what now? "When did he talk to you?"

"Earlier this week. He stopped by to ask me how long I've been renting the office from Jane and if I'd noticed anyone strange coming and going."

Good questions. Doc's office shared a wall with Calamity Jane Realty.

"Did you see anyone?"

"No." Doc crossed his arms over his chest. "Then he asked me about the albino. I listed what I'd witnessed at Mudder Brothers that night, told him about unloading his gun into the albino to no effect, and then being tossed around like I weighed nothing."

The memory of Doc's body hitting the doorjamb still made me wince. He'd been lucky to get away with just a slight concussion.

"What did Cooper say?"

"He didn't speak, just wrote everything down."

"Why didn't you tell me all of this before?"

"I haven't seen you much between then and now, and when I have, you've been pretty torn up about Jane. It just never seemed like the right time."

"Sorry." I looked down at my black shoes.

He lifted my chin, tracing my jaw. "There's nothing to be sorry for, Violet. You lost your friend. You needed time to mourn."

I blew out a sigh. "Right."

"How are the nightmares?" he asked.

"Still there."

For the last few weeks, I'd been sharing dreamtime with killers, demons, and lately, albinos. I'd been resisting sleep aids, but I wasn't sure how much longer I could stand slaying monsters every night.

Doc lowered his hand. "I have to run or I'm going to be late. Call me after you're finished with Cooper."

He'd have to get in line with Harvey.

"I will."

I wanted to step forward and wrap my arms around him, soaking up the safe, secure feeling I always felt when he was near. But we were in plain view, so I stepped back and patted the roof of his car. "Take care with that bottle."

He nodded. "When you want it back, you're going to have to come to my house and get it."

I knew what that meant. "Deal."

"And wear your boots."

He'd had a fondness for my purple cowboy boots ever since I'd dug my boot heels into him the first time we'd had sex.

"That may be a problem. Natalie has my boots." She'd borrowed them right before our friendship hit the rocks.

He frowned, taking off his sunglasses and cleaning them with his shirt. "I don't suppose she's broken her silence."

"Nope." I pointed at him. "But I'm not giving up."

Not on Natalie forgiving me.

Not on figuring out the whole Mudder Brothers mess.

"You never do," Doc grabbed my finger and tugged me toward him. "Which is one of the reasons I lose sleep at night, damn it."

I glanced around, looking for any gawkers, seeing none.

"Insomnia is more fun with friends," I said as his mouth lowered toward mine. "It could be worse."

He paused inches from my lips, his eyes crinkling at the corners. "Really? What's worse than my girlfriend chasing down a relentless killer albino who likes to decapitate his victims?"

His girlfriend. My heart flip-flopped, the silly thing. Didn't it know that thirty-five-year-old mothers weren't supposed to get such flutters?

"I don't know, maybe two relentless killer albinos," I answered, considering the albino's unaccounted for twin.

Groaning in his throat, he pushed my sunglasses to the top of my head. "And that's partly why I can't think straight during the day anymore."

"Oh, yeah? What else is bugging you?"

His dark eyes zeroed in on my mouth. "This."

He kissed me, taking his slow, sweet time with it. Achingly slow. His tongue teased mine, sending warm trickles down my backbone. Everything south of my bellybutton melted and pooled in my shoes.

Then he was done and gone, sliding into his car, leaving me all cranked up and sparking.

"Call me collect if you end up in jail, Trouble."

Grabbing my tote, I waved as he drove away, fantasizing about sneaking over to his house tonight and tying him to his new bed.

I turned toward Calamity Jane's back door and reality smacked me with a frying pan.

My boss was dead.

This hotel sale might be my last one as a Calamity Jane Real Estate agent if Jane's widower decided to shut us down.

Jane had taken me under her wing and carried me for almost three months with no sales. On top of that, she'd put up with my inability to have a normal agent-client relationship. There was no way another boss would tolerate my shortcomings.

As soon as it leaked out that I had a weekly contracted dinner rendezvous with Harvey, traded kid-sitting shifts with Jeff Wymonds, went on a couple of dates with Wolfgang the pyromaniac, broke Detective Cooper's nose, and ended up in bed with Doc, I would undoubtedly be explaining my assets to a job specialist at the unemployment office.

And that wasn't even including Cornelius Curion, my newest client. I doubted a new boss would be amused by the Abe Lincoln look-a-like who claimed to be a ghost whisperer, or with hearing that I'd joined Abe Jr. for not just one séance, but two.

My career was about to go the way of General Custer's.

I dug for my keys in my purse.

When I reached out to unlock the door, I realized it wasn't locked. Weird. I hadn't seen either Ray's or Mona's SUVs parked in the lot, but maybe one of them had walked over from Mudder Brothers after the funeral.

I took a deep breath and stepped inside, steeling myself

against the pinching loss I felt every time I walked by Jane's closed office door. I could smell Ray's Stetson cologne. I gritted my teeth, gearing up for another round of Rock'em-Sock'em with the dickhead.

The sight of the lights on inside Jane's office and her door wide open surprised me to a skidding halt. I stood on the threshold, frowning.

Somebody had mucked with the shrine. Where were the stacks of papers on the filing cabinet? The piles of receipts on her desk? The random blazers and scarfs, the wadded up pieces of paper strewn here and there, the empty bottles of Jack Daniels?

Besides Detective Cooper and his team of evidence collectors, nobody had touched Jane's stuff.

Until now.

The sound of a certain jackass's extra-loud, extra-fake laughter snapped me out of my stupor.

Ray! He must be the one who'd dismantled the shrine. He probably figured he had dibs on Jane's office after having sex with her in here almost two weeks ago.

Blech! My vagina still shuddered at the notion of him touching Jane that way.

I slammed her office door shut.

"Damn you, Ray Underhill!" I yelled and stormed toward the front of the office where Ray, Mona Hollister, and I all congregated each day. I didn't care if he was talking on the phone; this king-of-the-hill shit was going to stop right now. "Did you even wait until Jane's service was over before making your move on her off—?"

I swallowed the last of my rant at the sight of a strange blond guy with a pair of big broad shoulders over-filling the back of my chair.

Who in the hell was that?

I glanced at Ray, who hated me in plain sight with a sneer on his overly tanned face.

Darn. So much for the two of us forming a chummy new friendship after I had risked my hide to save him and his family jewels from a scalpel-happy albino.

The stranger spun around. A wide smile was carved on his face, joining the fans of crows' feet around his eyes and deep-set lines across his forehead. He was good looking in a used-to-be-a-surfer way and had managed to keep from going to seed south of his chin. I was trying to guess his age when he planted his feet and stood all the way up, up, up.

Holy shit! I took a step back, gaping all the way to the top of his sun-bleached-blond crew cut and back down to his clown-sized shoes. The guy had a good five to six inches on Doc, who stood a head taller than me.

Who ordered the Nordic giant?

Judging from his square-cut jaw and rock-hewn cheekbones, someone must have chiseled him out of a cliff that overlooked a Scandinavian fjord.

"Wow," I said aloud. Whatever else I'd been about to say had been knocked clear out of my head.

Thor, the God of Thunder, smiled down at me, his teeth tight, even, white rectangles, like extra-large Chiclets. Maybe he'd come looking for his big hammer. Maybe I could borrow it to knock that stupid smirk off Ray's face.

"You must be Violet Parker." His voice was as deep as he was tall. "I was just telling Ray that I was hoping to catch you here today."

Oh, no no no. Nuh uh. Nope. There was absolutely no way I was taking this guy on as another client. I had my fill with a dirty old man, a sexy medium, a frustrating ghost hunter, a soon-to-be single dad, and a crotchety detective. I drew the line at a blond giant wearing a green shirt big enough to make into curtains.

Heck, he probably wouldn't even fit in the Picklemobile unless I turned him lengthwise in the cab.

"You were looking for me? Really?" Pasting a smile on my face, I trekked around the monolith and dropped my bag on the corner of my desk. "Have we met bef—"

My desk phone rang.

We both looked at it. I saw the incoming number and recognized the area code.

"If you'll excuse me," I said to the giant, "I need to take this."

He nodded and spun my chair around, holding it out for me.

Nodding my thanks, I picked up the handset on the fourth ring. "Hi, Cornelius."

"I'd like to talk to Violet Parker, please," Cornelius said in my ear.

I rolled my eyes. How many times had he heard my voice now?

"It's me, Cornelius."

"Who's me?"

"Violet."

"Excellent. Your secretary is quick on the draw."

Cornelius wasn't an idiot; he just gave oblivious a new look, which included a top hat, a long black frock coat, and a cane.

"What do you need, Cornelius?"

"There's a slight problem with my funding for the hotel."

My knees gave out, my butt hitting my chair. "Define 'slight problem.'"

Ray snorted.

I tried to shrivel him alive with my glare.

"The money is sort of tied up at the moment," Cornelius said.

Turning my back to Ray, I said in a low voice, "You spoke previously of an abundance of cash."

"I know, and there will be … if we can dump the other property."

"The due date is in a week."

"Could we file some sort of extension?"

Maybe, but … "This isn't your taxes."

"I'm detecting some tension in your voice, Violet."

"You think?"

"Have you ever had your chakras realigned? It's very good for releasing tension and stimulating your mental health."

I was going to realign his chakras with my shoe.

"Cornelius," I said. I may actually have snarled between each syllable.

"Relax, Violet. I just wanted to test you and see how you'd respond to this kind of a situation."

"So you're joking then?"

"Not at all."

I closed my eyes for a moment and counted to five. "Would you like me to come over to the hotel and meet with you to discuss this more?"

"No. I have to go buy some socks and batteries."

The line went dead.

Criminy! I was going to kill him. It would be in all of the papers—Abe Lincoln slain again. The tabloids would name me as a long-lost relative of John Wilkes Booth.

I hung up the phone and turned back around. Two sets of eyes watched me—one wide and curious, the other narrowed and calculating.

Shaking off my Cornelius moment, I turned up the wattage on my smile again and faced off with Thor.

"So, what can I do for you, Mr. ...?"

"Jerry Russo." He strolled over and helped himself to a cup of coffee like he owned the place.

"Are you interested in buying a home in the Deadwood area, Mr. Russo?"

"Not at all. And you can call me Jerry, Violet."

First names already, huh? At least he was a friendly giant.

He used Mona's desk as a chair and took a sip of coffee. Grimacing, he set down the cup. "What I am interested in is watching you sell homes."

I frowned. Was he some kind of real estate voyeur? Next he'd want to fondle my For Sale signs.

"Watching me?"

He nodded. "You see, my ex-wife just passed away, leaving me as the sole surviving partner in a business venture we started together years ago when we were still married."

A low whooshing sound started in my ears.

"Your ex-wife?"

"Jane Grimes."

"So, you were Jane's ..."

"Husband. Her first one, anyway."

I thought she said her first husband was a client, not a partner. I remembered her telling me that when she'd warned me about dating Doc. She must have been in real estate before marrying Jerry and starting Calamity Jane Realty.

"Oh," was all I could think to say. The whooshing grew louder as anxiety flooded my brain. Here he was, the man who would determine my future in Deadwood. Now I understood the fake laughter I'd heard coming from Ray earlier, and I knew who'd cleaned up Jane's office.

Jerry shook his head, sadness lining his cheeks. "I'm going to miss my Janey girl."

Me, too, but I couldn't stop gawking at Janey girl's first husband. I'd always envisioned her ex-husbands smaller, more weasel-looking, not so juggernaut-ish.

Jerry clapped his hands together.

I jumped in surprise.

"I think it's high time we get this office up and running again," he said. "I hope you and my man Ray here are in it to win it, because Jerry Russo doesn't allow any losers on his team."

What about Mona? Had she already talked to Jerry? Was she feeling like a winner yet? Jane's death had hit Mona the hardest of us all. She'd worked with Jane for almost two decades.

Standing, Jerry towered over Ray and me. "Are you ready to go out there and show Deadwood what you got?"

"Yes, sir!" Ray shouted like the rat-bastard bootlicker he was.

"How about you, Violet?" Jerry asked.

My heart panged. Man, I missed Jane.

"Sure," I said with as much enthusiasm as I could muster two hours after the funeral service for my last boss. I'd have to be ready if I wanted to keep my job.

But first, I had an appointment with a gravel-chewing detective regarding the murder of my new boss's ex-wife, for which I'd somehow ended up on a list of "usual" suspects ... again.

Chapter Three

The glass doors of the police station were propped open. Deadwood's crime-busters apparently weren't worried about any convicts spilling out onto the street on this fine, sunny afternoon.

I crested the top step and skirted a pedestal fan blowing warm air in my face. The temperature inside the building felt a good ten degrees hotter than outside. Wonderful, now I'd really be cooked during Detective Cooper's grilling.

The cop at the front desk had his nose buried in the newspaper. Sweat beaded on his forehead and trickled down his silver sideburns. He smelled like his deodorant had run out for lunch and never come back.

I set my purse on the counter. "It's warm in here."

"Well, well, well," the cop said, setting his paper aside. A fat grin spread his chubby cheeks. "If it isn't the one and only Spooky Parker."

A couple of weeks ago, Cornelius had been hauled into Cooper's office for questioning about a case in New Orleans involving him, some exorcism attendees, and a now dead girl. During the interrogation, Cornelius had announced that one of the jail cells was haunted and asked if he and I could hold a séance for the ghost prisoner. End of story, beginning of new means of police harassment.

Biting my lip, I dead-panned the desk grunt. I'd promised myself on the way over to the station that I would not get into another insult-trading match with anyone carrying a badge and gun.

"So what brings you here today, Spooky? Hoping to assault some more police officers?" He snickered at his own joke.

Fanning myself, I forced a smile up my cheeks. "You're a

real Keystone Cop, aren't you?" Chock full of incompetence and buffoonery. "I'm here to see Detective Cooper."

He picked up the phone. "Spooky's here," he said and hung up.

I grabbed my purse and ambled over to the "Wanted" posters tacked to a corkboard, which hung above a couple of beat-up chairs.

"You should take it easy on the detective," Officer Wise-ass said, his jowls dripping onto the newspaper again. "He's the only one we got."

I should take it easy? Me? Cooper could slice through titanium with his razor-sharp tongue. Hell, I'd rather juggle porcupines naked than face off with him in his office this afternoon. "You tell your one and only detective—"

The door leading into the cops' den crashed open.

Cooper had shucked his suit jacket along with his tie since I'd seen him at the diner. His gray shirt looked like it had been tugged open at the neck, his hair a mixture of spikes and shark fins.

"Tell the detective what, Ms. Parker?" His voice was as stiff as his jaw.

I shrugged my purse strap higher up my shoulder and prepared to lock horns on the spot, but then I saw an underlying tiredness rimming his steely eyes. I hadn't noticed that earlier at lunch.

"That I might want some coffee with my interrogation today, please," I said, stepping past him through the doorway.

The air was a few degrees cooler inside the police department's lair. A handful of uniformed men filled the smattering of desks. I'd only ever seen two women in the place, and one of them had been wearing a suit and carrying a briefcase.

"Hey, if it isn't Rocky Parker," one officer called out, his face split by a shit-eating grin.

That was new. A little better than "Spooky," I guessed.

"Keep your eye on that one, Detective," another cop said, "she's a real knockout."

I grimaced and glanced over at Cooper, noticing a tic in his cheek. I kept my lips squeezed together until we were inside of

Cooper's office with the door closed, opting to skip the coffee today. The temperature in the room was almost cold.

"What's with the temperature flux in this place?"

He shrugged. "Every now and then our system gets confused."

Cornelius would claim the jailbird ghost had a hand in it and pull out an EMF meter. Me, I just sighed and fell into the torn vinyl chair opposite Cooper's desk.

"For future reference," I said, "I'd rather lie wide awake through a tonsillectomy than walk through this place."

"It's your own fault," Cooper said, rounding his desk.

"Getting harassed by *your* policemen pals is my fault?"

He sat down in his chair, leaning back with a creak. "I should have arrested you for police brutality."

"Criminy, we've done this dance," I said, crossing my arms over my chest. "I already said I'm sorry three times now for breaking your nose."

"And for knocking me out."

"And for knocking you out."

"And for stealing my gun."

"I didn't steal; I borrowed."

"And for giving me two black eyes."

I pointed at him. "That was part of the package deal included in the nose apology."

"And adding another murder to my caseload."

"Hey, I didn't kill George. Ask Ray."

My coworker was the one living witness to that fact.

"My life would have been simpler if you had. And leave Ray Underhill out of this." Cooper rubbed the back of his neck. "Thanks to both of you, I'm out there looking for some magical albino who disappeared in a puff of smoke. Do you have any idea how that flies with the chief?"

"Like a cow with chicken wings," I said, trying to lighten the mood.

Cooper's stony expression hardened even more.

Feeling like I was back in the principal's office after clocking little Jack Walker for peeking up my dress, I looked down at my fingers. They were all twisted together.

"And now I have another dead body on my plate."

That brought my chin up. "I had nothing to do with Jane's death."

"I'm not so certain of that." He stared at me for several silence heavy seconds. "Where were you Friday, August twenty-fourth?"

That was the day after the whole funeral parlor nightmare.

"In bed." Hiding under the covers.

"All day?"

"A good portion of it."

"Alone?"

I bristled at his question. Cop or not, that was too personal. "That's none of your business."

One eyebrow lifted. "Alone or not? Answer the question."

I just sat there and glared back.

He leaned forward, his forearms resting on his desk. "Ms. Parker, I'm simply trying to see if you have an alibi for the estimated time of Jane's death."

Did Elvis, Addy's chicken, count? "Alone."

"Hmmm," he said. That was it. I waited for more, but it didn't come.

"What is that 'hmmm' supposed to mean?"

"Nothing."

I cocked my head to the side. "Nothing, my ass. What's on your mind, Detective? Spit it out."

"In the newspaper a week ago, Jeff Wymonds stated that you and he were busy in his bedroom right before his garage exploded."

Argh! I could whack Jeff upside the noggin for that comment, but he'd probably think it was some kind of mating game ploy of mine. Jeff had big plans. Brady Bunch style plans. The guy needed a maid, not a wife, and I wasn't a good fit for either one.

"With as many suitors as you appear to have," Cooper continued, "I'm surprised that you didn't have company."

It's a good thing I didn't have Cooper's gun in my hand right then or I might have put a bullet in his toe. I had a feeling he was trying to rattle me, but after Jane's funeral and meeting my new boss, everything had been shaken out already.

I set my chin. "That was a cheap shot."

He pointed at his still swollen nose. "So was this."

"No, that was several self-defense classes paying off."

His eyes narrowed. "What kind of self-defense classes are you talking about? Karate? Jujitsu?"

"No, I'm talking about an off-duty police officer teaching a group of women what to do if someone sneaks up behind you and gets grabby."

"I wasn't sneaking."

"You didn't exactly call my name before tackling me."

"I didn't tackle you."

I counted to five. "Did you demand that I come here today to argue the semantics of our little wrestling match last week—which I won, by the way—or was it to talk about Jane?"

He pushed away from his desk and moved around to the front, leaning against it while staring down at me. It was a pure power play on his part, but I let him have it since I was feeling like Jackie Chan Jr. after what I'd done to Cooper's face.

"What were you doing Friday when you weren't in bed, Ms. Parker?"

I shrugged. "Watching TV, hanging out with my kids after they got home from school, talking to my Aunt Zoe—I live with her."

"I know."

Of course he did. "Do you know how long I've lived there?"

"Since March."

Ah ha! Last time we'd talked about when I'd moved to Deadwood, he'd been off by a couple of months. Someone had done his homework. Let's see how much digging he'd been doing. "Where did I live before then?"

"Rapid City with your parents."

"What's my weight?"

"About twenty pounds heavier than you claim on your driver's license."

I sputtered.

"Are you done testing me?" he asked.

"Maybe."

"Did you see anyone besides your Aunt Zoe, your daughter, Adelynn, or your son, Layne?"

Now he was just showing off. "Elvis."

"Your daughter's chicken doesn't count."

Figuring he'd probably already cornered Doc, I came clean. "My friend, Doc Nyce."

"All night?"

"What are you insinuating?"

"Don't play coy. I've caught you sneaking in his back door before, remember?"

"I wasn't sneaking." Okay, maybe a little that time, but only to see if his ex-girlfriend was in there with him. The jealousy bug had me all squirmy that day.

"Doc left around eleven," I told him. "And if you don't believe me, you can ask my neighbor Mr. Stinkleskine. He was out walking his dog when Doc left." Which was the reason the goodbye kiss had remained PG-rated.

"Then what?"

"Then I went to bed. Alone. All night."

He nodded. "Well, your story corroborates with Doc Nyce's as far as the evening goes."

"If you already knew all of this, why bust my balls about it?"

"Balls?" He glanced down at my black dress. "Testosterone would explain a lot about you."

"Did that hurt?"

"What?"

"Cracking that joke. I wouldn't think a hard ass like you could suffer that kind of structural tension without at least a wince or a grunt."

"You have no idea how hard I can be, Ms. Parker."

Harvey would have been guffawing all over that double entendre, slapping his thigh, hooting at the ceiling. I let it go without even a cheek twitch. "Why did you drag me in here this afternoon, Detective Cooper? Was there an actual purpose, or was it just to ask about my bedfellows and cry about your broken nose?"

His jaw shifted side to side like he was pulverizing granite between his molars. "You don't pull your punches, do you?"

"Not with you."

He smiled all of a sudden—a real honest-to-goodness smile that curved clear up to his crows' feet. The change almost hurt my eyes.

"I admire that about you, Violet," he said, and then his smile disappeared and the storm clouds returned.

Was that a compliment? I almost fell out of my chair. What just happened? Had I crossed into another dimension?

"I asked you here to ascertain your whereabouts the evening Jane Grimes was murdered and if you had an alibi, which it appears you do."

Blinking away my temporary smile blindness, I asked, "She was murdered Friday night?"

He gave a brief nod. "According to the coroner's report."

God, while I was sitting on the couch next to Doc watching John Wayne fall in love with a French whore in an Alaskan gold field, Jane was battling for her life.

"Was she killed down in the Open Cut?"

"That's police business."

"Was she shot or stabbed?" Or something worse?

"That's also police business."

"Have you talked to her ex-husband?" I thought of Jerry and added, "All three of them?"

"Again, police business."

I really, really wanted to reach out and pinch Cooper in the leg right about then, and ask him if that was police business, too. But he'd probably arrest me for aggravated assault and force me to sit in the haunted jail cell while I waited for Doc to post bail.

"Fine." I grabbed my purse and stood. "Since everything appears to be police business, I guess we're done here."

"We're not done, Ms. Parker." He took my purse from me and set it back on the floor, then pointed at the chair.

I took my sweet time sitting back down, smoothing my dress over my legs. "What else do you need, Detective?"

"Have you noticed any suspicious behavior between either of your coworkers and Jane over the last few weeks?"

Besides Ray having sex with Jane in her office a few days before her death? Actually, that wasn't suspicious, just disgusting.

I still cringed at the thought of his pants around his ankles. If only I hadn't seen his man-junk while he'd lain naked on that autopsy table in Mudder Brothers basement.

"No," I answered, still feeling the need to shield Jane's reputation from censure for that one slip-up. Although, now that I knew Jane had been murdered, Ray was back under suspicion and I was going to play the "what if" game when Cooper didn't have me under the microscope.

"Had Jane mentioned anything to you about someone following her or sending her threatening messages via email, a text, voicemail, anything?"

"Besides the jerk she was divorcing, no."

"Did you actually see or hear any threats from him?"

"No, I just heard Jane's complaints about him. Especially over the last few weeks."

"Why the last few weeks?"

"I don't know. Her divorce was getting pretty messy, I guess."

"Did he ever come to the office?"

"Not while I was there."

"Was Jane a heavy drinker?"

"No." I thought of the liquor bottles in her office, the thick smell of alcohol in the air at the end. "Well, not until lately. Her divorce really had her depressed. I think she was still in love."

Jane was one of the reasons my attraction to Doc had me chewing my thumbnails. Falling in love with him would mess me up and leave me sitting alone in a gutter somewhere, reeking of tequila, and having sex with some Neanderthal just because he said I looked "sorta pretty."

"Is there anything you know about Jane that would help me to find whoever is responsible for her death?"

I sat on that for several heartbeats, giving it serious thought. I wished I'd made more effort to get to know her on a personal level, but she'd been my boss first, friend second. I'd respected the boundaries set at the start. "No, I don't think so."

"I will assume if you stumble across anything—as you so often tend to—that you will contact me immediately."

"Of course," I said, and I meant it. Whoever killed Jane

ought to be brought to justice. She was good to me during a tough time, and I owed it to her to help Cooper find her murderer however I could.

"You're going to keep your nose out of this case, right, Violet?"

His use of my first name didn't go unnoticed. He'd shifted out of his hard-assed detective role, which meant he must be about finished chewing on me yet again.

"Yes." I had an albino to worry about. I didn't have time to figure out who killed Jane and why.

"You promise?"

"Do you want me to pinky swear with you?"

"It couldn't hurt."

Instead, I held up my left hand and placed my right over my heart. "I promise to let you solve the case, Detective Cooper." I couldn't resist throwing in, "for once."

He shook his head. "I should have just arrested you the first time I met you."

I stood, grabbing my purse again.

He walked toward the door. "What time are you coming over tomorrow?"

"You still want to have the open house then?" I'd already rescheduled it once due to Jane's death.

He nodded, grabbing the doorknob.

"Then I'll be there around one-thirty to set up." The showing started at two.

"Great, I'll let you in and then disappear awhile."

"You're not going to stay and help me bake some cookies? Wear an apron?"

"I'm leaving that to my uncle." He opened the door.

Warm air walloped me in the face. "Harvey's coming?"

"He told me you insisted he be there."

The big, fat fibber. I hooked my purse over my shoulder. Oh, well, some company might be nice if it was slow. "He does make a mean molasses cookie."

"Have you talked to Natalie Beals lately?"

Nat? That stopped me on the threshold. "No, why?"

Cooper shrugged. "Just curious. She seemed pretty upset

that night at the funeral parlor."

My neck warmed. Of course she had. She'd caught me kissing the man she'd been daydreaming about in happily-ever-after land.

"She was still acting odd when I stopped in to ask her about the whole ordeal the day after the incident."

Odd? That must mean *emotional* in Cooper-speak. "I'm sure sharing a walk-in freezer with a decapitated body wasn't something she could sleep off in one night."

He nodded, but I could see something unsettling in his eyes.

My stomach tightened. "What? Why are you asking me about Natalie?"

"There was something else she said that I can't make sense of."

"What?"

"She warned me to be careful if I went back to Mudder Brothers because of the albinos—as in more than one."

Had Natalie seen the other albino there that night? If so, where had he gone when the shit hit the fan? Had she seen him lurking around since?

Cooper leaned closer, his gaze piercing.

My spine broke out in a sweat. I couldn't tell if it was from the warmer air outside Cooper's office or standing too close to a man who wanted to handcuff me and force me to wear an orange jumpsuit.

"Ms. Parker, is there something about that night at Mudder Brothers that you're not telling me?"

Hell, yes. There were several cards I was holding close to the vest on that one. Most of them were way too weird to talk about aloud, especially in front of a detective who only saw in black and white, no color.

Hiding behind a smile that I could feel quivering on my cheeks, I shook my head. "I'll see you tomorrow, Detective."

I forced my feet to walk not run all the way out the front doors.

* * *

My Aunt Zoe's house had been sitting down the hill from Mount Moriah Cemetery for over a century. She'd spruced up the no-fuss Victorian decades ago, way before she'd invited me and my kids to share it with her for as long as needed while I tried my hand at this realty gig.

Her reputation for generosity in our family was exceeded only by her perfectly sweetened homemade lemonade, which was exactly what had my mouth watering when I parked Harvey's Picklemobile in the drive.

The old girl hiccupped when I cut the engine. Then she belched a cloud of black smoke from her tailpipe and wrapped up her gastrointestinal blues with a backfire finale in the still evening air. A dog up the street howled an encore—probably Mr. Stinkleskine's interfering mutt.

"Honey, I'm home," I said under my breath and shoved open the pickup door.

The scent of wood smoke tainted the evening air. The warmth of summer in the Black Hills was ebbing away. Fall's crisp breath required thick sweaters or lined jackets, especially after the sun dipped behind the hills and cast the gulches and valleys into darkness.

I found Aunt Zoe in the kitchen. Instead of her usual attire of faded jeans and a soft cotton blouse, she wore a silver silk tunic, black slacks with a fancy twirl at the bottom, and patent leather mules. Her long salt-and-pepper braid was twisted up into a snazzy knot on her head with elaborately designed chopsticks securing it. Her own custom glass bead earrings and matching necklace added a final pizazz to her ensemble.

Within the walls of her comfortable, pale yellow kitchen with Betty Boop accents, including the cookie jar she always kept filled for my kids, she stood out like Kathryn Hepburn in Dogpatch, Kentucky.

"Wow! You look gorgeous," I said, leaning my hip against the counter. "Do you have a hot date tonight?"

"I do, as a matter of fact. I'll probably be home around midnight."

"Are you going out with a certain captain of the Deadwood

Fire Department?"

"Absolutely not. One heartbreak a lifetime courtesy of Reid Martin is plenty for me, thank you very much."

That was the first time she'd mentioned anything about being heartbroken over the fire captain.

Reid might put out fires for a living, but he'd certainly lit one under Aunt Zoe at some period in the past and smoke still poured out of her ears whenever he came around. The last time he'd graced her kitchen, she'd gone down to the basement to find her shotgun shells. But dragging the truth out of her about what had happened between the two of them was about as easy as giving a kangaroo a French pedicure.

"Then who's the lucky guy?"

"The owner of a glass gallery from over in Jackson Hole is in town for a few days and wants to talk about commissioning some designs for delivery by next summer."

Aunt Zoe owned a gallery in town that specialized in glass art pieces—mostly her own designs. As a kid, I'd spent summers helping out in her workshop behind the house and running the register at the gallery.

"So, is this business or pleasure?" I asked.

"Well, if he places the order, it would be enough money to cover my gallery costs for six months."

"That would be wonderful." Especially since she had the added burden of me and my kids running up her utility bills here at home. Since we'd moved in, the only money she would take from me was for groceries. "So we're talking business only then."

"Not only. He looks like a slightly older version of George Clooney."

"Yum."

"He could also charm the crown off the Queen of England."

"Good looks and charm, that's a heady cocktail." He sounded a lot like Reid, only the fire captain looked more like Sam Elliott.

"Very heady. And my crown slips off much easier than hers."

I grinned at the wink she gave me as she slid the strap of her little black purse over her shoulder.

"So, should I wait up to count your hickeys?"

"Violet Lynn," she said, shooting me a coy smile, "you're too much."

"You don't fool me, Aunt Zoe. I've seen some of the men you've dated. You're not out there playing patty-cake with them."

"Well, that depends on your version of patty-cake."

She gave me a kiss on the cheek, and I could smell the exotic fruity scent of her favorite perfume that I hadn't ever been able to pronounce correctly.

"How are you now that the funeral is over?" she asked.

Aunt Zoe had been at the service today, too, but she'd sat closer to the front with some mutual friends of Jane's. Her friendship with Jane had been what had landed me the job. Months ago, she'd called in a favor and gotten me hired. Who'd have guessed we'd be attending Jane's funeral such a short time later.

"I'm okay." I opted not to tell her about my trip to the police station right before her date or anything about the albino that had me jumping at shadows. I'd catch her up when she wasn't about to go enjoy an evening off from me and my problems.

"It's time for life to go on now," I added.

She squeezed my shoulder. "Jane would want that from us."

I nodded, wondering if I should give Mona a call to see how she was doing or leave her be for the night. Her sobs when she'd first heard the news of Jane's death last week still echoed in my head and tore at my heart.

"The kids are upstairs playing Yahtzee," Aunt Zoe said. "Have a fun night."

"You, too." I followed her to the front door and closed it behind her.

I shucked my shoes and climbed the stairs, following the sound of kids giggling to my bedroom. There, both Addy and Layne sat on the wood floor playing the dice game.

"Why are you two in my room?"

Layne didn't even look up. "It's more fun to dump the dice on your floor than our carpet."

Addy smiled at me, her jaw working the bubble gum in her mouth. "Hi, Mama. Did you have fun at your friend's party?"

I hadn't told my kids yet about Jane's death, so I'd lied about her service, telling them instead that I had a fancy dress party to attend for work.

There were times in life I scared my kids with the truth, especially when it came to chasing a ball into a busy street or getting their hands too close to moving ranch machinery. But the murder of my boss wasn't one of those truth-needed moments.

"The party was okay," I told them while tossing my shoes in the closet, frowning at a couple of small chicken feathers floating about in there. "I'm glad to be home with you two, though."

Layne eyed my dress. "You look really pretty, Mom."

"Thanks, sweetie. I love you, too."

"Did you go to the party with a man?" he asked, feigning disinterest.

Layne had male-replacement issues, as in he feared that allowing another man to come into my life would erase my need for him. No matter how many times I tried to explain how incorrect that whole notion was, he couldn't shake his dislike for any guy who took more than a casual interest in me.

This was one reason I was being so careful with Doc. At the moment, Layne viewed Doc as my friend and was beginning to warm up to him. If he found out in this early stage of their friendship that Doc was my boyfriend—that word still made me grin like an idiot—the temperature between them would drop to freezing overnight.

"I went to the party with Mr. Harvey."

Layne admired Harvey for his worm catching abilities. Plus, with our age difference, Harvey was no threat.

I walked over to my dresser and grabbed a pink knit shirt and some yoga pants from my drawer. I had a while until Doc would show up on my doorstep, since he said he'd be working late down by Mount Rushmore, so no need to dress up to bake a frozen pizza.

"You should leave that dress on for dinner tonight, Mom," Addy said.

"I don't think so."

"Please. You look so beautiful in it."

"Thank you, Addy, but I'm not wearing this dress all night. I'm going to take a quick shower; then I'll throw something together for dinner."

"Will you make my favorite?" Addy asked.

"Lasagna?"

She nodded.

"That will take too long." And a lot more work than I was willing to put into dinner. "How about a frozen pizza instead?"

"Maybe I could help you with the lasagna."

"Are you even listening to me, Adelynn? And where are your glasses? You're supposed to be wearing them all of the time." As much as they'd cost, I wanted to see them on her face 24/7.

"They hurt my ears."

"That's because you're not wearing them enough. You better have them on when I get back." I ignored her protests and headed for the bathroom. "I'll be done shortly. Stay out of trouble."

There was something about death that made me need to wash my hair. I scrubbed shampoo into it twice and conditioned the hell out of my barely manageable curls. In the post-shower steam, I threw on my shirt and yoga pants and combed my fingers through my wet mophead. I had a couple of hours to get gussied up for Doc. The doorbell rang as if it'd heard me.

I froze, staring at the steamed up mirror. Doc was early.

"I'll get it, Mom," Addy called. I could hear her feet pounding down the stairs.

As I dug through my makeup drawer for some quick fixes, I heard the front door shut then the sound of a deep voice opposite Addy's excited tone.

I raced to my bedroom and kicked Layne out, telling him to go downstairs and help his sister entertain our company, and closed the door behind him. One look at my curls in the mirror and I squawked. I had some serious work to do taming my outer shrew with very little time to make it happen.

Fifteen minutes later, I cruised downstairs, my heart beating fast for fear that my children had somehow scared Doc off. With his being a bachelor for decades, his daily lifestyle didn't include sticky floors, dirty finger smudges, and chicken feathers. The sound of Addy's giggles coming from the kitchen lit a flame of hope in my chest.

I took a deep breath and then breezed into the kitchen, only to slam to a stop at the sight of Jeff Wymonds sitting at a candlelit kitchen table. And by candlelit, I meant there was just a single candle sitting there flickering in the bright room—no plates set, no silverware lined up, nothing.

"What's with the candle?" I asked. If he said the word *séance*, I was going back up to my room and barring the door.

Jeff leaned back in the kitchen chair and eyed me up and down, getting stuck in the down position, as usual. Jeff was a hips and butt kind of guy, which made me wonder if he used to be a dog in his past life. Finally his eyes returned northward. "You look hot with your hair all gelled like that, Violet Parker."

The ex-high school football player couldn't seem to get through his blond head that my name was just Violet, not a hyphenated name that rolled all together. Personally, I thought he'd taken too many hits to the noggin on the playing field, but he was nice underneath the bravado, and he loved his kids, so I put up with his lack of social graces.

"Thanks for inviting me over for dinner," he said.

What? I turned to my matchmaking daughter, my mother glare on HIGH. So that's why she wanted me to keep wearing my black dress.

Addy avoided my laser beams, stirring something in a big pot on the stove with her arm that was cast-free as of last week. As happy as I was to see her rebuilding her strength in the arm she'd broken back in July, I was less than thrilled with her motivation.

"What are we having tonight, Adelynn Renee?" I used her full name as I always did when she was in trouble. At least she was wearing her glasses now.

"Spaghetti," she said while she stirred.

I walked over and peeked in the pot. "Honey, you need to heat the water before putting the noodles in. Here, let me finish." I nudged her aside. The last thing I wanted to do tonight was listen to Jeff complain about his soon-to-be-ex wife who'd left him for another woman, or try to lure me out of my pants using his redneck-style bait—much of which revolved around how huge his tires were. But I couldn't be rude to a man who also happened to be a client, so I decided to rush through this one-course dinner and kick Jeff out of here before Doc made it back from his client's place.

"What did the insurance company say about your garage?" I asked him.

"They're going to pay for a new roof."

"Good." Jeff's garage roof had been a casualty at my first open house. The fire department had a nickname for me, too, now—"Four-Alarm Parker."

"At least the bitch kept the insurance bills paid up. She killed our credit, though."

There was the ex-wife crack. I chose to ignore it. "Good. We can promote a new garage roof on the listing."

I glanced out the back window at Addy, Layne, and Kelly, Jeff's daughter and Addy's best friend. The three of them were lying on the ground staring up at the sky. I envied their lack of worries about jobs, money, and killer albinos.

Addy's attempts to get me together with Jeff stemmed from her desire to have a sister, and Kelly could provide instant sisterhood without any messy babies. While she had a good idea with avoiding those messy babies, she just didn't understand that there was more to living with Jeff than her having a permanent slumber party pal. Someone had to cook his dinner and play dutiful wife: I burned most everything that couldn't be microwaved and I had authority issues. Sex with him was out of the question, no matter how drunk I got.

"Did I tell you that the bitch wants alimony? Can you believe that shit?" His sticky situation with his ex-wife was yet another reason I had no desire to hook up with him.

"That really sucks, Jeff. Maybe we can get your house sold soon and you can throw some money at her to see if that satisfies her."

"She'll never be satisfied. I knew that from the start, but she had such a cute ass in her cheerleading outfit."

And we were back to butts. I switched to talking about the weather while the spaghetti cooked.

I was carting the pot to the sink when the doorbell rang again.

It was too early for Doc, so that was probably Harvey. He must have seen Jeff's car in the drive when he stopped over at his girlfriend's, Miss Geary, our sultry neighborhood sexpot.

Harvey knew all about Jeff Wymonds and his preference for butts. He probably came to watch me dodge and weave Jeff's hands.

"Will you get that, Jeff?" I asked, not wanting to stop pouring.

"Sure." He disappeared through the kitchen archway.

I heard the sound of footfalls returning as I put the empty pot in the sink and reached for Aunt Zoe's homemade spaghetti bowl.

"Maybe you could help me with some money problems I'm having thanks to the bitch I'm divorcing," I heard Jeff say.

Was he really going to borrow money from Harvey? My inner Realtor perked up. How much cash was Harvey supposed to receive from that uncle with the mule? Enough to buy a place in town and worry about selling the ranch later?

I grabbed the bowl from up high and pulled it toward the shelf edge. A big plate next to it teetered, threatening to come down on my head.

"Yikes," I said, trying not to drop the spaghetti bowl while stopping the plate from falling.

"Here," Doc said, catching the plate.

Doc? I felt the blood drain from my face.

"Let me help." He took the bowl from my hands.

I looked up into his dark eyes, unable to read his reaction to Jeff greeting him at my door. "Hi, Doc."

"I hope I'm not interrupting anything by stopping by."

"Well, I … uh … Addy …" I trailed off, wanting to tell Doc the truth but not wanting to hurt Jeff's feelings.

"Violet and I are celebrating some good news of mine with a dinner date," Jeff explained to Doc.

Shit.

"A date." Doc's focus shifted from Jeff, to the candle on the table, to me. "How romantic."

Chapter Four

Over the years, one of my problems with having potential and actual boyfriends was that they tended to show up at the worst possible moments.

Like when that boy from my *Music of the Ages* college class caught me in bed next to his nearly naked Australian roommate, who'd invited me over to blow on his didgeridoo.

Or when that cute parole officer from my mom's bicycle club pedaled by while I was being handcuffed alongside a Pennington County Sheriff's SUV.

Or when Doc stopped by the house while I was making a candlelit dinner for an oversexed, wanna-be baby-daddy in my aunt's kitchen.

My track record with men had a lot of crashes and burns. As I stood there trying to gauge Doc's reaction to my situation, I crossed my fingers that tonight wouldn't end with any hearts exploding into pieces. Especially mine.

"It's not really a dinner date," I explained. "More of a celebration meal." Without looking at Jeff, I added, "Will you join us?"

When that didn't make any cracks in Doc's stony expression, I took the plate and bowl back from him and set them on the counter. Then I grabbed a stack of plates from the cupboard and handed them to him. "Please set the table."

Without giving him a chance to refuse, I took the spaghetti bowl over to the stove.

The screen door crashed open and two bundles of energy in the form of little girls shot inside.

"Dad," Kelly ran up to Jeff, her eyes wide, matching her smile. "Look what Addy found."

Addy followed on her heels, holding something cupped in

her hands.

Jeff gave the two his full attention. "What do you have there, Addy-girl?"

I joined the trio to see what my daughter had in her hands. Addy wanted to be a veterinarian when she grew up, and her usual "finds" were not allowed in the kitchen—Elvis the chicken included.

Addy opened her hands a crack and a squeak came from inside.

I jumped back. "No! Take it outside."

"Mom, you didn't even see it."

"I don't care." I pointed at the back door, where Layne stood frowning back and forth between Jeff and Doc. "That thing squeaks. It does not belong in this house. Outside now, Adelynn Renee."

Jeff cupped his hands around Addy's. "Come on, Addy-girl, let's take it out back and see if we can find something to put it in."

They walked together toward the back door. Layne moved out of the way to let the trio go by.

"Supper's almost ready," I called as the screen door closed behind them.

I glanced over at Doc and caught him frowning at the chair where Jeff had been a moment before. I could only imagine what he was thinking, and nothing I came up with helped my cause.

"Mom," Layne said. "I think I need a bandage." He raised his knee for me to see.

A scrape above his shin oozed blood between a smudge of dirt and a couple pieces of grass.

"Oh, honey, are you okay?" My knees popped as I squatted before him to inspect it.

"Mom, I'm fine." His face darkened as he looked over at Doc. "Don't treat me like a baby. I just need something to stop the bleeding."

"You also need to clean it first. Go upstairs to the bathroom. I'll be right there."

Layne avoided making eye contact with Doc as he passed.

I stood and turned back to Doc, who now watched Jeff and

the girls out the window, the crease still in place between his brows.

I opened my mouth to apologize for Jeff, Addy's critter, Layne's stiffness, and anything else I could throw in to smooth things over, but Doc spoke first. "He's really good with kids."

"Jeff?" At Doc's nod, I continued, "He'd better be; he has two of his own."

Doc looked over at me, his gaze guarded. "He's really good with *your* kids."

His comment hung between us, my brain picking up on the undercurrents rolling off him. I needed to tiptoe through this field of land mines.

"Jeff does okay," I said, "especially with Addy, since she's into the same things as Kelly. Plus, we take turns babysitting."

"Mom! Are you coming or not?" Layne hollered from upstairs.

"One minute," I called back. "Listen, Doc, this whole thing with—"

"Mom, I got blood on Aunt Zoe's shower curtain."

Crap! She'd just bought that one last week.

I touched Doc's arm, wishing he would wrap it around me and tell me everything was fine and dandy. "I'll be right back."

Upstairs, Layne sat on the sink counter swinging his legs, thumping the cupboards with his heels.

"Layne, stop kicking. You're getting dirt on the cupboard doors." I pulled open the drawer where Aunt Zoe kept her first aid supplies. "Here," I tossed him an old rag. "Get this wet."

"Why is *he* here?"

I faked nonchalance, wondering if Layne had picked up on the vibes between Doc and me. "Who?"

"Jeff."

Whew! "Addy asked Kelly and him to join us for dinner."

"He always stares at your butt."

Tell me about it. I took the washrag and dabbed at his knee. "He's probably just checking for chicken feathers. You know how Elvis is always roosting on my stuff."

"I don't think so, Mom. I think he wants to have a baby with you."

That stopped me mid-dab. "Where did you get that idea?"

"Addy says you're going to let her name the baby."

Wow. I grabbed the counter to ground myself. After raising two kids on my own, just thinking about having a baby made me feel like jumping out the bathroom window, shimmying down the ivy lattice, and running for the hills ... well, deeper into them anyway.

Apparently, the previous talk I'd had with Addy on the subject of Jeff and me and matrimony had bounced right off her bubble-gum-filled brain.

"Layne, I'm not going to have a baby with Jeff." Cross my heart and hope to die.

"Are you gonna have one with Doc?"

"No." I'd learned my lesson about having kids with hot guys who had relationship issues, and while Doc showed potential for a long-term plan, he'd left his last girlfriend as soon as she'd brought up marriage.

"Why is he here then?"

I returned to dabbing and cleaning. "Layne, there is something that you need to understand. I have friends who are boys, just like I have friends who are girls."

"So Kelly's dad is just your friend?"

"Yes."

"And Doc is, too?"

No. I hesitated. Lying outright to my son about Doc weighed heavy on my conscience for multiple reasons, especially when I expected the truth from Layne in return.

"Doc is a *really* good friend." I hoped that would suffice, but in case it didn't, I changed the subject. "What was in Addy's hands? Did you see it?"

"A mouse with a broken tail."

"Ewww." Why couldn't she be like her mother and run from creepy, crawly things like mice and spiders and albinos with snake eyes?

I ran the cold water, rinsing the rag, and thought I heard a door close downstairs. Jeff and the girls must be back inside. I hoped he'd made them wash their hands and kept his big mouth shut about his Brady Bunch fantasy with me.

Pulling out some first aid ointment, I smeared it on the bandage.

The growl of an engine made me pause. Was someone coming or going?

I slapped the bandage on Layne's leg, wiped my hand on a towel, and rushed out into the hall.

"Mom, it's crooked," Layne called after me.

Ignoring him, I took the steps two at a time and peeked out the front window in time to see Doc roll away.

Damn, damn, damn!

Back in the kitchen, Jeff and the girls sat at the table, where five dishes were set out instead of the six I'd handed to Doc earlier. Next to the candle, the bowl of spaghetti sat in the middle, all mixed together and ready for eating.

"So, Doc took off?" I tried to act as if I didn't want to throw myself onto the floor and kick my feet.

"Yeah," Addy said, scooping spaghetti onto her plate. "He said to tell you he needed to take care of something and he'd talk to you tomorrow."

Tomorrow? Crappity-crap. That didn't sit well in my gut, nor did the idea of eating spaghetti anymore. I dropped into the seat next to Kelly as Layne scuffed up behind me.

"Hey, Layne," Addy said around a mouthful of noodles. "Jeff said we could keep the mouse in his garage if we wanted to."

"That garage lost its roof," Layne grumbled, scooting a chair close enough to me that our legs touched when he sat on it. He couldn't be much more obvious about marking his territory short of peeing on me, which I'd had enough of when he was a baby.

"It'll have a new one soon," Jeff said, winking at me as he shoved a forkful of spaghetti in his mouth. He focused on Layne. "Then you and your mom and sister can come visit the little guy on weekend nights."

Or never. "I'm not really into mice," I told Jeff with a tight smile.

"Me, either," he said, his gaze dipping to my chest. "Is that blood on your shirt?"

I glanced down. How had Layne managed that? I didn't even

remember him touching me.

"Darn it, Layne." Pushing back from the table, I used the opportunity to make my escape. "I'm going to go take a shower and change."

"But you already showered, Mom," Addy said.

Shut up, sweetie.

Jeff's fork lowered. "It's just a little smudge."

I took my clean plate over to the cupboard and put it back. "I'm sorry, Jeff, but I have a nasty headache after today."

"Oh, that's right," Jeff said. "You went to Jane's f—"

"I went to Jane's *family gathering*, exactly." I shook my head quickly at Jeff.

"Her gathering, right." He'd caught on, thankfully.

"I hope you don't mind if I skip dinner. I want to lie down for a while, try to kick this headache. We can catch up another day about the roof."

"Sure. Holler if you need anything upstairs, Violet Parker. Anything to help you relax." Jeff hit me with another wink.

I considered super-gluing his peepers shut as a calming exercise. It'd be right up there with yoga at the moment.

"Layne, will you clean up after dinner and see Jeff and Kelly out?"

"Yeah, Mom." Layne smiled, obviously happy at the idea of shutting the door behind Jeff.

With a nod goodbye, I exited stage left.

Instead of showering again, I sat on the bathroom floor while I let the water run for a couple of minutes. Wasteful, yes, but extreme measures were sometimes needed when hiding from a client who wanted to make my womb his baby factory.

While I pretended to shower, I sent a text to Natalie, telling her about my new boss being a giant. Then I sent another one saying Cooper had asked about the "albinos" comment she'd made, asking if she'd seen any more since that night at Mudder Brothers. Since she'd stopped talking to me, I'd been sending her texts with the hope that she'd at least write to me. So far, I'd received nothing.

An hour later, Layne walked into my bedroom and caught me staring at the ceiling. I'd been contemplating calling Doc since leaving the bathroom, but every time I reached for my phone my stomach felt like I'd gulped Pop Rocks and followed them with a Coca-Cola chaser.

"What are you doing, Mom?" He smelled like spaghetti sauce.

"Trying to figure out if that's a spider or a black spot on the ceiling." Which was partly true. I loathed spiders.

"Everyone's gone."

"Good."

"Did you really have a headache?"

"Yes." His name was Jeff. "But I'm better now."

"Cool. Can Addy and I watch *Jaws* again?"

"Do you really think that's a good movie to watch before bed?"

"Yeah. I love it when they are out on Quint's boat." He cleared his throat and recited his favorite line from the film: "Saw one eat a rockin' chair once."

Chuckling at his impression of the late great Robert Shaw, I pinched his nose. "Fine, but don't tell your Grammy that I let you watch it. She thinks it makes me a bad mom."

Layne leaned over and kissed my cheek. "You're an awesome mom. So awesome that we never need a dad."

He really needed to work on his use of subtlety. "Point taken. Go watch TV."

"Thanks, Mom."

It took me almost another hour to get up the nerve to make the call to Doc. I was afraid to hear why he'd left, chewing my knuckles that it was something more than just Jeff sitting at the kitchen table.

I grabbed the phone and a jacket and went downstairs, stepping out onto the back porch. The cool night air cleared my head of the lingering webs of the day's sadness, frustration, and exhaustion. It also chilled my bare toes, so I tucked them under me and huddled on the cushioned lounge chair.

The smell of burning wood reminded me of long ago when I'd sit on Aunt Zoe's porch and stare at the stars, wondering what my future held. Now thoughts of things to come made me want to hide under my covers with a shotgun next to me.

Doc's phone rang and rang and rang and rang. I was about to hang up when the ringing stopped.

"Hello, Violet." His deep voice soothed, giving me the courage to dive right in.

"You left without saying goodbye."

"I did."

I waited for him to explain why, but he didn't.

"I didn't invite Jeff over here for dinner," I said. "Addy did."

"I figured."

"He's a client."

"And he's a friend," Doc said.

"Sort of. He helps with my kids."

"I noticed that."

Silence filled the line again.

"Did Jeff say something to you?" I asked, trying to figure out what had sent Doc running. Had it been just being around my kids?

"He told me he wants to take Addy and Layne to the Rec Center and give them some swimming lessons."

"Oh. That's nice of him." Especially since I was allergic to bathing suits—they made me break out in humiliation.

"You all make a perfect little family unit," Doc said.

"Wrong." I didn't like the sound of that for many reasons.

"Your kids like him a lot."

"Wrong again. Layne isn't a fan, and Addy just wants Kelly as a sister."

"Addy wants more than a sister."

Okay, technically, that was true. She wanted a father, who would do things with her like Jeff did with Kelly. But what Addy didn't get was that her father had walked out on her before she was even the size of a pea and was never coming back. Not if I could help it. She was stuck with me and only me.

"Doc," I decided to quit screwing around and get the truth out in the open so we could watch it flip, flop, and gasp in front of us. "This isn't really about my kids liking Jeff, is it?"

"No."

My heart panged. I was afraid of that. "I come as a package deal."

"Yeah."

I wished he'd stop being so fucking monosyllabic. Closing my eyes, I whispered, "Do you want to call this whole thing off?"

There was a pause from the other end of the line that felt long enough for the earth to revolve around the sun—twice.

"No, Violet," he said finally. "I don't."

I covered the mouthpiece and gulped several breaths. "What do you want to do then?"

"I don't know."

He didn't know? My best friend was no longer taking my calls because I'd allowed Doc to come between us and he "didn't know." I pulled the phone away from my ear and hit it on the cushions a couple of times.

We needed to talk about something else for now, before I pushed too hard for an answer and shoved him away in the process.

"I think I'm off Cooper's hit list," I said. At least I was for now.

"What did he say about Jane's murder?" Doc seemed to take the change of subject in stride.

"The coroner figures she died Friday evening when I was with you. Since our stories match up, Cooper's done sniffing around me."

"Did he say how she was killed?"

"No."

"Does he have any idea why she was killed?"

"He wouldn't tell me."

"Did he have anything else to say at all?"

"Yes. He cried about his sore nose and said he should have locked me up for assaulting a cop."

Doc chuckled. It sounded forced.

"He also told me to stay away from his case. You know, same shit, different day."

"I wonder how Jane's body ended up at the bottom of the Open Cut."

"You and the rest of the population in Lead and Deadwood. Cooper is being really closemouthed about this, which makes me curious about a few things."

"Violet," Doc warned, "promise me you won't get mixed up in this Jane mess."

"Are you afraid you really will have to bail me out of jail?"

"No, I'm afraid you'll end up just like her, dead at the bottom of the Open Cut."

I grimaced. "Well, there is that."

"And you have two kids."

We were back to me and my package deal. "I do."

"They need their mother alive and healthy."

"I don't think I've ever been considered 'healthy,'" I joked, trying to keep from falling back into our serious conversation pothole.

"I need you alive, too," he said.

When he told me stuff like that, I felt like rolling around in the grass with my tail wagging. It almost made me forget about his hesitation when it came to my kids. Almost.

"So, you're okay with my not being the epitome of health?" I asked.

"I like you just the way you are. All of you."

I lay back against the lounge cushions, wishing he were here next to me whispering that in my ear. "I like you okay, too."

"Just okay, huh?"

Grinning, I played with him, "Well, you're a little short."

"I'll strive to be taller for you."

"You could also use some practice between the sheets."

He laughed aloud. "You have no idea what I'm like between the sheets. You're too impatient to make it to the bedroom."

"My impatience is your fault."

"Your impatience is my undoing. You just go off in my hands."

"Well, you have talented hands."

"It's incredibly hot to watch you."

I unzipped my jacket, warming from the inside out. "Maybe I could come over after Aunt Zoe gets home and throw pebbles at your other bedroom window." I'd accidently broken one of them weeks ago, why not go for a double whammy?

"Or I could give you a key."

My eyes popped open. "A key?" That was like some kind of

commitment, wasn't it?

"I can't have you breaking all of my windows," he said.

I heard the screen door creak open.

"Mom," Addy called out from the doorway.

"Over here, Addy," I said, sitting up.

"Layne won't give me the remote so I can back up the movie to watch the scene where they open the shark's gut again. When I tried to take it from him, he pinched me."

"Like mother, like son," Doc said in my ear, snickering.

"You big baby," I whispered to him. To Addy, I said, "I'll be right there, sweetheart."

"Okay, but you better hurry or I'm gonna sock him in the nose."

"No hitting!" I said to her back. "Doc, I have to go."

"Come see me tomorrow."

"At work?" I asked. Doc worked every day of the week, pretty much like me. Building a successful business didn't allow for much time off.

"Yes, at work. I want to frisk you against my desk."

"Oh." Goosebumps rippled over my skin.

"Get some sleep for once, Boots, and dream something happy."

Chapter Five

Sunday, September 2nd

Early the next afternoon, I stopped at the Piggly Wiggly grocery store on my way to Cooper's house and almost ran over a zombie in the parking lot.

No shit.

There I was, merrily cruising toward an empty spot with cookie dough in the forefront of my thoughts—as it often was— and out popped a black-haired zombie with a torn, blood-stained shirt and hillbilly pants belted on with a rope. He was pushing a grocery cart with a six-pack of beer, laundry soap, and a loaf of bread.

And here I'd been worried about killer albinos. Silly me.

The zombie guy was gone by the time I grabbed the cookie dough and returned to the Picklemobile, making me wonder if my nightmares and the resulting lack of sleep were now expanding to include hallucinations about the walking dead.

Old Man Harvey's Ford truck hogged Cooper's drive, so I parked on the street.

Cooper opened the door before I reached his bottom porch step. His holey T-shirt, torn jeans, and bare feet made me do a double-take. Who was this laid-back looking guy and what had he done with Detective Cooper?

He squinted down his broken nose at me. "You're late."

Ah, there was the detective I knew and hissed at when he wasn't looking. My mistake.

I glared up at him. "There was a zombie at Piggly Wiggly."

That wiped the scowl off his face. He laughed, his carved features softening. "Did it try to bite you?"

"No. He bought beer and bread."

"Do you want me to arrest him?"

"That would require you to actually capture him first."

"Watch it, Coop," Harvey said, peeking around the detective's shoulder. "She's feisty this morning. She must not have gotten any last night."

Damn Harvey for being right.

"Can it, old man." I pointed the Picklemobile's key at Cooper's shirt. "Please tell me you're not wearing that today."

"What's wrong with my shirt?"

"It's your bullet-hole shirt." His proof that Kevlar was a necessity in his career. "Buyers don't need to be reminded that you own and carry a gun for a living."

"I own and carry several guns."

"Wonderful. You should start a club with bullet-hole filled jackets. Can't you put on a different shirt?"

"This is a different shirt from my other one."

I looked down at the wide circle full of tiny holes in the cotton—shotgun spray by the looks of it. The holes did appear smaller than before.

"Exactly how many times have you been shot?" I asked.

"I stopped counting after this happened." He pointed at his

shirt.

"Are you two going to stand there flapping your lips all day, or are we gonna have us an open house?" Harvey asked.

Cooper stood back to let me by. "What's in the bag?"

I slipped past, careful not to touch him lest he slap handcuffs on me for assault. "Cookie dough."

"What?" Harvey grabbed the grocery bag from me, his face crinkling in disgust when he saw the plastic roll in the bottom of it. "You can't serve pre-made cookies at an open house, girl."

"Why not? I'm going for smell not taste. It's an illusion."

"Those cookies scream cheap and lazy. Impressing buyers starts with showin' up in your finest duds, not letting them see your shabby old bloomers."

"You're ragging on me about cookies, but you have no problem with him wearing that?" I pointed at Cooper's shirt.

"He's skedaddlin' soon, so his skivvies don't matter none."

I looked back at Cooper, who'd closed the door and now leaned against it with his arms crossed, his frown back in its usual place.

"Where are you going?" I asked.

"Work."

"They fix that air conditioning?"

"No."

"It's good you're leaving. Buyers are more at ease if the owner isn't underfoot."

"You will be, too."

"Of course. It's easier to withhold evidence when you're not around." I made light of the truth, then turned to Harvey. "You ready to make some cookies?"

"Not them there little pieces of cardboard that taste like cow patties. I'm making some from scratch."

"Before you two start playing Betty Crocker," Cooper said, "I have a couple of rules."

Harvey and I both stopped, listening.

"Nobody goes in the garage—my bike's in there."

Cooper owned a shiny Harley that he liked to wash while wearing his bullet-hole shirts.

"They can look in the windows, but that's it."

"Okay," I said, "but before someone makes an offer, they're probably going to want to see it."

"A serious buyer can make an appointment for another visit. The second rule is absolutely nobody goes in the storage room in the basement."

"What's in the basement storage room?" Harvey asked.

"It's where I'm keeping all of my personal stuff while the house is being shown."

Cooper had personal stuff? What could there be besides guns? Gun racks? Gun cleaning supplies? Ammo? Cannons?

"No problem," I said. "But you should probably lock the door."

"I did." He held up a key.

"I'll hold onto that while you're gone," Harvey said.

"I don't think so."

"I'll keep it safe," Harvey said.

"You give in too easily to her." Cooper jutted his chin in my direction.

Why didn't Cooper want me in the basement storage room?

"What if we catch the place on fire while we're making cookies?" Harvey asked.

"Don't."

"I make no guarantees when preparing my masterpieces."

Cooper seemed to chew on that, his jaw flexing, then he held out the key to his uncle. "Okay, but you're in charge of making sure nobody goes in there, including both of you."

What was in the basement storage room?

"Do you understand what I just told you, Violet?" Cooper asked, as if he'd just read me my Miranda rights.

"Got it," I said.

"I mean not a single soul."

"Tarnation, boy! You wanna grab a Bible and have us swear on it?"

"Maybe."

"I want to sell your house, Cooper, not take all of your stuff." Shaking my head, I walked past Harvey to the kitchen. "Come on, Harvey. It's time to make this place smell homey."

Cozying up the inside of Count Dracula's castle might have

been easier.

A couple of minutes later, I heard the front door close.

After the sound of his engine disappeared, I breathed a sigh of relief. "Has Cooper always been so intense?"

He nodded. "He once arrested his grandma on his daddy's side."

"What?"

"Yep. She was three sheets to the wind and shootin' at the neighbor's pigs, claiming they were demons in disguise. Coop tried to stop her and ended up gettin' that there shirt he was wearing peppered with hot lead."

"Holy crap."

"Puttin' his granny in the hoosegow never did settle well with the rest of the family."

I grinned. I couldn't help it. Poor Cooper. Well, maybe it was more like poor Grandma Coop.

"What did Cooper have to say to you after lunch yesterday?" Harvey asked.

"Not much. He wanted the details on what I was doing Friday night—the night the coroner estimates Jane died."

"You have an alibi?"

"Doc."

"Lucky girl."

When it came to Doc, I was. Well, except for the fact that my having kids seemed to wig him out.

"Unfortunately, Cooper wouldn't give me any details about Jane or who they think murdered her. Or why."

I checked the time on my cell phone. I had ten minutes until we opened to the public. While I was staring at the screen, the phone started ringing, the number unfamiliar.

"Hello?" I answered.

"Violet, it's Jerry."

"Jerry?"

"Your boss."

It all came rushing back—big shoulders, big feet, big expectations. "Right, sorry. I haven't eaten lunch yet, so I'm a little scatterbrained."

"Are you ready for some company?"

"You mean prospective buyers?"

"And me."

"You?"

"I thought I'd come by today to watch you in action."

My shoulders tightened so fast it was a wonder my head didn't pop right off. The last thing I needed while playing hostess in Cooper's house was my new boss breathing down my neck. Well, from his height, he'd be breathing on the top of my head.

"Are you sure you have time to spare today?" I asked. Didn't he have bookwork to go through or a big hammer to polish?

"Plenty. I'll be there in a few minutes."

"Jerry, I'd rather you—" about that time I realized I was speaking to a dead line.

Shit! My boss was coming.

I glanced around Cooper's living room, hoping I'd taken care of every last detail. What about the bedrooms? The bathrooms? I hadn't even checked the toilets and shower yet to make sure Cooper had left everything clean.

"Harvey, I'll be right back."

I raced down the hallway, peeking in the guest bathroom where a vanilla-scented candle burned away. Cooper lit a candle? No, that had to have been a Harvey touch.

Next door down, the bedroom-turned-office was empty of everything but a desk with a polished oak top. Even the books had been lined up according to height. I needed to hire Harvey for every open house.

A little further back was Cooper's bedroom. I'd been in there once before when I'd first checked out the house with Harvey in tow.

Not much had changed. It still smelled like leather, only now mixed with pine thanks to the breeze rippling the gray curtains. Cooper's room was filled with black things—from the dresser to the headboard to the leather lounge chair against the far wall. Even the bedside lampshade was black.

Hitting the light switch, I started back up the hall then stopped.

Wait a second.

Heading back into his bedroom, I hit the overhead lights

again and walked over to that black-shaded lamp, taking a closer look.

"You've got to be kidding me," I said and tore the cord from the wall, carting the lamp to the kitchen where the smell of sweet molasses made my stomach purr.

"Harvey, what is this?"

He pulled a tray of molasses cookies out of the oven and dropped it on the burners. He spared a glance at the pistol that made up the lamp's neck. "It's a Peacemaker."

"Is it a real gun?"

"That's not just a 'gun,' it's a Colt .45, nickel-plated with a wooden stock. That there's a piece of history."

"Great. Wonderful. I'm in awe. Does it actually work?"

"Hell, yes. I bought that online for Coop's birthday a few years back. It's just glued to the base." He pointed a spatula at me. "It'll light up a crook so you can get a clear shot. You should get one."

I looked around for somewhere to hide the damned thing. "I can't have a gun in here during an open house."

Harvey pulled the basement key out of his pocket. "Stick it in the basement room with the rest of his stuff."

"Cooper said not to go down there."

"Well, don't dilly dally while you're there. Just open the door and shove it in. I'll get it out later before he even notices it's gone."

I grabbed the key. The steep basement stairs groaned under my two-inch heels. At the bottom, I made a left. I'd been down there once before during that first tour, so I knew exactly where to go.

The deadbolt on the door looked shiny and new. I unlocked it and felt along the wall for a light switch, clicking it on. The room was packed full of boxes and crates and a couple of corkboards. I could smell the cardboard over the scent of damp concrete.

What was the big deal with me not seeing this? It was just a storeroom. No naked babe posters, no sadomasochistic racks with spikes, no dead bodies. If this were Cooper's secret lair, he could use an interior decorator and some air fresheners.

I carried the lamp inside, weaving through several crates full of folders and papers, looking for something to set the lamp on without it falling over and possibly going off. I wouldn't put it past Cooper to have a loaded bedside lamp.

The end table with the two beer cans on it sitting in front of one of the big corkboards would work. I crossed to it, my gaze snagging on my name written on a notecard pinned to the board.

What? My grip tightened on the lamp.

I took a closer look. My name wasn't the only one secured to the board. There were several notecards with names, including Ray's, Mona's, George Mudder's, and Jane's ex-husband—the cradle-robbing one, not Jerry. All of the cards were grouped together in an almost flower shape with Jane's name in the center.

Ah, now I knew why Cooper didn't want me down here.

On the other side of the board, there were a few more names, most I didn't recognize, except for Dominick Masterson, the guy from the diner who was running for mayor in Lead.

Down in the bottom corner were several pictures. The shadows made it hard to see, so I pushed the end table aside, steadying the empty beer cans, and squatted in front of the board. Something shiny filled one of the photos, but it was still too dark to see it clearly.

I looked around for a flashlight or wall outlet and then remembered my cell phone. I set the lamp down on the floor and pulled out my phone, hit a button to light it up, and peered more closely at the picture with the shiny thing in it.

What I saw made my breath whoosh from my lungs.

No!

It couldn't be.

I pulled the picture free and held it up to my phone.

The floor tilted under my feet, then spun a couple of twirls. I shook my head, trying to clear it, and blinked.

A long, shiny hook that looked like it was wrapped with some kind of wicked sharp barbed wire filled the four-by-six picture.

I'd seen a hook just like it once before a couple of weeks ago. The albino had pulled it from his pocket when he was coming for me in the autopsy room at Mudder Brothers. Only the hook he'd threatened me with hadn't had any dried blood on it.

This one did.

"Violet!" Harvey's voice made me drop the picture in surprise.

My heart rattling in my throat, I picked up the photo, took a quick shot of it with my cell phone camera, and then pinned the picture back to the board in the same spot. Pocketing my cell, I moved the end table back to its original position and skirted around the boxes on my way to the door.

"Violet!" Harvey yelled louder.

"What?" I called from the open doorway.

"Pecos Bill is at the door. I think he rode in on a tornado. Should I let him in?"

Pecos Bill? What was he … Oh, Jerry must be here.

"Yes. I'll be right up."

Shutting off the light, I started to close the door then remembered the lamp. If Cooper saw it near the corkboard, he'd know I'd been in there snooping around. I raced back inside, grabbed the Peacemaker, and zipped back out, shutting off the light and locking up behind me.

Harvey scowled at me after I closed the door to the basement and leaned against it, my breath erratic.

"Whaddya doin' with that damned lamp? I thought you were gettin' rid of it."

Right, the lamp. I opened Cooper's pantry door and buried it behind a big plastic container labeled FLOUR.

I shut the cupboard door and turned around to find Jerry filling up the whole kitchen doorway. Wearing a white button-up shirt, a tie covered in different colored rectangles, and a pair of blue Dockers, he looked like a freighter ship docked in port.

His gaze traveled down my pink satin blouse and matching paisley skirt to my heels, his forehead furrowing. "You have dirt on your shirt," he pointed out.

I glanced down, dusting off some dust and spider webs. "Better?"

He nodded. "Those are pretty bright colors for an open

house. You might want to consider something beige next time so that you blend into the background, let the house shine brighter than you."

I refused to wear beige while my blood ran red. It made me look twice as wide and emphasized all of my skin's blotches.

"Violet's not much of a wallflower," Harvey said. "Especially with that hair."

"Yes, I noticed that." Jerry said while inspecting my curls. "Not much we can do about that, though, unless you feel like shaving your head."

"Uhhh." I wasn't sure if he was serious or not.

"I'm kidding."

"Oh, whew." I tried to get my mind back into the game, but my brain was still down in the basement hyperventilating about that bloody weapon.

"Maybe cutting off a few inches would help, though," Jerry said. "Or a straightener."

What? I touched my curls.

He rubbed his huge hands together. "Are you ready to open her up?"

Is that what the albino had done to Jane with that barbed hook? Opened her up? What exactly had Cooper found at the bottom of the mine's pit?

STOP!

I took a deep breath and pasted a smile on my face. It didn't want to stay on my lips.

How in the hell was I going to make it through the next few hours without locking myself in the bathroom and screaming into a towel until they called the guys with the straitjacket to come and take me to my new home?

* * *

There were no garage explosions at Cooper's open house, thank God. But Harvey did burn a batch of cookies, filling the house with smoke and setting off Cooper's fire alarms. All six of them.

Of course, just my luck, Reid Martin, Deadwood's fire chief and Aunt Zoe's ex, was talking to me in the front yard at the time, asking me if the guy he'd seen with Aunt Zoe the night before in Charles' Club, an upstairs lounge on Main Street, was more than just "a friend." I'd been trying to decide if I should tell Reid the truth when all hell broke loose.

Now, two hours later, I could still smell the burned cookies. The carbon particles must be embedded in my nose.

I pulled the Picklemobile into the parking lot behind Calamity Jane's, noticing Doc's Camaro SS parked in its usual spot, and cut the engine.

"One, two, three …" *Boom!* The exhaust scared several crows out of the pine trees overhead. They screeched their complaints at me as they flew away.

"Oh, get in line," I muttered.

I took two deep, slow breaths, then checked to see how badly my hands were shaking—only a slight tremble, barely visible. Good. Grabbing my purse, I stepped out into the warm afternoon sunshine.

Jerry had wanted to meet back in the office for a "team huddle," but he'd needed to run a couple of errands first, so I had a half hour to get my team spirit on.

The back door was locked meaning I wouldn't have to face off with Ray before getting critiqued by my new boss. Score!

It also meant Mona hadn't come into work yet. Maybe I should stop over at her house later, see how she was doing.

I tucked my purse in my desk drawer and slipped out the front door over to Doc's office. I had to tell him about the picture of the albino's barbed hook before my head burst. His office door was unlocked even though the sign on it was flipped to Closed.

Pushing it open, I called, "Doc?"

He was nowhere to be seen, but his laptop was sitting on his desk, the screen saver running.

"Be out in a second, Violet," Doc's voice came from the hallway leading to the back room, a place I knew well from our past escapades. If I hadn't seen that picture with the bloody hook, I'd join him back there and see if he could give me a private pep rally before Jerry told me everything that I had done wrong today.

I dropped into the chair opposite his desk and leaned back, pulling the bobby pins from my hair that Jerry had insisted I use to corral my curls so I'd blend better into Cooper's surroundings. I hadn't bothered explaining to Jerry that Cooper and I were like oil and vinegar—our molecules didn't mix well together because one of us was positively charged and the other was pissed off and always wanting to be on top.

"I can't stay long," I hollered back to Doc, shaking out my hair and then closing my tired eyes for a few seconds of much-wanted rest. "But I need to tell you what I found at Cooper's house today. You're not going to believe it."

Silence came from the back room. Then I heard footfalls.

Eyes still closed, I felt the air shift over me. My chair's wood arms creaked and then the whole thing scooted backwards a little with me in it. I imagined Doc leaning over me and pursed my lips, waiting for him to touch me like he usually did when we were alone.

Then I caught a whiff of cologne—sharp, zesty, not Doc's usual. I opened my eyes.

Detective Cooper's face was six inches from mine, every crease furrowed into one big squint. "What did you find at my house, Ms. Parker?"

Shit!

I gulped, my face flash-frying. "Smoke alarms," I whispered.

Movement over Cooper's shoulder caught my attention. Doc stood in the hallway, his face lined with a cringe.

"Smoke alarms?" Cooper said, trying to stare the truth out of me.

I nodded. "A lot of them. You must buy your weapons and alarms in bulk."

He pushed away from the chair, standing upright, but continued to stare down at me with his arms crossed. "Why do you smell like smoke?"

"Your uncle had a little accident."

His jaw clenched. "Do I still have a house?"

I nodded. "Reid was there to help."

"What was the chief of Deadwood's fire department doing at a false alarm in Lead?"

"Trying to find out if my Aunt Zoe was on a real date last night."

He seemed to swallow that without a second thought. "Was anyone hurt?"

I shook my head.

"How much burned?"

"Twelve cookies. They were a total loss. And a hot pad."

"Where was my uncle when this was happening?"

I hesitated. "Preoccupied."

"With what?"

"More like 'whom.' He was showing your bedroom closet to one of his old flames." Jerry had run to the store for more bottled water, leaving Harvey alone in the house with the wanna-be Brigitte Bardot in her black pleather top.

"My closet?"

"With the door locked."

He grunted.

"Why do you have a deadbolt on the inside of your closet door?"

"None of your business."

"Other than that little incident, the open house was a success."

Unfortunately, most of the visitors were Cooper's neighbors—the female variety—who'd come to see what the inside of his house looked like. Come to find out, he was a bit of a hermit in the neighborhood. No surprise there.

Several of the Cooper groupies wore tight or low-cut shirts and pouted when they found out he wasn't there to show them around. Reid sufficed for many of the ladies my age and older, his charm winning him several phone numbers in the end. I wondered if he was going to give up on Aunt Zoe and settle for one of the open house hotties.

"Any takers?" Cooper asked.

"Not outright, but we'll see what happens over the next couple of days."

"Do I need to hire some cleaners to get the smoke smell out

of my place?"

"No, it's mostly gone. I have your kitchen curtains in the Picklemobile. I'll wash them and bring them by tomorrow."

"Just leave them at the station."

If Cooper was trying to keep me out of his house because of the corkboard in the basement, it was too late.

I looked over at Doc, still watching us from the hall.

He raised a brow.

I grimaced back.

So much for unloading on him about that bloody hook. Judging from Cooper's reaction to my big mouth, I was going to have to sit on this insight until later when I could get Doc alone.

"Well." I stood up and collected my bobby pins from Doc's desk. "I should be going."

I tried to step around Cooper and he blocked my exit.

"Let me get this straight. You came rushing in here to tell Doc about my smoke alarms? That's it?"

No. "Yes." I felt my nose twitch. Yikes! My tell. I covered my nose.

"What's wrong with your nose?"

"It's itching. I think I'm going to sneeze."

Doc appeared next to us with a tissue, his eyes practically twinkling with mirth. He knew all about my tell.

I shot him a warning glare as I blew my nose, faking a couple of exaggerated blinks.

"Maybe you should go take care of that in the bathroom," he suggested, clearing a path for me, saving the day.

Still hiding behind the tissue, I scurried down the hall into his bathroom. I locked the door behind me and leaned against it, shaking my head at the hornets' nest I'd jammed my hand into out there.

I waited, staring at the curly blonde-haired monster in the mirror with dark smudges under her red-lined eyes. Add some streaks in my hair and I'd make a good Bride of Frankenstein.

How was I going to get out of this without having to suffer another interrogation in Cooper's office?

Or lose his trust as his real estate agent?

"Way to go, bonehead," I told Mrs. Frankenstein.

She stuck her tongue out at me.

"Very mature," I said and opened the bathroom door.

To my right, the back door beckoned. I tiptoed toward it. My hand was on the door handle when I heard a scuff on the floor behind me.

"I'll talk to you later," I called out and rushed out into the sunshine, yanking the door closed behind me.

I didn't waste time celebrating my escape in case Cooper was thinking about following me out and chomping on me some more.

I jogged over to Calamity Jane's back door and slipped inside the shadow-filled hall, locking the door behind me for good measure. *Who turned off the lights?* I wondered, heading down the hall toward my desk. Jane's door opened as I passed in front of it.

I looked over and up, expecting to see Jerry's huge frame.

Someone much shorter blasted out, slamming into me. My arms flailed as I stumbled forward, almost falling, until a hand caught and steadied me.

"Thanks," I said, looking around to see who'd tried to run me down.

A female zombie with milky white eyes and grayish-colored skin stared back. Torn flesh hung from her left cheek, black rings circled her eyes, and blood streaked down her chin and neck.

Without further ado, I screamed my head off.

Chapter Six

"Violet!" The zombie grabbed me by the shoulders and pushed me back against the wall. "Stop! It's me. It's Mona."

The sound of my coworker's voice coming from the blood-stained lips cut through my nightmare-come-to-life panic. I stood there panting, staring at the zombie, wondering if I'd starved my brain of so much sleep that it was turning normal people into the walking dead. Like some kind of zombie vision now stuck in place.

"Mona?" I whispered, blinking, trying to see her high cheekbones, porcelain skin, and full lips under the flaps of skin and crusted wounds. She smelled rubbery, synthetic compared to her usual cozy jasmine scent.

"Is she okay?" Jerry asked zombie-Mona, coming up behind her.

"*She* doesn't know," I answered for my coworker and tried to laugh, only it sounded like someone stepped on a cat's tail.

I wanted to ask if he thought Mona looked a little rough around the edges this afternoon, but I was afraid to find out that it was only me. There'd be no coming back from something as serious as walking and talking hallucinations, not without a mad scientist and a few well-placed bolts of lightning.

I heard the front door slam open.

"Violet?" Doc shouted.

"She's back here," zombie-Mona said.

"I heard her scream," he said, rushing toward me.

Jerry stepped back, making room for Doc.

I glanced back and forth between Doc and zombie-Mona. He looked normal, no freaky eyes or apparent cravings for brains.

"You okay?" Doc asked me, his face creased with concern.

"I don't know."

"What's wrong with her?" Cooper asked from where the hall emptied into the front office.

"I think I scared her," Mona said.

Cooper scoffed. "You think? Have you seen yourself lately?"

My focus whipped to the detective. "You mean you can see her …?" I gestured toward her face.

"Her zombie makeup?" he asked. "Of course. It's not that dark back here."

Makeup? "Could somebody please turn on the light," I asked.

The overhead fluorescent flickered on, lighting up Mona's face. Up close under the bright bulbs, I could see the streaks in her makeup, a portion of the flap of skin where the glue had loosened, the edge of her milky white contacts.

"Oh, God," I said, leaning my head back against the wall, feeling like such a huge freaking idiot. "I thought …" I clamped my jaws shut before I spilled too much.

Only Doc knew the truth about my vivid nightmares involving demons and albinos. I couldn't risk telling my boss or Cooper or Mona that I'd thought this was another lifelike nightmare similar to the one I'd had where my psychotic ex-client had melted right in front of my eyes. Coughing up that little nugget would make me sound like an escapee from the loony bin, and I doubted Jerry allowed nut-jobs on his team.

"You should sit down," Doc said and led me down the hall to my desk chair, his palms warm on my chilled skin.

Cooper stepped aside to allow us to pass.

To hide my trembling hands, I gripped the arm rests. Mona followed us out into the front room, Jerry didn't.

Doc went down on one knee in front of me, his eyes searching mine. "You good?"

"Yes. Sorry."

"Don't be." He sniffed twice and squinted at the far wall for a couple of seconds, his olive skin paling. "I have to go."

According to Doc, the Calamity Jane Realty office was haunted, and the entity wasn't the fun-loving kind of ghost that floated around joking with everyone like in Disney movies. Doc's visits to my office were usually short and often took place from the threshold, where he could make a quick escape, if needed, rather than deal with the side effects of interacting with the wispy remains of the past.

As much as I wanted to burrow into his chest and wait for the tremors to pass, I straightened my shoulders. "Okay. I'll talk to you later."

He opened his mouth like he had more to say, then shook his head and rose to his feet. His focus shifted to Cooper. "Ready?"

Cooper nodded, sending a smirk in my direction. "Unless Ms. Parker wants to press charges against the zombie for assault and battery."

I flipped him off, uncaring of our audience. He was lucky I didn't throw my stapler at his back as he walked away chuckling.

After the door shut behind Doc and Cooper, I lowered my forehead to my desk.

"I'm sorry, Violet," Mona said next to me. She squeezed my shoulder. "I was planning to take off my makeup as soon as I got here, but Jerry called me into his office first thing."

Lifting my head, I looked her up and down, noticing for the first time that she was only a zombie from the neck up. Her yellow T-shirt, faded blue jeans, and tennis shoes had no rips, tears, or blood.

"You're the second zombie I've seen today," I told her. "There was a zombie at the grocery store earlier."

She smiled, her teeth bright white in the midst of the dried blood framing her mouth and trailing down her chin. "We're in a play at the opera house. Today was the start of dress rehearsals."

"Up in Lead?"

She nodded.

Lead had a century-old opera house with a history full of gilded grandeur, world class entertainment, and famous visitors. It was also rumored to be haunted, like so many other buildings in the area. I had yet to walk inside the six-story building, but I'd peeked in the lobby doors recently after dropping off some of Layne's books at the library next door.

"I didn't know you were an actress," I said as Jerry joined us again.

"Mona and Jane have both dabbled in community theatre over the years." Jerry handed me a bottle of water left over from Cooper's open house. "Here, your throat must need some rewetting after that scream."

"Thanks." My cheeks warmed at his reminder of my banshee-like behavior. I uncapped the bottle and took a swig, wishing it were a glass bottle with the word TEQUILA printed on it.

"Jane was the actress," Mona said. "She just talked me into joining her on occasion." She looked down at her hands, her blood-encircled mouth curving down at the corners. "This time I wasn't planning to be involved in the production, but then Jane …" Mona cleared her throat. "The producer called a few days ago. I'm just filling in for her now."

Jerry put his hand on Mona's shoulder, which she shook off, flashing him a scowl.

I thought I felt a ripple of tension pass between them, but then it was gone, making me wonder how long they'd known each other and how well.

Jerry cleared a spot on Ray's desk and dropped onto it, his long legs stretching to the floor.

"When does the play start?" I asked Mona.

"The first of October. It runs twice a week for a month—a matinee on Saturdays and an evening show on Sundays."

"The play is a month away and you're already having dress rehearsals?" That showed how much I knew about community theatre.

"Peter Tarragon, the director, would've given Napoleon a run for his money on the tyranny scale. He insists this performance must go off without a flaw, including the makeup and costumes, and has fired cast and crew members on the spot for disobeying his orders."

She opened her desk drawer and pulled out a hairbrush and compact mirror. "Word backstage is that he's trying to grab the attention of a few bigger theatre companies to propel his career, so he won't accept anything less than perfection on stage and off. Today was our trial costume and makeup run. He had us go through in shifts so he could inspect the costumes one at a time. This coming week, we'll start rehearsing in full makeup and costume."

"What's your part?" I asked.

"The maid of honor."

"Always a bridesmaid, never a bride," Jerry said, watching Mona pull off her hairband and brush through her auburn locks.

"Maid of honor?" I said. "But you're a zombie. I don't get it. What's the play?"

Mona inspected her hair in the mirror then tugged on the loose flap of skin half-stuck to her cheek. "It's called 'Better Off Wed,' only the word 'Wed' is crossed off and replaced with 'Dead.' It's a zombie wedding musical."

I gaped at her. "Like with singing and dancing?"

She nodded and snapped the compact closed. "Jane had a solo performance in one of the songs at one point, which I'm not thrilled about, but for her I'll give it my best. She was a much better singer than I am." Her milky eyes grew watery. She turned away from both Jerry and me, grabbing the black duffel bag sitting on the floor by her desk. "I'm going to go wash this stuff off and change."

I watched her walk away until the bathroom door shut. Then I turned to Jerry. "I'm sorry about that screaming business." I waved toward the back hall. "I didn't expect to run into a zombie at work."

"As opposed to on the street where they belong." He grinned. "What a day. Burned cookies and zombies."

At least he didn't know about Harvey and his closet nookie. That was Reid's and my secret, along with the pain I'd seen ripple across Reid's face when I'd told him the truth about Aunt Zoe's romantic interest in her date last night.

"Is life always this entertaining here in Deadwood?" Jerry asked.

Besides the murders, ghosts, mediums, and albinos? "No. It just has your normal, small town fun."

He stood and stretched all the way up. I crooked my neck to see if he could tickle the high, tin-plated ceiling. Not quite. Damn, he was big. Where had Jane found him? Why had they split? I'd have to ask Mona. Judging from her actions and his words, she'd known him for a while.

"Are we ready to get our 'huddle' on?" I asked, wanting to get his critique of today's open house and my lack of success over and done.

He shook his head. "No. You look like hell, Violet."

Ouch. I cringed. He could use some coaching on his delivery.

"How about we skip the huddle," he continued. "We can talk about it in the morning."

I wasn't going to fight him on that. All I wanted to do was go home, put on my pajamas, grab the half-gallon of peanut butter fudge ice cream from the freezer, and slip into a dairy coma on the couch while Humphrey Bogart filled the screen. On second thought, skip the ice cream and bring on that tequila.

Thinking of Bogart made my chest ache for Natalie, my fellow Bogart groupie. I wished she'd give me a chance to explain what had happened with Doc. That I didn't want to hurt her, but I couldn't stop myself from playing with fire even while knowing I was going to get good and burned. After the whole mess with Doc and Jeff and the kids yesterday, what degree burn was yet to be determined.

I collected my purse from my desk drawer, my knees no longer knocking when I stood. "Tomorrow it is."

Jerry walked me to the back door, holding it open for me.

"Oh, Violet," he said as I stepped out into the warm, late afternoon breeze. "Do you know a Benjamin Underhill?"

A feeling of dread fell like an anvil, landing in the bottom of my gut.

Benjamin was Ray's nephew, who also happened to be a real estate agent—the very agent that Ray had been trying to replace me with for the last three months. Because Jane had hired me instead of Ben, Ray had had it in for me since my first day on the job. His continued attempts over the months to get me fired had helped our relationship remain thorny.

I'd actually gone to dinner twice with Ben. He was the kind of guy my mom would hook me up with—one who pulled out chairs and held doors and never claimed to smell ghosts. While I liked Ben in a let's-just-stay-peers way, his name on Jerry's lips roused my fear of being kicked to the curb.

"Sure, I know Ben. He's Ray's nephew. Why do you ask?"

Please don't say you're hiring him.

"I'm meeting Ray and him later for dinner."

Ray! That rat bastard!

I tried my best not to let my loathing for Ray spill out through my eyes. "Oh, yeah?"

"What can you tell me about Benjamin Underhill? Is he a team player?"

"A team player?" I repeated his question, stalling.

I didn't want to slander Ben. He'd never been anything but nice to me, although a little creepy with his undivided attention at times. On the other hand, Jerry getting chummy with Ben could mean the end of my job at Calamity Jane's, especially if Cornelius wasn't able to come up with the funds for the hotel deal and I was suddenly a one-sale agent again.

"I haven't worked with Ben enough to answer that." I decided dodging and weaving was my best strategy this early in the game since Jerry might be testing me on some level.

"All right. I'll find out for myself tonight." Jerry pointed at me. "Tomorrow, let's talk about your future with Calamity Jane Realty."

I'd rather lick a doorknob. "I'm looking forward to it."

* * *

Aunt Zoe met me at the door when I got home. Tonight she wore a long blue bohemian style skirt and a flowing white cotton top with blue diamonds embroidered on it. With her hair pulled back in a braid threaded with rhinestones and her cowboy boots polished, she had me whistling and cat-calling as I circled her.

"Another date with Mr. Wyoming?" I asked, catching a whiff of the exotic scent of her expensive perfume.

"We're heading down to Rapid tonight. May even do some dancing."

"You really like this guy, huh?"

"Yeah, I think I do."

As fond as I'd grown of Reid, I wanted to see Aunt Zoe happy. However, I couldn't resist testing to see if she really was done with the fire captain.

"I saw Reid today. He asked who your friend was at the lounge last night."

Her eyes narrowed. "That's none of his damned business." She grabbed her purse off the side table. "And you can tell him I said that next time he tries to nose into my life."

I guess she was done. "Okay."

"I'm not going back down that road again." She started out the door, came back and kissed me on the cheek. "Sorry, sweetheart. I want to hear about your open house at Cooper's. Tell me tomorrow over breakfast?"

"Sure. Have a fun night." I waited until she'd climbed into her pickup to close the door. "Sorry, Reid," I said. I went to see what my children were into, and if I could get a piece of the action.

Hours later, after feeding the kids some pepperoni pizza for supper, I sneaked upstairs and tried calling Doc for the third time. It kicked to voicemail after several rings. I hung up without leaving a message, just as I had before, and tossed my cell phone onto the bed. I needed to talk to Doc, not his voicemail. Besides, what I wanted to say shouldn't be recorded.

My phone buzzed, announcing a text message. I grabbed it, hoping it was Natalie replying to my message about the cookie disaster at Cooper's open house.

Nope—it was Doc: *Hi, Trouble.*

I typed back: *Where are you?*

Cooper's.

What? Why?

Playing poker.

For real? I frowned, not liking Doc carousing with the law. There must not be any ghosts hanging out in Cooper's house. Hell, the gun lamp had probably scared them away.

Before I could reply, another text came in: *Cooper says to tell you no texting during poker. Gotta go.*

"Cooper can shove it," I told my phone and stuffed it in my

sweat jacket pocket. A glance at the clock got me moving. Both kids had homework to finish before bed.

After cracking the whip, we watched a little TV, then brushed teeth and climbed into bed—well, they did, not me. I waited another hour before pulling the bottle of aged tequila down from the cupboard above the fridge. I didn't waste time with a glass, just leaned against the kitchen counter and sipped from the bottle. Staring at Aunt Zoe's Betty Boop cookie jar, I drank the smooth tasting liquor.

"You're lucky, Betty," I told Miss Boop, pointing at her with the bottle. "You get to eat all of the cookies you want and you still look sexy."

My phone buzzed in my pocket.

"I used to be able to pull off wearing a bustier like yours, but having kids really messed up my fun-bags." I took another hit of tequila and then pulled my phone from my pocket.

Doc had texted again: *I want to talk to you.*

I replied: *You still at Cooper's?*

No. I'm standing on your back porch watching you talk to the cookie jar.

Oh! I looked at the back door. On the other side of the glass, Doc beckoned me outside with his index finger.

I pocketed my phone, set the tequila on the counter, and opened the door, shutting it and the screen quietly behind me. "What are you doing back here?"

Doc stood in the deep shadows, nothing more than a dark silhouette. "Being quiet on a school night."

"Where's your car?"

"At home. I walked. After all of the cigar smoke at Cooper's, fresh air appealed."

I crossed my arms, wanting to touch him but following his Joe-cool lead. "So you're one of Cooper's poker buddies now, huh?"

"Does that bother you?"

"A little. I don't trust him not to whip out his handcuffs and haul me off to jail at any moment just because he feels like it."

"You want to know what bothers me?"

"What?"

"You screaming your head off today and scaring the hell out of me."

I grimaced. "Sorry about that. Mona really freaked me out."

"I'm not talking about your verbal reaction to Mona."

"What are you talking about then?"

"The panic I saw in your eyes."

"I thought I was hallucinating."

"When I saw you, I wanted to do this." He reached out and captured my elbow, tugging me into the shadows with him where he enfolded me in his arms. "But I couldn't. Not with an audience. *That's* what really bothered me."

I leaned my forehead against his chest. The faint odor of cigar smoke mixed with his cologne soothed away the day's rough edges, taking care of what the tequila hadn't. "I definitely could have used some of this right about then."

He lifted my chin, tipping my head back. I tried to see his face, but the shadows were too deep.

"Then you sat there in your chair, trying to hide your trembling."

"God, don't remind me. I felt like such an idiot for overreacting," I said.

His mouth touched mine, gentle, soft, slow; his lips caressed mine, taking their time. My heart rolled over and splayed out like a good puppy, vulnerable, smitten, his to treasure or crush. That couldn't be good. I moaned.

He pulled back. "I've been waiting to do that all day."

"Was it worth the wait?"

"I don't know." He walked me backwards until I was pressed against the side of the house. "I'm going to need to try it again to tell." Capturing my wrists together in one hand, he held them hostage above my head against the siding. His eyes glittered from the feeble light coming through the back door window. "Now what's this about me being short, little woman?"

I smiled up at him. "My new boss has several inches on you."

"I noticed." His lips moved along my jaw, teasing me with feathery kisses. "He looks familiar. I've seen him somewhere before."

My body swayed toward him, wanting more contact. "Maybe you saw him visiting Jane before I came to town."

Doc had been living in Deadwood about eight months before I moved up from Rapid.

"No," he said. "Somewhere else."

"I think he's from the eastern side of the state."

His free hand glided along the back of my neck, his body pressing mine into the house. "I don't want to talk about your boss anymore."

"So shut me up then," I said, wrapping my leg around his thigh.

He obliged, plundering my mouth, the easy warmth between us now a sizzling fervor.

"You taste like tequila," he said when his lips blazed a trail across my cheek. His hand slid down my neck, his palm covering my breast. "I want to drip lime juice on my favorite parts, sprinkle on some salt, and start licking."

My head swooned and not just in a lovesick way. I had a feeling the tequila I'd downed while talking to Betty Boop was catching up with me, and Doc's kisses weren't helping my ability to remain vertical.

Doc let go of my wrists and stepped back, slipping free of my leg hold. "We shouldn't do this here."

"I know." Groaning, I slid down the wall, aching. "The kids might hear us."

"And your aunt."

"She's on a date." I peeked up at him. "We could sneak upstairs to my bed."

"It squeaks."

"How do you know that?" He hadn't been in my bedroom yet.

"I heard it the other night when you were talking to me on the phone," he said.

"You were paying attention to the bed's springs?"

"I was imagining you naked on it."

"Really? What were we talking about?" I didn't remember getting heated up like I usually did when he started telling where he wanted to touch and how.

"You were asking me what kind of car you should buy when you get the commission from Cornelius's sale."

I giggled. "And you were thinking about me naked right then?"

"Violet, I think about you naked ninety percent of the time I'm talking to you, in person or on the phone."

"What about the other ten percent?"

"You're wearing something lacy."

A loud laugh escaped from my throat before I could corral it.

Doc covered my mouth with his hand. "Shhh."

That made me laugh even harder.

He changed out his hand for his lips.

My laughter died in my throat as he fired up my rockets again—all systems go!

He pulled away much too soon and tugged me over to the porch steps, drawing me down next to him. I resisted the urge to tackle him and drag him behind Aunt Zoe's juniper shrubs.

"So," he said, "tell me what you found at Cooper's house that nearly got you in big trouble at my office."

"Oh, jeez." I buried my face in my hands. "I almost swallowed my tongue when I opened my eyes and saw the detective standing over me instead of you."

"You should've seen your face." I could hear the grin in his tone.

I poked him in the ribs. "Thanks for the heads up on that. You could have warned me."

He caught my hand and laced his fingers through mine. "And say what? 'Violet, don't talk about Detective Cooper because he's standing in my back room looking at a book with old pictures of Mudder Brothers Funeral Parlor.'"

Cooper was looking at old Mudder Brothers' pics? Why? I'd have to ponder that later.

"Well, something like that certainly would have helped," I said.

He squeezed my hand. "Tell me what you found."

I glanced back over my shoulder, making sure neither of my kids was eavesdropping. "A corkboard with Jane's name pinned on it, surrounded by other names, including mine."

Doc was silent for a moment, and then said, "You think it's his case board."

"Is that what you call it?"

"That's what they call it on TV."

"There was something else on it." I stared out at the dark shadows hovering just beyond the glow of the house lights. "A picture of a barbed hook covered with blood."

"The murder weapon?"

"That's my guess."

I hesitated to tell him the rest, hating to say it aloud, as if giving it voice would make it more real, more dangerous. But I needed to tell someone, and Doc was probably the only one who would believe I hadn't been imagining things in that autopsy room.

"I've seen a hook just like it before, Doc. Only that one wasn't covered in blood."

I felt the weight of Doc's stare. "Where?"

"That night at Mudder Brothers."

"The albino?" he asked.

I nodded. "He threatened me with it."

"Shit."

"Yeah."

His thumb stroked my palm. "Are you going to tell Cooper?"

"How can I? If I say anything, he'll know I withheld information from him about that night at the funeral parlor, which will make him wonder what else I'm hiding. I don't need him sniffing around me any more than he already does."

"Violet, it isn't just a bottle you're concealing this time. It's a link to Jane's murder weapon."

"I know that, but Cooper's going to wonder how I came to know about Jane's murder weapon, which means he'll know I was in that basement room he ordered Harvey and me to stay out of. At the least, he'll fire me as his real estate agent, which will not win me any favors with my new boss." And with Ray and Benjamin on the sidelines waiting for me to stumble, I needed to look like I was still running strong.

"What's the worst that can happen?" Doc asked.

"I could end up in jail for a multitude of charges, including stealing evidence."

"Stealing evidence?"

"Yeah, there's that book from the Carhart house that I kept, the one that belonged to Lila." After the sadistic bitch had tried to use it to lure a demon into impregnating me, I figured I had a right to keep it handy in case something started stirring inside of me. And something had, only in my brain, not my uterus.

"Right," Doc said, sounding tired. "The book."

Doc was hiding the book for me in his closet, studying it, watching for more signs of the demon, Kyrkozz, who'd paid a visit to me in my nightmares a couple of weeks ago and warned me to "get out." If only I knew how to depart from where he was referring, I'd be happy to let the door hit me in the ass on the way out.

"Cooper might be able to help protect you," Doc said.

"You and I both know from firsthand experience that Cooper's gun didn't work on that albino."

We stared out into the darkness for several silent breaths. The surrounding pine trees muffled the usual ruckus from Deadwood—traffic, music, and laughter. If only they could block out the threatening elements, too.

"What are you going to do?" Doc asked.

"I don't know. That's why I needed to talk to you, to help me make sense of what that hook means."

"I don't want you to get hurt, Violet."

Were we talking about my crazy-for-Doc feelings here or a killer albino? I went with the latter, hiding behind a grin. "Me, either. Pain is not really my thing."

My pocket rang. I fished out my phone, figuring it was Aunt Zoe calling to tell me she was going to be really late—as in after-breakfast late.

Cooper's name showed on the screen. The detective must have bionic ears.

"It's Cooper," I whispered.

"You'd better answer it or he might show up on your doorstep with a search party ready to hunt you down. Again."

I wrinkled my nose at Doc and pushed the *Answer* button. "Hello?"

"Where's my Peacemaker?" Cooper asked.

"It's nice to hear your voice, too, Detective Cooper."

He huffed. "It's hard to read in bed without my lamp."

Cooper read? I imagined all sorts of firearm how-to manuals piled next to him on the nightstand.

"You're just afraid you won't be able to shoot the bogeyman. Although with the deadbolt on the *inside* of your closet door, you're kind of screwed."

"I'm not laughing, Parker. Where's my light?"

He sounded extra crotchety tonight, like he'd spent the night getting his chest waxed instead of playing poker with his buddies and drinking beer.

"I hid it in your pantry behind the flour container," I told him. "I can't have loaded guns at my open houses."

"But kitchen fires and garage explosions are okay?"

"I'm not going to dignify that with a response."

"Reid sends his love," he said. I could imagine the smirk on his lips right then.

"I didn't know you snuggled up with Deadwood's fire captain at night. How cozy for you two."

"He's passed out on my couch, wiseass."

"Does that happen often?" Or did it have something to do with Aunt Zoe seeing another man?

"Nope. Sleep tight, Parker. Tell Doc not to bite. Leave that to your zombie friends." The line went dead.

I stuffed the phone back in my pocket. "Did you tell Cooper you were coming here?"

"No. But he knows you kept calling me during the game."

"So Reid was there playing with you guys tonight?"

"Yes. Your fiery past was one of the topics of discussion."

"You defended my reputation, of course?"

"Of course," he said in mock seriousness then ruined it by laughing under his breath.

I lifted his hand and bit his knuckle until he pulled away, still laughing.

"Did Reid say anything about Aunt Zoe?" I asked. I doubted

he had but wondered nonetheless.

"No. But damn that guy can drink. Cooper mentioned handcuffing him to the couch so he wouldn't try to drive home."

Poor Reid. I bet I knew why he'd been drinking so much. Broken hearts were often drowned in bottles.

I heard the back door hinges creak and jumped up, yanking my hand from Doc's.

"Mom?" Layne said from the other side of the screen door. "I heard voices. What are you doing out here?" He turned on the back porch light.

I shielded my eyes from the brightness. "I'm talking to Doc."

"What's he doing here so late?" His tone made it clear he was not thrilled with Doc sitting in the dark with me.

"He's keeping me company until Aunt Zoe gets home."

"Why do you need company? You've been alone a bunch before."

Tell me about it. "Layne, go back to bed. You have school in the morning."

"I'm not tired."

"Now, Layne." He slammed the door.

"Dang it. Now Addy's probably awake."

Doc stood. "I should go."

I'd rather he just held my hand again, but reality had returned, along with the fact that my kids seemed to send Doc running in the other direction.

"I'll walk you to the gate," I said.

We strolled through the grass in silence, not touching.

I closed the gate behind him. "Thanks for stopping by."

"I'll see you tomorrow." He took a couple of strides and then stopped and walked back.

"Did you forget something?" I asked, hoping he had. A declaration of his undying love would have been nice. I'd even have settled for a declaration of undying lust with the hope that it would grow into something more.

"What happened to their father?" he asked.

I stepped back in surprise, not expecting a question about Rex, the good-for-nothing asshole who'd left me high and dry shortly after finding out I was pregnant.

"He didn't want kids." I gave the short and bittersweet version.

"When did they last see him?"

"Never. He left when I was pregnant and signed away all rights after they were born."

"Have you heard from him since?"

As a matter of fact, I had recently but not directly. Detective Cooper knew all about it, and while I often hated how tight-lipped he was, this was one of those times I was happy he didn't share secrets.

It turned out that Rex seemed to be trying to check up on me. It was because of him asking around about me that my business card had ended up in the hand of the decapitated body found in the old cemetery out behind Harvey's barn a few weeks back. I didn't know why Rex was suddenly interested in catching up nor did I want to. I wanted the bastard to stay the hell away from my children.

"No, I haven't," I answered, which was essentially true since he hadn't actually contacted me. "And as far as I'm concerned, my children never will either."

"Mom?" Layne called out again from the back door.

"Damn it." I growled in my throat.

"Go be with your kids, Violet," Doc said, walking away backwards. "I'll talk to you tomorrow."

Chapter Seven

Monday, September 3rd

I slept like hell.

Maybe it was the tequila. Or Doc's questions about Rex. Or Cooper and that damned albino's hook. Or a pea under my mattress. Whatever the reason, I had sweaty nightmares that merged together into a kaleidoscope of terror until I woke up in the midst of a muffled pillow scream. Then I dragged my tired ass to the shower.

While the hot water poured down my back, one fear that threaded through each scream-queen moment made my chest tight—what if my albino buddy was still alive? What if he'd killed Jane? Him still being alive after I buried a huge pair of scissors in his back, not to mention the whole spontaneous combustion and disappearing in a puff of smoke act, made my questions seem absurd to a rational person ... but *what if?*

I put my head under the water, replaying that final scene with the albino, trying to make sense yet again of something that was beyond logic. Wiping the water from my eyes, I gave up and grabbed the shaving cream.

The razor shook in my hands. I took a couple of slow breaths and tried not to lacerate my legs. Scabs weren't professional—or sexy.

Since the mess at Mudder Brothers, all I'd focused on was the albino's twin showing up on my doorstep, but maybe I had two albinos waiting for the right moment to upend my world—and one of them itching for payback. If only I knew with whom I was dealing ... or what. At least with Ray, I could see him for the snake he was and step on him before he struck.

I shut off the shower and dripped all of the way to my

bedroom. Gray clouds filled the sky outside my window. Fall was on its way, along with its much cooler temperatures. I grabbed a calf-length, wispy blue-violet skirt from my closet and a modestly cut matching tunic, avoiding any cleavage display since I had a "career" meeting this morning with my new boss.

My purple boots would have looked great with the skirt and drawn some much-wanted attention from Doc, but Natalie still had them. She'd probably written *Jezebel* all over them with a black permanent marker by now.

After rousing the kids and chop-chopping them to get dressed and brush their teeth, I headed downstairs, lured by the smell of fresh brewed coffee. Aunt Zoe was sitting at the kitchen table staring into her cup like she was reading tea leaves.

"How was your date last night?" I asked, pouring myself some caffeinated breakfast.

"Enlightening," she said, sarcasm present.

"What happened?" I pulled out the chair across from her.

She scratched at a crumb glued to the table. "I found out he's in the midst of a divorce."

"His choice or hers?"

"His."

"That's a good thing, isn't it? He's moving on."

"I don't want to get involved with a man who has been divorced for less than two years."

I grinned. "You think they're contagious?"

"I've been there, done that, and got my heart broken."

"When was that?" Was she talking about Reid?

"A long time ago."

"What happened?"

"He changed his mind."

No, that couldn't be Reid. He wasn't married to anyone.

Aunt Zoe had dated on and off over the years. Maybe the broken heart explained why she'd never settled down with one man.

I opened my mouth to ask her more, but she interrupted with, "How did the open house go?"

An obvious change of subject.

Sipping my coffee, I went along with the change to give her

some space for the moment. "We had a nice crowd."

"Anyone act interested?"

"Yep." Plenty—interested in Harvey and Cooper and Reid, but not in the house.

"Anything exciting happen?"

Besides some closet-nookie, a fire, and the discovery of Jane's murder weapon? "Not really."

Nothing I wanted to burden her with in her current Droopy-the-Dog state, anyway. I took a drink of coffee, searching for a way to return to the subject of men, particularly Reid.

Thunder from the stairwell announced the arrival of both kids at once, their bickering interrupted by an angry screech from Addy before they even stepped foot inside of the kitchen. It was no wonder Doc was keeping his distance. At the moment, I wanted to join him on the sidelines.

A second squeal from Addy had me on my feet.

"Criminy!" I pushed up my sleeves and went to play referee.

An hour-and-no-kids later, I sat in the Picklemobile in the parking lot behind Calamity Jane's with my cell phone in hand. I scrolled to Detective Cooper's number, then cancelled out of the screen and tossed the phone onto his clean kitchen curtains on the bench seat next to me.

I needed to talk to Cooper about that barbed hook and my albino pal, but how could I say anything without showing him all of my cards?

I reached for my cell phone, but pulled my hand back empty. If I called, he'd want me to come into his office. Once he got me there under those bright fluorescent lights, what was to keep me from spilling like an overflowing sewer grate under his brain-piercing glare?

Wait. Maybe if I were surrounded by other people, I could hide my telltale nose twitch better when truth-skirting became a necessity. I could even call in some backup to help keep me out of trouble.

I scooped up my phone and found Cooper's number. My heart pounded in my throat, which was just silly, damn it. Before I could chicken out again, I hit the Call button.

Cooper answered midway through the second ring. "Make it

quick, Parker, I'm in the middle of something."

Someone needed to teach him a little phone etiquette.

"I have your curtains." I rolled my eyes at how stupid that sounded as an opener and tried again. "I need to talk to you."

"I don't have time to talk right now."

"Fine. Meet me at Bighorn Billy's in an hour." I looked down at the seat next to me. "That is if you want your curtains back."

As extortion went, I could probably use some practice.

Silence came from the other end of the line. I wondered if he'd already hung up on me and looked at my phone's screen—no, we were still connected. "Did you hear me, Detective?"

"Are you holding my curtains for ransom, Violet?"

"Yes," I answered, and before I blurted out anything even more asinine, I hung up.

My heart was still pounding in my ears as I hopped out of the Picklemobile and slammed the door behind me. I'd set up a brunch date with the devil; what was next? Oh, right, a meeting with Goliath. Joy.

Crossing the parking lot, I noticed Doc's Camaro wasn't there, nor Mona's or Ray's SUVs. Unfortunately, Jerry's silver Hummer was.

Damn. I wanted nothing more than to head back home to Aunt Zoe's and just sit on her back porch watching Elvis the chicken peck at the ground until it was time to see Cooper. But since Ray had introduced his nephew—aka my possible successor, Benjamin—to Jerry last night, I needed to pull up my britches and at least act the part of a successful Realtor.

I stepped through Calamity Jane's back door, hearing the deep sound of Jerry's voice coming from Jane's ... or rather *his* open office door.

"Violet," he called out as I walked past on the way to my desk.

I winced and stopped, then backed up, hovering in his doorway. His face looked freshly chiseled, the smell of citrus and sandalwood overpowering any remaining traces of Jane.

"I'll call you back later," he said into his phone and hung up. His gaze traveled down my outfit, his forehead wrinkling as he finished with my strappy, high-heeled sandals.

What? There were no shaving cuts or bandages visible. If he was going to insist on my wearing pantyhose, I was demanding a raise in my commission rates for putting up with those binding torture devices.

"Shut the door and have a seat, please," he said, nodding toward the door.

Crudmongers.

I followed his orders, lowering into the chair across from him, pasting a smile on my lips.

Here it came, the comment on my lack of sales, the questions about what I was doing to lure buyers, the analysis of my wrongdoings after his open house observations yesterday, the reports showing my solo sale in three months, for which I could thank my boyfriend. I straightened my back, ready to be put through the wringer.

Tilting back in his chair, Jerry steepled his fingers over his wide chest. "When was the last time you had a makeover?"

My smile slipped a little. "A what?"

"A makeover. You know, someone helping you with your choice of clothing, makeup, and hair style."

I touched my curls, which were tamed with hair product today. "Uh, never."

"Hmm."

Hmm? What did that mean? Was I as much of a mess on the outside these days as I was on the inside?

He leaned forward, his forearms on the desk. "How well do you know Tiffany Sugarbell?"

The red-headed bombshell who used to have sex with my boyfriend? "We're acquainted."

"Then you know she works for one of the most successful real estate agencies in the Black Hills area."

"Yes." I also knew she was ultra-competitive in everything she did, including mattress bouncing, but Jerry didn't need to know that—or maybe he already had firsthand experience. "She's the agent I'm working with on The Old Prospector Hotel deal."

"Right. I've been studying their business model, and from what I can tell, they use Tiffany for more than just her know-how when it comes to real estate."

"What do you mean?"

"She's their hook."

"Hook?"

"Their lure, especially with male clients. They use her in eighty percent of their advertising pieces now."

Oh, that kind of hook. "Is that legal?"

"As long as she isn't exchanging sexual favors in return for a contract, sure."

Define *sexual favors*, I thought, remembering some of my less professional dealings with Doc when I was his agent.

"It's not exactly ethical," Jerry continued, "but this day and age when sales are hard to come by, more and more agencies are trying new marketing techniques."

His comment reminded me of Tiffany's advice a couple of weeks back about using my hair and cleavage to win sales. Had she been sharing what her new employer had enforced? Or was that just innate for the Jessica Rabbit twin?

"The way they are using Tiffany to attract customers got me thinking about you."

My smile fell off my face. I wasn't sure I liked the way this was going. "*What* about me?"

"Well, with some help from a professional and a little photo manipulation, I think you have the potential to bring us some more sales."

I blinked at his backhanded compliment. "What about Mona? Couldn't you use her?"

"Mona is a redhead. We don't want to look like we're copying Tiffany's agency. Plus, Mona has been around for a while and already has a reputation in place. You're still new in town with a reputation to build."

Oh, I had a reputation already building, one involving ghosts and killers. Apparently, he hadn't yet heard of "Spooky Parker."

"What are you doing tomorrow morning?" Jerry asked. "Do you have any appointments?"

His probing stare left me no fibbing room. "Not at this time."

"Good." He clapped his big hands together, the loud crack

making me flinch. "You and I are going to Rapid City."

"We are?"

"I'm taking you shopping."

* * *

Bighorn Billy's parking lot was only a third full.

I pulled in next to Cooper's police-issued sedan and cut the engine. The Picklemobile sputtered for several seconds before going out with her usual bang. After my pep talk with Jerry about how we could fix me up so I was as appealing to the male sex as my boyfriend's ex-hottie, I felt like going out with a bang myself—as in a serving tray upside Jerry's thick skull.

Pulling out my cell phone, I tried to call Cornelius for the fifth time since running out of Jerry's office with my pride between my legs. I really needed that big commission check from the hotel sale to be taken seriously as a real estate agent before my boss turned me into a Barbie Doll.

The call went to voicemail, as it had the previous four times. Cornelius's voice came on the line. "I prefer messages to be left in Morse code."

Why couldn't I find semi-normal clients? I waited for the beep. "It's Violet. Call me."

I had no idea how many series of Morse code clicks those four words took. Maybe for the next message I could just burp out S-O-S.

Hopping out of the Picklemobile, I headed for the restaurant's front doors. The dark gray clouds overhead were a great visual effect for going to meet my doom.

The smell of bacon and eggs hit me when I walked through the door. Buck Owens crooned from the overhead speakers about acting naturally. Good advice from the Buck-ster, but odds were before the week was up I'd be a runner-up for the biggest fool to hit the big time.

Cooper eyed me from the back corner booth, wearing a white button up shirt, a blue tie, a broken nose, and a scowl.

I ricocheted his scowl right back at him and joined him.

"Where are my curtains?" he said as a greeting.

"It's nice to see you, too, smiley. You'll get your curtains when we're done here."

I slid into the opposite seat and opened the menu. I needed something to chew on before I lunged over the table and took a chomp out of the detective glaring at me over his coffee cup.

"Done with what?" he asked.

"My interrogation."

"*You* are interrogating me?"

"Yes." The nervous jitters I'd had when I'd called him this morning were now buried under several layers of indignation, humiliation, and resentment thanks to Jerry.

"Did you order already?" I asked, looking up from the menu.

Cooper nodded. "For both of us."

Last time Cooper had ordered on my behalf, he'd gotten me a salad. Being the ever-present gumshoe that he was, he'd noticed my sad attempt at dieting.

I closed the menu and dropped it on the table. "You'd better have ordered me something with meat."

One blonde eyebrow lifted. "Feeling carnivorous this morning are we, Ms. Parker?"

"I filed my teeth on the way over."

"Lucky me."

The waitress brought over a cup of coffee for me. "Could you bring a second cup, please," I asked her.

She nodded and left.

At Cooper's squint, I said, "Company's coming."

"Who else are you extorting …" His attention targeted the door, his jaw tightening. "I should have known."

"Scooch on over, girl," Harvey said to me when he joined us. He looked more grizzled than usual, like he'd just rolled out of a bar.

The waitress delivered Harvey's coffee as I settled my purse against the wall.

"I'll have my usual," Harvey told her, sounding a bit gruff instead of his usual flirty self.

Cooper's rigid gaze measured both of us after the waitress left, his glare shooting back and forth. "What's going on,

Parker?"

"Breakfast," I said. "And a few questions."

His lips tightened. "What's he doing here?" he nudged his head at Harvey.

"I came for the free food," Harvey muttered.

"He's my backup." I took a sip of coffee and grimaced. Blech! Bitter. It was in desperate need of sweetener—so was Cooper.

"Backup? Are you going to read me my rights next?"

Lowering my cup, I leaned forward and didn't waste any more time. "How was Jane killed?" I kept my voice low enough for our ears only.

Cooper scoffed. "As if I'm going to share any of the details with you of all civilians."

"Was she murdered before she was dumped in the Open Cut?" I pressed.

He mimicked my elbows on the table pose, closing the space between us, his face full of furrows and crow's feet. "What makes you think she was dumped there?"

Oh, nothing, much. I just might have met her killer up close and personal. "It's a gut feeling."

The waitress brought our food, interrupting the staring contest I'd been having with the detective. She dropped a plate with a small pile of scrambled egg whites and a single piece of bacon in front of me, along with a small bowl of oatmeal. Cooper had ordered the same items, only with three times as much of everything.

"You got more than me," I said to him, picking up my fork.

He shrugged. "You're a girl. Every calorie counts."

It was no wonder his grandmother had shot him.

"I'll bring yours in a flash, honey," she told Harvey with a wink and waggled her hips as she left.

Harvey didn't seem to notice her prancing exit, fiddling with his spoon instead. Normally the old dog's tongue would match her waggle. I glanced at Cooper to see if he'd noticed his uncle's lack of piss and vinegar this morning, but he seemed too preoccupied with digging into his big fat pile of eggs to notice.

"What else does your gut tell you?" the detective asked me.

"It's my interrogation, not yours," I said, reaching for my one measly piece of bacon.

"Fine, but I'm not telling you anything, Parker. This is police business. Unless you own the property at the bottom of the Open Cut where we found Jane, you have no reason to stick your big nose into this case."

I begged him one bloody hook to differ. "Who are your suspects?"

"Besides you?" His glower challenged.

"Yes."

"None of your business."

I swallowed more coffee, assessing Cooper's stiff body language. Obviously, I was going to have to come at this from a different angle. "Did you know Jane was acting in an upcoming play up in Lead?"

"Yes." He stabbed a forkful of eggs.

"Have you interrogated the cast?"

"Of course, Inspector Clouseau. That's standard procedure."

"What did you think of the director?" If the Napoleon wanna-be was as much of a hard-ass as Mona had said, Cooper should get along chummily with him.

"He's five-foot-eleven, around two hundred pounds, Caucasian, Italian descent, and married. I'd pull his phone number for you, but that's police business."

Cooper's smirk had me itching to kick his shin under the table. He was toying with me and enjoying it. I wondered how much he'd enjoy my oatmeal poured over his head.

I glanced over at Harvey, who was still fidgeting with his spoon. I reached over and took it away, shooting him a what-the-hell look.

He frowned and shrugged. So much for any plans to tag-team against his nephew.

The waitress brought Harvey's food, flirting again, bumping him with her hip. She'd have had better luck rousing road kill.

When she left, the old bugger frowned at the pancakes stacked on his plate as if they were made of styrofoam. Instead of digging in, he scooted out of the seat. "I'll be back in a jiff."

I watched him cross the dining room and push into the

men's room; a flicker of concern lit in my chest. Something was wrong with Harvey. I'd have to corner him after I'd finished trying to draw blood from the piece of granite that was his nephew.

Scooping up the last of my eggs, I played dumb with Cooper. "Do you think this director had anything to do with Jane's death?"

"Nope."

"What about the rest of the crew? Any suspects there?"

"Parker," Cooper dropped his fork to his plate. "Do you really think you're going to get anything out of me? I interrogate criminals and suspects in my sleep. This is a waste of time for both of us."

I stared at him, fantasizing about plugging his mouth with my cork-heeled sandal. Then his words sank in and gave me an idea—a dicey idea, but maybe it would work. After raising two kids, I had a little interrogation experience of my own from which to draw.

My cowardly lion side tried to rationalize with me, talk me out of it. But if I gave up now, I'd be no closer to figuring out if my albino buddy was still alive. Or if he was responsible for Jane's death.

"Okay, Detective," I said, reaching across the table and stealing his last piece of bacon—part power play, part plain hunger. "If you're such an ace at interrogation, how do you go about prying critical case information out of someone as closemouthed as me?"

He glared at the strip of bacon in my fingers. "Are you saying that you have information about Jane's case?"

Did I ever! I raised my brows and shrugged.

"Is that the real reason you used extortion to get me to meet you here this morning?"

I chewed on his bacon in response.

A muscle in his jaw clenched. "You know that withholding evidence or information from me is a criminal offense, right?"

I pointed at the slice of orange on the rim of his plate. "Are you going to eat that?"

I was playing with fire here, but with Cooper it seemed that getting through his tough exterior required a blow torch and suffering a few third degree burns in the process.

Harvey returned, shaking his head at my look of concern. He slid in next to me, his focus zeroing in on his nephew. "Looky there, girl. You went and got Coop mad as an old wet hen."

Cooper's gaze didn't waver from me. "Parker, do I need to remind you that I am an agent of the law?"

"What do you think?" I nudged Harvey's shoulder. "Is this an example of the detective playing 'bad cop' with his interviewee?"

"It's definitely Coop being a sore-toothed cuss," Harvey answered, a hint of a grin showing under his beard for the first time since he'd walked in the door.

"I'm not sure I've ever even seen him in 'good cop' mode," I said.

"You do seem to be a burr under his saddle most days."

"Every day," Cooper corrected. "What aren't you telling me about my case, Parker?"

"I'm sure there is something in this head of mine that I've been meaning to say, but I just can't remember. Let's try a little more interrogating, shall we?"

Harvey sat back in the seat watching me with his bushy brows raised. "I do believe she's bent on making you out to be a chucklehead, Coop. You'd better git busy workin' your badge magic on 'er."

Cooper pushed his empty plate aside and shoved his chin out. I copycatted him, jut for jut.

"Where were you the night of Jane's murder?" he asked.

"Cold," I said without missing a beat.

"What do you mean, 'cold'?"

"I mean you're freezing. Not even close to the right question. Besides, you already know I have a solid alibi."

Harvey snickered.

The detective lowered his head, lining up his horns. "This is not a game, Parker. A life was taken."

"Oh, I know. But if it were a game, you'd probably lose."

"That's a stinger," Harvey said, rubbing it in. He picked up his fork and dug into his stack of pancakes.

"Tell you what, Detective, why don't you just present the facts to me, explaining the physical and circumstantial evidence you've collected, and I'll fill in where I think you're wrong."

Cooper's head tilted a little. "Or you could just recount your side of the story and I can verify it against what you've told me before."

"Nope, I'm tired of telling my side." I switched gears. "Hypothetically speaking, if I were a fellow detective on this case—your partner even—where would you have me start investigating? Interviewing your suspects again to catch inconsistencies or studying the evidence collected at the crime scene?"

"I'd have you look into your own background because I suspect that your history of time behind bars has tainted your ability to remain an honest officer of the law."

He had a point there. I just smiled.

He studied my smile like someone had tattooed hieroglyphics on my lips. "According to your friend, Natalie Beals, you witnessed an interaction between Jane and a coworker that may have played a part in the lead-up to her death."

He was right about an interaction, but I hadn't told anyone about Jane having sex with Ray a couple of days before her death. Not even Natalie.

"Nice bluff, Detective. After your little poker game last night, Doc filled me in on your tell."

"Now who's bluffing, Parker?"

"What was Natalie wearing the last time you saw her?" I asked, partly to knock him off course, but mostly because I was curious if Nat had had her cast removed yet.

Cooper's nostrils flared. If I hadn't been in a face-to-face standoff with him, I'd have missed it.

"What does that have to do with Jane?" he asked, his tone brusquer than usual.

"Just curious," I said. "Was Jane wearing her watch when you found her?"

I knew the answer was "No" because I'd found Jane's favorite pearl watch and a matching necklace in her office the day after Ray had identified her body. They had been sitting on her filing cabinet next to an empty bottle of whiskey.

Cooper hesitated. "Why?"

"Just curious," I answered again, and then it hit me—Jane hadn't been wearing that watch when she was killed.

Why not? With her constant to-do lists, she was often checking to see how much time she had left to tackle another task. Where had she been going that she would have taken off her watch and left it? Was that even an important clue? Or was I making something out of nothing?

Cooper's gaze sharpened. "If you know something that will help solve your boss's murder, Parker, you should tell your friendly policeman."

"Nice try, Mr. Good Cop," I said, chuckling. "But I can still see your saber teeth. You need to pull those puppies in when you role-play."

The waitress brought the bill. Harvey dropped his fork on his empty plate and pointedly looked from the bill to me. I wrinkled my nose at him and grabbed it. Cooper pulled out his wallet and threw a few greenbacks my way.

"As much as I enjoy your chafing company, Parker, I have an appointment I can't miss." He rose from the bench. "Can I have my curtains back now?"

"They're out in the Picklemobile."

I added some cash to the bill, left it on the table, and the three of us trailed out single file. Cooper jangled his keys while I fished his curtains from the cab of the pickup.

When I handed them to him, he said, "If you have something to tell me about Jane's murder, you need to cough it up and soon."

I looked up at him all wide-eyed and touched my chest. "Why whatever are you talking about, Detective Cooper?" I said in a fake southern accent.

"It's all fun and games, Parker, until somebody gets arrested." With a nod to his uncle, Cooper stalked off, climbed into his sedan, and peeled out of the parking lot.

I turned to Harvey. "What the hell was wrong with you in there? The deal was you help me pick Cooper's brain in exchange for food."

"You did a fine job on your own."

"Not really." In the process of interrogating Cooper, I managed to drag a clue out of my own head. The Marx Brothers couldn't have done it better. "So what's going on with you? Did somebody shoot your favorite cow?"

"Yeah, as a matter of fact."

"What?" I gaped at him. Harvey had had some weird shit going down at his ranch lately. Creepy, horror-movie weird. "Was it one of the whangdoodles?" I asked, using Harvey's nickname for the crazy hill-people who lived in Slagton, a mining ghost town located several miles back on the dirt road that wound past his ranch.

He put his hands on his hips and scowled out at the highway. "Beatrice dumped me."

Who? Oh, Miss Geary, Aunt Zoe's short-shorts-wearing neighbor and Harvey's girlfriend. "Well, you haven't exactly been faithful to her."

He scoffed. "It's not like we ever exchanged promise rings."

"Then why did she break if off?"

"She found herself a new stallion."

A stallion? "Is he younger than you?"

"Yeah, and her, too."

Way to go Miss Geary. "What are you going to do about it?"

"I don't know. I guess I'll have to find me another woman to take her place."

"What are you talking about? You have several women already."

"Yeah, but none like her. She sparkled." He grunted. "I'm gonna go home and clean my gun."

"You're not going to shoot the guy, are you?"

"What? Hell, no. I just need some alone time with Bessie to make me feel better."

I wasn't touching that one with a ten-foot pole.

With a nod, Harvey left me alone with the Picklemobile. I started her up, thinking about Harvey and his shotgun. That's what I needed, some alone time with my favorite toy. Not *that* toy. I meant Doc—my *boy* toy.

I rolled out of the parking lot and turned toward Lead,

deciding to swing into the Piggly Wiggly to grab some snacks for the kids' lunches for the rest of the week. Up in Lead, I noticed a small crowd of folks standing in front of the Historic Homestake Opera House. The sight of a black, Lincoln-like top hat rising above the group made me hit the brakes.

Cornelius!

A horn blasted behind me.

Oops! I hit the gas.

What was Cornelius doing at the … of course, the "haunted" opera house.

I made a quick left down a side street and cruised back around, parking near the big brick building.

Rushing along the sidewalk, I zeroed in on that black top hat and weaved my way through the small crowd of tourists to Abe Jr.'s side.

"Cornelius," I said, grabbing him by the wool coat sleeve. Wool? Today? Really? It wasn't that cold. What planet was he from? Never mind that. "Why aren't you returning my calls?"

He looked down at me through his little round sunglasses. "Violet, you're just who I wanted to see."

"Why? Did you find out about the money?"

"Not at all." He locked onto my arm and tugged me toward the open lobby doors of the opera house, the crowd funneling around us.

Someone in the pack had showered in a gardenia-scented perfume this morning, making my eyes water. A short guy jostled into me, stepping on my toes and then not offering an apology. The urge to bite him came and went. Maybe I was turning into a zombie. Why had I left the safety of the Picklemobile?

I tried to pull free of Cornelius, but his grip wouldn't loosen. "Why did you want to see me?" I asked him again.

He dragged me into the lobby, his gaze traveling from the tile-covered floor up the gold-painted walls to the ornately trimmed ceiling. A carved, wooden rail flanked a wide staircase to the right. On our left, several sets of doors opened into a semi-dark theatre.

"Welcome to the Historic Homestake Opera House," a petite white-blonde said from the fourth step up, her smile twice as big as she was. Her voice matched her small stature. I tried to figure out the color of her eyes, but they were too light to tell whether they were blue or gray from this distance, although they looked a little red-rimmed like she'd recently been crying or had allergies. "My name is Calypso, but you all can call me Caly."

Someone's parents must have been into Greek mythology or just big fans of Jacques Cousteau's ship.

"This morning, I'll be taking you back in time to the golden glory days of Lead."

The crowd tightened around us in front of the stairwell, shoulder-to-shoulder. Murmurs of appreciation sounded as they took in the finer details of the lobby.

Cornelius leaned down. "This place is said to be haunted by several ghosts," he whispered in my ear.

"I know," I whispered back, tugging to free my arm.

"Excellent. Then you're ready to channel them for me."

Chapter Eight

The Historic Homestake Opera House had aged over the last century like fine whiskey—its architectural refinements diminishing while its historical flavors grew more rich and robust.

According to Caly, our super-duper-chipper tour guide, a huge fire in the early 1980s had destroyed the opera house's roof and world-class pipe organ, along with most of the stained-glass chandeliers, gilded cherubs, and velvet seats. Charred plaster that still covered parts of the brick walls offered proof of the fiery tragedy that had played out in the theatre, but from where I currently stood, seeing the evidence of the work that had gone into rebuilding the stately playhouse, the fat lady hadn't sung yet.

"The flames may have tried to raze this heart of the community," Caly told us as she stood tall on the stage—well, tall for her tiny frame. "But its spirit prevailed, and from the ashes, a phoenix arose."

I moved closer to Cornelius, catching a whiff of pipe smoke from his wool coat. "I'll bet you a ten-spot that Caly writes poetry on the side," I said for his ears only.

"She's a Venus," he replied, all breathy-like. His cornflower blue eyes worshipped her from afar over the rims of his round, wire sunglasses.

I'd always pictured Venuses having long hair and lush curves, not short gelled spikes and A-cups. "More like a pixie."

"You think she'd marry me?"

"Why mess with a ceremony? Just stuff her in your coat pocket and run away to Neverland."

"I'm going to get her phone number."

I did a double-take, watching him comb his bony fingers through his black wavy locks. "You're kidding, right?"

He looked down at me. "Not at all. We're a perfect match."

Cornelius must have been sniffing pixie dust before the tour started. "You really think so?"

"She hears ghosts."

"How do you know that?" Was there a secret hand signal I'd missed?

"She said it when she led us in here."

"I don't remember her saying that."

"Well, she didn't exactly say, 'I hear ghosts,' but she gave away her secret when she mentioned that the theatre is haunted."

Boy, oh, boy, he was really reaching. I hated to burst his love bubble, but I hadn't noticed a single sign of attraction—more the reverse in her avoidance of eye contact with Abe Jr.

"Plus, it was in her gaze when she talked to me."

"You mean when she asked you to remove your hat?"

"Exactly. Then she winked at me a few times."

I didn't think those were winks. Caly seemed to be having trouble with her contacts, which explained her red eyes. But I didn't have the heart to squash his hopes.

Turning back to Caly, I listened as she pointed out decorative molding that had been recast using molds made from the few pieces of the original architecture that had survived the flames.

Through Caly's tales of the post-fire events, I came to have a whole new respect for those hell bent on returning the place to its former glory. Those who fought tooth and nail for funds to rebuild it, who volunteered their time to polish it back to its previous majesty, who helped fill seats by participating in community plays.

People like Jane.

It would be a cruel injustice if it turned out that her murder was somehow connected to this stately place where she'd spent so much time. Neither she nor the opera house deserved such an indignity.

"With time and donations from generous patrons, our theatre will return to its previous grandeur," Caly said, her light-colored eyes rounding, imploring, like a cute little kitty cat. I found myself liking her in spite of her perky boobs, butt, and everything else. She probably even had perky pinkie toes.

Dang, she was good at campaigning for a cause. I needed to hire her to help me convince buyers to pull out their wallets.

Cornelius reached into his coat pocket and pulled out a black leather wallet.

Hold on a second, Mr. Moneybags!

I took the wallet from him and stuffed it back inside his coat. We had bigger financial commitments to focus on first—like my career and his ability to kill it if he couldn't come up with the funds for that hotel.

As the tour continued, I tried to stick close to Cornelius, who was trying to stick even closer to Caly.

The bouncy nymph led us upstairs and then back down, sprinkling happiness along the way. By the time we'd covered the unrestricted areas of the building, including what used to be a library, a gentlemen's lounge, a sitting room for women, a bowling alley turned shooting range, and the bottom floor where concrete now filled the old swimming pool, I was trying to decide how much time and energy I could donate to help restore the brick structure since cash wasn't exactly overflowing my coffers.

Then I stepped outside under the gray cloudy sky and got hit with a cool breeze that smelled like rain and knocked off my rose-colored glasses. I was a single mom on the verge of losing my job with a boyfriend whom I didn't want wandering off just because he never saw me anymore. Maybe I'd take my kids to see the zombie play next month and call it good. When I looked back to see where Cornelius was heading next, I couldn't find him anywhere.

Nor Caly.

Crap. The last thing I needed was for the little blonde siren to convince Cornelius to write her a big fat check.

I returned to the lobby and stood in one of the theatre's open doors. Cornelius wasn't in there, but a handful of non-tour group folks were, moving pieces of set around at the back of the stage.

Two zombies dressed in blood-stained clothes stood in front of the stage on the temporary wooden floor that covered the musicians' pit. I watched for a minute or two as they took turns reading aloud from the sheets of paper in their hands, their grotesque faces and blood-smeared mouths mesmerizing even from a distance. One of them picked up a fake bloody arm from the stage and pretended to eat it like corn on the cob.

A shout from backstage made all three of us jump. I backed out of the doorway as the zombies returned to practicing their lines and taking turns hitting each other with the severed limb.

I needed to pay a quick visit to the little girls' room thanks to all of the coffee I'd downed at brunch while interrogating myself by accident in front of Cooper. I was tempted to ignore the Keep Out sign and hop over the velvet rope that sectioned off the refurbished women's sitting room and its small bathroom, but a few of the tour group folks were still milling about. Maybe I'd wait until I got up to the Piggly Wiggly to take care of business.

Now if I could just find Cornelius. I crept up the stairs, calling his name softly. The rooms up there and the upper balcony were sans Abe Jr.

What in the hell? A six-foot-plus top-hat-wearing ghost talker didn't just disappear into thin air.

Back downstairs I found the lobby empty. The last of the tour group had trickled outside and were heading across the street toward a restaurant with a couple of outdoor tables.

To the left of the theatre entrance was an unmarked wooden door that Caly hadn't taken us through on the tour. Maybe it led to an employee lounge or her office.

I sidled over to it, pretending to inspect the paint on the lobby wall next to it. After a quick glance around to make sure nobody was watching, I turned the handle. It was unlocked. I slipped through and closed the door quietly behind me, finding myself in a fluorescent lit hallway.

On the right was a set of stairs and stainless steel elevator doors. Another closed wooden door stood across from the elevator. The other end of the hall emptied through the frame of a doorway into what looked like a bathroom. My bladder panged at the sight, reminding me of other non-Cornelius matters growing more pressing.

Everything sounded muffled in the hallway, like I was a

spider trapped under an upside-down glass. It was a sharp contrast from the acoustic-friendly high ceilings of the lobby and theatre.

Ignoring the claustrophobic sensation tightening around my lungs, I stepped away from the door, peering down the hall. Maybe I could just slip quickly inside the bathroom without anyone noticing.

In the heavy silence, I heard what sounded like several sniffs from the other end of the hall.

Who's there?

A high-pitched sob answered.

That wasn't Cornelius. I glanced back at the door. Gray clouds and freedom beckoned. I could just call Cornelius later to see if he ended up offering to buy the opera house in order to impress Caly and then deal with that fallout on safer turf.

The sound of a woman weeping reached me, tugging at my mothering strings. Maybe it was Caly. Maybe she wasn't as chipper as she'd acted on the tour.

Tiptoeing down the hall, I paused at the elevator to listen again. A loud sob tore through the thick quiet. Two more followed, wrenching my heart.

I hesitated, stuck between the urge to comfort and the need to get out of there and go take care of business somewhere sob-free.

Compassion won. I tiptoed further down the hall. The weeping woman must be inside the open room at the end.

As I got closer, I realized two things—that the sign on the open bathroom door said MEN; and there was another room at the end of the hall, the recessed entry hidden from view. Propped slightly open with a yellow Caution—Wet Floor cone, the door had a WOMEN sign on it.

I inched up to the women's restroom, moving just outside the threshold. From my vantage point, I could see in through the partially open door. Natural light brightened the room, beckoning. The white and green tiles on the floor ran mid-way up the walls. White paint coated the rest of the way to the ceiling. The sniffles were amplified thanks to the lack of carpet.

I covered my mouth as I listened. I'd done my fair share of

crying in public bathrooms over the years, at times wanting to be left alone, other times needing a shoulder to lean on. Maybe I could whistle a little tune out here to let her know I was coming in, then fake surprise at finding her in there.

The honk of her blowing her nose made me grimace. From the sound of it, she'd been crying for quite a while.

I heard a rustling sound from within, footfalls coming toward me, and chickened out. Backpedaling into the men's bathroom, I hid out of view just inside. My bladder cramped and tickled in protest. I crossed my legs, my eyes darting to the urinals.

What in the hell was I doing? I was supposed to be going to the Piggly Wiggly for some snacks for the kids and now here I was hiding in a men's bathroom.

I held my breath, straining to hear the weeper. My stomach chose that moment to gurgle so loudly that most of Lead *and* Deadwood had to have heard it.

Rubbing my stomach, I tried to soothe it into silence. It was probably ticked off about the diet Cooper had put me on for breakfast. I couldn't blame it—I was still pissed, too.

The creak of a door hinge froze all internal rants against the detective. I did my best mannequin impression as the bathroom weeper's footfalls headed away from me.

Leaning my head back against the wall, I closed my eyes and waited for the sound of a door closing.

"Where in the hell have you been?" A man asked out in the hallway, his tone gruff, all bristly with irritation.

My eyes opened wide in surprise. Where had he come from? Had he seen me steal into the men's room?

"Relax, Petey," a woman said, who I assumed was the weeper by the plugged-nose sound of her voice. "There was something in my contact."

No way was that bathroom episode a something-in-her-contact ordeal. She'd been sobbing.

"Damn it, I told you to call me Peter while we're here. I will not tolerate your disrespect, especially in front of the rest of the cast."

"Yet it's okay for you to publicly reprimand me."

"You're supposed to be acting up there, not creating a bloopers reel. You couldn't even remember your lines last night, for fuck's sake. Do you know how humiliating it is for the director's wife to need continual cues?"

The director? Peter Tarragon, the director? After hearing about him from Mona, I had to see the man in the flesh. I stole a glimpse around the edge of the doorframe.

My glimpse turned into an all-out gape. At the other end of

the hall, Tarragon stood toe-to-toe with a zombie bride. Or maybe I should say THE zombie bride, since she must be the star of the play. Her white wedding dress was torn, the neckline splashed with fake blood. I couldn't get a good look at her face through her ragged veil, which made her even creepier. It was a good thing I'd chickened out on going inside the bathroom to comfort her. I probably would have peed my pants if I'd walked in and run into that mess.

Tarragon's profile looked the yin to the bride's yang. He was dressed all in black, from his porkpie hat to his tight shirt and jeans to his motorcycle boots. He reminded me of Gene Hackman in *The French Connection*, one of my dad's favorite flicks when I was a kid, except Tarragon had a goatee, longer sideburns, and a Roman type nose.

"It's not my fault I can't remember my lines." The bride shoved her veil back from her face, giving me a glimpse of a blood-streaked chin, gray-colored skin, and dark-circled eyes. "If you'd quit tweaking the damned script every night, I could get my lines straight."

"Damn it! Look at the mess you made of your makeup." He grabbed her jaw, turning her face to one side and then the other. "Your mouth and eyes are ruined. You're going to have to go back downstairs to makeup and have that fixed."

From where I stood, she still had no problems giving goosebumps.

The bride slapped his hand away. "It will only take a few minutes."

"That's a few minutes the rest of us have to wait for you to get ready yet again." Tarragon leaned in close, his body all threats and dominance. "One more time, baby," I could practically hear his lip curl around that endearment, "and I swear I'll ..."

"You'll what? Do to me what you did to Jane?"

Jane? My breath caught. Did she mean *my* Jane?

"Maybe," Tarragon said.

What had he done to Jane? Did Cooper know about this?

The zombie bride snarled. I half expected her to lurch forward and take a bite out of Tarragon. "Try it, *Petey*, and I'll tear your dick off and use it as bait out at Pactola."

Try what?

"That would mean you'd have to actually touch it again after all of these years." Tarragon grabbed his bride by the arm and jerked her toward the door. "Get down to makeup before I remove you from the equation permanently." He yanked the door open and shoved the bride through it, following behind her torn train of lace.

I counted to five after the door shut and then skidded into the women's bathroom. This cloak and dagger stuff required a stronger bladder. Many more of these close calls or zombie surprises and I was going to have to start wearing absorbent underwear.

I flushed and walked over to the sink, staring absently at a crack in one of the green and white tiles below the mirror.

What had Tarragon's wife meant about Jane? Was Peter the murderer? Could it be that simple? And why had Mrs. Tarragon been in here bawling her eyes out?

Wadding up the towel, I tossed it into the trash. It landed next to a crinkled and torn piece of paper, a smudge of red and black makeup streaked one corner. I did a double take. I knew that banner. It was a Calamity Jane Realty flyer.

I flattened it out on the counter, careful to avoid any water drops.

The sight of Jane's picture in the bottom right corner made my eyes water. I focused on the property for sale—the Sugarloaf building, one of the historic buildings on Lead's Main Street. It was also one of the properties Jane had asked me to research for her back in July. My eyes blurred again, dang it.

There was a rip at the top, like it had been ripped from a tack or nail. Blinking away my tears, I wondered if the zombie bride had been the one looking at the flyer, and if so, why had she wadded it up and thrown it away?

How well had she known Jane? Were they old friends or just cast mates?

I dropped the paper back in the trash. Had Cooper considered Tarragon's wife as a suspect? Could she be a missing piece that would help him solve the puzzle? I frowned at my reflection in the mirror. I had so many questions and nobody I could badger for answers.

On the way out the door, I dodged the yellow cone. The sight of Dominick Masterson standing in the doorway of the men's bathroom where I'd hidden only moments ago made me screech and stumble backward into the wall.

I covered my chest with my palm. "You scared the bejeezus out of me."

His smile didn't crease his eyes. "Sorry about that. I thought you were someone else." He pointed at the other bathroom. "Were you alone in there?"

I nodded. Was he looking for the zombie bride, too, like Tarragon? Was Dominick part of the cast? Or was something going on with him and Tarragon's wife?

A rolling sensation surged through my stomach. The hallway we stood in suddenly seemed too tight, the urge for fresh air and a wide open sky tugged at me. I rubbed my stomach again. Damn Cooper for not letting me eat a decent breakfast. Some of us girls aren't meant to look like stick insects with boobs.

Dominick's gaze combed my face. "Do I know you?"

"No." *But I know you.* "Not officially, anyway, but you might have seen me at Jane Grimes's funeral."

"That's it. You were there with Willis Harvey. What's your name?"

"Violet Parker. I work with Ja…" A wave of nausea rippled through me. My saliva glands kicked into gear, making me pause to swallow. "I mean 'worked' with Jane."

I glanced down the hall at the door I'd come through what seemed like hours ago.

He held out his hand. "Nice to meet you, Ms. Parker. I'm Dominick Masterson."

His hand felt like an unripe nectarine, a soft, smooth layer of skin covering a firm core. No calluses to be felt. I pulled back.

"Did you know Jane well?" I asked, wanting an explanation for his front row seat at her funeral.

"We go way back. She represented me on several properties in the area."

That still didn't justify the front row seat, but my stomach was in no mood to keep prodding. I needed to get outside or I'd be rushing back into the bathroom for a whole other reason.

"I should be going. It was nice to meet you, Mr. Masterson."

I'd made it to the elevator door when he asked, "Do you still work at Calamity Jane Realty?"

That made me stop, my Realtor radar picking up a bogey.

"Yes." I turned. Was it crass to hit on Jane's clients so soon after her funeral? Jerry probably wouldn't think so, but would Mona? I could picture Ray's purple face when he found out I'd managed to hook one of Jane's big fishes without even trying. "Are you interested in buying or selling some property?" I felt a little icky asking, but I had kids to feed and clothe and all that jazz.

"Maybe. I just might come calling, Ms. Parker."

"In that case," I walked back and handed him my business card, "you can call me Violet."

"Violet, it is."

I could feel Dominick Masterson watching me all the way out the door.

Outside, rain bounced off the sidewalk. I didn't let that slow me down. By the time I reached the Picklemobile, I was soaked, shivering from a mixture of cold water and turmoil. My stomach seemed to have slunk back under its rock for the moment.

I locked both doors and pulled out my cell phone. A drop of water splashed on the screen as I searched for Cooper's number. Before I could chicken out, I hit the Call button.

Four rings later, he picked up. "I'm getting tired of talking to you today, Parker."

"Too bad. It's your job."

"No, my job is to chase down the bad guys, not listen to a nosey blonde who has a wild hair. Make that many wild hairs."

"Are you making fun of my hair, Detective Cooper?"

"Maybe."

"What's next? Are you going to knock my school books out of my arms and snap my training bra?"

I heard static through the line. Or maybe it was more of Cooper's molars being ground off. "What do you want, Parker?"

"Is Peter Tarragon's wife one of your suspects for Jane's murder?"

"That's none of your business."

"That's what I thought." I didn't remember seeing her name on his case board. "Maybe she should be, *Mr. Detective.*"

I couldn't resist that jab. He shouldn't have made fun of my hair.

"Where are you, Parker?" he asked, his voice edged with a growl.

My cell phone vibrated. Another call was coming in. I checked—Cornelius's name showed on the screen.

"I have another call," I told Cooper. "Gotta go."

"Damn it—"

I cut Cooper off with the push of one little button. If only I could do that in person.

"Hello, Cornelius. Where are you?" I wrung water from my curls onto the vinyl seat bench, swiping it onto the floor. The fragrance of my peach-scented shampoo mixed with the oily smell of aged pickup. The rain still pounded my windshield, which was fogging up.

"In heaven."

"Right." I stuck the key in the ignition and turned it. The Picklemobile stuttered a little, acting like she wasn't sure she wanted to start, then caught and cranked to life. "Is that located in Deadwood or Lead at the moment?"

"Lead. Did you know the opera house has a basement?"

"Yes. I was on the same tour as you, remember?" I held my shivering hand over the vent, waiting for some engine heat to kick in. "They took us down to the bottom floor by the old bowling alley that's now a shooting range."

"That's not the basement. There is a level under that."

"How do you know?"

"I found it while I was following Caly."

I rolled my eyes. The sound of that girl's name was getting old quick. "She went down in the basement?"

"No, but I did. Only it's not really a basement. It's some old locker room with showers and the bottom of the pool."

"I thought they filled that in."

Cornelius had stood on the smooth, concrete-covered pool next to me.

"No, they just added a ceiling to the empty pool."

"Let me get this straight." I checked my mascara in the rearview mirror, wincing at the black rings. "You went underneath the floor that is really only a layer of concrete the length and width of the pool?"

"I walked around down in the deep end."

I tried to picture an empty pool capped with concrete. "Was there anything else in the pool with you?" Maybe they used it for storage.

"Just a drain," he said.

Why would they keep the pool but not use it?

"And the ghost you're going to channel."

Chapter Nine

It was moments like this when I considered going home, lying down on the couch, and spewing all of my troubles to Elvis—Addy's chicken, not the King of Rock n' Roll. Her indifferent clucks might do wonders toward soothing my ruffled feathers.

I glared at my cell phone several seconds before putting it back up to my ear.

"You want me to channel a ghost that lives under a concrete covered pool?" I asked Cornelius, just to clarify that we were on the same page.

"He may not actually live there," he explained.

"It's a man's ghost?"

"Actually, he's just a boy."

"What makes you so certain this boy ghost was there with you at all?"

"He talked to me."

Cornelius called himself a ghost whisperer. But after the last two séances I was coerced into attending, I'd say he was more of a ghost hummer.

I waited for him to elaborate. When he didn't, I took the bait. "Okay, what did he say?"

"I don't know. I couldn't hear him clearly."

"Then how do you know he talked at all?"

"He whispered in my ear."

Even if he was full of shit, that gave me goosebumps. "Why don't *you* go back and talk to him and we can skip the channeling."

"I can't."

"Why not?"

"He didn't like my hat."

I banged my head on the steering wheel a few times. "How

do you know that if you couldn't hear what he was saying?"

"He knocked it clean off my head."

"Maybe it just fell off." Blame gravity not a persnickety ghost, I thought, rubbing my forehead where I'd banged a little too hard.

"After I picked up my hat, the boy knocked it out of my hand. It landed at the pool's six foot mark."

Six feet and under … the pool. A coincidence?

"That's when the whispering stopped," Cornelius said.

I frowned out the rain-blurred windshield. This all sounded like some kind of parlor trick, but why would Cornelius try to put one over on me? I'd already joined him for two separate séances.

"We need to figure out how to sneak in the building later tonight," he continued. "Maybe I could convince Caly to join us."

Absolutely not! That was one bad idea stacked precariously on top of another.

"I'm busy tonight," I said, evading.

"What could be more important than talking to the dead?"

Never in my life would I have guessed I'd be asked that question, yet here I was, and Cornelius meant it with all seriousness. "Homework," I answered. "It's a school night."

"Skip class tonight."

"Not for me, for my kids."

"You have children?" he asked, sounding awed by the fact, as if they were mystical beings I controlled with my fingertips. "What are their blood types?"

I didn't even hesitate with my equally absurd answer. "Red."

"Ah, human then," was his comeback.

Some days I wasn't so sure.

"Violet, you need to be there to open the lines of communication for me."

"Do you always need someone to channel for you?"

"Yes, unless we're in the southern hemisphere."

I let that one fly right past me. "Isn't there someone you could call?" A fellow ghost buster? The short lady with Coke-bottle glasses from *Poltergeist*?

"My sister is in Australia trying to connect with the ghost of Ned Kelly and my cousin is unavailable."

"Unavailable for how long?" I could delay him for a week, maybe two.

"Forever. She's dead."

I grimaced. "I'm sorry, Cornelius."

"Me, too, but she died doing what she loved best."

"Channeling ghosts?"

"No, participating in an exorcism."

That was what the girl had loved best? Somebody should have gotten her a puppy. "What happened to her?"

"A couple of weeks prior to the exorcism, she opened too wide while channeling. One of the spirits took control."

Channeling widths varied? "What do you mean, 'took control'?"

"It possessed her."

Was that what happened to Doc when he was overcome by a ghost? Was his channel stuck wide open?

"We had to perform an exorcism to free her. But there were complications."

"What kind of complications?"

"The kind that stop your heart."

I covered my mouth mid-gasp. Last month, Cornelius had been hauled into the Deadwood police station and questioned about the death of a girl during an exorcism that took place down in New Orleans. Cooper had let him go, but Cornelius was still a person of interest. The girl must have been his cousin.

"We'll return Friday night at eleven-forty-seven." Cornelius stated, moving past the subject of his cousin. "We'll sneak into the under-the-floor pool area and try to connect with the boy ghost."

"No." I said without missing a beat.

"Why not?"

First of all, I had enough trouble with Cooper. I didn't need to get busted for breaking and entering. Second, I was too chicken shit to go in there at night, especially after the zombies I'd seen roaming around the place today.

But I didn't bother Cornelius with either of those reasons. "I refuse to channel anything other than my television until the sale of the hotel goes through."

I wasn't going to damage my professional reputation any further until I had a huge sale to stand behind.

"I told you that my funds are tied up."

"So are my channeling paths or hallways or doors—whatever you call them." I ground into gear and after checking the mirrors, pulled out into the street. "See if you can get those funds untied, Cornelius. I'll give you a call tomorrow."

"Violet—"

I hung up on him, using that little red button on my phone again. That was really starting to come in handy.

After stopping at home to change clothes, wolf down a peanut butter and honey sandwich, and morph from a wet ragamuffin into a curly-haired mess, I drove back to work.

Doc's car wasn't in the parking lot. His business really seemed to be taking off with all of the word-of-mouth help lately. Yet another reason we needed to be even more careful about keeping his sixth sense our little secret.

I opened Calamity Jane's back door and walked into a cloud of cologne. Whoa! Jerry's sniffer must be going bad.

Jerry's office light was on, but his desk sat empty. I heard the low thunder of his laughter coming from the front of the office. The shoulder scrunching sound of Ray's followed.

The sight of Benjamin Underhill sitting on the corner of my desk stopped me in my tracks. He wore a Black Hills State University T-shirt and gold gym shorts.

Instead of my stapler, a basketball sat on a stack of papers and fliers next to my keyboard, acting as a paperweight. Why hadn't I thought of that? A ball was perfect for throwing at Ray when he made one of his snide remarks. Although, it wouldn't leave a dent on the asshole's forehead like my stapler would.

"Hi, Violet," Ben said, practically vaulting from my desk. He held my chair out for me to sit—always the gentleman.

Jerry didn't move from his perch on Mona's desk. His gaze traveled down my emerald green tunic and navy slacks like I was a mannequin in a Fifth Avenue window, his forehead creasing. I resisted the urge to grab the long black raincoat I kept hanging in the corner and wrap myself in it.

I met Ray's curled lip head-on and returned my own love for him with an eat-shit-and-die glare.

"How have you been?" Ben asked as I dropped my purse on my chair.

"Great." Considering my day so far, I figured I should keep my answer monosyllabic but tried to make my smile at least look real.

Ben and I had a complicated history.

He'd gone from secret admirer to stalker to possible child kidnapper to creepy dinner date to friendly dinner date to his current label—nice guy who might accidentally steal my job out from under me.

At our last dinner date—the friendly one—he'd mentioned becoming something more than friends. I figured we already had four labels too many going for us.

Ben had his colored contact in today, which made his eyes both look blue instead of one of them being green. Unfortunately for Ben, he looked like a younger version of his uncle. While that made him attractive to many women, it made me want to snap him with a dish towel whenever I saw him.

Picking up the basketball, Ben grinned. "Jerry and I are going to go shoot some hoops over at the Rec Center. You want to come over and cheer us on?"

That explained why Jerry had on cargo shorts and a T-shirt so big I could have worn it as a dress.

"Sounds like fun, but I need to look up some listings," I lied. "Did you play basketball in school, Jerry?" With his height, I imagined he was a shoo-in for deep in the key.

Ray laughed, loud and ugly. "She has no idea who you are," he said to our boss.

Jerry shrugged. "It's been a while since I've been on the sports page."

I felt a fool's blush creeping up my neck. "What does he mean?" I asked. "Who are you?"

"He's Jerry Russo, Violet," Ben said, as if that should make it crystal clear. "You know, Jerry the Slammer?"

"Slammer? Were you a professional wrestler?"

A month ago, I'd met another ex-wrestler who went by the name of the Jugularnaut because of the constricting leg hold he'd lock onto his opponents' necks. He'd reminded me of a leather-covered refrigerator when I'd met him and his biker-babe wife. Unfortunately, they'd set their sights on the Carhart house up in Lead, which was temporarily off the market because of an attempted murder within its walls—mine.

Jerry had a similar build to the Jugularnaut, only taller.

"You'll have to forgive Violet, Jerry," Ray said. "She was too busy popping out kids to pay attention to your all-star ball career."

I had two children, not a clown-car's worth. Besides, if I had his age guessed right, I was still a kid when Jerry was running up and down the court on national TV. At least I assumed "Slammer" referred to a slam dunk now that I knew he hadn't been throwing aluminum folding chairs around inside a wrestling ring.

"Jerry played pro-basketball for over a decade," Ben explained in a much friendlier tone. "Until a shoulder injury ended his career."

"I could have gone back, but I didn't want to spend my sunset years with an arm I couldn't lift over my head." He stood and stretched said tree limbs, reaching toward the ceiling. "That's when I hooked up with Janey girl, bought a house from her, and convinced her to start a realty shop together—putting her brains together with my marketing potential as a local athlete. The business took off at a full court sprint."

"I bet," Ben said, all smiles. Admiration lit up his eyes.

I'd have to go online and look Jerry up after they left to play ball, see what he'd looked like in his younger years, read up on his history. Now that Ben and he were going to be basketball playing buddies, I needed my own angle on getting him to like me enough to keep me, more so if the hotel deal crashed down around me. I doubted being his clothes shopping pal was going to cut it.

I heard the back door shut. Turning, I met Mona's smile. She was in her normal form today with her long red hair coiffed, her lipstick subtle yet sexy, and her white sweater just tight enough.

The last time I'd worn a white sweater I'd ended up with handprints on my chest—Addy's. The silly girl had been trying to catch the toad she'd brought inside and handed to me without warning. I still worried about getting warts on my boobs after the thing jumped down the front of my shirt and got stuck in my bra.

Mona's eyes widened at the sight of Jerry standing there in his shorts, her focus holding on his legs for a moment. Then she turned away so fast she almost gave herself whiplash.

Jerry stared back at Mona and her white sweater, only he wasn't so fast to look away. He had no forehead creases this time either, damn it.

Ray's eyes were doing that wide, dreamy thing, just like Elmer Fudd when Bugs Bunny got all dolled up for him. "Is that a new sweater, Red?"

My cell phone rang. It was Doc, saving me from having to watch the drool start dripping down chins. I stepped outside, closing the door behind me.

"Your car isn't in the back parking lot," I said as a way of answering.

"I know. It's at the library."

"What's it doing there?"

"Waiting for me while I look at black and white newspaper pictures of The Old Prospector Hotel."

Knowing Doc as I did, I suspected he was trying to identify some of the ghosts who pretty much ran him over during our séance there a couple of weeks ago. "You usually walk to the library."

"I have an appointment with a client soon, but there's something I want you to see."

"With or without clothing?"

He chuckled, all deep and husky in my ear. "Without, Boots, but we'll get to that later."

A shiver rippled down my skin.

"I found a picture in a late fifties issue of the *Black Hills Trailblazer* that concerns me," he said.

I shook off all thoughts of Doc naked and focused on what he was saying. "What's the picture of?"

"The manager of the hotel back then."

"Is there something weird about him?"

"No, but he's standing in front of another picture on the wall that you and I need to see in person."

"Why?"

"I'll explain later. What are you doing tomorrow morning?"

"Going clothes shopping with my boss."

Silence came from the other end of the line for several seconds.

"Did you say 'clothes shopping' with your boss?"

"Yes, he wants to make me look more like your ex-girlfriend."

Again, silence.

"*MY* ex? You mean Tiffany?"

"The one and only."

"Oh, man. How's that working for you?"

"Guess."

"Why does he want you to look more like her?" he asked.

"For marketing purposes. Tiffany's company is using her in a bunch of their ads."

"And you're letting him?"

I kicked a pebble into the street. "It's that or hit the unemployment office."

"Did he say that?"

"Not in those exact words, but I can see the writing on the wall."

"Is he blind? You're ten times more beautiful than Tiffany without even trying."

I smiled up at the sun peeking through the clouds. "Such flattery will lure me into your bed."

"It's not flattery, and I was hoping to get you into my shower, too. What time does the shopping extravaganza start?"

"We haven't set a time yet."

"Good. Tell him you have an early appointment and can't be there before ten."

The Adams Museum clock chimed three times. "Where is my appointment?"

"At the hotel your ghost whispering pal is buying. You and I are going to find that framed picture that's visible in the background of the newspaper article."

"And then what?"

"I'm not sure. First we have to find out if what I fear is true."

"That sounds ominous."

"I know. I gotta go, Violet. Call me later."

And then he was gone.

I peered inside Calamity Jane's plate-glass windows. Jerry and Ben must have left for the Rec Center. Ray had his boots off and his polish out. Mona's fingers flew over her keyboard, her rhinestone reading glasses partway down her nose.

The scene reminded me of a Norman Rockwell painting. I'd title it: *Just Like Old Times.*

My heart squeezed a little. Damn, I missed Jane.

* * *

Tuesday, September 4th

The next morning dawned bright and sunshiny, and I didn't trust it one bit.

I met Doc in the parking lot outside of The Old Prospector Hotel. He was leaning against his Camaro SS when I sputtered up next to him in the Picklemobile and backfired to a full stop.

"I missed you last night," he said, looking quite rakish in his dark brown khakis and cream-colored button-up shirt. Some days I really couldn't believe this guy wanted to see me naked on a regular basis. He must need glasses.

"Harvey came over for supper and never left," I explained. "He claimed he needed some company, but I think he just wanted to spy on Miss Geary. We fell asleep watching *Hondo.*"

"I liked the book better."

"Me, too. Aunt Zoe was cooking pancakes for the old buzzard when I left. He's going to drop my kids off at school this morning for me." Of course, his offer was in exchange for a full report of what Doc showed me in the old hotel this morning. Nothing from Harvey came without some sort of a deal attached.

"Why was he spying on his girlfriend?" Doc asked, capturing my hand as we walked toward the front of the hotel.

"She left him for another man." I shot a sideways glance down Main Street, on the lookout for Natalie's pickup. This paranoia about being seen with Doc had to stop, but until Natalie broke her silence and told me she wasn't going to hate me for eternity, I couldn't help it.

"Harvey's pretty obsessed with this new guy," I said. "He kept grumbling about a younger stallion pawing the ground around his favorite mare."

"Well, a good mare is hard to come by," Doc said, grinning, and ushered me through the hotel's glass doors with his hand on my lower back.

I heard him inhale and did the same thing myself, sniffing the air. A blend of flowery perfume and stale cigarette smoke made my nose twitch. Deadwood's non-smoking policy inside of the casinos was still recent history. Cornelius would need to replace the worn carpet and gold wallpaper to get rid of the years of cigarette smoke embedded in the building.

Doc led me past Socrates, the full-size stuffed mule with a balding nose from too much petting over the decades. We leaned on the reception desk where my favorite hotel employee, whom I'd nicknamed Safari Skipper, was running the show.

She smiled wide when she saw us, her eyes lighting up. "Hi, you two! Are you here for another séance?" she asked loud enough to draw several stares from the sprinkling of slot machine gamblers within earshot.

"No," Doc said in a much quieter voice. "We're here to see the manager. I made an appointment with her."

"Be right back," Skipper bounced off.

I looked up at Doc. "She's way too cheery for this time of the morning. Someone must have spiked her Cheerios."

Skipper came back alone carrying a ring of keys. "My boss is on the phone right now, but she said I can show you the storeroom. I have to stay and watch you, though."

"That's fine," he said. "Lead the way."

We followed Skipper past the elevator.

"You doing okay?" I asked him.

Doc had been overrun by ghosts more than once in this hotel. While all previous encounters had been on the upper floors, and he claimed to be able to brace himself after that initial contact for the second go-around, I was always a little antsy about having him keel over at my feet.

"I'm fine. There's nothing here right now."

"How did you convince the manager to let you look in their storage room?" I whispered.

"I told her I'm Cornelius Curion's financial manager and I needed to take stock of the antiquities in the building for valuation purposes."

"Oh, you're good."

He winked at me.

Safari Skipper led us down a set of wide, carpeted steps to the finished basement equipped with a sound stage and microphone, walnut bar, and tables and chairs.

"We rent this out for receptions and parties," she explained.

I didn't bother telling her that I had already peeked down in the basement along with Cornelius when we'd first toured the building with Tiffany, Doc's lovely ex, who represented the seller.

Skipper took us down a narrow, concrete-floored hallway to a set of double metal doors at the end. Unlocking the deadbolt, she pushed one open and slipped inside. Light flickered on within.

"Here you go," she said, holding the door open for us. "If it's cool with you, I'll be out by the bar. I can't get good cell reception back here."

"That's fine," Doc said. "We'll try to make it as quick as possible."

I followed him through the doorway. "So, what exactly are we looking for in here?"

He frowned as he looked around the cluttered storage room. "I think I've uncovered something hellish."

I laughed.

He didn't, which sobered me up real quick.

"What do you mean?" I asked.

"If we can find that old picture, you'll see," was his cryptic answer. "Look over there in those tall cabinets against the wall, will you? The picture is from the late 1800s. It has three men in it; the one in the middle is sitting on a chair, holding a rifle."

I opened the doors of the cabinets, finding folding chairs, plastic totes labeled with "Christmas," tablecloths, and crumbling boxes filled with assorted odds and ends from what I guessed were previous promotions. I unrolled a Mardi Gras party banner from 1963. Cornelius was going to need to have someone go through all of this and figure out what was salvageable.

I paused for a moment, trying to imagine Cornelius running a hotel, sitting behind a desk, punching figures into a calculator and chuckled to myself. Maybe he'd keep the same crew to run the place for him while he held his séances from his private room. I hated to see anyone get fired, even Skipper.

"Any luck?" Doc called across the cloth-covered mounds separating us.

"No," I said, walking around a huge covered object shaped like a horse. I lifted the cloth. Nope, not a horse—a mule.

I lifted the drop cloth more. On the floor next to its front hooves were the words: *Plato—First Mule in the Black Hills.*

"No shit," I said half to myself. Why wasn't old Plato up there next to Socrates? Flipping the cloth over his nose, I saw how much worse for wear the old mule was—one ear missing, a scruff of hide hanging loose on his cheek, and a chunk torn away from one of his nostrils. I grimaced. No wonder; Plato the Mule would scare people away. Maybe Cornelius could use him at Halloween as a Frankenstein version of Socrates.

"Violet, come here," Doc's tone sounded grave, making the back of my neck tingle.

I covered Plato back up and made my way around some filing cabinets and stacked tables to where Doc stood in the opposite corner. On the floor next to him were several picture frames leaning against the wall.

"What?" I asked.

"Yesterday, I went to the library to find whatever I could about this hotel. I wanted to figure out the stories behind some of the thirteen ghosts that swarmed me during the last séance, right before you knocked me out."

"*Accidentally* knocked you out," I clarified.

His lips twitched. "Your elbow to my cheek was no accident."

"It's in the past. We should just let that go. Continue with your library story."

"Anyway, I was going through old newspapers and in one from June of 1956, there was a tribute article for the long-time manager who'd just passed away." He pulled a folded piece of paper from his pocket and handed it to me. "It has his picture, too."

I flattened the paper on top of a nearby shelf, then held it up for more light. Doc pulled a penlight from his pocket and handed it to me.

It was a copy of the newspaper article and picture, which was grainy, but the image of a man probably in his late sixties with thinning white tufts of hair on the side of his head and dark eyes smiled back at me.

"He looks like a friendly guy," I said.

"Sounds like it, too, if you read the article." He pointed at the framed photo on the wall behind the manager. "Look closely at that."

I held the paper closer, shining the penlight on the framed photo. It was as he'd described earlier—three men, the one in the middle sitting, a big-ass rifle resting across his knees. Two of the three had the old fashioned long handlebar mustaches, reminding me of Wyatt Earp. The third man was standing to the left of the chair. He looked older than the other two, his hair white where the other two still had dark hair.

"Are they early hunters?"

"Maybe. I needed to see the picture itself though to confirm something."

"What?"

"First, the date on it."

"What else?"

"If the guy on the left was really an old man or not."

"What do you mean? He looks older."

"I know, but look at his body. That's not an old man's body."

"True."

"Look at his eyes."

I did, but the picture on the wall was too small to see more than shimmers where the guy's eyes were. "It looks like they are reflecting the flash."

"That was one theory I had."

I frowned up at him. "And the other?"

He grabbed one of the framed pictures leaning against the wall. "See for yourself."

I took the framed picture from him. I could see where he'd wiped the dust off the glass.

It was the picture of the three men from the newspaper— one man sitting in a chair with his big-ass rifle, which was even more impressive in the real picture, two handlebar moustaches, one shock of white hair.

Only the guy on the left wasn't old.

And it wasn't the reflection of a flash in his eyes, either.

I gasped and wiped off more dust, shining Doc's penlight on him.

"He's an albino," I whispered.

"Yeah." Doc looked over my shoulder. "Is he the same one from Mudder Brothers?"

"No, how could he …" but I looked closer, trying to remember exactly what my albino pal had looked like. The nose looked similar, long and straight, the cheekbones were cut high, hollowing out the space below, his chin shaped the same. My heart hammered loud enough for Doc to hear it. "Is he?"

"I only saw him for a split second," Doc said. "I can't remember many details."

"I need to see him sneer to be sure, but he has the same face structure, the same body style. But how can that be, Doc? This picture is old."

Doc pointed at the tarnished brass plate nailed to the lower part of the frame with the words *October 1886* on it.

"It can't be him," I said. "It has to be one of his ancestors."

"If there were a long-standing family of albinos living here, don't you think Cooper would have some of them listed on his case board? The detective acted like he'd never seen an albino around here when I was explaining my side of the story."

"That's true. He and Harvey should have known about them." Even if they were from the sticks … or Slagton.

Doc took out his cell phone and took a picture of the framed photo. Then he stuffed the portrait back behind a stack of others leaning against the wall.

When he turned back to me, his dark eyes were wide, serious. "Violet, you need to walk away from all of this."

"Walk away from what? The albino? How am I supposed to do that if he has a twin who wants revenge?" Or if he wasn't really dead. I had no way of knowing since he had disappeared in a damned cloud of smoke.

"I don't know," Doc put his arms around me and hugged me close, my nose bumping one of the buttons on his shirt. "But there's something evil going on here. As much as that sounds like something from a B-rated movie, I can feel it."

I tipped my head back, smiling up at him, leaning on humor to keep my panic at bay. "You're right. That was totally a B-movie quote."

He kissed my forehead, then stepped back, freeing me. "I don't know if I can protect you from what's going on."

"Who says I need protection?"

His stare said it all.

"Let me rephrase that," I said. "Why should you have to be responsible for my protection?"

One of his eyebrows lifted. "Are you fishing for something in particular?"

Maybe. "Of course not."

He grunted. "I don't know why I feel like I have to protect you. I just do, and not just because I pine for you late at night while you're busy snoring away next to an old man during *Hondo*."

"Pine for me? Is that another B-movie quote?"

"Moon over you?" He grabbed my hand and pulled me toward the door. "Is that better?"

"That's more like a soap opera line."

He reached back, running his hand over my butt, first a caress, then a squeeze. "How about I'm hot for your body?"

"All of the above."

He shut the door behind us. I turned and pinned him against it, pulling him down, wanting to taste and savor him again before we returned to the public eye and I couldn't. His mouth yielded to mine as I pressed against the whole length of him, feeling the heat from his skin through my black knit top. His hands locked onto my hips, pulling me even closer. I kept the kiss tender, slow, provocative, teasing with the slightest of brushes with my tongue. My fingers delved into his hair, holding him still as I finished with a nip, suck, and final lick.

"Damn," he whispered when I pulled back, his eyes glazed. That was no declaration of love, but I'd take it anyway. Then the creases in his forehead returned. "Violet?"

Why the frown? I'd brushed my teeth and gargled twice with cinnamon-flavored mouthwash this morning since I'd known I'd be seeing Doc. "Yeah?"

"I want to visit Prudence again."

I blinked twice. "Prudence? You mean the ghost from the Carhart house up in Lead?"

"Yes, that Prudence."

My kiss made him think of a dead woman? Nice. "Why?"

"There is something that I need to see. Something she seemed to be doing with her hands before her killers got to her."

Prudence's death had been violent and bloody. "So you want to relive her death again?"

Doc's sixth sense involved experiencing a victim's demise firsthand.

"Part of it, yes," he said. "And I'm going to need your help."

Chapter Ten

After parting from Skipper in the casino, Doc and I walked out to the parking lot of The Old Prospector Hotel in silence.

I had no idea where his thoughts were, but mine were hovering somewhere between Albino Street and Prudence Alley. Both places had my stomach churning like a clothes dryer full of tennis shoes.

Doc gave me a quick kiss goodbye, his thumb stroking my cheek with a tenderness that made me wish we had more time. "Be careful today," he said.

"What's today?" After seeing that portrait, I was a little distracted. I tugged open the Picklemobile's door and climbed up and in.

"Your shopping trip." He shut the door behind me, waiting while I rolled down the window. "Try not to kill your new boss and leave his body in a dressing room in Rapid City."

"I give no guarantee." It all depended how many times I heard the word *Tiffany*.

"Call me tonight," he said, stepping back. "Even if Harvey shows up."

That meant Doc didn't plan on coming over to spend the evening with me. Was he going to be busy with work? Or did it have something to do with the two little beings sharing my life?

I cranked the Picklemobile to her usual sputtering rhythm, leaving Doc with a wave and a black puff of acrid exhaust.

Mona was the only one at Calamity Jane's when I walked in the back door. The scent of her jasmine perfume calmed me in the way that the smell of my grandmother baking molasses cookies always had.

I made a beeline straight to the coffee pot.

"Morning, Vi," Mona said, her fingernails clacking away on her keyboard.

"Morning," I returned over my shoulder.

My cup shook in my hand as I poured the coffee. I set the cup down on the counter and mouthed a few silent "Ohmms." Then I stuck my finger in the black go-go juice to make sure it wouldn't scald and gulped the warm, bitter stuff down in one shot.

Ahhh, that was better. Maybe I should keep a flask of tequila in my desk drawer.

The clacking stopped. "Someone stopped by earlier and left you a gift."

When I shot her a raised brows look, she pointed toward my desk.

One of my purple boots sat on my chair—the right one. The same as her broken leg.

Natalie!

Nat had borrowed my purple boots before she'd found out I was involved with Doc. I'd written off those boots, figuring she'd throw them in a wood chipper and send me the pieces—if she were feeling nice by then.

"How long ago was Nat here?"

"Actually, it wasn't Natalie who dropped it off. It was Jeff Wymonds."

Jeff? I moved the boot from the chair and put my butt there instead. Oh, God! Had I driven her to Jeff's bed? She'd slept with him a long, long time ago back in high school and sworn not to revisit his bed ever again, no matter how drunk she got. But then she hadn't counted on her best friend betraying her like I had.

Hugging the boot, I wondered what the significance was of delivering only one boot. Was it an olive branch? Or was Natalie just being practical since her leg might still be in a cast and she only needed the left boot?

I searched the inside of the boot for a message, written on paper or on the leather, but found nothing.

"Did Jeff leave any message?" I asked Mona.

"Yes. He said to tell you that he hired a crew to fix his garage roof, and they should have it done in the next two weeks."

"Nothing about Natalie, though?"

"Nope. He said she'd stopped by his place with it yesterday and asked him to give the boot to you the next time he saw you."

Damn.

I grabbed my phone and texted Nat: *Thank you for the boot.* I hesitated for a moment, then added: *I miss you.*

As I hit the Send button, the front door whipped opened. Jerry burst inside, moving like a locomotive. He was wearing shorts again, this time with a tank top that showed off his muscular shoulders, one of which had a nasty six-inch scar down it. The neck of his top was soaked with sweat, his face dripping.

"Hello, ladies. Sorry about my appearance," he said. "I forgot my gym bag in my office."

He screeched to a stop after passing by me and backed up, looking down at my boot.

"Killer boot," he said, grabbing it, holding it up. "You should wear these in some of our ads."

Until the other boot showed up, the ads would have to be one-legged. I could imagine the nicknames that would follow.

Without giving me the chance to reply, he handed the boot back to me. He knocked twice on Mona's desk as he strode toward his office. "Pretty necklace, Red," was his parting comment.

Mona watched him from over the top of her reading glasses until he disappeared from view, fingering the single teardrop emerald pendant hanging around her neck.

I heard him rummage around for a few seconds and then his footfalls moved toward the back door.

"Be ready to go when I get back, Violet," he hollered and then closed the door behind him.

What if I weren't? Was he going to drag me down to Rapid?

That was tough talk for a real estate agent with only one sale and another barely pending. I shoved the boot in my desk drawer and opened up my Day-Timer to the address book. Under the letter C, I found two phone numbers for Wanda Carhart—one for her house up by the edge of the Open Cut and the other for her sister's place, where she supposedly was living these days.

I didn't want Mona to hear what I was about to do, knowing she'd disapprove after my last disaster involving the Carhart house, so I scribbled the number on a piece of paper and pocketed it. "I'll be right back, Mona; I left something in the Picklemobile."

Closing the back door behind me, I made sure Jerry wasn't hanging around anywhere nearby and then hit the Call button.

I counted four rings. Maybe I needed to cruise by there tonight and try to catch Wanda in person. I hadn't talked to her since …

"Hello?" a female voice interrupted my reminiscing.

"Hi, this is Violet Parker. I'm looking for Wanda Carhart."

"This is Wanda." Her voice sounded stronger than I recalled, less quavery and ready to shriek at any given moment. "I've been thinking about you lately, Miss Parker."

Good, she remembered me. "Really? Are you considering putting your house back on the market?"

"No, that's not why."

Then what … "Oh, you heard about my boss."

"Yes, that was a tragedy. But it was Prudence who put you in my thoughts."

Besides Doc, Wanda Carhart was the only one around who "knew" Prudence. While Doc had relived Prudence's death, Wanda claimed to have conversations with Prudence on a regular basis. I still wasn't one hundred percent certain Wanda wasn't experiencing figments of her own optical delusions. She had spent years with an abusive husband and a deranged son. Both were slain in a vicious double murder by her neurotic daughter who now spent her life behind bars. Wanda may have created a world full of fictitious characters to keep her company. I probably would have, too.

"Have you been visiting with Prudence again?" I asked.

Had Wanda moved back home to the scene of the crime—make that both crimes, the double murder and attempted murder? Wanda's house had been the setting for my nightmares many a night.

There was a shuffling sound from Wanda's end of the line before she whispered, "She's my friend." Her words made me shiver in spite of the September sunshine warming my skin. "Prudence tells me things."

I hesitated a moment, then took the plunge. "What kind of things?"

"Things about bad people," she whispered still.

"She thinks I'm a bad person?" I asked. What did I ever do to Prudence besides not believe she existed?

"Not you, the others."

Others? How many others were we talking about here? "You mean like Lila and her friends?"

Lila had been engaged to Wanda's son, but all along she'd been having an affair with Wanda's daughter, Millie. Lila had manipulated Millie into murdering Millie's father and brother, and then into attempting to sacrifice me. That demon-worshipping bitch had been bad juju. For both Wanda's and my sake, it was a good thing Lila had fallen on her own knife.

"No, not Lila," Wanda said, muffled now like she was cupping the mouth piece. "Or her horrible, disgusting friends."

When Cooper had sorted out the details of the Carhart crime, he'd linked Lila to a group of demon groupies from down by Yankton. They all had shared a lovely tattoo of a goat head melting into a pig. They also had shared a book written in Latin with a lot of freaky pictures in it, including the aforementioned goat-pig drawing. After my near sacrifice, I'd grabbed the book before Cooper could bag it as evidence. It was the same book Doc now kept tucked away in his closet.

I leaned against the brick wall that divided Calamity Jane Realty from the back door of Doc's office, wanting the feel of something solid at my back. "Who then, Wanda? Who are the others?"

Who were the bad people in Prudence's world, besides the hooded executioners who'd slain her family and then brutalized her before slitting her throat?

"The ones who killed your boss," Wanda whispered.

What? "The ones who killed …" I repeated under my breath, feeling dizzy all of a sudden. I bent over, letting gravity help get the blood to my head. "Wanda, do you know who killed Jane Grimes?"

"No, but Prudence does."

"Ask her who it was."

"She won't tell me."

Damn these ghosts and their cryptic conversations. "Why won't she tell you?"

If Wanda said Prudence didn't like her hat, I was going to throw my cell phone on the ground and jump up and down on it.

"Because she wants to talk to you."

My knees wobbled. "Why me?"

"She said you are ..."

I heard talking in the background, then hushed conversation, as if Wanda covered the phone with her hand.

Prudence said I was what? Losing my marbles? Sleeping with a medium? Hanging out in a historic opera house with a ghost whisperer? Seeing albinos?

"Miss Parker?" Wanda came back on the line.

"Yes? What did Prudence say?"

"I can't talk right now."

I growled in my throat. "How about I stop by later today?" I could race over there after my shopping trip.

"No, that won't do. Could you come by the house tomorrow morning?"

I didn't want to wait that long to hear what Prudence knew about Jane's murder.

Wait a second. Did I really believe I could find out who killed my boss from a woman who had been dead for over a century? One who supposedly channeled her thoughts through Wanda Carhart, someone who'd recently experienced mind-blowing trauma and violent bloodshed, let alone decades of brutality at the hands of an abusive husband? I could just hear Cooper's cackles of mad laughter when I told him where I had gotten my inside information.

"Sure, I could come by your sister's house," I said. "Where does she live?"

"Not my sister's, come to my house. That's where Prudence lives."

I pinched the bridge of my nose. Whether I truly bought into the whole idea of Prudence or not, Doc wanted me to get him into the Carhart house. I needed to figure out a way to let him roam the place without Wanda present. That meant I needed to gain her trust, which in turn meant she'd give me her key.

"Okay, your place it is. How about nine-thirty?" That gave me time to drop off my kids at school first.

"Splendid, Miss Parker. Prudence and I will see you then."

I could hardly wait. Stretching, I noticed a spider web in the corner of Doc's back entryway, a small dead bee caught in the web. A fat, long-legged spider was starting to wrap him up for later.

"Violet!" Jerry called out from behind me, making me practically jump right up into the web.

"What?"

"Let's roll."

Grumbling behind my extra-wide smile, I followed him into the office, stopping by my desk to grab my purse.

"Where are you two off to this morning?" Mona asked, watching me swing my purse over my shoulder. Her face was lined with more than curiosity, but I couldn't figure out what.

"I'm taking Violet to get a makeover."

"Why?" she asked, eyeing my black knit shirt and red slacks.

"She needs a little smoothing around the edges before we put her up on billboards."

"Billboards?" I gaped at him. "I thought you were only talking about marketing flyers."

"I have big plans for you."

Mona searched my face. "What about what Violet wants?"

Violet wants a job, I thought, and tried to hide behind a fake smile. "It's fine, Mona. We'll be back in a bit."

I squeezed her shoulder in thanks and zipped out the back door.

My phone rang as soon as I stepped into the sunshine.

I pulled it out of my purse. It was Cooper.

"I need to take this," I told Jerry. "I'll be right there."

I hit the answer button as Jerry zigzagged through parked cars toward his Hummer.

"Hello, Cooper. Did you call to yell at me some more?"

The detective grunted. "No, I actually called to apologize for yesterday."

A small breeze could have toppled me. "You what?"

"I'm sorry for being so ... so ..."

"Rude and bitchy?" I supplied.

"Short," he bit out.

What in the hell was going on? "Is someone holding a gun on you right now? Grunt once for yes."

He chuckled under his breath. "No."

"Wow. Okay. Apology accepted."

"Now tell me why I should interrogate Tarragon's wife," he ordered.

I gave him a quick run-down of what I'd overheard yesterday at the opera house between Tarragon and his wife. I didn't mention the paper with Jane's picture on it in the bathroom trash.

"You're sure it was Peter Tarragon."

"Well, I've never seen him before, but his wife called him Petey and he said he was the director."

"Okay. Did anything else happen?"

I debated on mentioning Dominick, but Jerry had started the Hummer and was waving at me out his window to hurry it up. Impatient much?

"No, that was it," I said.

"Why were you in the opera house?"

"It's a gorgeous old building. I took a tour of it with a friend." I feared mentioning Cornelius's name would set off alarms in Cooper's head. "Then I needed to use the bathroom and ran into Tarragon."

A little bit of fibbing there, but mostly the truth.

"All right. I'll look into this some more."

Jerry backed out of the parking spot and sat there watching me, idling, blocking anyone who might want to come through.

"I believe Jane and Peter's wife go back a ways," Cooper said. "She may have noticed something about Jane during practice the night of her death."

Was Cooper actually sharing information with me? Holy crap! Was the world ending and nobody had bothered to inform me?

"Did Jane and Peter Tarragon get along?" I asked Cooper.

"I haven't been informed otherwise."

Jerry honked.

Damn him! Patience was not his strongpoint. I was really starting to see why Jane had divorced his tall ass. I held up my index finger, like I often did with my children.

"Are you going to add Mrs. Tarragon to your case board?" I asked.

Silence came from Cooper.

Dead silence.

Then it hit me. Oh! My! God! I'd mentioned his case board. The one hidden in his basement behind the locked door.

Shit, shit, shit!

Before I could make an even bigger explosion in Cooper's or my world, I hit the disconnect button and cut the detective off cold.

Practically jogging, I rushed to Jerry's Hummer, jumped inside, and said, "Let's get the hell out of here," slamming the door behind me.

My phone buzzed.

I stuffed it in the bottom of my purse, leaned my head back, and closed my eyes.

I was so fucked.

* * *

When I was a kid, my mother used to take me shopping and pick out pink, frilly dresses with darling little bows and hearts all over them. She'd buy me patent leather shoes and would style my blonde curls into a Shirley Temple-like do. Then she'd prance me in front of her friends and sisters like a miniature show pony and they'd "oooh" and "ahhh" all over me.

She never asked if I wanted to wear the ridiculous Pepto-Bismol costumes. She never listened when I said the lace was making me itch or the shoes were pinching my feet.

Her princess-in-pink parade finally came to an end the day I wore one of her fancy tufts of lace during a mud-ball fight with

Natalie and her cousins. Mom came unhinged and sent me to my room, where I cut the muddy dress into pieces and then proceeded to butcher my curly mop. When my father came home and found me crying in the middle of a pile of tattered lace and blonde curls, he put an end to the family beauty show circuit once and for all with a promise to shave all of our heads bald if Mom didn't stop.

After that, Mom took up quilting and won lots of blue ribbons at the fair. I let my hair grow back and wore jeans and T-shirts like all of the other kids. And we all lived happily ever after … well, until my little sister, Susan, made it her mission in life to take everything that was mine and make it hers, including my children's father. The bitch.

Whipping into Aunt Zoe's drive, I slammed on the brakes. The shopping bags on the passenger side of the Picklemobile fell to the floor in a jumbled heap.

Glaring at the bags, I growled under my breath. Mom and Jerry would have gotten along like two peas in a pod.

Criminy. A freaking pink satin suit.

I mean really, who was going to buy a piece of property from a real estate agent wearing that ridiculous outfit? Only Barbie's boyfriend Ken, and that's because he had to put up with living in Barbie's pastel townhouse with that damned silly poodle of hers in order to get laid. Poor sucker.

The late afternoon sunshine still held court in the sky, but from a lower angle so that it shined directly into my eyes instead of over my head. Par for the course, I figured.

Natalie would have laughed her ass off over this whole mess, cracked a joke, and made me laugh, too. But Natalie still wasn't talking to me, not even to text me back.

I grabbed the bag with the pink suit, along with the ones with the white cashmere sweater dress that my children were sure to stain by just looking at it, and the fuschia June Cleaver-style day dress. In the ad with June's dress, Jerry'd probably want me holding a frying pan with bacon and wearing bright red lipstick.

Seriously, did Tiffany have to put up with this shit? Her ads said: *Smart and sexy Realtor here to serve your needs.*

Mine were going to scream: *Blonde bimbo here for you to bang while you buy a house.*

Grumbling all the way up Aunt Zoe's front porch steps, I shoved open the front door, threw the bags on the floor next to the stairwell post, and stomped toward the kitchen to get a stiff drink—something hard and potent that would make me forget my afternoon in hell.

I walked through the arched entry to the kitchen and found Aunt Zoe and Harvey sitting at the table, hands hovering over her Betty Boop cookie jar.

"Holy shitballs of fire!" Harvey shouted loud enough to make me wince. He burst out laughing. "Hot damn, I didn't know the circus was in town this week. Where'd you leave your red nose?"

Crap, I'd forgotten about the makeover Jerry insisted I get. I wrinkled my non-red nose at him as I headed to the fridge. "You bray like a donkey, old man."

That only made him wheeze harder.

"Look at those eyelashes." Aunt Zoe walked over to where I stood in front of the open fridge door. She grabbed my jaw and gently twisted it to one side and then other. "How do those even stay on?"

"They look like someone glued spider legs to her eyelids," Harvey said.

"They're a little long," I conceded.

"A little?" Aunt Zoe smiled. "I can feel a breeze when you blink, child."

"I just hope they don't rip off my eyelids when I remove them," I said.

I grabbed a cold Corona from the door shelf. That would work. I joined them at the cookie jar, stealing two chocolate chip cookies from Harvey's pile.

"What's with all of the goop on your face?" he asked.

"My boss took me shopping today."

Aunt Zoe's gaze narrowed. "You mean Jane's first husband?"

Last night after supper, I'd told her and Harvey about who was running the show down at Calamity Jane Realty. They were now both up-to-date on most of the current happenings, except for Cornelius and his opera house ghost, the old albino portrait, Prudence possibly knowing Jane's killer, and my slip in regard to Cooper's case board.

I grimaced at the thought of Cooper and shoved a whole cookie in my big mouth, barely tasting the chocolate.

I'd received three very terse voicemails from the detective throughout the course of the day. Judging from the amount of swear words per message, it was a good thing I'd left the hills and him behind. After much thought, I'd decided the best way to handle Cooper's current level of fury was to avoid him until after Christmas, or at least until he didn't want to shoot me on sight.

"Remember how I told you Jerry wanted to try a new marketing idea," I said. "Well, I'm it. He wants to use me to bring in more clients—especially males."

"Are you gonna pose in your birthday suit?" Harvey asked.

"Hell, no."

"Gotcha," he said, "just topless then."

I reached across the table and pinched his forearm. "Would you get your mind out of the gutter, old man."

"What? I guaran-damn-tee you'd get a bunch of new clients knocking down your door if you showed your hooters." His gaze lowered.

I crossed my arms over my chest. "Quit thinking about my boobs."

"I'm not. I'm thinking about Beatrice's and the names we gave them. One was called—"

"Stop right there," I said, cramming a cookie in his mouth.

"How do you feel about being used like this?" Aunt Zoe asked. "Like you're some piece of man-candy."

Aunt Zoe's feminist roots still held strong. She was one of my main influences and cheerleaders when it came to taking charge and being the sole provider for my children without needing to lean on a man for help.

"Jerry promised me today that all of the ads would be tasteful," I told her.

"No cherry licking then," Harvey said, "or bending over to pick up the newspaper in a little swishy cowgirl skirt?"

Aunt Zoe and I both wrinkled our noses at him.

He blinked. "What? I'm just trying to think outside of the box."

"These ads are not going in *Penthouse*," I said, stealing another cookie from the crusty old cowpoke.

"I was thinking more along the lines of some of those fancy men's magazines with the sexy babes on the front," Harvey said.

"So, they'll be tasteful," Aunt Zoe said, her arms crossed now, her eyes squinting in obvious distaste. "But you're still being treated like an object."

"I know," I said, tipping back the Corona. I could have used a lime wedge. "But I need this job, and if it does bring in new buying clients," something I was in dire need of at the moment, especially if Cornelius flaked out on me, "then it's worth swallowing my pride for now."

She nodded slowly, but her neck seemed stiff. "I don't like it. You're beautiful just the way you are."

"I don't like it, either, and you're biased about my looks."

"I am."

"She is," Harvey said around a cookie, his beard stretched wide from his grin. "I think you're just so-so. But that there goop on your face sure makes it more fun to look at ya."

I slapped him on the arm.

The doorbell rang.

"I'll get it," Addy yelled from the living room.

"What are we having tonight?" I asked Aunt Zoe. "You want me to order some pizza?"

"Harvey's cooking for us."

I sat back. "Really? Beans and biscuits then?" I taunted, knowing he was ten times the cook I was.

"I was thinking more along the lines of flank steaks on the grill, risotto, and some sautéed vegetables. Cherry pie for dessert."

Drool almost ran out of my mouth. "You have cherries on the brain, old man."

He shrugged. "They're Beatrice's favorite."

Correction, he had Beatrice Geary on the brain.

Addy came skidding into the kitchen. "Mom!"

"Slow down. You shouldn't be running with a sucker in your

mouth." She shouldn't be eating suckers this close to dinnertime, either. "What is it?"

"Oh, my molies, Mother! What is on your face?" she asked, coming closer for an inspection. She smelled like her grape sucker. "Are those spiders on your eyes?"

"It's makeup," I said, nudging her back out of my face. "You almost put my eye out with that sucker stick."

"Sorry," she tried to touch my right eyelash, but I knocked her hand away.

"Where are your glasses, Addy?"

"On my dresser."

"They need to be on your face. Who was at the door?" I asked.

"Some guy. He's still there. He wants to talk to you."

It was probably another salesman. Last week it was roof gutter systems; the week before, it was satellite television. I turned to Aunt Zoe. "Will you go see what the guy is selling? I look like I fell into a vat of makeup."

"It's not a sales guy," Addy said. "He said to tell you if you don't come to the door, he's coming back later tonight with a warrant."

Chapter Eleven

Straightening my shoulders, I warned Addy to stay in the kitchen and went to meet Cooper's gnashing teeth. My feet dragged as I crossed the living room.

Through the screen door, I could see the detective's profile. In the soft, early evening light, his body looked rigid and tense, posed to strike. His fists were clenching and unclenching at his sides. His shoulders bent inward like he was barely holding in the beast.

Something down the street seemed to have captured his attention—probably a baby harp seal he planned to club when he finished beating on me.

I thought about keeping the screen door between us as a layer of protection, but I doubted anything less than a brick wall would suffice against his huffing and puffing. Stepping out on the front porch, I pulled the main door shut so my family wouldn't have to witness the carnage.

He was on me before the screen door *thwapped* closed, backing me into the door jamb, his expression all tight-jawed and squinty-eyed. With my blood pounding in my ears, I tried to hold my ground in the face of his fury.

"What in the hell were you doing in my basement?" he said, his voice a deep growl. His aftershave smelled minty-cool, matching the ice shards in his gaze.

I dragged my tongue out from its hiding spot behind my tonsils. "Good evening, Detective Cooper."

He just snorted.

Going head to head with him would only result in my getting mine bit right off, so I opted for an off-the-wall response. "Would you like to stay for supper?"

"I explicitly told you *not* to go down there. I even deadbolted the fucking door!" A vein in the middle of his forehead pulsed.

I glanced down at his open jacket to see if he were packing tonight. *Dammit*. Of course he was.

Trying not to let him see my gulp, I said, "Your uncle is going to grill some steaks."

"But you just couldn't keep your damned nose out of my business!"

"We're having cherry pie for dessert." I strove to keep my tone calming. Nice beast. Good beast. How about a Scooby Snack?

"I should have known better than to trust that key anywhere within a fifty mile radius of you!" His left cheek began to tic.

I cringed, waiting for his head to explode. "We have ice cream in the freezer, too."

"I'm so fucking sick and tired of finding your ass at my goddamned crime scenes."

I was pretty sure this was the most I'd heard Cooper swear since I'd begun pissing him off regularly. "I could get you a pre-dinner drink. We have tequila, whiskey, and some—"

He grabbed my arm and yanked me closer until we were almost nose-to-nose. His lips curled in a snarl. "Do you have some kind of death wish, woman?"

"Vodka," I finished, my voice squeaking on the last syllable. I cleared my throat. "It's bacon flavored."

His chest rose and fell fast. His wrath seemed almost tangible, like a sparking aura that would shock if I risked a touch.

His grip on my arm became vice-like, bruising. "Have you heard a single fucking word I've said through all of that crazy hair?"

All right, that was about enough. I yanked my arm free and poked him in the chest hard enough to make him grunt. "Listen here, Mr. Detective, you can chew on me for sneaking a peek at your precious case board, but do *not* make fun of the hair."

He searched my face, and then he stepped back, frowning at me as if he were seeing me for the first time tonight. "What in the hell is on your eyes?"

"Fake eyelashes."

"Are they supposed to be sexy?"

"For your information, they're supposed to make me look like a fashion model." At least that is what the salesgirl claimed as she stuck them onto my eyelids.

"It looks like you glued long-legged centipedes to your eyes."

Okay, I got it. Nobody liked the fake eyelashes. I didn't either.

"Do those things throw off your balance?" Cooper leaned in to inspect them, lifting his hand like he was going to touch one. "They almost look alive."

I knocked his hand away, just like I had Addy's. "Don't touch the lashes."

He shoved his hands in his pockets. "Why is your hair all gooped-up like that?"

"It's called styling gel, and again, I have a fashion model thing going on here."

"Fashion model, huh?" His lips twitched. "You could scare children with that face."

"So could you. Now, if you're done chewing my ass up one side and down the other, I will explain why I know about your stupid case board."

His angry glare returned in a blink. "I'm all ears."

And I was all eyelashes. "You left that damned Colt .45 hand gun lamp in your bedroom during the open house and I had to hide it before my boss came and saw what a lousy prep job I'd done."

"Hey, my house was clean. I even put those vanilla candles in the bathroom like Uncle Willis insisted."

Cooper had been the one who tidied up the place? I imagined him with a dust mop in one hand and a semi-automatic machine gun in the other.

"Clean, yes, but that's not the same as having it prepped for show. Anyway, my boss was already on the way and I had to hide your stupid gun lamp. Harvey suggested I stick it inside of the basement room and lock the door so nobody would find it and accidentally shoot somebody."

His jaw tightened as he chewed on that for a moment. "Fine. That flies. But why didn't you just stick it inside of the door and walk away?"

"I got distracted by your case board."

"Bullshit. That board was tucked away in the back of the room. You just couldn't resist seeing what I was hiding. Admit it."

There was no way I was admitting anything that could be used against me later in a court of law. "Why is my name listed on the board?"

"Because you're a suspect."

I planted my hands on my hips. It was that or strangle him with them. "I didn't kill my boss, Cooper."

He shrugged. "I know that, but I might as well keep you on there until the next crime. You're like herpes—you show up when shit gets tense and never fully go away."

Centipedes and herpes. "You're always so warm and fuzzy to me."

"Being a teddy bear isn't in my job description. I find the bad guys and throw them in jail."

"And harass innocent women caught in the wrong place at the wrong time," I couldn't resist poking the non-teddy bear a little when he kept stabbing me with his own sharp sticks.

He scoffed. "You were sneaking around a mortuary looking for God knows what. Don't try to pretend you're all pigtails and pink lollipops, Violet Parker. I have your number."

That's what had me sweating. I kept my desire to leap off the porch and yip-yip-yip all of the way to Doc's house in check behind a fake grin. "I prefer a pony tail and cotton candy, Detective."

His pinched lips made me wonder what he was damming behind them. "How many people have you told about what you saw on my case board?"

"Uh …" I didn't want to get Doc in trouble.

"Don't lie to me, Parker."

"Tarnation, Coop," Harvey said, coming around from Aunt Zoe's side gate. "What's with all of the squealin' about your godforsaken case board?" Apparently a certain suspender-wearing shotgun lover had been eavesdropping. "I didn't see a single name on your list that ain't already been thrown in the ring as a possible killer by the boys up at The Golden Sluice."

"Jesus H. Christ." Cooper scrubbed his hand down his face. His glare narrowed on me. "I should have known you'd drag *him* into this."

The funny thing was I distinctly remembered telling only Doc, not Harvey. The old buzzard must have sneaked down into Cooper's basement and taken a peek for himself.

Cooper pointed at me, his pissed-off cop mask back in place with its granite crust and rough edges. "I swear to God, Parker, if I catch you messing with my investigation one more time, I'm going to arrest you for obstruction of justice."

The intensity of his gaze acted as an effective exclamation point. I took a step back.

"Define 'messing'," Harvey said, leaning against the porch rail.

"One. More. Time." Cooper shook his finger in my face with each word. "I'm not fucking around anymore."

"Got it," I said, dead serious. Call me kooky, but I really didn't want to go to jail.

After a final growl, Cooper strode to his unmarked police sedan parked at the curb. Through his passenger window, he kept us in his crosshairs as he drove away.

"Dang," Harvey said, climbing the steps to stand next to me. "That boy's mad as a bee stung dog."

"When did you look at his case board?"

"I didn't."

"Then why did you act like you did?"

"I figured you'd been sandpapered enough for one night."

I snapped the old boy's suspender playfully. "Thanks for saving my bacon."

"It's my job. You sure have a way of getting Coop's tail all bristly. If I didn't know better, I'd think he's sweet on you."

That reminded me of Natalie and her theory about Cooper lusting after me. Natalie just had lust on the brain. At least she had before I broke her heart.

"He's not sweet on me," I said. It was time to put an end to that whole unfounded notion.

"I know."

"You do?" I asked.

"Yeah, I said 'If I didn't know better.'" Harvey spared me a sideways smirk. "He's sweet on someone else."

My mouth gaped. "Who?"

"I'm not tellin', so don't even bother badgerin' me about it." He nodded across at Miss Geary's house. "You think her young stallion is in there with her right now?"

My mind was still wondering about Cooper's secret crush, but I gave a cursory glance across the street. "I don't see his racy black sports car."

"Maybe she lets him park in her garage like I used to."

"Is that supposed to be a double-entendre?"

"Why do you have to make everything dirty?" he asked.

"I'm just following your lead."

He grinned. "You're an apt pupil."

I grinned back. "Thanks."

We both watched Miss Geary's house while the crickets started warming up.

"I need you to go somewhere with me tomorrow morning," I told him. "You busy?"

"Nope. Where're we headin'?"

"The Carhart house. I have to talk to Wanda." And her ghost.

He grunted. "Giddy up."

* * *

Wednesday, September 5th

True to his word, Harvey stood on my doorstep the next morning at eight o'clock, all spit-polished and bushy-tailed.

Aunt Zoe was still sleeping after a late night working in her glass workshop out behind the house, so I fixed some toaster waffles to go with the store bought orange juice I put on the table. Ignoring the grumbles from Harvey about the lack of real breakfast food, I managed to herd everyone out the door without rattling the windows and doors.

Fitting all four of us in the cab of the Picklemobile for the ride to school would have been a tight squeeze, so Harvey chauffeured us in his extended cab pickup.

"It smells like dog back here," Addy said as we sat at a red light.

Harvey looked at her in the rearview mirror. "Old Red usually rides in that seat when we go out checkin' on my herd."

"Mom says pets don't belong inside vehicles."

I scowled at her, knowing exactly where this was heading. "Now is not the time for another protest about animal rights," I told her.

"If we don't stick up for them, who will?"

"Shut it down now, Adelynn Renee."

"Yeah, shut your big yap," Layne said, shoving his sister into the side window. His tiredness from staying up too late last night was showing its bully face. Who knew a book on the geology of the Black Hills could be so riveting, but there he'd been at midnight, hiding under his covers with a flashlight in hand.

"Layne, knock it off and say you're sorry," I said, giving him a hard stare.

He mumbled something that vaguely sounded like, "Sorry."

I turned back to his sister, who was rubbing her head where it had connected with the glass. "Addy, do you really want to go another round with me about this? Remember, you're still in big trouble for painting Elvis's feathers with my mascara brush."

"I told you, Mom, Elvis needed racing stripes for the competition."

"And I told you to stop using my toiletries on your pets."

Turning back toward the front, I heard muffled wheezes coming from Harvey. I poked him in the ribs, and he wheezed some more.

"Why do you have to check on your herd, Mr. Harvey?" Layne asked. "Do some of the cows get lost?"

"Lost, stolen, even shot. Old Red is pretty good at sniffing in the wind and finding a missing heifer."

That dog was also good at finding missing human heads, like the one belonging to the decapitated body the yellow lab had dug up out in Harvey's cemetery—the body with my business card still clutched in its hand. Turned out the head was still on the property. Old Red had found it in the defunct outhouse behind Harvey's barn. Now if only the dog could find the rest of the body that went with the torn scalp and human ear that Harvey had found in his bear trap a couple of months ago.

Addy sighed. "I sure wish we could take Elvis with us when we go places in the Picklemobile."

I ignored her billboard-sized hint and stared out the window at a couple of teenagers hugging on the sidewalk. His hands were on her butt, her arms inside his fleece jacket. Ah, young love. My heart panged for Doc, darn it.

I blinked back to reality and my daughter. "That chicken is not allowed inside the pickup. Period. I have enough trouble keeping her feathers off my clothes."

"Elvis molts on you because she loves you," Addy said.

Harvey pulled up in front of the school and let the engine idle. He turned around in the seat and grinned at Addy. "Maybe tonight we can make a chicken carrier you can tie in the back of the Picklemobile so Elvis can travel along without messin' up your momma's glad rags."

"Yes! Can we, Mom?"

"We'll talk about it after school," I said, tired of thinking about that dang chicken this early in the morning. I stepped down to let both kids out my side. After I planted a kiss on the tops of their heads, I sent them on their way.

When I crawled back in the pickup, Harvey was messing with the radio dials. I pulled my dark green knit sweater over my matching short sleeve shirt. It was supposed to warm up into the seventies today, but it sure didn't feel like it this morning.

Harvey settled on a station playing Willie Nelson's *On the Road Again* and headed up the highway that took us through Central City and then on into Lead. Not a half mile out of Deadwood, we passed Reid. He was driving the big red dually truck that had the fire station's namesake on the side.

"Damn," Harvey said, "he looked like he's been rode hard and put up wet."

Harvey was right. Reid appeared drawn, almost haggard. "Maybe he's not a morning guy," I said.

"Maybe he's got barrel fever," Harvey said.

"What?"

"He's been bending the elbow too much." When I continued to frown at him, he added, "He's hungover. Do I have to teach you the English language, girl?"

I ignored his smartass grin. "Maybe Reid just needs some more caffeine." I always needed more. Feeding it to me intravenously would be easiest some mornings.

"Is your aunt still all puckered up about him?"

"If that means wanting to shoot him on sight, then yes. I don't know what happened between those two in the past, but she can't seem to forgive and forget."

He shook his head. "Life is too short for holdin' grudges. You must have gotten that bull-headed streak of yours from her."

"I'm not bull-headed. I'm determined."

"That's not what Doc calls it."

What does Doc call it? "Leave him out of this."

"No can do."

I tried to divert him. "Did you ever talk to Doc about your uncle's mule?"

"Not yet. Did you get a hold of him last night after I left?" he asked.

"No, it was way too late." Many more nights of Harvey staying until all hours of the morning in Aunt Zoe's living room and I was going to go over to Miss Geary's myself and beg her to take Harvey back. As much as I enjoyed the company of the ornery coot next to me, I missed Doc—even the sound of his voice on the telephone.

"You need to tell him about Coop's threat to arrest you," Harvey said, turning left down Lead's main drag.

"I doubt he wants to hear about that." It would only make him groan, and not in the good way I preferred.

"Humph." It was more of a sound than a word coming from Harvey. "I disagree. That boy's taken to you like a lean tick to a fat dog."

"You do realize you just called me a 'fat dog,' right? I'm going to have to bite you now."

"Don't go gettin' all lathered up. That's just a turn o' phrase.

You know Doc would wanna be told about Cooper threatenin' to throw you in the pokey."

"I'm not going to get thrown in the pokey." At least I didn't plan to end up there.

I watched the houses go by out the window. After Cooper's latest warning, I'd decided to toe the line and keep my nose free and clear of his business, Wanda and Prudence aside, that was.

"By the way," I told Harvey, "as far as Cooper is concerned, this morning's visit is about selling the Carhart place. Got it?"

He nodded. Wanda Carhart's drive was just ahead on the right. Harvey pulled in and cut the engine.

"You sure you want to face this demon today?" he asked, his fingers still on the wheel.

I didn't have much of a choice. I didn't know how else I could get Doc inside Wanda's house without breaking and entering, and Cooper didn't need any extra reasons to arrest me.

"As much as I ever will be."

"We could just talk to her on the porch," he offered.

I stared up at the two story house in all of its Gothic-Revival-style finery with its steep cross gables and point-arched windows. The new layer of cheery paint all trimmed in chocolate brown reminded me of a summer morning and flower-filled garden, the front porch begging for a swing and some glasses of lemonade.

Here it was, the site of my near sacrifice. The house was like an oleander flower, beautiful yet deadly. Prudence and the Carharts weren't the only victims of its poisonous past; there had been another murder committed decades ago. One born of jealousy—of love soured into hate.

I'd avoided driving anywhere close to the Carhart house since I'd been carted out of it in an ambulance a few weeks ago.

"I'll be okay," I told Harvey.

I glanced up at the attic window, staring at the white lace curtains, half expecting them to be drawn back by a woman in an old fashioned, high-necked dress stained with blood. Goosebumps rippled up my arms.

"As long as Prudence plays nice," I said partially under my breath.

"What are you talking about?" Harvey asked.

"Wanda says the ghost who lives here wants to talk to me."

"The same ghost that warned you about staying away from one of the mines?"

I frowned at him. "How did you know about that?"

"I sat next to Wanda last week during Jeb Haskell's funeral."

"Criminy! Another Haskell died?" That was the fourth Haskell to die since I'd moved to Deadwood this spring. "How many more are left?"

"Enough to fill the Mudder Brothers parlor, lobby, and porch."

When I just gaped at him, he added, "Those Haskell boys had a hankerin' for wide-hipped women who didn't believe in birth control."

"This world needs more men who hanker for wide-hipped women," I said, considering the girth of my own hips since having twins.

His blue eyes sparkled. "This world needs more wide-hipped women who like to ride—"

"That's enough!" I hopped out the door before he could finish that sentence.

Hoofing it across the yard in front of the house, I wrapped my fingers around the wires of the eight-foot high chain-link fence that edged the property, staring through the wire diamonds. On the other side, past a narrow strip of land covered in knee-high dry grass, the earth fell away, forming the uppermost dirt ring around Homestake's non-operational Open Cut mine.

Harvey joined me, linking his fingers in the fence, too.

"You have to wonder how her body got down there," I said, peering across the half-mile width of the pit to the different colored bands of earth lining the other side.

"Word at the bar is that there were no tire tracks on the mine floor before Johnny Law arrived. No footprints around the body, either."

"How can that be?" I stood on my tiptoes to see as far down as I could, unable to see the bottom at its twelve-hundred foot depth. "Short of her being dropped from a helicopter, which somebody around here would have heard."

"That's the stumper."

"No prints," I whispered. I thought of the bloody hook on Cooper's board. Did anyone other than Cooper know about that? Well, Cooper, me, Doc, and whoever analyzed and shelved the evidence. "Any mention of a murder weapon?"

"Nope. Plenty of jaw flappin' about it, though."

I opened my mouth, wanting to tell Harvey about the hook, but hesitated. On one hand, he was a good friend who helped me whenever I needed it and supported me when I was up against his very angry nephew. On the other, if word got out about that hook, Cooper would know it was me who ran my mouth.

"Spill it, girl," Harvey said. "I'm all ears."

I glanced over to see him watching me, his gaze searching. "You have to promise to tell no one."

"My lips are glued tight."

"I mean absolutely nobody. Not even that dog of yours."

He snorted. "Old Red is a vault, and I swear on my uncle's sacred firewater that I won't let out a peep. Now grease your tongue and let 'er rip."

My gaze returned to the Open Cut, now shadowed thanks to a cloud covering the sun. "Remember that albino I told you about who chased me down at Mudder Brothers?"

A couple of days after the whole Mudder Brothers ordeal, I'd given Harvey an edited version of what happened, ending it with just a disappearing act rather than a miraculous puff of black smoke.

"The one Cooper is on the lookout for?" he asked.

I nodded. "When the albino and I were in the autopsy room, he pulled a barbed hook out of his suit jacket and threatened me with it."

"Like a Captain Hook hook?"

"No, a little bigger and covered in multiple sharp points, like it'd been wrapped with barbed wire minus the wire."

Harvey grimaced. "Sounds hair-raisin'."

"Cooper found that same hook somewhere near the body."

"How do you know?"

"A picture of it was on his case board." I looked at him. "There was blood all over the hook in the photo."

"Did you see pieces of flesh on it?"

I winced. "I didn't look that closely." I hadn't wanted to.

"Was it the exact same hook or just a look-alike?"

"I don't know."

"So, your albino pal may still be slinkin' around town even though you embedded those big scissors in his back."

"Possibly."

He stared out at the Open Cut. "You need to start sleeping with Bessie."

"I'm not sleeping with your shotgun. I'll blow my own toes off."

"Does Doc know all about this?"

"Yeah."

"Then he should be sleeping with you."

"I have kids."

"Even more reason to have him there with you. Or y'all with him."

"We can't sleep at Doc's." I wasn't going to force him into having an immediate family, using his need-to-protect against him like that. That was a sure-fire way to make him kick up dust on his way out of town. "Besides, the kids don't know about us."

"What's the big secret? Natalie knows now, why don't they?"

"It's complicated."

"You're just one big bowl of 'complicated,' girl." He crossed his arms and leaned back on his heels. "If you won't sleep with Bessie or Doc, then I'm going to have to share your bed."

"Absolutely not."

"Well, I'm not sleepin' on the hard floor at your feet."

"Harvey, I'm fine. I don't need a babysitter."

"Yeah, you do, but you're too mule-headed to realize it." He pointed toward the mine. "My thinkin' is the murderers came out through one of them there mine drifts in the side of the pit and somehow launched her onto the bottom. Maybe they used one of those pumpkin chuckers I've seen on TV."

My eyes welled up. We were talking about Jane like she was someone we hadn't known, someone whose perfume I could still smell if I thought about it.

"Unfortunately," Harvey continued, "Cooper was one of the first on scene, and he ain't tellin' what condition she was in when he found her."

I swiped at my eyes, hoping my mascara wouldn't give away my tears. "Where do those mine drifts lead to?"

"Homestake, one way or t'other." He jutted his chin toward the tall shaft buildings that covered the elevator pulleys up on the hill on the other side of the Open Cut. "These northern hills are honeycombed with drifts, shafts, and the like thanks to Homestake."

"So you think whoever is behind this has access to Homestake's main shafts?"

"Yep. Could be the killer works for that big science lab they built under Homestake."

According to Layne, my little scientist, the neutrino lab was located 4,850 feet under the gold mine. He'd ridden his bike all of the way up to Lead in July to hang out at the science festival that the research facility put on each year. Later that night, he'd filled my head with all sorts of words like "dark matter" and "mass" until my eyes glazed over.

Harvey frowned through the fence at the Open Cut. "Something's goin' sour in the Hills." The gravity in his tone made me frown along with him.

"You think Cooper can stop it?" Whatever *it* was.

"I sure as hell hope." He patted me on the back. "Now let's go have us some tea and crumpets with Wanda and that chatty ghost of hers."

Chapter Twelve

I could see Wanda's silhouette behind the white lace curtains in the front window. At least I assumed it was Wanda who was watching us.

Harvey and I climbed the front porch steps. The paint on the Carhart house was several weeks old but still smelled fresh under the warmth of the mid-morning sunshine. The door inched open as I raised my knuckles to knock. I half expected Vincent Price's low-pitched, creaky-sounding laugh to echo around me.

"Hello?" I said, pushing the door wide, stepping inside.

Wanda stood at the other end of the foyer filled with Tiffany-style stained glass sconces and twin lamps. Pastel shades of red, yellow, green and blue light dappled over her faded yellow gingham dress with several bees embroidered above her ample bosom. Her long gray hair was secured in a single braid that draped over her shoulder. She looked the same as she had the last time I'd seen her over a month ago, except for her smile, which took up her whole face. The mouse-like woman who used to study my feet the whole time I talked to her seemed to have been sent away along with her whack-job of a daughter.

"Good morning, Miss Parker," She slipped past me and Harvey to shut the door behind us. "I see you brought my old friend."

At the sound of the deadbolt clicking, I froze, my chest tightening, my breath getting all tangled up in it. The foyer shrunk around me, too narrow, full of too many people.

Harvey nudged me. When I didn't move, he pinched my lower back, down where I was storing up a decent supply of fat for the upcoming winter months. I jerked away, aiming a glare his way. The ornery bird needed to come up with some non-bruising ways of pulling me back from the edge of panic.

Harvey chuckled as I rubbed where he'd pinched, then he turned back to our hostess. "Good mornin', Wanda. You're lookin' like you feel good enough to dance the hokey pokey all by yourself."

Wanda tittered. A month ago, she was screeching at her own shadows, cringing in corners. Apparently, having her cruel and abusive family members all killed or shipped off to prison had lightened her disposition. Go figure.

She led us out of the foyer and into the sitting room with its birch flooring. The place smelled of vanilla, just like I remembered. The caramel wood tones and islands of cream-colored shag carpet were still plush, the ambiance still serene with a touch of old-time elegance. One would never know of the violence the room had witnessed.

A new rug covered the area where Lila had bled out while staring at me with her sightless eyes. That much blood had a way of staining memories long after it was all mopped up and gone. I knew from experience because the dark pool was still fresh in my mind, the coppery scent lingering in the back of my nose.

"Would either of you like something to drink?" Wanda asked. "I have tea, coffee, or snake oil."

Snake oil? For breakfast? Seriously? I was tempted. It might keep my shoulders from riding piggy-back on my earlobes until we left this place. But I doubted my new boss and fashion consultant would be giddy if he smelled anything stronger than coffee on my breath when I got back to Calamity Jane's.

"I'll just have some tea," I said, then remembered Wanda's previous obsession with a lack of ice when I was here last month. "Unless you have ice water."

Wanda's brow wrinkled. "I'm sorry, Miss Parker, but the freezer is broken."

Had that been the reason for the lack of ice all along? Something that simple? If so, why had Wanda been so uptight about it?

"What about you, Willis?" Wanda asked.

"Nothin' for me." Harvey grinned wide enough for his gold teeth to show. "I'm not touchin' your pa's homemade snake oil again. One tip of your flask during Haskell's funeral and I nearly fell ass over teakettle into the casket."

Wanda snickered. "Daddy's recipe always gives a good kick. I'll be right back." Her long dress swished as she walked away.

"Is this where you saw Millie Carhart and her long-legged girlfriend French kissing?" Harvey asked, taking my mind off Wanda's lack of ice cubes. He crossed over to a window that looked out onto a small flower bed, the same window I'd peered out in the past.

"Yeah, but that's all I'm going to say about it, so don't expect a play-by-play."

"Fine, killjoy."

"Get over here and sit next to me." I patted the burgundy leather sofa.

"I need to scout out everything if I'm gonna be your bodyguard. Where did you and the spitfire get into the wrestlin' match?"

There'd been no wrestling, more like a claw and scramble 'til the death duel.

"Over there." I pointed at the sideboard where Lila and Millie Carhart's collection of macabre knives had been laid out. The chair I'd been tied to was gone, of course, as was the grandfather clock I destroyed in my struggle to escape Lila and her sharp blade. A fleeting memory of the malicious glee that had lit up that crazy bitch's face made me shudder.

Harvey dropped onto the couch cushion next to me and patted my leg. "How about you take me out to lunch today?"

"I already took you out once this week. That fulfilled our deal until next week."

"That one didn't count. I was off my feed."

I snorted. "It's not my fault your tummy was sad about Miss Geary finding a new boyfriend."

"First of all, darlin', men don't have tummies. Second, if my memory serves me right, you ordered me to come to breakfast with you to act as backup with Coop."

"But you fell down on the job," I reminded him.

"That don't matter none. I showed up for the dance, that's what counts." He rubbed his stomach. "All of this Sherlock

Holmes business works up an appetite."

Wanda entered the sitting room carrying a tray with one mug and a plateful of blonde brownies. I could hear Harvey's lips smacking as he reached for a couple. My hand was right behind his. We shared groans of appreciation for creamy icing and moist brownies. If it wasn't for the dead woman who was supposed to be floating around the place and my recurring nightmares of hooded figures slicing me open in this very room and feeding my blood to an orange-eyed demon, I could have sat here happily stuffing my cheeks all morning.

I took a sip of the lukewarm tea, tasting a hint of nutmeg and something spicy that I couldn't place. After a couple more sips, I shoved another brownie in my mouth as a sweet chaser.

"Miss Parker," Wanda said, lowering into the matching burgundy leather chair next to the sofa, "I'd like to hire you again to sell my house." She leaned forward, looking eager, as if she hoped I'd pull a For Sale sign out of my ass and plant it in her front yard this very moment.

I stopped chewing and stared at her. Had she been tipping her infamous flask in the kitchen? Had she forgotten that the last time I'd put this house on the market, I'd almost ended up hanging out with Prudence the ghost for all of eternity? Did she think I could just waltz through here with potential owners and not have flashbacks that would send me racing back outside gasping for air?

"You don't have to give me your answer right this moment," Wanda said. "But I'd be willing to pay you a higher percentage than normal, just like before."

Just like before, huh? "How much higher?"

"An extra ten percent."

Harvey whistled. "That's mighty generous."

Wanda clasped her hands together. "Well, I'm getting along just fine now what with the inheritance I got, so money isn't as much of a concern. I'm gonna miss Prudence's company, but this house is filled with memories that are far from happy— memories I'd like to try to bury so I can enjoy my sunset years."

"Prudence won't pack up and travel with you?" I asked, serious. I wasn't quite sure how this ghost thing worked for

Wanda. Hell, I wasn't sure of anything having to do with the ectoplasmic crowd, but after all of the inexplicable events I'd witnessed over the last few months, I was open to learning.

"No. This was where she raised her son, where she and her husband enjoyed many happy memories. She's too attached."

"Isn't it also the place where she died?" I asked, curious to hear from Wanda if her version of what happened to Prudence might be different from the horrific demise Doc claimed to have experienced while sniffing around in Prudence's memories.

Wanda didn't answer. Instead she looked down at her clasped hands. I was about to ask my question again when she nodded and said, "Yes, but she wants me to tell you those men can't hurt her anymore."

"Prudence is here right now?" I asked, glancing at Harvey to see if I could read any doubt or disbelief on his expression.

He was too busy licking the frosting off a brownie to even notice my attention had shifted to him.

"Of course," Wanda said, as if I were being a silly ninny. "She's here all of the time."

Harvey reached for another brownie.

I knocked my knee against his leg, frowning at the half-empty brownie plate. He scooted further away from me, dropping crumbs on the white shag rug in the process, and then dove into his brownie.

Focusing back on Wanda, I asked, "How does Prudence feel about your leaving her?"

Wanda went quiet again, staring at her hands. I kept expecting her to do something with them, something David Copperfield-like that resulted in a white dove poking its head out from her cupped palms.

But nothing happened.

The clock ticked.

Something *tinked* over by the front window.

Harvey chewed, swallowed, and then licked his fingertips.

"She'll be sad," Wanda finally spoke, "but she understands it's time for me to move on."

"Move on to where?" Harvey asked.

"I'd like to get a condo down in Rapid," Wanda said.

"Maybe one down in Arizona, too. Somewhere warm when the snow falls."

I cleared my throat. "So, is that what Prudence wanted to talk to me about today? Selling her house to someone new?"

"Oh, no, that's what *I* wanted to talk about. Will you help me?"

I thought of Ray's howls of laughter when he found out I'd signed on to sell the Carhart house again, of Mona's disapproving frown, of Jerry's … Jerry's what? Would he approve of my selling a house with such a sordid history? Would he think it was bad for Calamity Jane's reputation, or would he be wooed by the almighty dollar?

At my hesitation, Wanda's eyes grew watery. "Please, Miss Parker. You're the only real estate agent who will come within a stone's throw of the house after Millie's mistakes. Help me escape from all that happened here."

I wasn't totally fooled by Wanda's weepy plea. Twenty bucks said the waterworks were an attempt to get me to agree. But knowing what I did about Wanda's experiences within these walls, I believed there was some truth behind her sales pitch.

What would Aunt Zoe say when she found out I'd taken this place on again?

And Doc?

Oh, crap—Doc. I'd forgotten about his being my whole reason for calling Wanda yesterday. At least if I gave her a contract, I'd be able to get him inside the place alone with Prudence.

"Would you be willing to drop the price another twenty thousand, if I have any trouble selling it?"

She nodded. "I just want to be free of it."

I couldn't blame her. I did, too. It spooked the crap out of me. "Okay," I said, crossing my toes that I wouldn't live to regret this.

Wanda reached out and squeezed my hands between hers. Her palms felt coarse, like she'd been handwashing burlap bags for years. She closed her eyes.

Figuring she was going to thank me, I opened my mouth to tell her it was no problem.

Before I could speak, she cut me off with, "Stay away from the mine, Violet."

Only it wasn't the wavering voice that usually came from Wanda's lips. She sounded younger, her tone more melodic with an almost mid-Atlantic Eastern accent, like a young Katharine Hepburn or Grace Kelly.

I shook my head feeling a bit like I'd been tipped on my side and everything had slammed into one ear. I tried to pull my hands free, but Wanda held on tight.

"Stay away until you've read the book," Wanda continued in the voice that was strangely soothing, yet chilling all at once, leaving the hairs on the back of my neck sticking up. "You have much to learn."

The book? The same one Lila had stashed upstairs in this very house? The one I'd sneaked out of here that Doc was currently hiding for me? The one written in Latin that I couldn't read?

All of the saliva drained from my mouth, leaving my tongue flopping like a marooned fish. "P-P-Prudence?" I stuttered. "Is that you?"

"I saw them throw another into the hole," Wanda said in the odd voice, her eyes still closed. "I saw them throw it like it was nothing more than a bag of potatoes."

I gaped over at Harvey to make sure I hadn't been cannonballed into some freaky hallucination.

He sat staring at Wanda, his whole body frozen with a brownie held midway to his lips. His eyes darted to me and then returned to our happy-go-lucky oracle.

I tried to get past this being some bizarre delusion and grasp what Wanda had said about the *bag of potatoes*. "You saw them throw what, Prudence?" I asked, half-expecting Wanda to open her eyes and start laughing, the joke on me.

"The body," she said. "They threw the body in the hole. They threw it all of the way down."

"Who?" I asked, scooting closer in case she whispered. I didn't want to miss her reply. "Who threw the body?"

"The undead ones. Two of them."

Undead? I mouthed the word *zombies* to Harvey. He nodded

and shoved the last of the brownie in his mouth.

"But it didn't take this one," she said, sounding puzzled, bewildered. "It always takes the bodies, but not this time."

"What didn't take the body, Prudence?" I asked.

"Why didn't it take the body?" she seemed mired in her own question, her grip loosening.

I grabbed onto her as she tried to pull free, not wanting to break contact, disrupt whatever conduit we'd created. "What didn't take the body, Prudence?" I asked again.

Wanda moaned, her eyes still closed. Suddenly her grip returned tenfold, my fingers squeezed in a painful clasp. Her eyelids flew open, revealing the whites of her eyes, her focus literally turned inward. She hauled me toward her in a strong tug, yanking me half off the couch. Before I could right myself, she leaned forward and sniffed the crook of my neck, stopping at my earlobe.

"It's as I thought," she whispered, her breath hot on my ear. "You will be the next one."

Terror seized me, hugging the air from my chest.

Then Wanda's hands slid free of mine and she blinked back to normal, her eyes no longer rolled back, her smile returning with a hint of timidity.

"More tea?" she asked, as if she hadn't just scared my soul into the next state.

"No!" I shot to my feet and rushed toward the foyer. Fresh air! I needed fresh air ... and maybe a defibrillator.

After a brief struggle with the deadbolt, I surged out the front door and leaned against one of the thick porch posts, sucking in lung-filling breaths.

Harvey came up behind me and touched my arm. "You okay, girl?" He handed me my purse, which I'd run off and left.

"No," I said, letting go of the post to cling to him. "I don't think so."

"Your hands are hotter than a nun's knees." He touched my cheek and forehead. "But the rest of you feels just fine."

Wanda stood on the threshold, holding the screen door open. "Should I call an ambulance?"

"No, I'm fine." The last thing I needed was Reid or Cooper

catching wind of my being here. "Things just got a little ..."
disturbing, hair-raising, spooky as hell, "claustrophobic in there."

"We should probably get goin'," Harvey said to Wanda.
"Violet's been down in the joints lately."

I'd been what? In what joints? Where?

"You should have told me earlier," Wanda said to me. "I
have some wonderful herbal tea that will take care of all of your
aches and pains. I drink it every morning."

Homemade herbal tea? That might explain the freak show
that had just happened in her sitting room. What was in that tea?
Had she slipped me one of her homemade herbal concoctions,
spurring me to start hearing voices? What was that strange spice
in my tea?

"Maybe next time," Harvey answered for me, leading me
toward the steps.

"Will you be bringing by a sales contract later, or should I
come down to your office to sign the paperwork?" Wanda asked.

I'd forgotten all about the house sale. "I'll call you after I get
everything typed up and you can stop down." I wasn't coming
back to this house while she stood inside of it.

I let go of Harvey when we reached the bottom step, feeling
almost back to normal, the invisible corset no longer constricting
my lungs.

"Oh, Willis," Wanda called, still standing in the doorway.

We both turned.

"Be sure to tell that sweet nephew of yours that he should
come by for more tea and cookies sometime soon."

I only knew of Harvey having one nephew, but maybe there
were multiple *Coopers* running around the Hills. I shuddered at
the notion of Cooper having a clone—I'd rather face off against
the albino twins.

"Are you talking about Detective Cooper?" I asked.

"Of course. He was very kind when he stopped over last
week. And what a wonderful sense of humor he has. He must get
that from you, Willis, because his daddy was a real pisser."

I blinked. Cooper? Sense of humor? Wanda must have been
drinking her special herbal tea that morning, too.

"What was Coop doing here?" Harvey asked.

"He asked me some more questions about the call."

Harvey's gaze narrowed. "What call would that be?"

"The one I made about the body," Wanda explained, as if the *Black Hills Trailblazer* had run a front page story on it that we'd apparently missed. "Prudence insisted. She was so upset about it all."

I frowned. "So, Detective Cooper came here to ask you questions about Jane Grimes' murder?"

She nodded. "Twice—the night Prudence was so distraught and a couple of days later." She smiled, staring off toward the Open Cut. "He's so well-mannered. And my," she touched her chest, "what a handsome man he's grown into."

Well-mannered? The same man who cussed me out on my front porch last night? I would have laughed aloud if my heart wasn't ramming into my ribs, trying to break out and high-tail it down the road. We needed to leave before Cooper or one of his crew stopped by for more milk and cookies.

"We need to get the hell out of here," I said under my breath to Harvey.

If I had known Wanda was part of Cooper's murder investigation, I'd have insisted she meet me somewhere that offered more cover from the cops and less potential for me winding up in jail.

"Good to see ya, Wanda," Harvey said, grabbing my arm and tugging me toward his pickup.

I waved at Wanda as I beat feet after the old buzzard. "I'll call you soon."

Neither of us said another word until he'd backed out of the drive and the Carhart house was shrinking in my side mirror.

"Damn," Harvey said, shooting me a bushy-browed grimace. "I'm not sure what just happened back there, but it was a hell of a long ways from ordinary."

"Which part? The news about Wanda being the one who called in to report about Jane's body or the parlor trick where she whispered cryptic warnings and scared the crap out of me?"

"That was no parlor trick, girl, and you darn well know it." He made a right turn. "Now I know Wanda's banjo hasn't been tuned right ever since she married that no-good drunk, but that wasn't Wanda holdin' your hand. It wasn't her voice, and those sure as shootin' weren't her words."

He slowed to a stop and shot me a frown before turning left onto Lead's main drag, heading down the hill toward Deadwood.

"What did she mean about reading some book before goin' in a mine?" Harvey asked. "What book?"

I pinched the bridge of my nose, worried about what I was about to disclose for multiple reasons. After hearing Prudence's warning, getting busted by Cooper for withholding evidence was now the least of my fears. But could I be putting Harvey at risk by telling him the truth?

"Damn it, girl," he said with a growl, as if he could hear the waffling in my head. "If you don't tell me, I'm going to start pinching again."

He was right. He'd stuck his neck out for me with Cooper and practically held my hand back at Wanda's. It was time to come clean. Mostly clean, anyway. Besides, those pinches hurt.

"Wanda—I mean Prudence—was referring to a book I took from the Carhart house after the big showdown with Lila. A book they were going to read from while sacrificing me to some demon." At least that's what I'd assumed when Lila had carried the book into the room while dressed in her sinister-looking brown robe.

"What's in this book?" he asked.

"Scary pictures and a lot of Latin words."

"Does Coop know about this book?"

I shook my head. "And if he finds out now, I'll need three lawyers to save me from spending ten years in prison for withholding evidence."

"Where are you hidin' it?"

I didn't want to out Doc in case everything went south. "A safe place."

We rolled to a stop, caught in a traffic snarl. Up ahead of a line of traffic, I could see the flashing hazard lights of a delivery truck.

"So, why would Prudence want you to read this demon book before you go into some mine?" Harvey prodded.

"I don't know." Cross my heart and hope to die on that

answer. Prudence's warning made no sense, especially since the only Latin I knew was printed on the money in my purse.

I looked out my window and realized we were sitting in front of the Lead library; the Historic Homestake Opera House was just ahead on the right.

In one of the large plate-glass windows of the art gallery that fronted the opera house building, a movie-sized poster advertised *Better Off Dead—A Zombie Wedding Musical*. An image of Mrs. Tarragon in her zombie bride outfit filled the top two-thirds of the poster. The title was plastered across the bottom third in a font that dripped blood on Peter Tarragon's name and directing accolades.

After the heated conversation I'd heard between the two of them, the poster took on a whole new meaning.

"How well do you know Peter Tarragon?" I asked Harvey.

"Enough to know he thinks the sun comes up just to hear him crow."

"Do you think he's capable of killing someone?"

"Girl, we're all capable of killin' someone. It's just a matter of if we choose to pick up the hatchet or not. Now Tarragon may be pretty puffed up with air, but that's all it is—just hot air."

As the vehicles ahead of us eased around the delivery truck, Harvey inched forward, grumbling under his breath. We reached Siever Street and Harvey took a right, escaping the backup.

"I overheard Tarragon and his wife fighting yesterday," I explained to Harvey. "She said something about not letting him do to her what he did to Jane."

Harvey grunted. "Did you tell Coop about that?"

"Sort of. I made some interrogation suggestions. That's when I slipped about seeing his case board."

At the junction with Julius Street, Harvey paused in the middle of the street, letting the pickup idle. He craned his neck to look out my window.

From this corner of the block, the side and back of the tallest part of the opera house was visible—all six stories that led up to the roof high above the stage of the theatre. Around the backside, four doors placed at different theatre levels split up the layer upon layer of orange-brown brick; the black wrought iron railings and steps leading down from them looked sturdy in spite of the building's age. A set of double glass doors exited out the bottom of the structure at street-level, a flight of concrete steps leading to the ground.

Harvey took a hard right and backed into a narrow gravel parking lot across from the historic brick building.

My gut tightened. "What are you doing?"

He shut off the pickup and scratched his beard. "She said the undead ones threw Jane's body in the pit."

Yeah, I remembered. Prudence's voice replayed in my thoughts, giving me goosebumps again. "We shouldn't be here, Harvey."

"Let's go beat some bushes, see what we can shake loose."

I jammed my feet against the floor. "Absolutely not."

"Just a quick looksee."

"I'm not going in there."

"What're you scared of? Them zombies aren't real."

For one thing, running headlong into a killer wasn't on my to-do list for this morning. For another, "If Cooper catches me within twenty feet of the Tarragons, I'll be behind bars before you can say, 'Boo!'"

"Cooper's not around right now."

"How do you know?"

"I was on the lookout for his car as I was driving. It's nowhere around. Besides, it's Wednesday."

"What's so special about Wednesday?"

"Didn't you look at his calendar last weekend?"

"No, why would I?"

Harvey shook his head at me. "If you're going to keep up this sleuthing on the side, you need to pay attention better."

I didn't want to sleuth on the side. I didn't want to sleuth out front either. I just wanted to raise my kids, sell real estate, and enjoy a lot of peanut butter fudge ice cream and Doc—separately or together, I wasn't picky.

"Coop had a note on his calendar about a dentist appointment this morning." Harvey glanced at his watch. "He should still be down in Rapid."

So that's where he had his incisors sharpened. "What if he

skipped the appointment?"

"Why would he do that?"

"To catch me doing something I'm not supposed to."

"Coop's world doesn't revolve around you. Besides, I don't think he'll really arrest you. He's just snarlin' at anything that moves because he's frustrated with not figuring out who's killin' who." Harvey shoved open his door. "Come on, I'll show you some parts of this old place that they don't cover on that fancy tour."

I stayed put. "How do you know about these secret parts?"

"You kiddin'? My uncles both worked for Homestake. I spent a lot of time growing up in this old building, bowling with my aunts, taking swimmin' lessons, and watching dime movies back when they used to show flicks in the theatre. Hell, my initials are probably still etched in the underside of one of the tables up in the old library."

He stepped down onto the ground. "Come on."

I shook my head. "I'm not taking any chances at getting caught."

"Chicken."

I stuck out my tongue. "You can call me Elvis Jr."

"Fine. You stay here and keep an eye out for Cooper. If he shows up, distract him."

"What? How am I supposed to distract him?"

His gold teeth showed. "Flash him."

"You said he's sweet on someone else."

"Hooters are hooters, girl. If you flash him, he'll be temporarily blinded and drift off course long enough for me to make my escape."

"I will not—"

He slammed his door on my refusal, and then hitched across the street, slipping inside the street-level back doors.

The pickup engine ticked as I sat there alone, watching the traffic inch by at the top of Siever Street. I inspected my fingernails, checked my hair for split ends, picked the lint off my suede skirt, and tried not to think about Wanda, Prudence, Harvey, or Cooper.

Five very long minutes had dragged by when I noticed a

white and black taxi cut through the traffic and make a turn toward me down Siever Street. The taxi pulled up next to the sidewalk and a familiar top hat popped out of the front passenger side.

Cornelius!

What was he doing back at the opera house? Was he meeting Caly?

I watched him pay the cab driver and start walking up the sidewalk toward the front of the block, his cane clacking on the sidewalk loud enough for me to hear.

"It's not my business," I told Harvey's pickup.

Cornelius was a big boy. If he wanted to waste his time and energy on a little pixie who had shown absolutely zero interest in him besides asking him to take off that damned hat, that was his prerogative. His broken heart was not my problem.

But maybe I should give him a call, see what he was up to today. We could meet later, talk about other options if this hotel deal fell through.

I fished my cell phone from my purse and called him.

Cornelius paused as he rounded the corner, pulling out his phone.

It rang for a third time in my ear, then a fourth.

He looked at his phone for another ring, then shook his head and stuffed it back in his coat pocket.

The ringing stopped and his voicemail kicked in.

Hanging up the phone, I yelled through the windshield, "You big bozo!"

Cornelius continued along the sidewalk, swinging his cane now, looking happy as could be as he disappeared from my sight around the front of the old Stamp Mill building that occupied the corner of Siever and Main.

I tossed my phone back in my purse.

Well, damn. Now what?

Only I knew exactly *what*.

Grabbing my purse, I climbed out of the pickup, locked the door, and raced up the sidewalk after the love-smitten fool.

Chapter Thirteen

I was halfway up the block, following in Cornelius's footsteps, when I heard my phone ringing. It came from somewhere in the depths of my purse. I kept climbing toward Main Street while rummaging through the inside pockets, trying to find the blasted thing amongst my makeup, business cards, wallet, a small field guide on dinosaur bones Layne must have stuck in there, and a sticky unwrapped sucker—*dang it, Addy!*

Something vibrated against the back of my fingers. *Ah ha!* I pulled it out just in time for it to stop ringing.

"Of course," I muttered and looked to see who'd called, pressing *OK* through the low battery warning.

It was Doc.

"Crikey."

It buzzed again, this time a text appeared on the screen from Doc: *Need to talk to you. Call me when you can.*

My thumb hovered over the Call button as I rounded the corner. Beyond the old Stamp Mill building, Cornelius stood in front of the opera house, shaking hands with Dominick Masterson. I stopped short. Caly the Pixie stepped out from the concave marbled entryway wearing a huge pair of black sunglasses that made her look almost fly-like. She held open one of the glass doors, then she followed the two men inside.

What in the hell was going on? Caly hadn't given Cornelius the time of day yesterday, so what was with today's sudden interest?

Was Dominick actually meeting with Cornelius and Caly? What exactly did Dominick Masterson do anyway besides trying to get elected for mayor? Maybe he had an office somewhere in the building.

I tucked my phone back into my purse. Doc would have to

wait. I had questions to get answered.

Passing the plate-glass windows of the Stamp Mill building, I raced to the entrance as fast as my mule heels would carry me. If Lady Luck were on my side, I'd find Cornelius right inside the doors and catch him before he disappeared with Caly into the bowels of the opera house. If not, I'd be left to wander through shadow-filled halls and empty rooms, risking a face-off with another zombie or worse—Tarragon.

When I opened the front glass doors, there was no one in sight. Frickety-frack!

My heels clacked along the tiled floor as I looked through the inside windows of the art gallery on one side and empty office space on the other. At the stairwell, I hesitated, unsure whether to go up or down.

You should go back to the pickup, a logical voice in my head urged.

Oh, please. After having had a mid-morning tea party with Prudence the ghost, it was a little late to listen to logic.

I scraped my teeth over my lower lip, worrying about it. Why did I care if Cornelius got his heart broken by a spiky-haired sprite? Why did I have this need to protect him from Caly's rejection? It wasn't my business if Cupid's arrow was buried hilt-deep in his boney ass. He was just a client.

Well, okay a client and sort of a friend.

And a fellow séance groupie.

And a fellow town oddball.

Dang it. What was he thinking by laying his feelings out like street vendor wares to be pointed at and made fun of by Tinker Bell's twin?

The sound of shoe soles scuffing across a linoleum floor echoed up the stairwell.

Moving down the first step, I waited, listening, wondering if Cornelius was returning to that pool room and the hat-hating ghost.

A door closed somewhere below. Footfalls followed, and then another door shut. A car honked on the street behind me, surprising a gasp from my lips and scaring me down another step.

With one last look behind me to make sure nobody was watching, I headed down the rest of the stairs. At the bottom, I passed what looked like a janitor's closet on the left, a mop and bucket half full of dirty water blocking the entry. A couple of feet further landed me at a closed door on my right and a long, fluorescent-lit hallway on my left. I recognized the hallway as the one we'd been in yesterday. It led past the door to the bowling-alley-turned-shooting-range and then through a set of double doors to where the pool had been decades ago. If Cornelius had come to talk to the boy ghost, he must be close. I needed to figure out which of the doors down here would take me to the area under the pool he'd told me about.

I tiptoed down the hall. In spite of the fact that there were people on the floor above me, I felt alone in the big old building. It reminded me of walking through my high school after a basketball game, the usual din of shoe squeaks and laughter quieted for the night. My hands grew clammy even though it was the middle of the day.

This sneaking around stuff was for the cats. I wiped my damp hands on my skirt. If Harvey jumped out to scare me, I was going to strangle him with his suspenders. Where had that buzzard gone, anyway?

I passed a set of bathrooms on my left and then the old bowling alley on my right. Beyond that was an elevator, then the stairs that we'd come down yesterday during the tour. Outside yet another closed door on my left, I hesitated, trying to remember if Caly had let us know what was behind it. Something told me this wasn't the door I needed, so I continued through the double doors and down a short flight of steps to what used to be the pool room.

As I stood there on the bottom step looking at the two doors on my left that bracketed the edge of the concrete capped pool like a pair of parentheses, the door closest to me opened. A woman in white flew out. Blood stains covered the front of her wedding dress.

I knew that bloody dress. Tarragon's wife, minus the zombie gore and veil, closed the door and leaned against it. Tears streamed down her cheeks, her chest heaved either with sobs or from running; I couldn't quite tell which.

She hadn't appeared to notice me so I took a step back up the stairs toward the double doors, not really sure I wanted to get mixed up in whatever had her crying this time. My heel scraped across a step.

She looked over at me, her eyes wide, watery.

Crap!

I opened my mouth to say something but had no clue what. I tried to smile instead, but my mouth felt all crooked and loose on my face.

She sniffed. "You shouldn't be down here."

At that moment, I absolutely wanted to be anywhere else but *down here*. I cleared my throat. "I was just looking for—"

"They'll see you."

They who? Security guards? Janitors? Cooper's boys in blue? "I'll just explain that I'm looking for—"

"You don't understand," she interrupted me again. "She'll hurt you."

Just for looking … wait, now it was a *she*? "Who's 'she'?"

Tarragon's wife shoved away from the door and grabbed my arm. "I can't talk about it. She'll know it's me." She tugged me up the steps behind her.

I tried not to trip over her blood-splattered train.

She dragged me through the double doors, opened the door I'd hesitated outside of a moment ago, and shoved me inside. I stumbled into what looked like a supply room, almost knocking over a box of paper cups.

"What are you—"

"Shhhh," she hissed. Following behind me, she drew the door shut with a quiet click and enclosed us in darkness.

The room smelled like cardboard, floor cleaner, and a hint of sweat. Wait—I sniffed my armpits. Good, it wasn't me.

Her dress rustled in the darkness. "Deadly things come in tiny packages," she whispered, as if we'd been in the midst of a discussion about package sizes. "Remember that if you want to live."

Hmmm. Receiving cryptic advice from a spooked zombie bride in a dark supply room had not been on my schedule today.

The urge to bust out through that door and get the hell out of Dodge had me shuffling my feet.

"Um, you know," I said, trying to sound calm like my pulse wasn't racing. "I think I'll just go back the way I—"

"Shhhh."

I stood quietly and counted to thirty, listening, thinking that Mrs. Tarragon's brain might have broken under the stress of living with a man who sounded like he was an arrogant dickhead.

The clacking of heels on the floor outside our hideout and the alternating hiss and pause of something being dragged along stopped my ponderings. My heart beat like a tribal drum, so loud that I was sure Mrs. Tarragon would shush me again.

We waited in the dark for another minute after the clacking and dragging sounds disappeared, me with bated breath, her with her satin dress *swizz-swizzing* at each little move. Then she opened the door a crack and peeked out. Without warning, she opened the door wide. The hallway fluorescent lights made me recoil and squint.

"All clear," she spoke softly, hauling me out into the hallway with her.

I looked up and down the hall and saw no zombies or albinos, nobody at all. Still, the urge to run, not walk, through the double doors, over the pool, and out the glass exit doors beyond zinged down my legs.

"What's your name?" she asked.

"Violet Parker." Oops. It might have been smarter to lie. I blamed Prudence for my loose lips—she'd upset my inner apple cart this morning with her surprise party, scrambling my brain. My brief stay in the dark supply room hadn't helped straighten my thoughts out any either.

She pointed at my head. "You were at Jane's funeral. I remember your hair."

"I worked for Jane." Shutting up was probably the better choice, but someone else seemed to be controlling my mouth.

"You're a Realtor?" she asked.

I nodded. Since we were getting all warm and chummy, I dared my own question. "How well did you know Jane?"

Her eyes welled up.

Oh, man, more tears. This woman was one big leaky faucet. I started to reach for her, to console her, but she reared back from my touch.

While I was deciding if I should be offended, Mrs. Tarragon told me, "Jane was one of my best friends."

"I'm sorry," I said, unsure of what to do with my hands, which seemed to want to comfort her even after being rejected.

"She also slept with my husband," she whispered, her face pinched in pain.

"Oh," I managed to croak out. I held onto my purse with both hands to keep from hugging the poor woman. "I'm very sorry."

"Me, too." She swiped at her eyes. "Especially now."

Movement over by the stairwell caught my eye.

Dominick Masterson stepped into the hall, looking back up the stairs and talking to someone behind him as his feet turned in our direction.

Cornelius? Thank God, I'd found him.

The low sound of Dominick's laughter reached me at the same time his follower moved into my line of sight.

It wasn't Cornelius.

Panic bells rang in my head, clanging like a submarine's diving alarm. All hands below deck, I was going down, down, down.

Detective Cooper's rugged face looked even craggier under the fluorescent lights. He seemed to look my way in slow motion, his unyielding gaze turning into a searing laser beam as it locked onto me.

I took a step back. My first instinct was to hide behind an invisibility cloak and become one with the wall. My second instinct was to run like hell.

Mrs. Tarragon balked at the sight of them and let out a little screech. She seemed to be channeling my reaction. Then she practically sprouted wings and flew back down the steps and through the door she'd burst from earlier, leaving me alone to gurgle and sputter.

Dominick did a double-take when he noticed me, his eyebrows arching, the corners of his mouth following suit.

"Hello, Violet," he said, as if we hadn't just met yesterday in a hallway that was as off-limits to me as this one.

I wasn't sure if his remembering my name was good.

Dominick walked toward me, his smile curving higher with each step. Cooper followed, his expression all glare, granite, and fractured fault lines.

"You look lovely this morning," Dominick said, his voice velvet, his eyes soft enough to match it.

My stomach fluttered as if someone had roused a colony of bats that had been snoozing there. A mixture of pleasure and nausea roiled inside of me—the latter I blamed on the irritation sparking off Cooper.

"What are you doing down here, Parker?" Cooper's voice sounding like he'd been gargling firewater.

"Looking for a friend," I answered, standing tall against the brunt of the fury surging from him. I focused on Dominick. "Maybe you've seen him. He wears a top hat and looks a little bit like Abe Lincoln."

"Mr. Curion?" At my nod, Dominick said, "Yes, he had an emergency come up and left without an explanation."

What emergency? I wasn't sure whether I should be relieved or more worried. "In that case, I'll leave you two to your business and see if I can track him down elsewhere."

I left through the double doors, bee-lining toward the set of glass doors behind me—the same doors Harvey had entered. I just hoped the old buzzard's truck still waited for me. If not, I probably had enough adrenaline pumping through my veins to sprint down to Deadwood.

"I'll call you later," Dominick called after me. "I want to speak with you about something Jane was working on for me."

I winced at how that might sound to a certain detective. Glancing back, I winced again. The expression on Cooper's face should have turned me to salt. Great. Just great.

"You have my card," I told Dominick and tried not to crash through the glass doors in my haste to escape handcuff free.

The safety of Harvey's pickup beckoned. I clomped down the back steps, my feet trying to run out from under me, my pulse rampant, my breaths short and quick. Without even bothering to check whether anyone was watching, I reached up under the wheel well for the spare key, then vaulted in through the passenger door, slamming it behind me and hammering the lock button.

What in the hell had just happened in there?

I leaned forward, burying my face in my hands. Why had Tarragon's wife hidden me? And from whom?

What was that sound outside the supply room?

When had Jane slept with Peter Tarragon? Was he another Ray-like mistake at the end?

Had the zombie bride killed Jane for having an affair with her husband?

Had Peter killed Jane for who-knew-what reason?

Was Cooper going to kill me for talking to Tarragon's wife?

Why had Cornelius had to leave so quickly?

Where in the hell had Harvey gone?

Why was Cooper in there talking to …

Something tapped on the glass window next to me.

I shrieked and scooted toward the middle of the bench seat. I looked over at Detective Cooper, who stood on the other side of the glass, his neck and face all stretched tendons, throbbing veins, and blotches of red. A groan bellowed in my chest.

As I stared at him in horror, he held up a pair of handcuffs and tapped them against the window, making that same tapping noise again.

Oh, hell. This probably wasn't going to go well for me.

"Cooper," I said, raising my hands in defense. "It wasn't what it looked like."

"Open the door, Parker," he said, his lips barely moving.

"I really was looking for Cornelius."

"Don't make me drag you out of there."

"I swear I wasn't trying to find out anything about Jane."

"You can explain down at the station. Now open the damned door."

"I'd rather not."

"That's too bad." He dug in his pants pocket and pulled out a set of keys. I should have known he'd have a spare set to his uncle's truck. "Because now I'm really pissed."

Really? What had he been before, just mildly enraged?

The lock popped open. Cooper yanked the door wide.

"Come on, Cooper. You've made your point. You don't need to arrest me. I'm staying out of your business, I swear."

He swooped in, grabbed my right hand, and snapped a handcuff on my wrist. Dragging me outside, he spun me around and latched the second cuff with my wrists in front of me.

"You don't need to do this, Cooper. I'm innocent."

He grabbed my upper arm and towed me around the front of the pickup and down several cars to where his police sedan sat.

"Coop!" Harvey's voice called from the back doors of the opera house. "What in the hell are you doin', boy?"

I held up my cuffed wrists for Harvey to see. "You were wrong," I yelled across the street. "He meant it."

Cooper pulled open the back door of the sedan, scowling down his broken nose at me. "I didn't want to do this, but you forced my hand, Parker."

What a load of bullshit! I wasn't forcing anything. I'd been looking for Cornelius. But listening to reason was apparently beyond Cooper's ability at the moment, so there was no use wasting any more breath trying.

I glared up at him, the injustice of being hauled to jail for no good reason burning a hole in my gut. "Detective," I said, imagining how good it would feel to head butt him right now and break his freaking nose again. "Are you really going to be this much of an asshole?"

His nostrils flared. "Violet Parker, you have the right to remain silent." He shoved me inside the backseat and then leaned down to glare in at me. "And I suggest you keep your big mouth shut."

Then he slammed the door in my face.

* * *

In jail by noon—an accomplishment my mother would be so proud to hear her middle child had achieved.

I paced the jail cell, still waiting for my one freaking phone call.

Damn Cooper! The son of a bitch took my phone with him before locking me up in this stinking cage. I had kids to pick up from school, for fuck's sake.

My feet ached from standing in this urine-scented shithole for the last hour. Limping over to the cot, I wrinkled my nose at the stained wool blanket covering it. I could only imagine the disgusting things crawling in the fibers. No way was I sitting there. I walked to the opposite wall and leaned against it, taking off one of my shoes and massaging the ball of my foot.

I heard the buzz and click of the steel door to the outer holding area being opened. Expecting another one of Cooper's police buddies had come to give "Spooky Parker" more crap, I didn't bother looking over and kept rubbing my foot.

"Hello, Boots," the sound of Doc's deep tone jolted me. I dropped my shoe.

He grabbed the bars and peered at me through them, his dark eyes raking over me, his forehead wrinkling at what he saw. "It appears that you've finally managed to push Detective Cooper off the deep end."

"I didn't push." I slipped my foot back in my shoe and leaned against the wall, matching his frown with one of my own. "He jumped and took me with him."

Doc rubbed his chin. "Hmmm. He has a slightly different version. Something about you sticking your nose where it doesn't belong one too many times."

"Cooper has a nose fixation. I think it has something to do with me breaking his." *The big baby.*

Doc nodded. "Could be."

"Did he call you?"

"No, Harvey did. He said to tell you he'll pick up the kids after school."

"Good." It's the least the old man could do after taking me to the opera house and assuring me I wouldn't end up in jail. I bit my lower lip. "You weren't busy with a client were you?"

"It doesn't matter. My girlfriend needed to be bailed out of jail. That was a first for me."

"A first, huh? Doesn't that just make me feel special?" While I was trying to make light of his actions, my voice sounded husky with emotion.

"You should," his eyes darkened. Something hungry flared behind them, luring me closer. "You are."

Holy cow! When Doc said things like that my heart practically launched up and out of my throat and plastered itself in the palm of his hand. I gulped the silly, bouncing organ back down into my chest and gripped the bars to ground myself.

"Thank you. And thanks for rescuing me from the clutches of the villainous, cruel Detective Cooper."

He shrugged. "All in a day's work. So now what?"

I spread my arms wide. "You spring me."

His grin reached the corners of his eyes. "What's in it for me?"

"Name your price."

This time when his gaze traveled over me, there was no frowning involved. "My bail-you-out-of-jail charge is pretty *stiff*."

"Stiff?" That made me smile. "Great pun."

He winked. "I was trying to come up with something about doing the jail house rock in honor of your love of Elvis, but I couldn't make it work."

"Oh, you make it work very well. If you get me out of this joint, I'll show you just how well." I wiggled my eyebrows, making him chuckle. "Although, I hear conjugal visits are all the rage, so you may regret not leaving me in here."

Doc glanced at the cot. "I think I prefer my own bed."

I preferred a room sans a urinal with a half-chewed blue cake covering the drain.

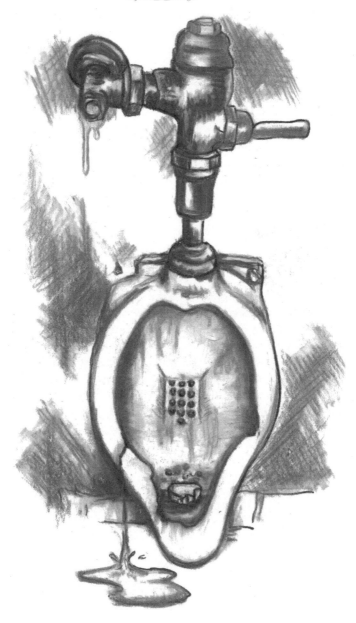

Reaching through the bars, I scraped my finger down his chest. "What do you say, Rocko?" I asked, doing my best impersonation of a 1940s Hollywood starlet. "You and me, we got us a deal?"

"Definitely." He captured my hand before it got into trouble. "But Cooper wants to talk to you before he'll let you out of here."

Damn it! "You mean out of jail?"

"No, the station. He's waiting in his office. You think you can face him without vaulting his desk and going for his throat?"

Probably not. "Of course. What do you take me for?"

"A very pissed off woman with a mean left elbow."

I held up my hands. "My claws are not extended. Besides, I would love a chance to explain why throwing me in this cell was another grand fuckup on his part."

Doc grimaced. "Yeah, see, I don't think that's going to go over well with him. Maybe you should let me do the talking."

"Maybe you're right."

He walked over to the outer steel door and rapped three times, motioning through the small square glass window.

Ten minutes later, I had my personal belongings back and had scoured my hands in the women's bathroom. After touching up my battle makeup and applying some lip gloss, I followed Doc to Cooper's office. I practiced deep breaths while silently chanting:

I will not strangle the nice policeman.

I will not strangle the nice policeman.

I will not strangle the damned, irrational, tight-assed …

Doc stepped back to usher me inside Cooper's office.

"You may as well join us, Nyce," Cooper said. "Close the door behind you."

After pulling the door shut, Doc leaned against it, crossing his arms over his chest.

Cooper sat behind his desk, his fingers steepled together, his gaze flat yet ominous.

"You wanted to talk to me," I said, clasping my hands behind my back. I was doing my darnedest not to sound like I wanted to bare my teeth at him.

"Sit down," Cooper ordered, nodding at the chair across from his desk.

I obeyed, playing nice. Doc stayed put by the door, watchful, giving us space.

"Why were you talking to Helen Tarragon when I explicitly told you to keep your nose out of my case?"

So much for starting with the weather. My hackles got nice and bristly, ready to begin our usual circle and lunge dance.

"What is it with you and my nose?" I asked. "Do you have some kind of freaky nose fetish?"

Cooper's jaw hardened so fast I could have sworn I heard it splinter.

Doc cleared his throat, warning me.

Right, no fighting. I regrouped, taking another deep breath, and then explained, "I ran into her in the hallway while looking for my client, Cornelius Curion."

I didn't bother with explaining which door she'd come out because it didn't seem important.

"So you made nice with Helen and then started drilling her about Jane?"

"No," *you big lug head.* "I asked if she was okay, since she was crying." *Again.*

Cooper's expression remained hard and unmoving. "Then what?"

"She told me I wasn't supposed to be down there—"

"She was right."

Let me finish!

I squeezed the arms of the chair and continued. "She said that 'they' would see me, and then that 'she' would hurt me. When I asked who would hurt me, she said she couldn't say because the person would know it was her. Then she pulled me into a storage room and hid me in there for several minutes, shushing me when I tried to ask why we were hiding, giving me some kooky advice about deadly things coming in small packages."

Cooper leaned forward, his forearms tense, his body language crackling with hostility. "Are you fucking with me, Parker? Because I will happily revoke your freedom and throw your ass back in that cell for the night."

I pointed at my face. "Do I look like I'm fucking with you? Trust me, I'm well aware that you'd give your left nut to lock me up for a week. I'm trying to tell you the truth if you'd stop being so goddamned, thick—"

"Violet," Doc interrupted, touching my shoulder. "What happened next?"

I sat back in my chair. "Somebody walked by outside the closet. It sounded like they were dragging something. Then we waited, and when the coast was clear, we stepped outside. That's when you came along," I told Cooper.

"You're telling me that you didn't ask her any questions about Jane's murder."

"Not about Jane's murder, no."

"Stop splitting hairs or I'm getting the cuffs back out."

I looked back at Doc. "Aren't I supposed to be assigned a lawyer by the court at this point?"

"Did you ask Helen about Jane?" Cooper bit out each word.

"All I asked was how well she knew Jane. That was it, I swear."

"What was Helen's answer?" Doc asked.

"She said they'd been close friends for years."

Cooper stared at me hard enough to see clear through my skull to the other side. "What else?"

"Well, she sort of mentioned that Jane had … uh …" I hated to tarnish Jane's reputation, but I also hated the idea of spending the night on that nasty cot. "She'd slept with Helen's husband."

Cooper's mouth wrinkled in disgust. "That's unfortunate."

"She'd had worse," I muttered, thinking of Ray.

"Who's worse than Tarragon?" Cooper asked.

Crudmongers. I probably shouldn't have started down that path. "That's not important. The point is that these pieces of information are all that Helen had told me before you showed up and scared her away."

He cocked his head to the side. "Parker, was Jane sleeping with someone besides Tarragon prior to her death?"

I should have known he wouldn't let it go. I took his

question literally on purpose. "No."

He watched me for a moment. I picked at a loose piece of vinyl on the chair arm while trying to maintain eye contact.

"Let's try this again," Cooper said, straight on, no blinking. "To your knowledge, was Jane having sex with someone other than Tarragon before she was murdered?"

I sat there, weighing the consequences of telling Cooper about Ray and Jane versus the results of keeping my mouth shut and having Cooper find out later and then throwing me back in jail for some other cockamamie reason.

"Damn it, Parker. I don't need this bullshit. Just answer the fucking question."

And yet another pun, I thought. "Yes. She was, but it was just a one night stand."

"Who?"

I closed my eyes so I wouldn't have to see his anger when I came clean. "Ray Underhill."

"And how long have you known about this?"

"Since Jane told me the morning after—two days before she was murdered."

A flurry of cursing blew my hair back. I risked opening my eyes when he quieted.

"Is there anything else you would like to tell me about my case involving the murder of Jane Grimes?"

I glanced at Doc. He stared back, his expression hooded, unreadable.

"Yeah," I said, focusing on Cooper. "I'm pretty sure she was killed by zombies."

Chapter Fourteen

Cooper sat so still I didn't think he'd heard me. The only sign of life was the slight pulse at the base of his neck where he'd loosened his tie.

Something about that pulse made my upper lip sweat. I shifted in my seat. "Two zombies, probably," I said, thinking of my earlier conversation with Prudence via Wanda.

His squint settled even deeper into the corners of his eyes.

"Could have been three, I guess," I said rubbing my chin, "with one waiting in the getaway car."

Cooper looked over my shoulder at Doc. "Get her out of here before I do something I'll regret later."

Glad to make my escape, I grabbed my purse from the floor next to my chair. "Alrighty then. You have what you need from me, so I'll head back to work."

I made it as far as the open door.

"Parker."

My shoulders seized up at the tension strangling his vocal cords. I grabbed Doc's arm in case Cooper had changed his mind and tried to drag me back to that stinking cell.

I slowly turned around.

His eyes were hard and cold, like little steel ball bearings rolling around behind his lids. "What else are you withholding from me?"

Besides the fact that I got my inside information from a ghost who also told me something in the bottom of the Open Cut was supposed to have dragged Jane's body away but didn't?

"Nothing that I can think of at the moment."

"Are you sure there isn't something more about Ray you'd like to share?"

Ray? I doubted the detective would buy into my various

conspiracy theories involving that horse's ass. Besides, I could tell by Cooper's hardpan glare that anything I said was going to ricochet off him and slam me in the face.

I shrugged. "For a man who thinks he's cock of the walk, Ray has a rather unimpressive penis."

Doc had a short coughing fit behind me.

Cooper's right cheek twitched. "I was referring to my case with Jane Grimes."

I pursed my lips.

"Or your involvement with the Mudder brothers."

MY involvement with … The furnace in my gut flared. "Contrary to what you think, Detective, I know very little about that whole Mudder brothers' deal." Something I was trying to rectify now that I had disappearing albino issues. "I was merely in the wrong place at the wrong time."

The tilt of his head cried bullshit, which made me want to snarl and paw the ground, considering the lives—including my own—that had been at risk due to his damned police-business-only mantra.

"Listen," I said, stepping toward Cooper, my finger out and pointing. "You were the one keeping secrets about Ray's involvement in that whole fucked up mess, putting us all at risk. If anything had happened to Natalie or Doc …" I paused, trying to control my rage before I swelled into a big, green monster and started breaking things.

Cooper stood so fast his chair slammed into the wall behind him. He planted his palms on his desk, challenging me. "Be careful where you point that blame, Parker. I'm not the only one holding cards close to the vest. You're still hiding shit from me. I can smell it on you."

I closed the distance between us in three strides, leaning across his desk, accepting his challenge. "Watch where you stick that nose, Detective. It might end up broken again."

"Okay," Doc interrupted. "I think we're done here." He wrapped his arms around my waist, lifting me clear off the floor, and carried me toward the door like I was a big doll. "We'll be in touch if we hear anything more about either case, Detective," he called over his shoulder.

"Parker, you'd better stay the hell away from the opera house!" Cooper hollered after us.

Outside Cooper's office door, Doc set me on my feet, his body blocking me from returning to chew on Cooper some more, damn it.

Pulling the door closed behind him, Doc frowned down at me. "Well, tiger, that could have gone better. You hungry?"

Huffing, I shook my head and stormed toward the front desk. "Wrongfully accused again," I announced to the small crowd of policemen hovering around the coffeemaker.

Doc followed me out into the front room. "Violet, wait."

I stopped at the glass doors, looking back.

He handed me his car keys. "I forgot something. I'll meet you at the car."

Forgot what? I didn't like the sound of that, but I also didn't like the big, stupid grin on the jowls of the police officer staffing the desk. Without another word, I pushed outside, sucking in the fresh air of sweet freedom, and bounded down the steps.

When I reached Doc's Camaro SS, I leaned back against it with my arms crossed. The metal felt warm through my clothes, calming.

Now that my blood pressure was no longer red-lining, I was able to think rationally about Cooper and the widening chasm between us that made all of our conversations happen at a shouting level.

He wanted to know everything. That was all good and fine, but he'd made it clear with the subject of the albino that he couldn't handle hearing everything. No matter how many times he drilled me, my answer was still the same—the albino disappeared in a puff of smoke. As much as I'd love to have a rational explanation for what had happened, there wasn't one.

I had to accept that.

So did he.

With all of this freaky stuff going on, I needed Cooper to have a little faith in me, but the only thing he seemed to have faith in was his gun. I had no idea where to go from here with that hardheaded man.

A ray of sunlight peeked through the clouds and warmed the

top of my head. I fished my sunglasses from my purse and found a folded piece of paper stuffed next to them. I unfolded it, wondering what part of a horse's anatomy Layne had drawn for me now.

But it wasn't a drawing.

It was a printed note with large, bold capital letters:

WE WANT WHAT BELONGS TO US!

The words sucked the breath from my chest.

I wadded up the note with shaking hands and stuffed it back into my purse. Behind my sunglasses, my gaze darted around, scoping out the police station windows, the parking garage behind me, the Rec Center, and the neighboring playground across the street. I tried to act nonchalant while dewy with sweat, feeling like Bambi's mom caught in the crosshairs.

My legs went weak with relief at the sight of Doc coming out the station's front doors, pulling on his sunglasses as he trotted down the concrete steps.

His brow wrinkled as he drew near, his fingers taking the keys from my hand. "Are you okay?" he asked, opening the passenger door for me.

I shook my head and crawled inside, sinking into the warm leather seats. The scent of his cologne wrapped around me, easing my skittishness. "Let's get out of here."

Doc shut my door and then joined me, sliding behind the steering wheel. "What is it? Something Cooper said?" he asked, keying the Camaro SS to life.

"I'll show you when we get home."

He stared at me from behind his sunglasses for a moment. "Yours or mine?"

Spending the afternoon in his place, letting him and his hands help me forget about all of these bizarre events for a short time would have been nice, but I hadn't even been into work yet today. Jerry was going to have my head if I didn't get my ass in there. "Mine, please."

He nodded, rolling out of the parking lot and onto the road. His palm drifted from the gear shift to my thigh. I covered his hand with mine, leaning my head back against the seat.

"What did you forget in Cooper's office?" I asked, staring blankly out my side window, wondering which of the police officers might have slipped me that note and what it meant.

"Something I needed to talk to him about."

Me? I wanted to ask, but it sounded insecure. As Harvey had reminded me earlier, not everyone's world revolved around me.

"Bail money?" I prodded.

"You were free ..." he squeezed my thigh, "this time."

I grimaced. "I owe you for coming to my rescue."

"I thought we'd already established how you'll pay me back for any hardship—in my bed, preferably naked, but I'll take whatever I can get."

Lifting his hand to my lips, I kissed his knuckles. "You called earlier wanting to talk to me about something."

He turned into the Presidential District neighborhood, making a left toward Aunt Zoe's house.

"I opened the bottle," he said.

"What bottle? You mean the black one from the crate at the funeral parlor?"

He gave a brief nod. "I was tired of staring at it, wondering what was inside."

I jackknifed upright. "What's in it? Blood? Poison? Some kind of potion or elixir?" I'd read one of Addy's young adult fantasy books the other night in the tub and had witches, love potions, and were-fairies on my mind.

"Mead."

"Mead? What do you mean *mead?*"

"Fermented honey and water."

"I know what mead is, I just don't understand why Ray would have been hauling around crates of it. It's not like mead is in high demand."

Why was that albino willing to kill Ray over mead?

Doc pulled into Aunt Zoe's drive, parked behind the Picklemobile, and cut the engine.

"It was high-quality mead," Doc said. "Not any of that watered down stuff."

"You tasted it?"

"How else was I going to figure out what it was?"

My lower jaw fell open. "You could have died."

"I started with just a drop and knew what it was as soon as I tasted it. The flavors were really complex and they blended well, which tells me that whoever made it knew what they were doing. I'm pretty sure it had been cellared for more than just a few months."

When I didn't respond and kept staring, he added, "We could see about having it tested in a lab somewhere if you don't believe me."

"I believe you." I sat back, surprised by his knowledge of fermented honey. "You drink mead often, do you?"

He grinned. "It's the elixir of love."

A love potion it was, then. "Really?"

"Sure, it greases the wheels of procreation. Humans have been using it for millennia—the Vikings, the Celts, the Egyptians."

I held up my fingers in a cross gesture to ward off evil spirits. "Keep it away from me. I'm allergic to procreating."

"You're good at practicing, though."

"With the right partner," I said and poked him in the thigh. "How do you know so much about mead?"

"I grew up around bees. I learned how to make it early on."

That must mean he'd grown up in the country, right? I tucked away that nugget of information. I wanted to drill him for additional details, but I was gun-shy. In the past, when I'd pushed him for more about his history, he'd pretty much walled me out. I didn't feel like taking up my battering ram right now, not after the morning I'd had.

I climbed out of his car, skirting the front, and leaned into his open window. "You coming inside?"

"What about the kids?"

"They're at school for a couple more hours."

"Oh, right. Your aunt?"

"Her pickup is gone. She must be down at her gallery."

He lifted his sunglasses, hitting me with a suspicious squint. "You're not going to get me inside and try to seduce me are you?"

I wasn't ruling anything out. "I stink like a pee-soaked concrete block."

"I love it when you talk dirty to me."

"And I need to get to work before my boss hears that I haven't been in yet today because I was a little detained this morning."

"He's probably already heard. Jailhouse gossip is juicy stuff. Didn't Andy Griffith and Barney Fife teach you anything?"

Chuckling, I tucked my hair behind my ears. "Oh, that reminds me of what I wanted to show you. I found something in my purse after I got it back from Evidence." I took out the wadded up piece of paper and handed it to Doc.

He frowned at it then took it from me.

"See you inside," I said and headed toward the porch.

His car door slammed as I crested the top step. I held the front door for him, shutting and locking it behind us.

"What the hell is this?" he asked, holding up the rumpled paper.

"I don't know. Either someone slipped it in my purse recently and I didn't notice it until today, or someone at the cop-shop wants something I have."

Aunt Zoe's mantel clock chimed the half-hour, spurring me. I started up the stairs. "Come on, we can talk more while I get cleaned up."

When I reached the landing at the top, I realized Doc wasn't on my heels. Instead, he stood with one foot on the first stair, frowning down at a rainbow-colored tennis shoe in his path. Addy had neglected to do as told and put her shoe by the door where it belonged.

"Sorry about the mess," I said.

He frowned up at me, his complexion a tad paler than usual.

"What's wrong?" I asked, starting back down the steps. "Do you smell a ghost?" He'd never had any ectoplasmic reactions before in Aunt Zoe's house.

He cringed, shaking his head. "I told, I don't *smell* ghosts. I should never have described it that way to you. It's much more than just a smell. It's more of an olfactory sensation triggered by the presence of … I don't know, a field of energy …

but it's intelligent, it communicates."

"You mean a ghost."

"No. But yes."

I paused, two steps up from the shoe, eye level with him. "You know what, never mind that. What's the holdup here?"

I needed to put some time in sitting behind my desk before Jerry hired Ben to sit there in my place.

Doc's gaze roved around my face. I could only imagine the mug-shot look I probably had going, all un-glammed with spirals of hair sticking out every which way. I tried to smooth my hair, which was nearly impossible without a jar of petroleum jelly.

"The way you went at Cooper surprised me," he said.

I sucked air in through my teeth, blushing a little at my public display of temper. "Something about that guy really ticks me off. I think it's those Alpha Male hormones he oozes." I twisted my lips. "I should probably back down when he challenges me like that." Otherwise, I might be issued an orange jumpsuit, and orange always made me look like I'd been bitten by a vampire, all pale skinned and dark eyed.

"No way, tiger." Doc kicked Addy's shoe aside and took the next step. He slid his hands around my shoulders and pulled me against him. "When you charged him ..." He brushed his mouth over mine, making my lips tickle.

I draped my arms around his neck. "Yeah?"

"That was sexy as hell."

"Well, then," I kissed the slight dimple in his chin. "You should hear me get after Addy when she uses my toothbrush to clean Elvis's feet."

His chest rumbled. "Poor Addy."

I stepped back and grabbed his hand, tugging him up the stairs after me. "Figures you'd take her side."

One step into my bedroom reminded me that I'd been rushed getting out of the house this morning in my efforts to keep from waking Aunt Zoe. Three different outfits were strewn across my unmade bed and wrinkled leftovers from the last few days were scattered around the floor. My closet spilled out loose shoes and fallen hangers, my dresser was covered with the kids' school papers and half-empty perfume bottles, the attached mirror partly hidden behind pictures of my children.

Doc paused in my doorway, leaning against the frame as his eyes traveled around my messy boudoir. I gave him bonus points for not wincing.

"I was in a hurry this morning," I explained with warm cheeks, opening my underwear drawer. "My room isn't usually this messy."

Liar, liar, pants on fire. It was usually messier, strewn with Addy's clothes and random pieces of Layne's anatomical models.

"Is that a chicken feather on your pillow?"

"Probably." I didn't even bother looking.

"This reminds me of my mom's bedroom."

I stopped, my hand buried in satin and lace. He'd never mentioned his mother before, never mentioned any family at all. After his earlier comment about the bees and mead, I took a chance and asked, "Where does your mom live?"

"She's dead," he said in a quiet voice.

My chest panged for him. I pushed a little more. "How long has she been gone?"

"Since I was a kid."

I nodded, keeping my focus on my drawer full of underwear, afraid that any eye contact would slam the window that I'd somehow opened. "Your dad?"

"He died with my mom. Their truck went off a mountain road during a blizzard."

My eyes smarted for a young boy left parentless, making me blink several times. "Who raised you?"

"My grandfather."

I plucked out a pair of lavender satin underwear and a matching bra. "Where did he live?"

"Colorado. Up in the mountains."

So, Doc wasn't dropped off by an alien spacecraft or created as a top-secret government project. He was just a guy from Colorado. Wait—I remembered something he'd said back when I was showing him houses. "I thought you said you were from back east."

"No. That was where I was living for a few years before I moved here."

"Ah, I see." I shut my drawer. "Doc?"

He dragged his gaze up from the bits of satin in my hand. "What?"

"Thanks."

His brow wrinkled. "For what?"

"Telling me about your family."

He took a step toward me but then stopped. "I like your kids, Violet."

That surprised me and made my stomach tighten with anxiety. I waited a few heartbeats and then asked, "Are you going to follow that with a 'but'?"

"Do you want one?"

No! But it was time to face this shitstorm head on. I crossed my arms. "What I want, Doc, is honesty. I come with kids, I'm a package deal. If there is a 'but' involved here, I need to know now." Before I fell totally ass-over-teakettle in love with him.

"Okay." He raised one eyebrow. "How about this—I like your kids, *but* I'm afraid I might somehow jeopardize them."

"Jeopardize how?" By bonding with them and then leaving us all broken hearted someday?

He smirked. "Are you kidding?"

"Nope. Spell it out for me."

"As we just rehashed on the stairs, I can detect ghosts."

"Ghosts can't hurt my kids." At least I didn't think they could. But being that I had about a thimbleful of knowledge on the spirit world, I reserved the right to change my mind.

"I'm not talking about the ghosts hurting them. If it gets out that I have this sixth sense, and your kids are associated with me, they could be picked on and bullied in and out of school. They don't need that stress on top of the angst of being at a new school in a new town."

Boy, he'd sure put a lot of thought into this "but." It made me wonder if that had something to do with why he'd left wherever he'd been living back east. "Were you picked on when you were a kid?"

"No."

"Well, see—"

"I was homeschooled because of my sensitivity to ghosts."

But his parents … "Your grandfather?"

He nodded.

"But you're a financial planner. You had to have some kind of advanced schooling for that, didn't you?"

"My grandfather died when I was seventeen. I tested my way into college."

First his parents, then his grandfather, damn. I focused on the less emotional aspect. "And the ghosts didn't bother you there?"

"No, they did. I quickly figured out where I couldn't go, worked on how to cope with my sensitivity. Most of the time I could avoid confrontations, but not always."

"By confrontations, do you mean reactions like you had when Prudence passed through you?"

More like bulldozed him. She'd literally laid him out flat for several minutes.

"Yeah, pretty much."

Prudence's essence, or whatever it was called, must be powerful. After the way she'd overtaken Wanda this morning, like she'd just flicked a light switch on and then off, I had to wonder if she were one of the stronger ghosts Doc had encountered. And if so, why? Something due to the violent way she'd died or something within Prudence herself?

"So, why do you need to go in the Carhart house?" I asked. I wasn't jumping for joy at the idea of returning to that place anytime soon. Just thinking about Wanda's eyes rolling up in her head gave me goosebumps. "Why see Prudence again? You've already experienced her death."

"I've been experimenting with something. I think I can go back to a short time before her death and see more."

"More than the last minute or so?" Typically, he was limited to their final breaths, according to what he'd explained to me.

He nodded.

"How come you couldn't do this before?"

"Because I've always fought being taken over, trying to block the energy rather than receive it. I think that has limited me."

"But you couldn't block it all?"

"The burst of energy expelled at death is too powerful. After all of these years, I still haven't figured out how to repel that last surge."

"So can you go back to any time in their lives now?"

"No. I'm still restricted to the final moments. But instead of trying to block the final energy flow, I'll try to be open to it."

Having no ghostly radar at all, I tried to make sense of that as best I could.

"It's hard to explain," he said, apparently picking up my puzzled vibes. "With Prudence, I hope to see what occurred before those men broke into her house and killed her. If it was just some random murder or if there was a reason they chose her family. And like I said before, I want to see what she was doing with her hands."

"What's driving this? Something you read about her family in the library?"

"I can't stop thinking about those teeth," he said. "Why did she have them? What does that mean? There is something about them that I can't put my finger on."

"Maybe it was just some weird coincidence that she had them? Maybe they were in the house when she bought it, left behind by someone with a creepy hobby."

"I need to know for sure. And I need you there with me."

"Why me?"

"To drag me out early so I don't have to get hit by the big surge of energy at the end. I don't know if this is really going to work and what will happen to me if I get slammed with something as powerful as that."

Talk about a little pressure. "Wouldn't you rather have Harvey there?" I would.

"Violet, you know you're the only one who has been able to pull me out when I go under." He cocked his head slightly. "What's with the hunched shoulders and head shaking? Where's the tiger who went for Cooper's throat?"

"That tiger had forgotten that she'd talked to Prudence this morning."

Doc stared at me like he was trying to use telekinesis to bend me like a spoon. "What do you mean?"

I started with the less crazy-sounding part of the explanation.

"Harvey and I went to talk to Wanda after we dropped the kids off at school. When we got there, she said she was interested in selling the house again."

"You didn't sign a contract again to sell it, did you?"

I held out my free hand, palm up. "How else was I going to get you inside without her around unless I had the key?"

"Damn, this is my fault then." He raked his fingers through his hair, leaving a few locks askew. "What's your boss going to think of this?"

"I don't know. I'll see when I get to work." Speaking of work, I glanced at the clock. Crap! It was time to move this conversation train out of the station. I kicked off my heels. "Hold onto these." I handed him my wad of clean underwear without thinking and slipped past him, heading toward the bathroom only to realize I still needed to tell him about Prudence. "Come on," I said, waving him to follow me.

He filled the bathroom door frame, his shoulders looking strong and broad and sexy. I dragged my gaze away, reminding myself that work called—there was no time to play.

"So how did Prudence actually speak to you?" he asked, looking down at the underwear balled in his hand. "I thought you can't see ghosts."

"I can't." I pulled out the bobby pins keeping most of my hair secured and shook loose my curls. "Wanda was sitting in the parlor, chatting with me about selling the place, and then she touched my hands. That's when everything got weird."

"Weird how?"

I reached inside the tub and turned on the water. "All of a sudden," I said over the noise of running water, "her voice changed, sounded younger and stronger." I unzipped my skirt and let it fall, my short slip still in place. "Then Prudence started talking to me."

I looked up while unbuttoning my shirt and caught him frowning at me. "If you don't believe me, ask Harvey," I told him while shucking my shirt. "He was there. He saw it, too."

Tightening my short terry cloth robe over my bra and slip, I reached in and tested the water, still cool. When I looked back at Doc, his forehead was still lined. If he thought Prudence speaking through Wanda was frown-worthy, he wasn't going to like what came next.

"She warned me to stay away from the mine until I read the book," I said. "And then she said I had a lot to learn yet."

I unclipped my bra through my robe and slipped it off through the arm holes, tossing the pink lace on the rest of my jail-tainted pile. My slip and underwear came next, the robe shielding me the whole time. I'd come back later to scoop up the clothes and dump them in a bag to go to the dry cleaners.

Doc looked at the pile of clothes, his jaw taut.

"I know what you're thinking," I said.

His gaze slid my way. "What am I thinking?"

I tested the water, perfectly steaming. Now if only I had some 14-grit sandpaper to scrub off the filthy microbes probably trying to burrow into my skin.

"Could you turn around for a moment?" I asked, untying my belt.

He raised one eyebrow. "That's not what I was thinking," he said, then turned his back to me.

I tossed my robe onto the dirty clothes pile, since it was now covered with jail germs, and crawled behind the dark-blue shower curtain. Grabbing the soap, I scrubbed fast and hard, then wet my hair.

"You're thinking," I continued, speaking over the spray, "that my studying the book is a mistake." I shampooed and rinsed, then let conditioner sit in my hair. "For one thing, you don't have the time or patience to read it to me, since I can't read Latin."

I rinsed again, sticking my head under the spray before adding, "And you're thinking that my reading through the book will only make my nightmares seem more real, more terrifying."

Shutting off the water, I wrapped a towel around me before I stepped out of the tub. Doc now leaned against the wall next to the light switch, watching me, his face still criss-crossed with high tension lines.

"And you're probably right about the nightmares," I told him, grabbing Aunt Zoe's robe and tying it around me. "But maybe it's time for me to roll up my pant legs and wade through the book with you." I loosened the towel underneath the robe, pulled it off, and wrapped it around my wet hair. "Let me throw on some clothes and then you can tell me where I'm wrong. Be right back."

I barefooted it back to my bedroom and closed the door behind me. A glance at the clock made me chew on my knuckles. Standing in front of my closet, I tried to decide what outfit would please Jerry the most. If I were wearing his idea of the perfect real estate agent outfit when he found out I'd been in jail over lunch, maybe he'd think twice before giving me a pink slip.

Pink! He seemed to like pink. I grabbed a straight-hipped dark pink skirt and a pale pink silk blouse. That would do it, feminine yet professional.

My bedroom door banged open, making me jump. I whirled around, taking a step back as Doc stalked toward me. My pulse revved up at the intent blazing in his dark, dark eyes.

"You forgot something, Boots." He dangled my bra and panties between us. "But I didn't."

Chapter Fifteen

S top right there," I told Doc as he bore down on me, took the skirt out of my hands, and tossed it on the bed. "I have to get to work."

"You were wrong," he said.

"About what?" I asked, shielding myself behind my blouse.

"My thoughts, the book, several things." He tugged my shirt away from me and sent it after my skirt.

"You don't think Prudence was talking about the demon book?"

"I have no idea." He grabbed my arm and pulled me toward the bed. "I stopped thinking about that damned ghost when you dropped your skirt."

Before I could catch my balance, he swung me around and kissed me, bending me backwards, his hands everywhere at once. By the time his mouth left mine, my robe was untied and gaping. His thumbs hitchhiked south along my spine, tickling the tender indents of my lower back.

"Doc," I said, trying to regain my breath, my balance, my senses. "I have to get to work."

"You just stripped in front of me." His lips brushed over mine again, this time tender, seducing me into seeking more. "And then you took a shower. That's fantasy material, Boots. You're not going anywhere until we finish this."

I clung to him, a bit bamboozled, yet still aware that the sight of my full frontal nudity in the bright afternoon light along with my lack of makeup might turn Doc into a pillar of salt. "I wasn't trying to be sexy."

"You don't have to try, Violet." He slid his palms down over my hips, cupping, hauling me closer. "Not for me."

His scent mixed with a whiff of his cologne teased my

senses, luring me, making me want to touch, to taste his skin.

Oh, hell, Jerry could wait. I framed Doc's face with my hands and brought his mouth back to mine, tugging on his full lower lip with my teeth, teasing with flicks of my tongue, not quite committing.

"Kiss me, woman." His voice had a thick rasp to it.

I obeyed, taking my sweet time, savoring how his mouth alone could make me tingle in some spots and flutter in others.

Trailing my fingers down his shirt, I stopped at his belt, scraping over his stomach through his shirt. "Doc?"

"What?" He tipped my chin up, his mouth burning a trail down my neck.

"Prudence told me that zombies threw Jane in the pit, and that something usually takes the bodies, but it didn't this time."

"Is there some reason you're telling me this right now?" he asked against my skin.

"Yeah, because once your pants come off, I tend to get distracted."

I moved my hand lower, teasing, not quite making contact … yet.

Pressed against him, I felt his groan rumble up from deep in his chest. "Touch me, Violet," he said softly as his tongue traced my ear.

Touching seemed too tame, so I grabbed him through his pants and then squeezed, rubbing at the same time.

"Is this what you meant, Doc? Or would you like it more if I used my nails on you?" I scraped up his khakis, then pressed back down with the heel of my palm.

"Vixen," he said, his hand covering mine, adding more pressure.

"How about my tongue?" I pulled his mouth down to mine, giving him a demonstration. "Is that what you want?"

He took my hand and slid it inside the front of his pants. "I want—"

"Violet?" Aunt Zoe's voice called up the stairs, penetrating the rush of blood in my ears.

Snatching my hand free, I stumbled backward into the bed. Doc caught me before I fell, righting me. He grabbed my robe lapels and pulled them closed, then handed me my unmentionables.

I could hear Aunt Zoe's footfalls coming up the steps.

Crap! Damn! Shit!

"I'm in my room getting dressed," I called, surprised at the steadiness of my voice as I struggled into my underwear.

Her footfalls stopped. "Where's Doc?"

How did she know he was—oh, right, his car was sitting in the drive. I looked at Doc, wondering what to say. I couldn't lie to her.

Doc's gaze zeroed in on my nether regions while I slipped on my bra. "I'm watching her dress," he called out, a grin curving his lips.

My cheeks warmed. I shot him a what-the-hell glare.

Aunt Zoe's chuckle tumbled through the open door.

Doc winked and kept watching as I adjusted the "girls" so they were pointing in the right direction without falling out the sides.

"I'm sorry to bug you two," Aunt Zoe said, "but your boss stopped by my gallery looking for you, Violet."

Jerry was looking for me? Uh, oh. I needed to hurry up and get to Calamity Jane's. I buttoned my blouse.

"He said he couldn't reach you on your cell phone," Aunt Zoe added.

I'd forgotten all about my cell phone thanks to that fight with Cooper and the note I'd found in my purse. The battery had to be long dead by now.

"What did Jerry want?" I asked, stepping into my skirt.

"He came to see if the rumor was true," she said.

I looked at Doc, my gut contracting in dread. "What rumor?"

"The one about you being in jail."

* * *

"Is there such a thing as a secret in this damned town?" I asked Harvey and Aunt Zoe later that evening after supper was over and all but the dessert dishes were cleared away. The smell of baked chicken still filled the room, adding comfort to the already homey, yellow kitchen.

"Sure," Harvey said, scraping his fork across the bottom of his plate, trying to get every last crumb and dollop of strawberry-rhubarb pie. "Just ask Coop. He's always snoopin' into other people's business and learnin' their secrets."

"I'm not talking to Cooper at the moment," I grumbled, spinning my fork on the table. "He went too far today."

Way too far. In fact, I'd be damned lucky if my job weren't a thing of the past, with all of the sweating and struggling to stay employed over the last few months for naught. Tomorrow morning at nine I'd know for sure. That's when I was supposed to meet Jerry at Bighorn Billy's, according to the note that had been taped to my desk phone when I'd finally made it into work this afternoon.

Mona had been the only one at Calamity Jane's when I showed up. Ray was out for the afternoon, showing some properties around Spearfish, and Jerry had had an appointment in Rapid that included dinner and drinks.

When I'd joked with Mona that I'd picked a good day to land in jail, she'd dropped the other shoe—she'd taken a message for Jerry after he left regarding Ray's nephew, Ben. The call was from a previous employer, which meant Jerry was checking into Ben's references.

I'd rested my forehead on my desk, trying to think up ways of blackmailing Cornelius into buying that damned hotel. Stapling strawberry jam to a wall would have been easier.

Then I sent a text to Natalie: *Need an apprentice? I'm about to lose my job to your old friend, Ben Underhill. Will swing hammer for food.*

She didn't text back.

The rest of my afternoon had been much calmer until I'd dropped my cell phone in the toilet. And on that note, I'd called it a day and come home to shove my face in Aunt Zoe's cookie jar. Unfortunately, Harvey had beaten me to it and left me a lone chocolate chip and some crumbs.

The urge to crawl under my covers and convince Doc to come over, lock the bedroom door, and finish what we'd started before the outside world had interfered had me fidgeting, but he wasn't answering his phone. I needed to wait for my cell phone to dry out so I could try texting him and see if he'd left me any voicemails.

Aunt Zoe reached across the table and took my spinning fork away. "Violet, that's enough moping and grousing about Detective Cooper. What's done is done. I'm sure he had his reasons, no matter how off-base they seem to you and me." She placed my fork next to hers. "Now tell me again what Helen Tarragon said about Jane."

I'd already gone over this, but Aunt Zoe had been running water in the sink at the time, so she must not have heard it all. "Helen didn't say much, just something about Jane being a best friend who also slept with her husband."

Aunt Zoe stared at me hard enough to make me begin to question my memory of that moment in the opera house. Had Helen said anything else?

"Did Helen mention if Jane's affair with Peter was recent history or old news?" Aunt Zoe asked.

I shook my head. "And I didn't get time to ask her anything else before Cooper showed up with Dominick. But judging from what I heard Helen say to Peter a couple of days ago in that other hallway, it sounds like the affair was more recent."

After the kids had left the supper table to go watch television, I'd caught Harvey and Aunt Zoe up on the conversation that took place during my accidental eavesdropping on the ever-so-loving Tarragons.

Aunt Zoe planted her elbows on the table, rubbing her temples. "This doesn't make any sense."

"What?" I asked. "Jane having an affair with Peter, or Peter killing Jane?"

"Or Helen killing Jane?" Harvey threw in, laying his fork across his plate. "We can't cross her off the list. You know the sayin'."

"Hell hath no fury like a woman scorned?" I asked.

"No. The one that goes, 'Women—you can't live with them, you can't sleep with their best friends.'"

I guffawed. "That's not a saying."

"It is in the Book of Harvey. My Uncle Jeb left his wife for her best friend. Then he up and left her friend to go back to his wife." Harvey crossed his arms over his chest. "Peck of trouble like none other."

"Why? What happened?" Knowing Harvey, I expected a shotgun to come into play.

"Jeb's ex-partner swooped in and stole both women out from under him. The three cut and run to some old mining town in Nevada and started a chicken ranch. They made hay and then rolled in it and ol' Uncle Jeb died poor and lonely."

I just looked at Harvey for a moment, letting that slide right out my other ear, and turned back to Aunt Zoe. "What doesn't make sense about what Helen said?"

"Peter and Jane having an affair."

"Why not?"

"They were an item a long time ago, after he left his first wife but before Peter and Helen got together."

"Maybe those old feelings never died," I said.

"No, they were dead."

"What makes you so all-fired sure?" Harvey asked.

Aunt Zoe stood and grabbed his plate, frowning down at him. "Because I'm the one who took Jane to the ER after Peter asked her to be his wife and she refused."

"ER?" I said, "What happened?"

Aunt Zoe scooped up my plate, too. "He gave her one hell of a shiner."

"He hit her?"

Aunt Zoe nodded. She carried the plates over to the dishwasher, shoved them inside, and then slammed the door shut. "And after she fell, the son of a bitch kicked her in the side."

I thought back to the way he and Helen had been in each other's faces in that hallway, the anger rippling off of him.

"Was that back when he was still hittin' the joy juice every night?" Harvey asked.

"Yeah." Aunt Zoe leaned on the counter, looking out the window into shadows beyond. "Peter had to go to AA as part of his sentence, along with spending thirty days in jail and doing some community work."

The judge must have found Peter as offensive as I had upon first sight.

"That's why Jane and Peter having an affair doesn't make sense," Aunt Zoe continued. "Jane wouldn't have gone back to Peter, not after what he did to her."

"But he's been sober for a long time," Harvey said. "Maybe time fogged her memory when it came to good ol' Petey."

"Jane did seem to be at an all-time low point when it came to self-esteem," I added. "Sleeping with Ray was proof enough for me."

Earlier, while blasting off to Harvey and Aunt Zoe about Cooper's half-assed interrogation, I'd shared my secret about Ray playing hide the pickle in Jane's office.

"No." Aunt Zoe turned around, sorrow fanning out from her eyes. "Jane's pain ran deeper than some bruises and a cracked rib. She'd asked me to take her to the ER that awful night because she'd started bleeding."

Oh, damn. I knew what was coming next and my heart ached for Jane all over again.

"She lost her baby," Aunt Zoe finished. "Peter's baby."

A memory resurfaced from a couple of weeks before Jane had died. She'd told me to take the afternoon off and go spend time with my kids. At the time, I'd seen the grief in her eyes and wondered why she hadn't had kids, figuring it had something to do with her need to succeed in business. Now I knew why—Peter. The bastard.

"She never could get pregnant after that." Aunt Zoe joined us back at the table. "So she put all of her energy into her other baby—Calamity Jane Realty."

This whole mess must have happened after Jerry and Jane divorced then. It was no wonder the thought of losing her business to that two-timing asshole she'd married had sent her into a drunken spiral.

I squeezed Aunt Zoe's forearm. "Is that why Jane gave me the job at Calamity Jane's? Because you helped her through all of that? Is that the favor she'd owed you?"

"Not just that," Aunt Zoe said. "It took her a while to get

rolling after losing the baby. I was there to lean on at first."

Helen Tarragon's words echoed in my head. "So, when Helen asked Peter, 'Are you going to do to me what you did to Jane?' Do you think she meant hit her?"

"That or kill her by accident while drunk," Harvey said.

I turned to Harvey. "You said he wasn't drinking anymore."

"As far as we know. Maybe he's tippin' when nobody else is lookin'. Maybe Jane found him in the middle of a bender and said something that lit his fire, just like old times."

The three of us sat there in silence for a moment, passing frowns around the table while in the living room the kids argued over who got to pick the next movie.

Aunt Zoe leaned forward. "I still want to know why Helen would tell you Jane was having an affair with Peter."

"Maybe she knows something more about what happened all of those years ago," I suggested. "Maybe Peter never got over Jane."

Harvey stroked his beard. "Maybe Petey lied to his wife and told her he was having an affair with Jane to make her jealous."

"If that is the case," I said, "then maybe Helen killed Jane out of jealousy." She had sounded pretty damned scary when she'd told Peter she'd rip his dick off and use it to fish with at Lake Pactola.

Aunt Zoe sighed. "There are a lot of 'maybes' at this table. Here's one more for you, Violet—maybe you should go see Detective Cooper and talk to him about all of this, let him wade through it before someone else I love ends up dead at the bottom of the Open Cut."

"I'm not talking to that handcuff-happy jerk."

"Stop being so stubborn," she said.

"I'm not being stubborn. Every time I try to talk to him, he threatens me in some new inventive way." When Aunt Zoe just squinted at me, I added with a shrug, "Plus, he makes fun of my hair."

"Fine. Just promise me you won't go near either Helen or Peter alone."

"I'll stick by her side," Harvey said.

Aunt Zoe grinned. "I was thinking more along the lines of

Doc. You get distracted too easily by the opposite sex."

"Me?" Harvey sputtered. "Have you ever watched Doc when Violet's near? He follows her around like she's a heifer in heat—always sniffin' around her, pettin' her, gettin' her all frisky and cow-eyed."

"Doc does not do that," I said, smacking the back of Harvey's hand. Doc was sniffing around for a whole other reason that had nothing to do with me or anyone else whose blood still ran red. "And could you not refer to me as a cow? Why not a mare in heat? Mares are pretty. Better yet, a unicorn in heat."

Aunt Zoe leaned back in her chair. "Then we're back to Detective Cooper. He might be the best bet to stick close to you."

"Nope. I'm not going near that man. I'm done trying to get along with him. From now on, I'm flying under his radar."

One of Aunt Zoe's eyebrows crept up. "Isn't he still your client?"

"Well, except for selling his house."

Although, after our last bout, I fully expected to receive his contract in the mail, full of bullet holes.

"Did you tell your aunt about agreeing to sell the Carhart house again?" Harvey asked.

I glared at him. "Not yet, you bucketmouth."

"Do you really think you can sell it after last month's fiasco?" Aunt Zoe asked.

I couldn't tell either of them that the real reason I'd agreed to sell it was so Doc had a chance to hang out alone with Prudence, so I just shrugged. "It's worth a try. That Britton couple was still interested in it last time I talked to them, but then it went off sale due to the whole police investigation mumbo-jumbo."

Harvey stood, shaking out his leg. "I need to go drain my lizard. Don't forget to tell her about Prudence and the book, too." He dropped that bomb and then left me to face the mushroom cloud alone as he shuffled off toward the bathroom.

I burned a hole in his backside with my evil eye.

"Tell me what about what book?" Aunt Zoe asked.

Here went nothing. I told her about the demon book, where I'd gotten it, when I'd sneaked it out, the gist of what was inside of it, and the mention of the "book" this morning—only I said Wanda warned me about it, not Prudence. I also avoided revealing Doc's role in all of it, hiding his sixth sense and anything that might cause her to glance in his general direction.

"And Detective Cooper knows nothing about this book?" she asked.

Jeez, she really was liking the sound of Cooper's name tonight. "Nope. Nada. And I'd like to keep it that way." I gave her the threatening look I usually reserved for Addy and Layne.

Aunt Zoe tweaked my nose. "Nice try but that doesn't work on your elders. Who's this 'Prudence' Harvey mentioned?"

"The ghost that lives in the Carhart house." I hesitated, not sure how much I wanted to reveal to someone who shared my flesh and blood, someone whose opinion of me as a sane person I valued more than my own most days. "I kind of fibbed about Wanda warning me about the book—it was really Prudence the ghost talking through Wanda." I watched Aunt Zoe closely, waiting for her to smirk or laugh or insist I start taking medication.

Her eyes narrowed slightly. "What makes you so certain Prudence was referring to this particular book?"

I scooted to the front of my chair. "You mean you believe that a ghost talked to me through Wanda?"

"You thought I wouldn't?"

"Of course I thought you wouldn't. You're the most level-headed person I know."

"Violet, I've lived in Deadwood a long time. I've seen a lot of things happen here. Some come with rational explanations, others don't. After a while, you have to either check yourself into a mental institution or decide to believe there are things in this world that are beyond reason. This incident in Wanda Carhart's house sounds like it falls into the latter class."

I gaped at Aunt Zoe. After tonight's revelation about Jane and ghosts, I felt like I was meeting the real Zoe for the first time. Until now, she'd just been my funny, loving aunt. Now she was a stranger full of stories, full of memories, full of experiences—all that had nothing to do with family, with me. It kind of knocked me sideways.

Then she smiled and patted my cheek, and she was back to being my favorite aunt who made the best homemade lemonade around.

"Close your mouth, Violet." After I obeyed, she said, "Are you absolutely certain Prudence was referring to this demon book?"

"What other book would she be referring to?"

Aunt Zoe started to say something, then stopped, her gaze searching my face. Whatever she saw made her look down at her hands and frown. "What do you think Prudence meant by you having a lot to learn yet?"

"I don't know. I guess to brush up on my demonology, since that's what Lila and her evil not-so-do-gooders were all giddy about."

"Hmmm," was all she said.

Since Aunt Zoe hadn't laughed me off yet or called for a padded wagon, I whispered, "Sometimes I wonder ..."

No, maybe I should keep my mouth shut.

"You wonder what, Violet?" Aunt Zoe's gaze was intense, her hand squeezed mine, seeming to urge me onward. "Say it."

I took a deep breath and plunged right into it. "I wonder if one of the demons in the book is real."

Aunt Zoe stared at me, not laughing at the idea even a little.

"I had a nightmare about one," I continued. "I could even smell the stench of sulfur coming from him, feel its heat." Feel its spittle on my face when it screamed at me.

Again, her eyes scoured my face, looking for what, I didn't know. "But you have doubts," she said, not asking.

I squirmed on my seat. "We're talking about ghosts and demons here. Fairytales. After that comes werewolves, vampires, and headless-horsemen."

"Yes, but fairytales are often based on true events."

Goosebumps prickled my skin. "Can't we go back to talking about who murdered Jane?" I'd rather stick to the flesh and blood players in the game.

"I think you need to leave Jane's murder to Detective

Cooper and put your energy into figuring out what Prudence meant about the book."

"Aunt Zoe, we don't even know if what she's talking about is real. I'm still not fully convinced Wanda wasn't playing some elaborate parlor trick on me just to mess with my head. I did help put her only remaining child in prison, if you remember. She probably has some grudges stacked up."

"Who has a grudge?" Harvey asked, hurrying back into the kitchen.

"You get lost somewhere? The bathroom is just down the hall." I was still bristling about him throwing me under a bus about Prudence and then leaving the room.

"Prostate was being mule-headed, just like someone else I know. Same thing happened this morning at the opera house; you were being mule-headed then and I couldn't rush my piss, so Coop got to you before I could come to the rescue."

So that's where Harvey had disappeared to.

"What did I miss?" he asked, dropping into his chair.

"Violet is going to bring me this demon book," Aunt Zoe said.

"I am? Why?"

"Because I'm your aunt and I told you to."

For some reason, the thought of her seeing the book made my armpits sweaty. Partly, I felt this overriding sense of guilt for stealing it, but mostly I was afraid she'd look at the book and find it quite silly and *then* call for a straitjacket along with the padded wagon. "But it's all written in Latin," I said.

"I'm not surprised. I want to see it."

"You're not going to be able to read it."

She smiled at me, looking a bit like Alice's Cheshire cat. "What makes you think I can't read Latin, Violet Lynn? I'll have you know, your great grandmother insisted I learn how to read Latin when I was Addy's age and went to great pains to teach me. I've kept up my reading ever since."

"Really?" When she gave a single nod, I pressed, "Why did she insist you learn Latin?"

"Someday I'll explain it all to you. For now, I want that book."

Chapter Sixteen

Thursday, September 6th

By the next morning, my cell phone had dried off after its swim in the toilet, but something wasn't quite right with it. The volume kept going up and down at random and there were black lines through part of the screen that no amount of shaking or banging on hard surfaces would erase.

On the upside, I could still retrieve and hear most of my voicemails, several of which had come in from Jerry during my lovely field trip yesterday to Con College.

The other two were from Doc, who'd called me on Aunt Zoe's home phone last night when he couldn't get through on my cell. He'd wanted to know when we could finish what we'd started earlier in my bedroom, and then he gave me the play-by-play of exactly how he'd "finish" me. My libido sat and whined, but between Harvey's snores from the couch and the kids taking turns needing one more drink of water and then one more trip to the bathroom before they could fall asleep, reality lulled all of my passion-filled hopes back to sleep for the night.

Reality sucked.

If only my life took place in the pages of a romance novel. Then Doc and I would get days to frolic in bed, exploring every inch of each other's bodies. Instead, I spent my nights with two kids, a chicken, or a crusty old man. Not to mention the demons, ghosts, ghouls, and creepy clowns who tore through my dreams. Stephen King should write my tell-all biography.

I pulled into the parking lot at Bighorn Billy's and parked the Picklemobile in the back of the lot next to a couple of other ancient metal pickups. A Bluetick hound dog sat in the driver's seat of an old blue beast with white and chrome trim. It barked at me when the Picklemobile backfired.

I glared through the closed window at its bared teeth. "Don't judge."

Dodging fat raindrops falling from the cloud-filled sky, I rushed through the three-quarter-full parking lot toward the restaurant's front door for what I feared might be my last meeting while still on Calamity Jane's payroll.

In my race through the rain, I hadn't seen Jerry's Hummer anywhere, but I was a few minutes early. I lucked out and landed a booth where it would be easier to hide under the table when the shit hit the fan. Coffee was all I ordered. I doubted I'd be able to choke down any food this morning since my stomach felt like it had a pair of pissed-off badgers tussling inside of it.

The waitress had just poured my coffee when Ray sauntered in, followed by Mona. What were they doing here? My face blazed. Was Jerry going to rake me over the coals in front of an audience of my peers?

Mona saw me and grabbed Ray's arm, pulling him along behind her. She slid onto the booth seat next to me.

Ray scowled down at her. "This booth isn't going to work, Red. Jerry's legs are too long. You two will be all tangled up under there."

Mona opened the menu. "We'll make do. Sit."

I was too mortified to do anything more than sip my coffee, all the while imagining the various Shakespearean tragedies that might play out shortly for the Bighorn Billy's crowd. I'd left my vial of poison at home, so I'd have to settle for suicide by fork during the climax.

Ray settled in across the table, kicking me on purpose and then offering a smirk-filled apology. I was busy loathing him with my eyes when Mona said, "Knock it off you two. Jerry's here."

I dragged my gaze off the orange-faced orangutan in time to see Jerry grab a menu from the hostess podium on his way over. He slid into the booth. His shoulders filled half of the bench seat, bumping into Ray, but he didn't complain.

He greeted each of us in turn, his eyes lingering on Mona before landing on me. I tried to read his expression for impending doom on the horizon, but all I got was a clear gaze and a smile. A Magic 8 Ball would have given me more of a clue on the surety of my future in Deadwood real estate.

After the waitress stopped by and took our orders, Jerry clasped his big hands together on the table in front of him. "Mona told me that Jane liked to have regular meetings here to catch up on what each of you are doing, discuss any problems you may have run into, and deliver group announcements." His focus shifted back to Mona. "Since you're sort of the team captain, Mona, why don't you start?"

Mona waited until the waitress had finished pouring coffee and then proceeded to fill us in on the status of her contracted properties in an even-keeled, matter-of-fact tone. When I grew up, I wanted to be like Mona, sexy bombshell sweaters, silky scarves, and all.

Ray was up next, his report topped with a good dollop of gloating and superiority about the bidding war going on over his most recent contract—a ranch northwest of town with six hundred and forty acres that spread through a couple of valleys dotted with multiple fresh water springs.

Having to check in after Ray always felt like being the follow up band to the Rolling Stones. His swansong included a big, fake smile and an announcement that it was his goal to bring in the first sale for our new boss.

What a freaking kiss-ass. I "accidentally" buried the toe of my pointy shoe into his shin while crossing my legs under the table.

He grunted.

"Sorry," I said and sipped some black coffee. Its bitterness paled next to the acidity in Ray's gaze.

His eyelids tightened into little slits. "Violet has some exciting news to share, don't you, Blondie?"

That was the first time he'd used my nickname in front of Jerry, who cast a frown at Ray before focusing on me.

I lowered my coffee cup, not liking the way Ray was practically licking his chops. I had plenty of exciting news involving ghosts, zombie brides, and albinos, but I had a feeling Ray was getting his sneer on about something else—probably my getting thrown into jail. Hell, I was surprised he hadn't dropped flyers from the sky to spread his joy about the whole mess.

"That depends on what you think is exciting, Ray," I said.

"She's agreed to try to sell the Carhart house again," he told the table while staring me down.

How did he …? Oh, shit. I'd left the contract on the printer, totally forgetting about it after I'd dropped my phone in the toilet yesterday and scampered home all defeated and ready to raise my white flag.

"Oh, Vi," Mona said, mixing her words with a sigh.

Ray's face was alight like Christmas had come early and Santa's elves had been replaced with tassel-clad pole dancers.

"What's the story on this Carhart house?" Jerry asked.

"It's the scene of multiple cold-blooded murders," Ray said. "Including one involving our very own Violet 'Spooky' Parker."

I kicked his shin again. The faceful of animosity he returned reminded me of the Bluetick hound from the parking lot.

"Is this true?" Jerry asked Mona.

"Unfortunately, yes," Mona said. "Except the part about Violet being involved. She was more of an observer. Lila Beaumont died by tripping and falling on her own knife according to the police report. She just happened to be chasing after Violet at the time of her demise."

Jerry's eyebrows slammed into his hairline. "You're gonna sell a house you were almost killed in?"

"It's a beautiful house," I said, still standing firmly by my opinion of the place even after all that had happened within its walls.

The waitress brought our food, silencing any response the other three had, giving me a moment to corral my rattled thoughts. I hadn't expected Ray to attack on that front. I'd planned to tell Mona on the side, and then Jerry, and let Ray pounce on it after it was old news.

After we were alone again, Jerry leaned his elbows on the table. "Based on what these two are telling me, Violet, that sounds like a pretty ballsy move."

"Ballsy?" Ray snickered. "I'd say it's more stu—"

"That's enough, Ray," Mona said in a tight tone, casting an imploring glare at Jerry.

"She's right, Ray," Jerry said. "Why don't you drop back and play defense for a bit." He took a bite of his toast, eating half of it in one chomp. "Violet, what's your plan for unloading this place as soon as possible?"

I had a chicken I wouldn't mind sacrificing to the realty gods, a gerbil, too. I nibbled on the dry toast I ended up ordering while considering my answer. "Make a few phone calls to previously interested parties," like the Brittons, who'd loved the old place, ghosts and all. "I thought I'd also put some ads out in a few markets where the murders weren't front page news."

"What about an open house?" Jerry asked.

"No way," Mona beat me to the punch. "The whole town of Lead would show up just to tour the scene of the crime. It would be like opening a freak show attraction at a carnival."

"Freak show, hmmm." Jerry eyed me while chewing. "That gives me an idea."

An idea involving me that was inspired by the words *freak show*? I cringed, pretty damned sure his idea wasn't going to include me baking homemade cookies for potential buyers. "What?"

"Just hear me out on this."

He said that as if I had a choice, apparently forgetting who signed my paychecks.

"We could have two versions of our ads—one with you in the pink suit with pink lipstick and soft hair, looking all sweet and angelic; and then the other ad with you wearing a black dress and dark kohl around your eyes, looking sexy and dangerous."

"I'm not sure that will sell houses," I said, still cringing, choosing my words with care. It might sell shotgun shells and deer piss to hunters over at the hardware store, maybe even a box of condoms or two at Piggly Wiggly for any nearsighted, lonely fellas, but not real estate.

"We're not trying to sell houses with these ads, Violet," Jerry explained. "We're trying to sell you, which in turn sells houses and makes Calamity Jane Realty more money."

"I don't like it," Mona said. "It seems desperate and borderline tacky, not to mention you'd be toying with Violet's professional reputation."

Amen, sister! I squeezed Mona's leg in thanks.

"I disagree, Mona." Ray took Jerry's side, of course, because his head was so far up the boss man's ass. "We could even use Violet's nickname on the ads."

"Pipe down, rub-a-dub," I said to the rat bastard. "You're trying way too hard now."

"The idea is worth considering," Jerry said, seeming to forget that I had to go along with the whole wacky concept for it to leave the drawing board. "If anything, it's a good way to experiment with our target audience and see if the folks around here prefer the bad girl or good girl look. From the results, we can build our next marketing campaign."

Mona dropped her fork on her plate with a clatter, her eyes spitting sparks across the table. "Really, Jerry? When will it be Ray's turn then to wear the black eyeliner, tight clothes, and padded jock?"

I did a double take at her. She must have seen Ray's penis, too.

Mona continued, "Or is this going to be a way to exploit only the females under your employ?" Mona asked.

Instead of taking offense at her stab, Jerry's grin took a flirting bend as his gaze traveled over her pinched features. "I haven't seen you this ticked off in a long time, Mona. Not since …"

Mona scooped up her fork and pointed it at Jerry's face.

"Don't even go there."

Go where? I wondered. What the hell had gone on between these two in the past?

"I'm serious, Jerry," Mona continued. "You need to step back for a moment and take off your marketing hat, because it seems to be blocking your view of what's right and wrong."

"Actually," Jerry said, "I was also thinking of putting some ads out showing the newest member of our little family."

My lower gut cramped in a pseudo labor pain. "We have a new family member?"

Jerry's smile was supposed to be reassuring, I assumed. Instead, it filled me with dread. "Yes. Benjamin Underhill has accepted my offer to join us as another associate broker."

Great, Ben would have the same title as me. That would make it easier for him to step into my shoes when I got fired.

"He'll start next week," Jerry continued. "So, if any of you would like to air any grievances about my hiring another employee, say your piece now, because after breakfast I don't want to hear any whining."

Across the table, Ray was one big gloating head. "I think you've made a smart choice. Ben's a good kid. I'm sure he'll succeed where others fail." Ray looked at me.

Really? Was that the best he could throw at me?

"I'm looking forward to teaching him everything I know," he added.

"Well, that should cover his first hour of training," I said with a smile of my own.

Mona laughed and then covered it with her napkin.

I joked, but there was a challenge in that statement that made me scrape off some tooth enamel. Mona had been my mentor from the start. She'd guided me and protected me along the way. Now Ray had his own puppy to train, and I had no doubt he was going to do his best to have Ben jumping through rings and spinning this way and that for treats every chance he got.

I glanced at Mona. She fiddled with her spoon, two rivulets between her perfectly arched eyebrows. "Benjamin seems like a nice guy," she said. "But do you think it's wise to hire someone related to Ray?"

Ray growled but kept his big mouth shut.

"You have an issue with nepotism?" Jerry asked.

"I have an issue with encouraging competition between coworkers. We are supposed to be one team all working together for the good of Calamity Jane Realty."

Jerry rubbed his jaw, watching her fingers on the spoon. "What makes you think we won't be on the same team anymore?"

She looked at Ray. "A gut feeling."

She'd caught on to Ray's challenge, too. No surprise there. Mona had become one of the all-time top sellers in the Black Hills by watching over her shoulder as she climbed.

Jerry reached across the table and touched her arm, patting it a few times. "Your gut's wrong. We'll now have a five-man ... er, five-person team that will be invincible, you'll see. Trust me on this."

Mona pulled her arm away. "I trusted you once before."

Jerry's cheeks reddened. He picked up his coffee cup, hiding behind it. "That was different. This time, it will work. Especially after we get some fresh ads out there with Violet and Benjamin on them, appealing to a new customer base."

His words didn't ease my own dueling badgers. Besides, I hadn't agreed to anything yet.

The rest of the brunch passed by with slurps of coffee and some talk about what Jerry had learned last night at his appointment with one of the higher-ups in the South Dakota Real Estate Commission.

When we all stood to leave, Jerry touched my shoulder. "Hold up a second, Violet." He turned to Ray and Mona. "We'll see you two back at the office."

As soon as they were out of earshot, he pointed at the bench seat where Mona had sat. I dropped into it obediently. He kneeled on the other bench, looking down at me.

"You were in jail yesterday," he said.

No mincing words for Jerry, so I followed suit. "Yes, I was."

"Why?"

"I was in the wrong place at the wrong time, and Detective

Cooper from the Deadwood Police Department locked me up as a way of teaching me a lesson."

He raised one eyebrow. "I have a feeling you're not telling me a big part of the story, but I won't prod this time. However, I strongly suggest you avoid that 'wrong place' in the future. I can spin the jail thing this time, but if it happens again, I don't think I can save your professional reputation."

I squeezed the bridge of my nose, hating that I was having this conversation with my boss of all people.

"Is Detective Cooper still wanting you to sell his house?"

"Yes." Unbelievably.

Jerry crossed his arms, his big forearms bulging like Popeye's. "Interesting."

Not really. Cooper was just good at compartmentalizing me into two roles: real estate agent on one hand; nemesis on the other. In my world, Cooper was someone to hide from, period.

"I have a rule, Violet. It's pretty simple—five fouls and you're out. That means you get four chances to screw up. On the fifth, I fire you. Consider yesterday's trip to jail on working time your first foul."

Fair enough, I guessed. Although I'd consider a trip to jail more like two fouls, or a technical foul, but who was I to argue?

"Any questions?" he asked.

"Yeah, how do I get this foul removed from my record?"

His lips flat-lined. "Sell that hotel."

* * *

I missed Natalie.

I missed her smiling eyes, her easy laughs, and her sharp wit.

I missed drinking beer with her in the dark, ogling our favorite silver-screen actors on TV, trying to out-swear each other when nobody else was around, and sharing conspiracy theories over the phone late at night.

But most of all, I missed her being by my side no matter what, come hell or high water, zombies or albinos, vindictive sisters or pissed off cops—like Cooper and whichever chicken

shit had left me that anonymous note yesterday with words that
still shadowed my thoughts.

From my current viewpoint in Gordon Park, which
neighbored the Rec Center, I could watch the Deadwood Police
Station while I twisted slowly in one of the swings. I just wished
Natalie was twirling in the swing next to me, like she had so
many times before. She would know the names of all of the cops,
where they lived, who suffered from what addiction, who was
screwing around on their spouse, and which ones I should add to
my suspect list.

She would also know exactly what to say that would make
me laugh about Ray and his annoying congratulatory phone call
to Ben that had driven me out of the office this afternoon.

I'd grumbled and growled all through the parking lot behind
Calamity Jane's, my frustration bubbling over in spite of
Deadwood's warm sunshine and fresh pine tree *eau de parfum*.
The squeals of children's laughter had lured me to the
playground, where a mother had been pushing two little girls on
the swing set. After the trio had left, I'd snagged a swing, spying
on Cooper and his buddies while revisiting old playground
memories with Natalie and more.

Since we were kids, Nat had always been next to me, holding
my hand during the hard times, like when I'd found out I was
going to be an unwed mother of twin babies whose piece-of-shit
father wanted no part in their world. Nat had been there to lift
me out of my funk and convince me that things would be all
right. She'd breathed with me through the kids' delivery and
celebrated their growth and achievements every moment since.
She was the sister I'd always wanted instead of Susan—the sister
I loathed.

The weight of Natalie's silence since that night in the
basement of the funeral parlor hurt my heart more every day, the
ache growing sharp and spiny in my chest.

I leaned my head against one of the swing's chains. If only
she hadn't convinced herself that she'd fallen for Doc, confusing
lust for love yet again. I'd never been able to understand how a
girl so pretty and smart could be filled with so many insecurities.
Except for Doc, she was always falling for the guys who

promised her the moon and then delivered stinky cheese with a side of infidelity.

I watched two cops step out of the police station and hop into a police car, their laughter rolling across the asphalt and grass separating us. They wheeled out of the parking lot and headed toward Main Street. Maybe I should start following some of these cops, trailing them to see if they were up to anything suspicious.

That sounded like something Mr. Big-Shot Detective might do to find out some answers. Hell, the hard-ass was probably watching me right now, waiting for me to make my next move.

I checked my cell phone, hoping to see a return text from Nat.

No such luck, damn it.

Since I had time on my hands and Nat on my mind, I typed her another text: *Jerry hired Ben. If I can't get Cornelius to buy that damned hotel, I'm really screwed. Ack!! I forgot to tell you that someone at the police station left me a threatening note yesterday, saying I had something of theirs they wanted back. WTF? Miss you!*

My cell phone rang as I hit the Send button on the text. Unfortunately, it wasn't Natalie, but rather Cornelius, who I'd been trying to reach since right after Jerry dropped his breakfast bomb on me.

"Speak of the top hat," I said under my breath and took the call. "Hi, Cornelius."

"I need you to come up to Mount Moriah immediately," he said without preamble.

Mount Moriah was Deadwood's historic cemetery, the town's version of Boot Hill, with such famous residents as Wild Bill Hickok, Calamity Jane, Charlie Udder, Seth Bullock, and more. I would have been less surprised if Cornelius had started our conversation with: *Four score and seven years ago …*

"Did someone die?" I asked.

"Several people have died, actually, but that's not important."

"Since when is death not important?" I twirled back and forth.

"Violet, stay focused. I need you to bring me seven double-

D batteries, a fifty-foot extension cord, a pair of jumper cables, five unscented candles, two pairs of rubber gloves, and some sea salt—the kind with the speckles in it, not that mineral-free stuff."

I stopped twirling. "Come again?"

"You should probably be writing this down."

With what? My invisible pen? I listened as he listed the items again and tried to plant them in my memory. I waited for him to finish saying, "Double-D is a bra size, you know, not a type of battery."

"Have you researched that thoroughly?"

No, I had never researched batteries in my life. But I had briefly hit the double-D cup range when I turned into a milk machine right after having twins. However, I really didn't want to explore this subject any further with Cornelius, so I changed it. "Why do you need this stuff?"

"I'll show you when you get up here."

"Cornelius, I have a job to do." I spun in my swing, winding the chains overhead together. "I can't just jump when you call."

"You sound irritable and tense. Have you cleansed your chakras lately?"

"No." Not since ... ever.

"When did you last have them aligned and balanced?"

"Well, I had to choose between the Picklemobile's tires or my Third Eye," I said with a definite snippiness in my tone.

"And now I'm picking up frustration from your energy field. I tell you, the reception on these new cell phones is incredible."

Wait until he caught my live vibe when I saw him next. Beating him with my purse seemed too docile at the moment; maybe I'd roll him down the mountainside like a wheel of cheese.

"How soon can you get here? I have a ghost I need you to channel. You're going to really dig this one."

"Cornelius, I'm a Realtor. Not some kind of conduit for your ghostly friends."

"You being a medium has everything to do with your success in sales."

Ha! Then I was one hell of a shitty medium. "I'm not coming up to that graveyard unless you promise me we'll talk about the hotel sale. We're running out of time."

"In more ways than you know," he said, and whistled a bit from the Twilight Zone soundtrack.

I sat up straight in the swing. "I'm serious."

"Fine, okay. I have news for you anyway that will probably make you happy."

Happy news? That would be a nice change. Usually all of the news I received made me want to soak my head in a barrel of beer.

I stared across the park grounds at the police station. I could either stay here and try to figure out which of the cops coming and going was the one who'd put the note in my purse, or go back and sit through more of Ray's snickers and snide grins and try not to slip him any of the rat poison Jane had stored under the bathroom sink, or go pay a visit to Deadwood's famous history makers while sitting next to an Abe Lincoln doppelganger.

"Give me an hour," I told him.

"That's too long. Make it forty-seven minutes. Time is ..."

He never finished that sentence, just disconnected, leaving me twisting in the breeze.

Since I had to hit the Piggly Wiggly to grab several of the things he'd ordered me to bring, I hopped to my feet. I returned to Calamity Jane Realty long enough to grab my purse from my desk, telling Mona I was going to see a client and returning Ray's leer with a fly-by double-birdie on my way out the door. What I wouldn't do to jam a whole can full of peas up his nose.

There was another zombie roaming the parking lot of the Piggly Wiggly. Actually, he might have been the same one as before. He beat me inside the grocery store. I found him in Aisle Six reading the back of a box of bandages.

"Hi," I said, grabbing a bottle of peroxide and tossing it into my basket. We always needed more of it thanks to Layne's experiments. "You're in the play, right?"

If he wasn't, I reserved the right to scream my head off and run the other way.

"What play?" He raised one half-bloodied eyebrow. It fell off and splatted on the floor, revealing his regular dark brown eyebrow underneath.

I bent down and picked his eyebrow up, handing it to him with a smile. "My name is Violet, by the way. You seemed to have lost this."

"Thanks, Violet-by-the-way. That one keeps falling off today." He took the rubbery piece of fake flesh from me and stuffed it in his shirt pocket. "My name's Zeb."

No shit. Zeb the Zombie. Doc was going to love this detail later when I filled him in on my day.

"Nice to meet you, Zeb. I think I saw you here last week. Do you always grocery shop in costume during a play?"

"I'm in between cars at the moment, so I walk up here after rehearsal and buy what I need and then call my neighbor, who comes to pick me up."

"It sounds like you have a nice neighbor."

He shrugged, turning back to the first aid sundries. "She's lonely and I'm single."

Harvey and Zeb should form a club. Then Harvey could crash at Zeb's house every night and I could get me some sex.

I needed to ask Zeb about Peter Tarragon, but I couldn't figure out how to swing the conversation toward Petey boy, so I plowed in head first. "Isn't Peter Tarragon directing that play?"

"Yeah," Zeb looked at me out of the corner of his eye. "You a friend of Tarragon's?"

"No, I just know of him." I purposely left that vague. "I've heard he can be a real hard-ass with his cast."

"Most directors like to be hard-asses, in my experience. I think they believe it makes them appear more in control than they are."

I hoisted my basket higher up my arm, getting the feeling that I wasn't going to get any further with picking this zombie's brains. "I should probably get going." I had a cemetery to rush to. "It was great to meet you."

"Tarragon would get a lot further with his cast if he'd stop trying so hard to impress certain folks and focus on directing the play."

Maybe ol' Zeb wasn't quite done. "By 'certain folks,' are you talking about that theatre company supposedly interested in hiring him?"

"No. That theatre company is most likely a rumor that Tarragon started to impress the locals into coming to the play. I'm talking about the way he kisses the executive producer's ass … pardon my French."

Zeb's ear fell off and landed at our feet. I grabbed it and handed it back to Zeb. "Who's the executive producer?"

"Dominick Masterson," he said. "You know, the guy who's running for mayor?"

"Yeah, I know Dominick." Sort of. "He seems like a nice guy." That would explain why Dominick seemed to be at the opera house more often than not.

"Oh, he is." Zeb tossed three boxes of bandages in his basket and then looked up at me, his black rimmed eyes serious, making a few creepy-crawlies inch up my arms. "As long as you stay on his good side."

"And if you don't?"

"You could end up like me."

What? Dead? Zombified? A secondary actor in a local play? Carless? "Like you how?"

Zeb looked over my shoulder, his face splitting in a grin. "Hey, boys, what are you two doing up here in Lead?"

I looked over my shoulder and did a double-take at the two Deadwood cops sauntering toward Zeb and me. Both men in blue were tall, one bone thin and the other a bit pudgy.

Crap, now what? It couldn't be a crime to talk to a zombie in Lead. I highly doubt the town's forefathers had that much foresight, so there was no way Cooper could arrest me for it.

"We're keeping an eye out for troublemakers," the tall, thin one said, his eyes twinkling as he nodded at me. "Always good to see you, Ms. Parker."

Had Cooper told them to follow me around? I wouldn't put it past him. Then again, maybe these two were the ones responsible for putting that note in my purse, in which case I wanted to put several miles between us.

I patted Zeb on his fake blood speckled shirt sleeve. "Nice to meet you, Zeb. Maybe I'll run into you again here."

"You should come down to the opera house. I could

introduce you to Peter, if you'd like to try to land a role in a future play."

Hell, no. After what I'd seen and heard about him, Peter Tarragon had mental issues. The official report hadn't been filed yet, but he was just one breakdown and bottle of whiskey away, I was certain. Besides, if Cooper caught wind of my stopping at the opera house and talking to Tarragon, he'd lock me up in his basement until he'd solved Jane's murder. With the detective's current track record, I could waste away to nothing before that happened.

Since the two cops were standing there witnessing our little exchange, I had to play it safe. "Thank you, Zeb, but I'll have to pass. I can't act my way out of a paper bag."

Zeb leaned in close. "Neither can a certain director's wife," he said under his breath, "but that didn't stop her from getting a lead role in spite of the whole cast's objections."

Chapter Seventeen

After a sluggish start, the Picklemobile chugged up the steep hill to Mount Moriah Cemetery, sputtering a little at the top right before I turned into the parking lot. I pulled into a spot a little way down from an idling tour bus.

"You made it, baby," I said, patting her dashboard, making the dust fly. The old girl was starting to act up on me. I seemed to remember something Harvey had said about her not liking the cold weather much.

I checked my voicemail—Cornelius had called three more times since I'd left Zeb the Zombie at the store.

"Yeah, yeah, yeah, I know, you need your supplies." I slammed the door, leaving the electrical cord and jumper cables in the pickup. I could only imagine what the caretakers might think if they saw me carrying means of transmitting electricity and shock therapy into a cemetery. Those two cops from the grocery store would be showing up here in short order, dragging me to the station again.

As I hiked up the paved road to the graves, catching whiffs of diesel from the tour bus along the way, I thought about Zeb's comments back in the store. Yet again, I wondered why Helen had been crying in the bathroom at the opera house that first time I saw her.

Zeb had made it sound like the whole cast wasn't thrilled with her being made the lead in the play. Had she been in tears because of something a cast member had said to her? Maybe several people in the play had been treating her badly because of the preferential treatment she'd received. Hadn't Peter chewed her out about taking too long with her makeup and making the cast wait for her to be ready again?

Now that I knew Peter was Dominick Masterson's puppet, I

was even more curious why Dominick had been waiting outside the Ladies room that day. Did it have something to do with Peter? Or was Helen given the lead role because something was going on between her and Dominick? Something under the covers maybe? Granted she was a few years older than him, but some guys were into older women.

Or did Helen's connection with Dominick have something shady to do with Jane's death?

For two whole seconds I thought about telling Cooper what Zeb had told me, and then I scoffed. Avoiding jail was key to keeping my job, and that meant staying clear of Cooper—and the opera house.

I found Cornelius's long, skinny frame parked in a canvas-style director's chair next to Wild Bill's fenced-in grave. His Abe Lincoln top hat sat askew as he scribbled furiously in the margins of some book. A herd of name-tagged tourists from the parking lot bus wandered by, several craning their necks to see what Cornelius was scribbling. I did, too, but his chicken scratches were worse than Elvis's.

"What are you writing?" I asked.

He looked at me from behind his round sunglasses and then closed the book. "What's this I hear about you going to jail?"

Several of the passersby screeched to a halt, not even trying to hide their eavesdropping. I waved at several of them. *Nothing to see here, skedaddle on back to the bus.*

I leaned closer to Cornelius and lowered my voice, "Where did you hear that?"

"Your coworker with the smelly feet told me."

My vision hazed with red. "Ray stopped by to see you?"

He nodded.

"When?"

"Last night. He came by to see if I was settling into the hotel okay and offered to take me out for a drink."

What?!

Ray must have gone to see Cornelius after I'd left yesterday. I should ask Jerry how many fouls he'd hit the dickhead with for trying to steal my client.

What was Ray up to now, besides trying to get me fired? The

rat bastard had to have known Cornelius would tell me about his visit. I'd have to sniff around this one a little before I went all monkey-nuts on Ray, jumping on his back and pummeling the crap out of him.

"Did you go out for a drink with him?" I asked.

Cornelius didn't even hesitate. "Of course not."

Good! He must have seen through Ray's false charm. Cornelius might be a bit odd, but he wasn't daft.

"I didn't like the color of his aura." He tapped my arm with his pencil. "I would try to avoid spending too much time with him if I were you."

No shit, Sherlock.

"You should have called me when you were in jail," he scolded. "I'd have come there."

"Thanks but my boyfriend bailed me out." Jeez, I sounded like a crack addict.

"Oh, I wouldn't have bailed you out."

"You w— Why not?"

"I'd have joined you with my EMF meter, along with the new EVP recorder that arrived a few days ago. I've been wanting to test it against my old recorder. Channeling that ghost living in the back corner cell would have provided the perfect opportunity."

I sighed. I needed to find less opportunistic friends. Or find Cornelius a hobby to distract him from all things ghosts: maybe even a girlfriend—but not Caly. Her "everything-is-beautiful" bubble would tempt me to grab a sharp pin each time she got within popping reach.

"Why don't you go to the station and test the meters on your own?" I was tired of being his test dummy.

"I tried, but they wouldn't let me in unless I was there to report a crime or visit a prisoner. After I explained I was there to visit a prisoner, one who might be trapped for eternity if not freed, I was escorted from the building."

That reminded me of why I'd ended up in jail in the first place. "I saw you outside of the opera house yesterday when I was on my way to the store."

That was sort of a lie. I'd also seen him ignore my phone

call, but I decided not to mention that tidbit, or that I had just come from having the crap scared out of me by Prudence the ghost.

"I don't recall that moment," he said.

"You were standing there with Caly and Dominick Masterson."

"Dominick who?"

The guy you shook hands with and followed inside, I wanted to say, but that would give away how closely I'd been watching him. "Masterson. He's running for mayor in Lead."

"Oh, you mean Caly's partner," he said.

Dominick was Caly's partner? What kind of partner? Or was Cornelius just applying that term loosely? I waited, hoping he would clarify, along with why he'd been at the opera house and what had transpired there; instead he pointed at the grocery bag in my hand. "Did you bring my double-Ds?"

"There is only one D on these batteries," I muttered and shoved the bag at him. Apparently, he was moving on to the next subject whether I liked it or not. "What am I doing here today, Cornelius, besides being your gopher girl?"

He dug through the bag. "I need you to ask Wild Bill some questions for me about the hotel."

"I'm your real estate agent, not your personal medium."

He looked at me over the top of his round sunglasses. "You can't hide who you are."

He said that as if he knew who I was. Heck, I didn't even know who I was these days.

"Fine," I said. "Maybe I could wake up Wild Bill and ask if this hotel sale will go through."

"He's not a fortune teller, Violet."

Silly me. I'd forgotten he was just a ghost.

"Did you bring the jumper cables?" he asked.

"They're in the pickup." I gave him a suspicious squint. "You aren't planning on playing Dr. Frankenstein and bringing someone back to life, are you?"

"Not in the daylight," he said without jest.

I took a step back. "For the record, I refuse to be any part of a corpse reanimation."

"I jest, Violet. I'm not that passionate about the dead." His lips did that lopsided thing that I was pretty sure was supposed to be a smile. "Besides, it's a clear day. We'd need lightning to jump start a corpse's brain."

"Not funny, Cornelius." I had no doubt that Ray would love to add necrophilia rumors to my ghost-loving reputation.

"Since we're on the subject of resurrection," he said, "you should know that we don't need to wake up Wild Bill. Somebody else already did that."

I looked at Bill's grave, remembering how months ago Doc had told me that the reason he'd stuck around town was partly because of Wild Bill, whom he'd run into down on Main Street.

Had Cornelius seen or heard something about Doc and his ghost-sensing ability?

"How can you tell?" I asked.

"There are candle wax drips on the back of Bill's monument."

Candle wax? Whew! I highly doubted wax could have lasted through the elements since Doc had come to Deadwood a year ago. "So you think he was woken up recently?"

"There was no wax here last week."

"How can you be certain it wasn't someone paying homage to Bill? I bet he has a lot of fans out there. I mean, not just any guy can pull off that long moustache and all of that wavy hair for over a century."

"I'm not absolutely certain," Cornelius said. "That's why you're here, to help me ask him about the wax and the blood."

"What blood?"

"The drops of it mixed in with the wax."

Eww! I circled around the back of Bill's grave. Wax drops dotted the dark bronze surface. The blood was visible only on the gray concrete base.

"What makes you think Bill's hanging around here?" I asked.

The old guy could be a meandering spirit. After all, Doc had run into him downtown. That made me curious if ghosts actually wandered the countryside like cows on the range, or were they corralled to a certain area based on some supernatural force?

Dang. This would all seem less wacky if I were drinking

alcohol. Maybe I should start carrying a flask.

"I can feel a presence," Cornelius answered my question about Wild Bill.

"Well, I *am* standing right next to you," I joked.

"You're right. Step back." After I obliged, he took off his sunglasses and stuffed them into his coat pocket, then cocked his head and closed his eyes. "I can still feel it. He's here with us."

"How do you know it's Bill? It could be Calamity Jane." I pointed at the adjoining plot. "Her last wishes were to be buried next to him. Maybe she hangs out here, watching over him."

The thought of Calamity Jane sitting here all alone over the decades made my chest twang again. Poor ghost.

"It doesn't feel like a female," Cornelius said.

Female ghosts feel different from males? Now that I thought about it, Doc once mentioned he could sense the difference between genders, even age groups.

"You feel it right now?" I asked.

"Yes. Can't you?"

"The only thing I feel is tired."

He studied me for several seconds like I was the first of my kind. "Come here."

"Why?"

"Just come over here." When I obeyed and stood in front of him, he said, "Now close your eyes."

I narrowed them instead. "Why? What are you going to do?"

"Just trust me, Violet."

"I'd rather just sell you a hotel."

"That will come in time."

"We're almost out of time."

"So file for an extension. I need a little longer to round up the cash."

He said it like I should have thought of it weeks ago. "What if the seller won't agree?"

"Then throw in another twenty thousand in earnest money."

My jaw dropped. "Seriously?"

"Yes."

Sweet. That gave us a little breathing room. "So was that the good news you mentioned earlier on the phone?" It wasn't the good news I was hoping for, but it was better than not getting the deal at all.

"No. The good news is that I may have an 'in' on sneaking us into the under-the-floor pool in the opera house so that we can make contact with the boy who didn't like my hat."

Cornelius and I had vastly different definitions of what "good news" was.

Recalling our earlier phone conversation, I asked, "So, how is that good news about the hotel?"

"It's not," he said. "You mentioning the hotel just sparked my memory that I'd made that arrangement."

I pinched him on the shoulder.

"Ow! What did you do that for?"

"Because you frustrate me, Cornelius."

"That explains why you can't feel the presence I'm sensing. Your receptors are blocked by your emotions."

I scowled at him. "Who sent you to our planet?"

He stood up and pointed at his chair. "Sit here."

"No."

"Don't you want to see Wild Bill?"

"I'd rather see a green bill—make that a case of them, enough to pay for a certain hotel."

He continued to point at the chair.

"No way. There's a tour group wandering around here."

"I can see them leaving right now, so sit."

I grumbled under my breath and sat in the chair. "I really don't have time for this, Cornelius."

"Now close your eyes."

I glanced around to make sure nobody was watching us besides the crows.

"I said close them."

"Fine." I did as told. "Now what?"

"I want you to picture a candle flame in a dark room."

A cool breeze skimmed my face. The scent of the pines seemed stronger, as if shutting down one sense cranked up another. "A big candle or a little one, like a birthday candle?"

"It doesn't matter. Just picture the flame. Watch how it dances and flickers as the air moves it."

I pictured a flame, then flashed back to the sight of my old Bronco burning in the parking lot behind Calamity Jane's last month and felt my shoulders tense. Taking a slow breath in through my nose, I pushed that memory aside and went back to the candle.

"See the line of smoke trailing up from the flame, fading into wisps and then nothingness."

Fading wisps and nothingness. Got it.

"Get rid of all of your preconceived notions about the flame, any worries about the fire, and just feel the warmth emanating from it."

I imagined how a candle flame felt when I ran my hand over it, when I snuffed it out with wet fingers. I pretended to lean close to the flame, letting the heat warm my nose, my cheeks, my lips.

"Now unfocus your mind's eye and sense the glow around the flame, the balance of light near the center, the shifting shadows."

My shoulders slumped. I let my head fall forward, my jaw go slack, and thought about the flame.

Cornelius began to hum quietly, the sound lulling me even deeper into relaxation. My fingers relaxed, curling slightly, my thighs and hips settled into the canvas. I concentrated on that candle, amazed how the flame danced to the rhythm of Cornelius's humming.

He really did have a pleasant voice. It was no wonder the ghosts liked it, the clarity of his tone, the way I could practically hear his vocal cords vibrating.

As I watched the shadows dance with the flame, the whispering of the pines overhead faded, the deep pulsing of Cornelius's hum the only sound. The heat of the candle filled me throughout; even my toes felt warm.

"Now look beyond the flame, beyond the glow," he whispered in my ear, seeming almost to come from inside of my head. "Look deep into the shadows, finding comfort in the darkness."

I looked, the sea of blackness soft like chenille, inviting. I stepped toward it, reaching out to touch it.

"Do you see anything in the darkness, Violet? Do you see any movement at all?"

It was so dark. The shadows curled all around me, like smoke shifting over my skin, almost tickling.

I stretched my hand out further, trying to feel the black softness on the tips of my fingers, trying to—

Something grabbed my wrist and yanked.

I stumbled forward into the dark. When I caught my footing and looked around, the candle's light was gone, not even the glow visible.

Everything was black. Cold and black. I could feel shadowy fingers crawling over me, digging into my skin, trying to burrow inside of me.

The grip on my wrist tightened. I tugged against it, but it crushed like an iron band. The flesh felt rough and bumpy, like alligator skin.

I tried to scream, and the blackness filled my mouth, coating my throat, muzzling me. I tried to cough free of it, but inhaled even more.

I couldn't see, I couldn't …

Hot breath blew against my face, the rancid smell making me retch, my stomach roiling.

"I can smell it on you," it said, its voice thick, each word gruff and rasping.

Terror chilled me to my core. I knew that rotten egg smell—sulfur. The last time I'd gagged on it, my ex-client had melted in front of me and torn off his own face.

I could hear its breath rattling in and out, the hot, sulfur gusts blowing my curls so they tickled my eyes and cheeks.

It was so close. Too close.

It tugged and squeezed my wrist until my fist spread open. Something hot and wet circled my exposed palm and then trailed up my forearm.

A tongue.

Oh, my God! Something was licking me!

"I can taste it in your flesh." Its hot breath rippled over the wetness on my hand.

I couldn't speak, I couldn't move, I couldn't think.

It started to lick my palm again.

Without thinking, I grabbed the slimy muscle and yanked as hard as I could. It let go of my wrist and scratched at my arm, but I squeezed tighter, pulled harder, grabbing on with both hands.

Its hellish scream pierced my head.

I screamed back, using the weight of my body to tug harder, feeling its tongue begin to tear away. Claws dug into my arms, my stomach, my thighs, shredding down my legs.

It thrashed but I held, not letting go, ripping the flesh.

"Violet!" It screamed somehow around my hold on its tongue.

With one last heave, I tore the thick, slimy tongue free.

"Violet!" It yelled again over its own squeals of pain.

What? How could it …?

"Wake up, damn it!"

It grabbed me by the shoulders, the squeals fading, the black surrounding me lightening to a soft gray.

"Violet, open your eyes."

I knew that voice.

"Come on, Violet," Cornelius ordered, "open them!"

I obeyed, and in a breath, the trees returned to their whispering and Cornelius swam into focus, his cornflower blue eyes wide.

"Where are your sunglasses?" I asked.

He gaped at me for a moment, and then let go of my shoulders, leaning back against the iron fence around Bill's grave.

"Violet," he said, holding his chest. "You scared the holy hell out of me. What just happened? What was going on inside your mind?"

I blinked several times and sniffed, still picking up a hint of sulfur in the back of my nose. "I think I had another nightmare."

"You weren't sleeping."

"I must have been."

Cornelius looked at me for a moment. "Do you have these kind of nightmares often?"

"Sort of."

"That explains why you look like you've just come out of a

dryer most times I see you."

"Hey, there's no reason to get insulting."

"How long have you been having these nightmares?"

Since I killed Wolfgang. "For a couple of months."

"Hmmmm." He stroked his goatee. "What did you see in the nightmare?"

"I couldn't see anything; it was pitch black."

"Then why all of the screaming?"

"I was screaming?"

"You scared off the crows. Luckily, the tour bus was revving up to roll out of here, so we didn't have an audience."

"I thought *it* was screaming."

"What was screaming?"

"The thing that was licking me."

"There was something licking you in your nightmare?"

"Yeah. When I reached out into the darkness, it grabbed me and then licked my palm."

I noticed then that I had both of my hands clenched tight. My fingers ached as I eased them open, my palms drenched in sweat. A lot of sweat. Slimy sweat.

I looked down at the little bubbles in the creases of my right palm. My heart throttled up, banging in my ears. Sweat didn't make bubbles, did it? No, but spit did. I sniffed my hand; the stench of sulfur was subtle but there.

"Violet, did you hear me?" Cornelius interrupted my panic attack.

Gulping, I wiped my hands on my skirt. It had to be just sweat. "No, what?"

"There was a reason I didn't tell you to reach out with your hand, only with your mind. You don't touch. You never, ever touch."

"Why? What happens when you touch?" Besides getting grabbed and licked?

"Well, I don't know exactly, but my grandmother was very strict about that when she would have me practice reaching out—no fingers, just thoughts." He kneaded his hands. "Did it say anything?"

"No," I lied, afraid of what I'd done.

He stroked his goatee some more. "Violet, have you ever considered that you might not actually be just a medium?"

"No." I hated to blow out his birthday candles for him, but I wasn't even a medium.

My phone rang, making both of us jump.

I looked at the screen, but the name was blacked out thanks to the toilet incident, the lines much worse now. I was going to have to get a new phone, damn it.

I had to take the call. It could be the kids. "Hello?"

"I need you to come down to the station, Parker."

What? He couldn't have heard me screaming clear down there, could he? Talk about nightmares! I swallowed the urge to scream again, and calmly told Cooper, "No."

"Parker—" he started.

"Am I under arrest?"

He growled. "Don't start that again."

"I'm not coming down there, Detective. If you have something to say to me, say it now."

Maybe I'd get a new number with the new phone and keep it unlisted. That wasn't going to work. I was a real estate agent. Cooper's agent. I needed a Plan B.

"Fine, meet me at Bighorn Billy's," he said.

"No." He wasn't going to call all of the shots, damn it. "You meet me in a location of my choosing."

"Is this some kind of pissing contest, Parker?"

"Yep."

He growled again. "Where?"

Nowhere. After the nightmare I'd just screamed through, I really wasn't in the mood to lock horns with Cooper. "In the Deadwood library."

"What?"

"You heard me." At least if we were there, he couldn't yell at me. He'd have to keep it to very tense whispering. "Be in the South Dakota room in fifteen minutes."

I hung up on his curses.

"I gotta go talk to the cops." Carefully, like I was ninety instead of thirty-five, I stood, testing my legs for any last shakes from the nightmare.

"We'll have to make contact with Bill another time."

Or never. "I'll talk to the seller's agent," who just happened to be my boyfriend's gorgeous ex, "and see if we can get a couple of weeks' extension on the sale."

"I'm coming with you."

"To the library?" Cooper would not be happy if I brought backup.

"To the parking lot. The battery on my rental is dead. I tend to have that effect on anything with batteries."

That explained the jumper cables. "Why did you need the mineral salt?"

He fell in beside me, his chair in hand. "The hotel only has over-processed table salt. I need the extra minerals."

"And the extension cord?"

"For my boombox."

Who used a boombox anymore? "I thought that's what the D batteries were for."

"No, I just like to keep seven batteries on me for good luck."

And here I'd always thought a rabbit's foot seemed odd.

"The candles and rubber gloves?"

"Those are self-explanatory," he replied.

Ah, no, they weren't, but I dropped the subject.

It took us an extra ten minutes to get Cornelius's black rental car running, which made me five minutes late getting to the library. Cooper's sedan was still pinging and ticking in the parking lot when I walked by it. I climbed the library steps, wishing I'd seen Doc's car parked there, too. I could use his broad shoulders, especially after having my palm licked.

I stepped inside the library, the smell of varnished floors and old paper welcoming. The sight of Cooper standing by the main desk with Tiffany Sugarbell, Doc's flame-haired ex, hanging off his bicep stopped me in my tracks. Her full, pouty lips made me long for a fly swatter.

What in the hell was she doing here? I hadn't seen her Jeep in the parking lot. Had she come with Cooper? Was she the woman Cooper had the hots for? That would be just my luck—my two headaches hooking up.

I walked over to them, sucking in my gut as I tended to do

when the ultra-competitive she-devil made an appearance.

Tiffany noticed me first, her smile fading around the edges. I could see her shoulders stiffen as I neared, making her all-star rack perk up even more under her tight blue sweater. In her pencil-thin white skirt and two inch heels, she looked straight off one of Addy's Barbie Doll boxes. All she needed was a smart little purse and a picture of Ken in her locket.

Cooper turned toward me, his face stony, his bulldog-covered tie crooked and loose, like he'd been leashed by it and tried to tug free. "You're late, Parker."

"Shit happens," I said, in no mood for his usual ass chewing extravaganza.

Tiffany's eyes bulged while Cooper's lips thinned.

"Really, Violet," Tiffany whispered, making a point of glancing around the big, nearly empty room. "You can't talk to your clients like that."

I'd like Tiffany to walk a mile in my heels and see if she didn't lose a little of her glossy coat.

"Cooper's not a typical client." He came with bullet holes and handcuffs.

Her laugh was husky, all coated with sex. She leaned into Cooper's arm, brushing those centerfold boobs against his arm. "Tell me about it," she practically purred next to his ear. "I was just telling the detective to give me a call if he needed help with anything."

Like unzipping his pants with her teeth? Sheesh, she was throwing herself at Cooper. Doc was right about her. Someone needed to slap her upside the head with some self-esteem.

"Anything," Tiffany emphasized. "I've been around longer than Violet. I know a few tricks when it comes to selling that I haven't shared with her yet."

Oh, come on! Like I needed any more kicks while I was down for the count. Ray and Jerry had already bruised me up enough, not to mention my experience with that freaky licker. The last thing I wanted to do today was arm wrestle Miss Perfect for a client.

I bared my teeth and tried to force my lips into a smile. "I don't know, Coop. Do you think Tiffany will let you handcuff her like you do me?"

Tiffany's lips parted with a gasp.

Yeah, take that, bitch.

I looked up at Cooper and ran smack-dab into two icy blue chips trying to freeze-ray me. "If you're done getting your ego buffed by my associate, how about we take care of business. I've got other appointments this afternoon." Like the standing one I had with my couch and the Duke on the TV.

He pointed at the door to the South Dakota room. "Go, Parker." His voice sounded like he'd been gargling with rock salt again.

"Always good to see you, Tiffany," I lied with a parting nod, and then I remembered Cornelius and the hotel situation. "I need to talk to you about the hotel sale." Tiffany represented the seller on that deal. "How about I call you later this evening with the details?"

Her big, bright smile returned, her mode flipping from sexpot back to real estate agent. "Sure, Violet. I'm having dinner with an old friend, but I'll be done early."

It had better not be Doc, or I was going to go all Godzilla on him and fry his jewels with my laser eyes.

With a wave goodbye, and a mumbled "good riddance," I clomped across the waxed wooden floor toward the room reserved for South Dakota books and information.

Cooper followed me into the room and shut the door behind him, leaning against it, caging me all alone with him and his temper.

I tried to find a positive thing to say. "Your nose is looking better."

His chin twisted slightly, his eyes narrowing.

"What?" I asked when he remained silent, hiding my trembling hands behind my back.

"Handcuff you?"

"Well, you did."

"Yeah, and then I threw your ass in jail. What the hell were you playing out there?"

"Chess. She's trying to take my queen."

"I'm no queen."

"You know what I mean." I crossed my arms. "Listen, if you want her to be your agent, just say so and I'll rip up our contract. I promise it won't hurt my feelings." Okay, that wasn't completely true. Even though working with Cooper was like stringing a barbed-wire fence without leather gloves, he was still MY barbed-wire fence. She could go find her own.

"We're not ripping up any contracts." He shoved his hands in his pockets. "I don't want her to be my agent."

"Then why didn't you tell her that?"

"I don't have to. It's none of her business."

I rolled my eyes. *Men!*

"Now can we cut to commercial on this soap opera and focus on the task at hand?" he asked.

"What task? In case you don't remember, you didn't converse with me on the phone, you just ordered me about, as usual."

"Quit your whining, Parker. Here's the deal. Peter Tarragon called me this morning and told me that his wife has been taking depression medication for a few months."

Helen was on depression meds? Was that why she was crying in the women's bathroom at the opera house?

"I need you to tell me in detail everything you know about Helen Tarragon."

"Is that an order?"

He sighed, leaning his head back against the door. "Will you please tell me what you know about Helen?"

I chewed on his request for a moment. "That depends."

"On what?"

"Do you promise not to yell at me?"

"Yes, fine."

"Or handcuff me again?"

The ridges down his cheeks softened. "I thought you liked it when I handcuffed you."

"I like it about as much as you like it when I take your gun and shoot at albinos."

That hardened his face right back up. "No yelling and no handcuffs. Now spill it. We need to get down to the bottom of this damned mess with Jane."

I pursed my lips, not liking his tone at all. If we were going to start sharing information, he needed to soften up a bit.

"Spill it, *please*," he corrected.

"Everything?"

He nodded and so I opened my mouth and let 'er rip, starting with when I heard her sobbing in the bathroom. I went on to tell about her fight with Peter, and then repeated the details from when I ran into her again in that lower hallway. His facial expression rippled and flattened like a sheet in the wind as I shared details. In the end, I even threw in what Aunt Zoe had shared about Jane's past and what Zeb the Zombie had told me at the store, making Cooper pinkie swear that this last bit of information could not be used in court or shared in a report.

He refused to hold up his pinkie, but gave me his word he'd keep it to himself.

When I finished, I raised my eyebrows and asked, "What do you think? Did Helen kill Jane, or is she just a pawn?"

"I think you've got chess on the brain." He opened the door.

"Wait!" I called as he started to leave.

He paused and looked back.

"I thought we were going to share information and figure out who killed Jane."

"The only things I agreed to were not to yell at you or handcuff you."

"What? That's not fair. I showed you my cards."

"I thought we were playing chess, not poker." When I glared, he pulled out his wallet, flipping it open and holding it out to me. "You see this?"

"Yeah, it's a tin star. I've seen them many times before packaged with cowboy hats and plastic pistols."

"This means that information only needs to flow one way, towards me."

"You're such an asshole, Cooper."

He tipped an imaginary hat at me. "Until we meet again, Parker."

I grabbed a magazine from a nearby rack and threw it at the door as he closed it behind him.

Chapter Eighteen

Friday, September 7th

When I opened my eyes the next morning, two realizations hit me at once. The light flooding in my window was brighter than it should be for seven o'clock and something was clucking in my closet.

A glance at the clock confirmed my anxiety was for good cause—I'd overslept by forty-five minutes. My cell phone's technical difficulties seemed to now include its alarm feature.

Dang it!

"Addy!" I scrambled out of bed and stuck my head out into the hall. "Come and get your chicken!"

Back in my room, I slipped on my robe, shooed Elvis from my closet, grabbed some clean underwear—a matching set today, since I'd be hanging out with Doc—and closed the bedroom door behind me.

"Addy!" I called from the top of the stairs. My stomach rumbled in excitement at the smell of pancakes drifting up the stairwell. *Pancakes?* Aunt Zoe must be having a Betty Crocker moment.

"I'm coming, Mom, sheesh!" Addy tromped up the steps, still in her pajamas.

"Don't you 'sheesh' me, Adelynn Renee. You know that chicken is supposed to be locked up each night, not roosting in my closet … again."

She walked by me grumbling under her breath about chickens getting no respect.

"And get dressed for school!" I hollered after her then raced down the stairs to corral Layne. When I found him, he was already dressed and sitting at the table, fork in hand, digging into a stack of pancakes covered in powdered sugar and strawberries. Aunt Zoe sat opposite sipping coffee, her plate left with just sugar and syrup residue.

"You're late," Harvey said from his spot by the griddle. Wearing one of Aunt Zoe's ruffle-lined Betty Boop aprons, he looked extra grizzled this morning after yet another night on the couch. He shoved a plate full of pancakes in my hands, sprinkled on the sugar, and then dumped a ladle full of strawberries over the top.

"I don't have time for food," I told him.

Harvey pointed a spatula at me, giving me the evil eye under a crinkled caterpillar eyebrow. "Eat. I'll take the kids to school this morning."

Oh, well then … I grabbed my fork, sat next to Layne, and dug in, swallowing a couple of sweet bites before looking up at Aunt Zoe. "Why didn't you wake me earlier?"

"I peeked in and you were sleeping so soundly that I didn't want to bother you. Did you take a sleeping pill last night?"

"No."

I tried to remember what I'd done last night after talking to Doc. Oh, right, I'd lain in bed and cursed at the ceiling, frustrated with Cooper for not answering any of my questions about Jane and Helen Tarragon after all I'd shared with him. At some point, mid-rant, I'd fallen asleep.

I stopped eating for a moment and realized what had changed. "I had no nightmares."

That was weird. I hadn't had a nightmare-free sleep since I'd spent the night at Doc's house weeks ago. Hmmm. Maybe things were going back to normal. Or maybe my brain was too exhausted even to try to scare the crap out of me anymore. Either way, I'd had a full night's rest. Add to that the stack of fresh pancakes in front of me, help getting the kids to school, and a date with Doc, and I suddenly felt like swinging my feet under the table. Life was good.

If only our date weren't in a haunted house with a ghost who kept trying to get chummy.

Aunt Zoe watched me eat for several seconds, her face pinched in thought. "Did anything happen yesterday that might have contributed to eliminating the nightmares?" she asked.

I chewed on her question and a mouthful of pancakes. What had happened yesterday? Let's see, I'd received a warning from my boss, chatted with a zombie, conjured up a freaky-ass dream at the cemetery, and spilled my guts to Cooper, who might be dating my boyfriend's ex-girlfriend. Nope, each one of those things should have spurred more nightmares, not gotten rid of them.

"Not that I can think of," I told Aunt Zoe.

Harvey cleared his throat, catching my attention. "Did you pay a 'social visit' to your 'financial planner'?" he asked, making the quote marks in the air while winking at me.

In other words, did I go to Doc's and get laid? I scowled at the dirty old buzzard. "No, Harvey, I did not." *Unfortunately.*

He shrugged and went back to cleaning up the griddle.

I noticed Layne's eyes on me and chuckled at how he was practically inhaling his pancakes. The poor kid needed a parent who could cook something other than fried eggs and tomato soup from a can. "Slow down, Layne. You're going to choke."

He made a show of eating in slow motion.

I reached over and messed up his hair. "Did you get all of your homework done last night?"

He'd been busy with his nose buried in a book called *Deadwood's Dead: True Tales from the Living* while I helped Addy with her two-page essay about the book *Treasure Island*, one of my favorites that she had neglected to read for class.

"Of course, Mom."

Layne was my studious child; Addy was the stubborn one. I'd love to take credit for Layne's interest in all things brainiac, but he'd gotten that from his father. Addy was filled to the brim with my genes, except for the color of her eyes.

"That book you were reading about Deadwood—was it for a report you have to do?"

He shook his head. "I'm trying to see if the rumor Doc told me about Wild Bill is true."

Doc? "When did you talk to Doc?"

"At the library yesterday."

It appeared Deadwood's library was a popular hangout these

days. Had I just missed Doc? Was that why Tiffany was there? Were they doing something together in the South Dakota room? Why hadn't Doc mentioned on the phone last night that he'd seen Layne at the library? Was it because he was hiding that he'd been there with Tiffany and Layne had caught them?

Whoa! Back 'er down there, Ms. Cray-cray. I shoved another bite of pancakes in my mouth to keep from asking my son if a pretty red-haired lady had been there with my boyfriend.

Doc had not given me any reason to distrust him so far. It wasn't his fault that my history with men rivaled the Badlands in terms of rockiness. Besides, this time felt different. I was older, Doc was far from my typical picks, and I wasn't letting the sun rise and set on his attentions. Although I wouldn't mind letting the sun rise and set while being on the receiving end of his lust-filled attentions.

With the ugly, green-headed beast in my head chained up again, I asked Layne, "What did Doc tell you about Wild Bill?"

Was it anything to do with someone trying to rouse Bill from his Mount Moriah beddy-bye with candles and blood? I had yet to tell Doc about my tongue-ripping merriment with Cornelius from yesterday. Some stories were better explained with animated hand gestures.

"He said it's rumored that Wild Bill is petrified due to the calcium carbonate in the soil he was originally buried in, but Doc thinks it's more likely he was mummified or fossilized."

While chewing, I tried to imagine what a petrified century-plus old body would even look like. I'd lay my bet on Bill being a dusty old mummy.

Addy raced into the kitchen, dressed for school with her chicken under her arm. She set Elvis outside the back door and turned to me. "Mom, can I stay over at Kelly's tonight?"

It was a Friday night, but … "You didn't read the book you were supposed to for school, remember?"

"Awww, come on, Mom. That's the past, let's just move on with our lives and find happiness in love and forgiveness."

Aunt Zoe chuckled and stood, squeezing my shoulder as she passed me on the way to the sink. "Your mother would be proud of her for that one," she told me with a wink.

"Good try, Addy," I said, pushing my empty plate away. Emulating her hippy grandmother was not going to help her cause. "I'm sorry to punish Kelly by keeping you away from her, but you have a book to read."

"But I have another book to read and write about for next week."

"Well, I guess you'll have to skip TV this weekend, too."

An explosion of whining and foot stomping followed. After I'd said my piece, I headed upstairs to get ready for my date with Doc and Prudence. I heard Harvey's pickup rumble away as I stepped from the shower.

When I got back downstairs, Aunt Zoe was nowhere to be seen, which probably meant she was out back in her glass shop, so I grabbed my purse and left. The fewer people who knew what I was up to today the better. I'd especially made sure to cover my ass with Jerry, leaving him a voicemail that I was showing a house to a client this morning and would be in sometime after lunch. Not exactly a lie, since I'd be *showing* Prudence to Doc in a *house*.

Doc was leaning against the trunk of his Camaro behind Calamity Jane's when I chitty-chitty bang-banged into the parking lot. Dressed in a dark maroon flannel shirt with the sleeves rolled up, a pair of faded blue jeans, and brown cowboy boots, he was just a Stetson hat short of throwing his leg over a saddle and riding off toward the horizon.

I admired the view, letting my imagination ride off with him and then some. My body responded in fine mating form, throbbing in places that left me tingling.

Jeez! What was wrong with me? Was I ovulating?

I pulled up in front of him and cranked down my window, telling myself to play it cool—no drooling.

"Hey, stranger," I said, pushing my sunglasses up. "Looking for a ride?"

Doc strolled over and leaned on my window frame. His hair gleamed in the morning light, looking almost blue-black. Shadows angled his face, adding an air of ruggedness that made me want to explore the texture with my fingers.

"That depends," he said, his voice throaty, his gaze locking on my lips.

The heady scent of him drifted inside the cab, making my pheromones bounce around like Mexican jumping beans.

His eyes traveled down my neck, darkening as they slid into the deep neckline of my pink cardigan. "Are you glittering?" he asked.

I looked down at where the silver zipper tab lay nestled in my cleavage. The sunlight streaming through the Picklemobile's front window hit me at chest-level, making the shiny flecks infused in my new coconut-scented lotion sparkle.

"Let's see," I said and made a point of peeking down the front of my sweater. "Hmmm." I let my sweater fall back into place and dragged my fingernail along the swell of my breast, flirting with him from under lowered lashes. "It appears I am— all over."

His focus jerked back to my face, his lust in plain sight. "Prove it."

My heartbeat got all hectic. "You're smoldering again."

"I haven't stopped smoldering since you dropped your skirt in front of me, Boots."

"Oh, really?" I purred. I should probably end this little game of seduction before someone lost control and melted all over her seat, but Doc was so fun to tempt. "Do you like to watch me take my clothes off?"

"I like to watch you, period. Touching is even better."

"Prove it," I threw back at him.

His grin surfaced, looking both playful and seductive. "I will, vixen. I will. And when I do, you're going to pay for all of the cold showers I've been taking lately."

"We could skip our visit to Prudence and go back to your place."

Doc shook his head at my suggestion. "I think it's your turn to smolder for a bit."

"I don't smolder." I just plain combusted, like a Phoenix, only with less flash and more screams.

His hand slipped down to trail up my pant leg, from my knee along my inner thigh. "Are you sure about that?"

Those dark, dark eyes of his nearly suckered me into

grabbing his hand and hurrying him along. Instead, I stopped his hand just before he hit the point-of-no-return. Responsible mothers didn't participate in foreplay in parking lots, I reminded myself, and neither did employees at risk of losing their jobs. I made a T with my hands. "Time out."

One of Doc's eyebrows lifted.

"It's been too long and I've been aching for you way too much, especially after last night's call." His detailed description of his latest shower-idea had left me writhing. "If you keep traveling up that path, I won't want you to stop, and with my luck, my boss will drive by right about the time I start screaming your name." I removed Doc's hand from my leg and placed it back on the door frame.

"You've been aching for me, huh?"

I was too discombobulated from his flirting to play it cool, but I was still armed with sarcasm. "I haven't reached the point of writing your name with little hearts around it on my notebooks yet, so don't get all cocky on me."

"Cocky?" Doc's grin spread, creasing his eyes, which sparkled with mirth. "I'll try, but you do make *it* hard."

Good looks and quick wit—it was no wonder he'd had me at "I want to buy a house."

My cheeks warmed as if my brain weren't totally corrupted by now. I matched his grin. "Then try to keep your cockiness in your pants so I don't get into any more trouble with my boss. I'd bet my mother's collection of John Denver records that Jerry's official rule book doesn't allow foreplay in Calamity Jane's parking lot."

"Jerry has a rule book?" Doc asked.

"We're talking at least another foul. Maybe two."

"What do you mean 'another' foul?"

"I already have one for going to jail."

Doc scoffed. "He's giving you fouls now?"

I nodded. "Life is one big basketball game to Jerry. He used to play for the pros, you know. His nickname was The Slammer."

Doc snapped his fingers. "That's where I know him from."

"I got one foul for going to jail. Four more and I'm done. I can't afford to foul out."

He shook his head. "You need a new boss."

"Don't say that too loud. After what happened to my last boss," *poor Jane*, "Cooper might hear you and throw you in jail, too." That reminded me of something I forgot to ask Doc last night on the phone. "Is Cooper dating Tiffany?"

He shrugged. "I have no idea."

"So Tiffany didn't mention Cooper the last time you talked to her?" And when exactly was the last time Doc had talked to the hussy? Yesterday in the library?

Doc chuckled and tugged on one of my loose curls. "Violet, the last time I talked to Tiffany was in front of The Old Prospector Hotel with you standing there next to me. I don't recall her mentioning Cooper's name at that time, do you?"

I frowned, wanting to stuff my insecurities in a box and toss it down one of Homestake's mine shafts. "Was I that obvious?"

"Your eyes gave you away."

I looked away, trying to hide my peepers from him. "I wish you'd picked an uglier ex-girlfriend," I grumbled.

He caught my chin and turned me back toward him, rubbing his thumb along my bottom lip. "I wish I'd met you first and avoided that pothole altogether."

"Yeah, but I'm full of potholes."

He tipped his head to the side as if considering my words. "You're not a pothole—more like the Grand Canyon."

What did that mean? "That doesn't seem like a good thing."

"You're looking at it through the wrong lens."

What lens should I be using? Probably a wide-angle one after all of those pancakes I gorged on this morning.

Doc stepped back from my window. "Now are we going to see a ghost or not?"

"Might as well since we're not gonna have sex."

He laughed aloud. "I'm going to enjoy watching you smolder, Boots."

I pointed my thumb toward the passenger side. "Get in before I shut off this damned truck and drag you off behind a tree."

I'd planned to drive to the Carhart's for good reason. If

Prudence's show and tell session today was anything like the one Doc had experienced last time, we'd be returning with him half comatose in the seat next to me.

Doc zipped around the back of the Picklemobile and climbed in next to me.

I waited for him to belt himself in before asking, "Is there anything we need to do to prep for this?"

Like dust off the Ouija board? Round up some Rune stones? Buy more double-D batteries?

"Nope."

"Are you ready?" I sure as hell wasn't. Knowing that he trusted me to keep him out of trouble in the netherworld had me sweating in unlady-like places. I couldn't even keep myself out of trouble in *this* world.

"I'll be ready after I take care of one thing."

"What's that?"

He pulled me toward him and kissed me, hard and hungry, almost bruising. My internal furnace flared, lighting me on fire Phoenix-style again. I sank my fingers in his hair, pulling him even closer, hitting him with my own need.

"Smolder, Boots," Doc whispered against my lips. "Smolder." Then he retreated as quickly as he'd attacked, leaving me stranded, breathing hard and sparking.

"Okay, now I'm ready," he said, chuckling at my huffs and snarls. "This is the part where you put the pickup in drive and hit the gas."

I certainly felt like hitting something. Shifting into gear, I steered the Picklemobile toward Lead.

Just when I thought I had a grip on the reins of this thing between Doc and me, he cracked the whip and my libido shot off yet again at a full three-beat gait.

"How much time do we have alone in the house?" Doc asked.

I'd let him know last night that I was able to get us into the Carhart house without Wanda there, convincing her to go shopping while I showed the place.

"I told her that I needed at least an hour."

"She doesn't know it's me?"

"No, she didn't ask and I didn't give names. I think she just wants to be free of the place." Which made me feel bad since I was giving her false hope today. I'd have to make it up to her by selling the damned haunted house.

"Can't say I blame her." He let his head rest against the seatback, closing his eyes, going silent.

I glanced at him several times on the three miles up to Lead, giving him space to prepare for whatever was about to happen. I just wished there were a guide book for whatever I'd need to do to get him back safely.

I rolled into the Carhart's drive and then cut the engine.

Doc opened his eyes and looked over at me. "Your forehead is one big wrinkle." He grabbed my hand, lacing our fingers. "Tell me why."

To start with, "What's going to happen once we get inside the house?"

"I don't know."

"Wow," I said, my sarcasm back for another round. "Surprisingly, that's not comforting at all."

"Sorry, Violet, but this is what I deal with every time I enter someplace that might be haunted. Prudence may rush us as soon as we step inside, or she may not even show up for the party."

"What happens if she rushes us—rushes you?"

"I let her lead me down her memory lane without any of my road blocks in place this time."

Even with his blocks in place last time, she'd knocked him flat. What would it be like with his defenses down?

"So, I sit there and wait for you to wake up?" I should have brought something to knit.

"No, you watch me, make sure I don't stop breathing, count to thirty, then pull me back out. You'll be my lifeline."

That "don't stop breathing" part made my hands tremble. I looked out the front window at the Carhart house, not wanting Doc to see my panic. Lifelines are supposed to be calm, not scrambling for paper bags to breathe into so they didn't pass out.

As much as I wanted to call this whole thing off, I tucked away my fears of losing him and focused on the task at hand. "Is thirty seconds long enough?" He'd been under three times as long last time with her.

"Time moves differently when I'm in *their* world. I need long enough for Prudence to relive the memory so I can see what she was up to before her killers arrive. Then you can work your magic and pull me out before I get slammed with the surge of energy that will come with her death."

Right, the surge that could fry his brain. "What if I don't know what magic to do?"

"You do. You've done it before."

He sounded so sure of me. I wished I felt the same.

His hand touched my leg, comforting. "Violet, I know you can do this. If I weren't sure of it, I wouldn't go in that house."

"What happens if I can't?" I whispered, grimacing.

"I don't know."

"Again, not comforting."

"Welcome to my world," he said and squeezed my thigh. "Let's go get this over with."

The porch steps didn't creak, but the front door did as it swung open. My feet didn't need many more reasons to turn around and run the other way, especially after my last visit to this spook-joint with Harvey in tow.

Doc shut the door behind us and deadbolted it, sealing us inside.

When I nailed him with a wide-eyed glance, he caught my hand. "She's just a ghost. She can't hurt you."

"It's not me I'm worried about at the moment."

"I like it that you're worried about me." He pulled me toward him, his gaze narrowing to an exaggerated squint. "Damn my eyes," he said, sounding a little like Clint Eastwood, "I find that kind of touchin'."

His impression of Hogan from *Two Mules for Sister Sara* didn't quite hit the mark, but he made me smile anyway. "I think I like your impressions of Bogart better than Clint."

"I collect blondes and bottles, too," he mimicked Bogart in *The Big Sleep*, and then led me into the sitting room where Harvey and I had scarfed down brownies.

I breathed in the now familiar scents of the Carhart house—vanilla and a hint of floor wax.

Doc stood in the center of the room, sniffing for a whole other reason.

"Is she close?" I asked, checking the pallor of his skin—still normal.

"No, but she's here." He pointed at the chair next to him. "Is that where Prudence spoke through Wanda?"

I nodded, skirting the chair to peek out the front window at the Picklemobile, my touchstone of normalcy.

"Let's go upstairs," he said.

Without a word, I followed him up to the bedroom where Prudence had accosted him the last time we'd toured the place.

I watched him walk to the dresser, noticing how he used the furniture to steady himself. "Are we getting hot?"

His skin had paled enough to be noticeable, but not as drastically as I'd witnessed before when Prudence had hovered in the doorway.

"Yeah," he looked behind me into the hall. "She's close."

Goosebumps prickled my arms. "She's not standing right behind me again, is she?"

"No. I think we need to go up into the attic."

"That sounds like what someone would say in a slasher movie right before getting chopped into pieces."

"She's just a ghost, Violet," he reiterated.

"Yeah, but a chatty one."

"Better than one with a grudge, like Wilda."

I shuddered at his mention of Wilda Hessler, the long-dead sister of my first client. Wolfgang Hessler had tried to burn me alive in his upstairs bedroom. I'd never forget the acrid odor of lighter fluid as Wolfgang poured it around me while claiming his dead sister sat in the corner watching with glee.

The ghost of Wilda Hessler still had me double-checking shadow-filled corners, especially after Cornelius told me a few weeks back about a blonde girl ghost who'd approached him in a dream and wanted him to relay the message that I was invited to her tea party.

I peeked down the hall, wondering if Prudence were standing there waiting for us. "Doc, do you realize how absurd I would have found this conversation back when I first met you?"

When I looked back, Doc's smile was tight. "You've come a long way, baby."

"Yeah." Considering what I'd witnessed at the Mudder Brothers with the albino, I'd have preferred being in the dark about it still. "You feel up to climbing a ladder? It's the only way into the attic."

"Onward ho," he said without gusto.

I lifted an eyebrow. Maybe if I kept things light and playful my panic wouldn't run rampant. "I may be easy, big boy, but I'm no 'ho.'"

He followed me into the hall. "Oh, you're not easy."

I stopped below the attic trap door. "Really? What am I then?"

"Complicated."

"Hey!"

He tweaked my nose. "As in not boring. Complex works, too."

"If we're going to stick with C-words, I have a better one. How about 'charming.' As in irresistibly charming. Or charismatic."

His face had taken on a grayish hue, but he played along. "How about 'confusing'? As in spinning me every which way, keeping me guessing."

He was one to talk, but I resisted punching him in the shoulder since he looked about ready to keel over.

"I prefer more positive adjectives," I said, grabbing the long-handled hook I'd learned about a month ago when Millie had sent me up into the attic to get what turned out to be Prudence's box of goodies. "Like 'captivating' and 'compelling.'"

Even Millie had known about Prudence. She'd first described the ghost in her attic as: *The old lady who lives up there. The dead one.* Back then I'd had to bite my lip not to smile, thinking she'd been optically deluded. That was long before Prudence had made a point of changing my mind.

I hooked the metal ring in the trap door and pulled it open. Dust floated down, circling us, carrying the scent of old cardboard and musty dropcloths.

"You're forgetting one of my favorite words for you," Doc

said, wiping at the sweat beading on his upper lip, a telltale sign that we were close to the source, aka Prudence. He pulled down the rickety ladder attached to the door.

"You mean 'cute'?" That word always made me feel like a puppy with floppy ears. I pointed at the ladder. "I'll go first," I offered, in case I needed to lend him a hand up.

At his nod, I climbed. I'd forgotten how dust-blanketed the attic was. Wiping my hands off, I glanced around and groaned. What kind of an idiot wore black pants in a dusty attic?

Doc came up after me, his complexion almost waxen. I caught him by the arm and tugged him up the last few rungs. The thought of getting him back down if something went wrong with this experiment made my chest tight.

I looked around the room, trying to ignore my anxieties. If Millie was right and Prudence had been up here for most of her after-life—what a dreary place to spend eternity.

"Well, you are often quite cute," Doc said, picking up where we'd left off. He swiped at the spider webs trying to ensnare him. "But I was thinking of 'caring.'"

"Caring?" I rasped around the dust coating my vocal cords. "You like that I'm caring?"

"Oh, shit," Doc gasped. He leaned down, bracing his hands on his thighs, his eyes closed, his breathing labored.

I touched his back, bending next to him. "Let's go back down."

He shook his head.

I rubbed his tense muscles. "What can I do?" My gaze darted around the attic, trying to see what I couldn't. Where was she? How close? I tried to shield him with my body even though I knew it was useless.

"Show me where you got the box of teeth," he said.

I'd forgotten that he knew I'd found them up here. I'd hidden that tidbit from Harvey and from Cooper, who now had possession of the teeth.

I zigzagged through the half-rotted cardboard boxes, the dropcloth covered furniture, past the dust-coated baby crib frame and old chests, making my way over to the shadowy corner of the attic where the cupboard leaned against the wall.

My mouth now tasted like attic. I should have brought a water bottle along. I could have used it to splash Doc back to the present.

Doc followed, stumbling several times but catching himself, his skin now ashen.

"Here," I said, opening the cupboard door. "This is where I found it. Millie said it had been hidden here since she was a child."

Millie was no spring chicken, so I guessed the box with the teeth and other goodies had been stowed away for at least a half century. Unfortunately, Millie would be spending the other half-century of her life behind bars. I wouldn't be writing any country ballads about Millie's life since she'd been more than willing to sacrifice me in order to appease her girlfriend, the bitch from hell.

Something thumped heavily behind me. I whirled around and found Doc on his hands and knees.

"Doc," I raced to his side, squatting next to him, holding him steady. "Doc, talk to me."

"I need to lie down."

"No!" He might never get back up.

"Just for a minute."

Panic rose from my gut and started climbing my esophagus. "Let's go back downstairs, Doc. We can do this another time."

"No better time," he whispered, and collapsed into me, knocking me back on my butt with his weight.

"Doc?"

His body went limp in my arms, half draped over my lap. I pulled my legs free and rolled him onto his back. Kneeling over him, I lowered my ear to his heart.

Thump-thump. Thump-thump. Thump-thump.

Whew!

Gulping a mouthful of dust, I used my sleeve to wipe away the sweat on his face and began to count under my breath. "One-one thousand. Two-one thousand. Three-one thousand."

I grabbed his hand, his skin felt so cold! "Five-one thousand. Six-one thousand."

Using both hands, I tried to use friction to warm him up.

"Nine-one thousand. Ten-one thousand."

Behind his closed lids, I could see his eyes moving rapidly back and forth. I checked his pulse; it raced, matching mine. "Thirteen-one thousand. Fourteen-one thousand."

Shit! How was I going to wake him? I should have talked to him more about that. "Fifteen-one—"

Doc's hand squeezed mine. His eyelids fluttered open, his dark eyes locking onto mine.

I could have cried in relief. "Oh, Doc. Thank God you woke up."

"Violet," he said, only his voice sounded off, higher, strained. "You have taken too long."

"What do you mean? It's only been fifteen seconds."

"It may be too late." His mouth was moving oddly, like a ventriloquist's doll. "Too many have been freed." His voice had taken on that mid-Atlantic Eastern accent I'd heard come out of Wanda's mouth days ago. Fear scuttled up my spine on spider legs.

I froze, my breath wheezing from my throat. "Who am I talking to?"

"You know who I am, Violet Parker." Doc's hand squeezed mine harder. "Time is fleeting. We must not play such games."

Holy fuck!

"Prudence?" I squeaked.

Chapter Nineteen

I once had a blind date with a good-looking guy who met me at my parents' front door with his ventriloquist's dummy in hand—or rather *on* hand. Trying to be an optimist, I looked forward to an evening full of puppeteer jokes and followed him to his car. I smiled through our three-way conversation over mini-corn dogs and put up with the dummy's suggestive whispers in my ear through the barbecued ribs. But when the apple pie à la mode was served and that plastic hand started moving up my thigh under the table, I knocked my chair over in my haste to escape to the bathroom, where I scrambled out the window and called Natalie to come rescue me.

Kneeling there in the Carhart's attic next to Doc while Prudence used him like her own wooden dummy, I fought that same impulse to scramble out the nearest window and call someone to come to the rescue.

But that someone would be Doc.

I was on my own here with a ticking clock and a dead woman.

"What do you want from me?" I asked, wondering if this were just another nightmare I'd wake from any minute.

Doc's mouth moved before the voice came out. "You need to find the timekeeper."

Time keeper? Did she mean a watch? We had found a locket in that box from the cupboard, along with some cufflinks, wooden toys, and the teeth. But no watch of any kind.

Doc's body jerked, then began to shudder so hard that his heels bounced on the floor.

Damn! How long had it been since he went under? Fifty seconds? A minute? I had to get him back here with me.

"Doc, wake up." I tugged on his hand that still clutched

mine.

He twisted away from me hard enough to pull me down on top of him, my nose bumping into his jaw. I pushed up, trying to tug free of his hand so I could catch my balance and start pinching and elbowing or whatever it took to drag him out of there.

His eyes were closed, his face scrunched in pain.

"Doc!" I yelled. "Open your eyes."

The shudders grew more violent. I tried to force his mouth open, afraid he'd bite his tongue or swallow it, but his jaw was locked tight.

"Come on, baby," I said, yanking my hand from his and straddling him.

Shit! Shit! Shit! What should I do?

An idea hit me. I straddled him and planted my knees on his wrists to restrain his hands. Leaning down, I held his face as still as I could and kissed him. His mouth shook and trembled under mine but gave nothing back. For a second, as I tried to coax his lips to life, I thought I smelled something slightly floral and sweet-scented coming off his shirt, like irises. After a couple of seconds of no response I sat up, searching his face for some clue that he was coming back to me.

His eyes flashed open wide.

"Doc?" I bent closer, trying to see clarity and recognition in his gaze. "Are you okay?"

"Bring me the librarian!" Prudence's higher voice commanded.

I screamed and slapped Doc across the cheek hard enough to knock his head sideways.

His shudders stopped. Between my thighs, I felt his muscles relax, his body sink into the floorboards.

My palm stung. I closed my fist around the pain, ready to swing again if Prudence sat up to bite me.

"Doc?" I whispered, afraid to lean down near his face.

He groaned and mumbled something.

"What did you say?" I asked, cringing at the sight of the red mark spreading across his cheek.

His head turned slowly, his dark eyes blinking open. "I said," he spoke in his usual deep voice, "my cheek hurts like a son of a bitch."

I chewed on my lower lip. "Yeah, I, uh, tried something new this time."

"No shit." He grimaced. "Could you kindly remove your knees from my wrists?"

"Oh, sorry." I crawled off and kneeled next to him. "Do you think you can stand?" *Because I want to get the fuck out of this attic!*

He pushed himself into a sitting position, rubbing his wrists and then touching the pads of his fingers to the red splotch on his face, wincing. "Yes, but give me a second."

My gaze darted around the attic, wondering where Prudence had gone. While I couldn't "feel" her presence, something told me that she hovered nearby. As much as I wanted to help Doc stand, I was afraid to hold his hand until we stepped outside of this damned place.

Over by the cupboard where I'd found that box a month ago, I saw a broom with a wooden handle and pushed to my feet. I carried the broom back to Doc and held out the handle for him to grab.

He frowned at the broom for a moment then turned to me with the same expression. "I know it's dusty up here, but I'm not really feeling up to sweeping at the moment, thanks."

"It's to help you stand up."

"Did I somehow contract cooties while I was out?"

"No, but I don't want to touch you right now."

"First you punch me, then the only way you'll touch me is with a four foot pole." He managed a grin, albeit a shaky one. "I feel like we're growing apart more and more every day, Violet."

I lightly jabbed his shoulder with the end of the broom. "I didn't punch you, smartass. I just slapped you."

"You *just* slapped me. See, like I said earlier, you're so caring."

I shook the broom handle in front of his smirk. "Here, grab it and I'll pull you up."

He latched on and I pulled him to his feet. He stumbled, but held onto the broom handle and steadied himself.

Lowering the broom, I noticed his trembling hands. "How

are you going to get back downstairs?"

"The ladder seems like the best plan of action, unless you plan on flying us out of here on that broomstick."

"Keep it up and I'll beat you with it."

"What are the warning signs of an abusive relationship again?"

I waved him off and walked over to the ladder. "You'll understand better after we're out of this house and I explain what happened."

I also wanted to hear what else Doc had found out, if anything, when he switched places with Prudence.

"How about I climb down first," I said, tossing the broom down before me and then putting my foot on the first rung. "Then maybe I can help you ... somehow."

I climbed down the ladder, grabbed the broom, and looked up at his face as he peered down through the trap door.

"Violet, you need to remove that broomstick from the equation while I'm climbing down."

Good idea. I tossed it aside.

He started down the ladder, pausing partway to rest his head on one of the rungs.

I reached up to help, but hesitated, wondering aloud, "Maybe I can touch your butt," and manage not to open the door to more one-on-one time with Prudence.

Doc looked down over his shoulder. "I'm definitely going to be touching yours."

I grabbed him by the hips, wincing in anticipation of more ghostly chit chat. As soon as he had both feet on the floor, I stepped back out of reach and told him, "Wait over there and I'll close it up."

He didn't argue, just leaned against the wall and watched me with his red cheek and labored breath.

We made it down to the foyer without stumbling or touching. I held the door for him and then locked up afterward, pocketing the key with a sigh of relief.

I caught up with him as he started down the porch steps and wrapped my arm around his waist, letting him lean on me for support.

"Touching is okay now I take it," he said.

"I hope so." If that ghost was still inside of Doc, it would probably be the end for us, romantically anyway. Prudence making a cameo appearance in the midst of sex would land me in a convent.

I glanced back at the upstairs windows. Were the lace curtains moving? Chills rippled up my arms. I swore I could feel *her* gaze on me.

Hurrying Doc along to the Picklemobile, I shut the door behind him. When I climbed inside, I stuck the key in the ignition and then lowered my head onto the steering wheel. My shoulders dropped an inch.

Life was normal again … for now.

Doc's hand on my back made me tighten again.

Prudence?

"Relax, Violet," his low voice lulled me. "You did it. You pulled me out."

I turned my head, letting my temple rest against the wheel, and noticed Doc's olive color returning. The red mark my palm had left didn't contrast nearly as much. "I'm sorry I slapped you."

"Better your palm than your elbow like last time. It took almost two weeks for that black eye to fade." He rubbed his red cheek. "Ready to tell me what happened back there?"

No, but I was ready to gulp some tequila. "You first."

Doc stared out the front windshield at the Carhart house, his expression haunted. "Not until we get back to my office."

"Maybe you should go home for the day, take it easy."

He chuckled and settled back into the seat, closing his eyes. "You're just trying to get me into bed, minx."

Not really, but he wouldn't have to twist my arm. "I'll throw in a massage."

Flirting aside, he looked exhausted, which was my fault for not pulling him out sooner.

One of his eyes opened. "Tempting. I'll take a rain check on that."

"To the office it is then."

We rode in silence, my hands gripping the steering wheel to

keep the tremors at bay. By the time the Picklemobile backfired her resignation in the parking lot behind Calamity Jane's, Doc's complexion had returned to normal.

A glance in the mirror made me flinch—I still looked white as a ghost. Prudence was rubbing off on me.

"You need help?" I asked Doc as he shoved open the door.

"No, but I need you. Come on." He led the way to his door, his shoulders stiff under his attic dust-covered shirt. I brushed off his back as he unlocked the door and ushered me inside.

I walked in front of him down the shadow-filled hall toward the sunlit front room. Halfway there he caught my arm and pulled me to a stop.

"What happened up in that attic, Violet?" His gaze searched mine.

The need to wrap my arms around his waist and bury my nose in the hollow at the base of his neck tugged at me. I took a step toward him, craving the soothing scent of his skin to settle my nerves, like that tequila I wanted. "Prudence happened, and she scared the bejeezus out of me."

"You saw her?"

"Sort of ... but not."

His head tipped to the side. "How exactly can you 'sort of but not' see her?"

"She talked to me."

"But you couldn't see her?"

"No, I saw you. She spoke through you."

He stepped back, releasing me. "How did she ... ?"

"She made your mouth move, only it wasn't quite right."

"Holy shit." He scrubbed his hand down his face. "That must be why—" His eyes narrowed. "How long was I out?"

The moment of truth. "Well, she kind of distracted me." Trapped under the weight of his stare, I lowered my purse to the floor and came clean. "About a minute."

He gave a slow nod. "That explains it."

"What explains what?"

He rubbed his jaw and leaned his shoulder against the opposite wall. "What did she say to you?"

Wrapping my arms around my middle, I thought back to

those thirty odd seconds in the Carhart attic. "She told me that I was running out of time and said something like 'too many are free.'"

His forehead wrinkled. "You need to find a less cryptic ghost to play with."

"I'd rather stick to playing with the living." I hugged myself tighter to still the tremors that cranked up at the memory of talking to Prudence. "She also told me to find a timekeeper, which I assume means some watch, but I don't remember a watch being in that box I found, do you?"

He gave a slight shake of his head. "So, did she just make my mouth move or did she animate my body, too?"

"Well, she made you squeeze my hand, but mostly it was just your mouth. Oh, and your eyes. They moved around like Howdy Doody's." I did an imitation of the old puppet, which made the furrows in his forehead sink deeper.

"Is that why you slapped me?"

"No. I slapped you because I was afraid."

"Of me."

"Of Prudence. Of you not waking up before she hurt you." I paced the hallway. "I tried to yell at you to get you to come back, but you wouldn't budge. So then I had this bright idea to kiss you awake."

"But I didn't wake up?"

I shook my head. "You're no Sleeping Beauty."

He chuckled. "I don't have the hair to pull that off."

"That's when Prudence showed up one last time. She shouted at me to bring her a librarian, moving your lips, which I'd been kissing seconds before. That freaked the ever-lovin'-holy hell out of me."

"I can imagine."

"*That's* when I slapped you." I stopped in front of him, stroking his cheek where I'd left my mark on him. "I'm sorry I took so long to pull you out. You had to relive her death again, didn't you?"

He caught my hand and held it, his thumb stroking my palm. "It wasn't your fault, Violet. Prudence is more powerful than any ghost I've come across."

"Because she was able to take control of your body?"

"That and because she wouldn't let me out."

I thought back to the way his body had shuddered. He must have been fighting to get back to me, to the present. "What happened while you were in her world? Was it different from before or did you just relive the same events in more detail?"

"The scene of her death was the same with one exception—I realized that what I originally thought was fear driving her struggles while her killers held her down wasn't that at all. It was rage."

"She was angry about her family being slain?"

"Maybe. Probably. I don't know. But she was making threats that I hadn't heard the first time because I was so overwhelmed by the shocking acts being done to her."

The horror of Prudence's death still stole my breath. I laced my fingers through his. "You made it through that final energy blast, though."

"Your slap came before it hit." He lifted my hand and kissed the back of it. Then his mouth tilted downward. "There is something else."

"What?"

"You know that box of teeth you found?" At my nod, he continued, "Well, I figured out their purpose."

"The teeth have a purpose?"

"Prudence had several of them in a pocket in her dress. She was holding some in her hand when she was killed."

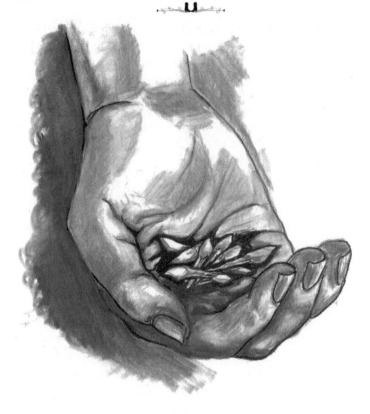

"You mean she was carrying teeth around?"

"I think they were hers."

"You mean her own teeth? Like she'd just returned from the dentist?"

"I mean that puzzle box held *her* collection of teeth."

"Who collects teeth?" That was just creepy, right up there with collecting toenails.

"Maybe they're trophy teeth."

"So, you think she was collecting them all along, storing them in a box in the attic?" He nodded briefly, like he didn't like agreeing with me. "Where did she get them? The local dentist?"

"My guess is a bit darker."

I blinked up at him. "You think she's a killer?"

"Deadwood had its fair share of hired guns back then."

"That may be true, but a killer who collects teeth? Prudence?"

"When she pulled the teeth from her pocket, she admired them."

"Admired how?" He let go of my hand and showed me, holding out his palm and running his finger along it, reminding me of Gollum from *The Hobbit* and his precious ring. I gaped. "Really?"

He gave a single nod.

"Okay, so she's officially a freak show. But she still could have gotten them from a local dentist."

"Maybe, but three of the five canines in her hand had blood on them with pieces of the root still there, like they'd been recently ripped out."

I recoiled. "The prostitute! The one in Cornelius's hotel. Didn't you say her murderers ripped out her teeth before they killed her?"

"Yes."

"Was Prudence one of them? You said they wore burlap bags over their heads, too, like those who slit Prudence's throat. Maybe her own people turned against her."

"I don't know." He leaned his head back against the wall. "That could be, but it doesn't feel right."

"It would make sense about her rage during her death," I said. "She'd been betrayed."

"True, but there is something about all of this that's not lining up. I need to think about it." He tugged me closer, settling me between his legs.

I wrapped my arms around his waist, letting my forehead rest on his chest. The steady thump of his heart was a comfort in the midst of the chaos that was becoming "normal" in my life.

"Those men wearing the burlap sacks with cutout eyes," he said, "they would make great fodder for your nightmares."

I scoffed. "They'd have to get in line behind the Licker."

"The Licker?"

I forgot that I hadn't filled him in on what had happened up at Wild Bill's gravesite, so I gave him the short version—me dreaming again, the darkness, something licking me, me ripping its tongue out.

"Christ, Violet." He hugged me. "That's some horrific shit."

"Yeah, and here's the bell-ringer—my palm smelled like sulfur afterward and had what looked like little spit bubbles on it." I laughed, but it sounded hollow.

He pushed me back and frowned at me. "That doesn't sound like just a nightmare."

"Don't go there, Doc. I already have in the middle of the night and it made me want to hide under my bed." Either I was sliding down a steep slope into insanity, or it was real—all of it. To be honest, I couldn't decide which was worse.

Doc cupped my cheeks, studying my eyes, letting his focus drift down to my lips. He inched downward.

I pressed my hand against his chest, stopping him. "Are you going to kiss me?"

His mouth curved upward into a lopsided grin. "I was leaning in that direction, unless you have an objection."

"Not really an objection, it's just I'm …"

"Not in the mood?" he asked.

"Nervous," I finished.

"You're nervous about kissing *me*?"

"No, I'm nervous about kissing Prudence again."

"Ahhh." He caressed my cheeks with his thumbs. "Trust me, Violet. Right now in this hallway it's only me." His lips brushed against mine. "And you." He kissed me again, slow and soft, melting my fear, my resistance.

I pushed up on my toes and kissed him back with more force, growing frenzied. He tasted salty, sexy, safe. He was my rock, my sanity. My tongue delved and danced with his. I wanted more. I tore at his shirt buttons, hearing something rip in my haste to touch his skin, to have his flesh rubbing against mine, to feel him inside of me, taking me.

"Damn, Boots," he said, his voice rough around the edges. "You turn me inside out when you kiss me like that."

"Like what?" I unbuttoned his pants, yanking the zipper down.

He shoved me back against the wall. "Like you want me to tear off your clothes and take you right here." His mouth covered mine, owning it. His tongue worked a few new tricks that had me writhing against his thigh, which he was pressing into my groin.

"I do," I gasped. "I want you deep inside of me."

A growl rumbled from his throat. "God, your mouth is incredible, so soft. And your breasts …" His lips trailed down my cleavage, his hands cupping, his thumbs circling through my sweater. "They glitter and smell like coconuts. Do you know what that does to a guy?"

I reached down and touched him through his jeans. "The intent was to get you a little excited."

His laugh was muffled by my skin. "I'd appreciate it if you wouldn't use the word 'little' when your hand is on my fly."

He tugged the front of my sweater and bra down and just ogled me. "Damn," he said. "I've never met a woman who makes me so—"

Someone pounded on the back door.

We both froze, looking at each other.

"Did you lock the door?" I whispered.

He nodded.

The pounding rattled the door again. "Doc?" Cooper called from the other side. "You in there?"

I hissed at the door.

"I messed up your sweater," Doc said, adjusting himself before zipping up.

No, he'd messed up everything under my sweater. I fixed my bra so my breasts were back on the inside and ran a hand through my hair.

"Ready?" he asked, grabbing the knob.

"No! Wait." I scooped up my purse and raced toward the bathroom.

"Coming," Doc yelled through the door, unlocking it.

"Okay," I whispered and shut the door, leaning against it. I hit the light and looked at the flushed woman in the mirror frowning back at me.

What was Cooper doing here? And why now, when Doc and I finally had a moment alone?

I heard the back door shut and the mumbling of low voices.

I pressed my ear to the wood, hearing Cooper say my name as they passed by outside the bathroom door heading for the front. Was he here to ask Doc about my whereabouts again? For what? I hadn't done anything lately. At least I didn't think so.

The rumble of voices faded. They must have gone out front. I counted to ten and flushed the toilet, then ran the water for a moment. Smoothing my sweater down over my pants, I shut off the light, opened the door, and headed out to undoubtedly butt heads with Deadwood's cuddly and loveable detective once again.

Cooper's eyes widened at the sight of me.

I'd surprised him. Good. Why was he coming around Doc's back door?

In a blink, Cooper's shields lowered and his usual hardpan expression fell into place. The fading bruises from the black eyes I'd given him at the funeral parlor along with his broken nose added an ominous feel to his glare. "I thought I smelled you."

I hunched my shoulders, ready to crash horns right out of the gate. "What's that supposed to mean?"

"Your perfume. I noticed it when I walked in. Am I interrupt—" he turned back to Doc and cocked his head to the side. "So, that's what happened to your left cheek. You didn't run into *something*, you ran into her hand."

Doc must have fibbed about the red mark on his face.

Cooper's chin swung back in my direction, his gaze accusing. "Are you some kind of sadist, Parker?"

"What?" My cheeks reddened to match Doc's mark.

"You tore his shirt, too," he said, pointing at the button I'd torn loose earlier.

Damn his see-it-all detective eyeballs.

I held Cooper's stare while my face counted down to spontaneous combustion. "It was an accident," I explained.

"Yeah, so was Doc's black eye and my broken nose." Shaking his head, he chuckled. He looked at Doc and pointed his thumb in my direction. "What do you see in this bruiser?"

Doc dropped into his chair and leaned back, grinning up at me. "Well, she has these purple boots …"

Ack! No sex talk around Cooper. That was my cue to leave. I hitched my purse onto my shoulder. "I should get back to work. Call me later."

"You're staying put," Cooper said.

I focused on Cooper, my glare on high-beam. "Excuse me, Detective?"

"I need you to answer a few questions."

"Ha! If you think I'm going to spill my guts again after the way you refused to share information yesterday, then you've been sneaking bags of Mrs. Maryjane from the evidence room and toking behind the police station."

"Really, Parker? Mrs. Maryjane? Did you just get back from touring with the Grateful Dead?"

I sneered back and crossed my arms. "Ask away, Detective, but I'm not feeling very chatty at the moment."

"When was the last time you talked to Helen Tarragon?" he asked.

That seemed harmless enough. "That day in the basement of the opera house, right before you threw me—an innocent taxpaying civilian—in jail."

"Innocent?" He snorted. "What about your friend, Cornelius Curion? When did you last see or talk to him?"

"Yesterday, before I met you in the library."

"You're sure?"

"Yes. Why? What's this about?"

"Peter Tarragon reported his wife missing this morning."

"What?" I looked at Doc, whose frown mirrored my thoughts.

"While she hasn't been gone for twenty-four hours yet, she's on my suspect list now and you know how I feel about my suspects leaving town."

Yes, we'd had that discussion a couple of times now. Interesting that Cooper had added Helen to his list. Was that because of my information on her or something else he'd learned and wasn't sharing? "Why did you ask me about Cornelius?"

"One of the zombies from the play claims Helen got into a newer, black, four-door sedan last night after practice. The guy behind the wheel was wearing a top hat."

Damn that hat!

"That's the last anyone saw of her," Cooper continued. "You don't happen to know what kind of car your friend Cornelius is driving these days, do you?"

Considering that I'd just helped him jumpstart his newer, black, four-door rental sedan yesterday afternoon in the Mount Moriah Cemetery parking lot, I had a vague notion of it, yes.

Cooper's jaw hardened as he watched my face.

Shit.

Chapter Twenty

Saturday, September 8th

Luckily for Cornelius, as well as my future as his real estate agent—heck, anyone's agent—Helen Tarragon hadn't truly gone missing.

Cooper had contacted me last evening while I was cracking the whip on Addy to write her book review for school. He gave me the news that Peter Tarragon had called. Helen had shown up. Apparently, she'd gone on a bender after Cornelius dropped her off at The Golden Sluice bar up in Lead and crashed for the night at a friend's place without calling home.

"So you're saying that Peter cried wolf," I had said into the phone, chuckling at my own cleverness.

Dead silence was the detective's response.

Either someone had filled Cooper's funny bone full of lead at some point in his past, or that funny bone was lodged somewhere deep in his colon. My bet was on the latter.

My Saturday zoomed by, thankfully. The realty gods seemed to have taken pity on me and sent three new clients my way within one afternoon—a "hat trick" according to Jerry, who spoke English as a second language after Sports Speak.

In between talking about potential digs with the newbies, I left several messages for Cornelius, wondering why in the hell he'd been hanging out with Helen Tarragon anyway. She was old enough to be his mother. What had happened to Caly, the love of his life?

Tiffany finally got back with me about the hotel sale extension. The owner was "considering" taking the extra earnest money and extending the final date. I wondered if their "maybe" was a way to get me to push Cornelius into making the sale happen faster. They didn't get that I was already pushing hard on Abe Jr.; much harder and I risked a hemorrhoid, for Christ's sake.

Doc was down in Rapid all day, working with a new client, so I didn't get a chance to slip into his office, draw the shades, and rip his clothes off. Nor could I prod him for more tell-all about his prolonged tour of Prudence's pre-death memory.

As I gathered my purse to head home for the evening, I paused to enjoy a moment of serenity that I hadn't felt in what seemed like months.

Ray had been out with clients all afternoon—another blessing from the realty gods. Looking over at his desk, I wondered what it was going to be like to work under the same roof with both the horse's ass and his nephew. Would they team up on me? Would Jerry run interference? Would Mona have to constantly play referee? Would I foul out due to cramming my tape dispenser down Ray's throat? Would I ever stop using stupid sports references?

Jerry-speak seemed to be contagious.

I stopped by Mona's desk on the way out to leave her a message about Tiffany and the hotel sale, since she was still acting as my mentor on the deal. Even her pens smelled like her jasmine perfume.

"Violet," Jerry called as I tried to tiptoe past his office.

I backed up. "Yeah?"

He wore a pair of wire-rim glasses that made him look like a jock-turned-ESPN-commentator. "I booked the photographer for Monday morning. I'll drive you and Ben down to her studio in Rapid City. We'll need to leave the office by nine."

God, this was really going to happen. *Correction*, a voice in my head said, *YOU are going to let this happen.*

What was I supposed to do? I argued back. The way I saw it I had two options: Do the ads and keep my job for another day—or don't do the ads, which would probably equate to my losing my job and then having to move back in with my parents, who were currently housing my evil sister in my old room. Susan would kill me in my sleep, given a five-minute window and a butter knife, in order to take what was mine—my children. The thought alone made me shudder with a mixture of rage and horror. Charles Dickens' street urchins had fared better than my two would under Susan's care.

"Violet, did you hear me?"

"I should be here by nine," I repeated.

"Well, yes, but I also reminded you not to forget the outfits we bought."

Hiding my cringe took a conscious effort. "Right. The outfits."

"Do you have a little black dress you could bring along, too?"

Yep. It was one of Doc's favorites, but I wasn't sure I wanted to sully it by association with this stupid ad. "I'll have to look in my closet."

"Please do. I have another idea that might offset that jail incident."

In addition to his "bad girl/good girl" idea? Splendid.

"How about I dress in black and white stripes and wiggle my hips while I sing *Jail House Rock*?" I joked. "We could plaster the Internet with it."

Jerry tipped his head to the side. "Maybe, but we'll try my idea first."

Crap. That smartass comment had backfired. I'd better make my escape before he started hooking up my chain gang.

"Well, unless you have anything else, I'm heading home."

He shook his head. "I'll be out of town tomorrow. If you need anything, Mona is playing point guard."

And we were back to sport-speak. I managed to make it out the back door without having to high-five him goodbye. I checked my phone as I crossed the parking lot. It only took one smack of it against my leg for the screen to appear.

Still nothing from Natalie—no voicemail, no missed call, no text message. Damn. I'd hoped my last text about Cooper possibly lusting after Tiffany followed by another message suggesting we spy on his house would have gotten a response.

Pocketing my phone, I climbed into the Picklemobile and cranked her up. The old girl seemed to hesitate a little until I gave her some gas to clear her throat.

If Cooper and Tiffany were really an item and Natalie wasn't willing to take one for the team by seducing Cooper away from that red-headed siren, I'd have to resort to Plan B. Was it illegal to bug a cop's house if I had no intention of using the recording for anything other than to plan my revenge on my competitor?

Shifting into reverse, I sulked all of the way home about Natalie. Since childhood, her specialty had been making me laugh. Life without my favorite clown sucked some of the color out of my world, leaving many days painted in a sad sepia tint.

I hadn't texted anything to Natalie about what I now thought of as "The Prudence Hour"—the show where the guests were dying to get invited and the interviews were a real scream. That was just between Doc and me.

And Prudence, of course.

Harvey's truck was parked in front of Aunt Zoe's house again when I got off of work. I was beginning to wonder if he'd moved in without anybody telling me.

The house smelled like charbroiled meat, making me drool all over myself before I even kicked off my shoes. The old buzzard had dinner ready when I strode into the kitchen—steak, salad, and roasted potatoes with a tart lemon meringue pie for dessert. Beaver Cleaver's dad had never had it so good. I could get used to this kind of treatment way too fast, which would mean I'd be popping buttons on my pants in no time.

After dinner, I cornered Aunt Zoe while we were alone in the kitchen sharing dish duty. "Do you think it bothers Miss Geary that Harvey is sleeping across the street from her?"

Aunt Zoe shrugged. "Judging from that sporty black Jaguar parked in her garage night after night, I think Miss Geary has her feet in the air too much to spend her time worrying about where Harvey is."

"Aunt Zoe!" I gaped in fake outrage at her, and then ruined it by laughing.

"What? We should all be so lucky to have a black sports car parking in our drive every night."

True. I'd take a certain black Camaro SS with white rally stripes, please.

"I could really use something young and racy these days,"

she continued, holding out a dripping dish. "It's been too long since I've had some fun."

I took the wet dish from her and started towel drying it.

"Reid drives a red pickup," I said, risking getting a cupful of sudsy water dumped over my head. "It's not racy, but it's big and tough." When she didn't reply, I put away the plate and added, "It may not be as fast out of the gate as those young sporty cars, but I'll bet it handles well and rides smooth."

Aunt Zoe held out the last plate for me to dry. "I don't like red."

Liar. "Why not?"

She pulled the drain plug harder than necessary. "Because it means danger."

"It also symbolizes vitality," I said.

"And anger."

"True." I put the plate away and closed the cupboard door. "But also passion and love. I think you could use some red in your life again."

"No." Her tone was crisp, final.

I tossed the towel on the counter and crossed my arms. "Why not?"

"Because I'm not going to go through that again."

"Through what?"

She grabbed the towel and dried her hands. "Falling for that son of a bitch."

Now we were finally getting somewhere. "He wants you back."

"What he wants is something that used to be here. That's gone now. He just hasn't accepted it yet."

I frowned at her. "We're talking about your heart, right?"

"Yes, we're talking about my damned heart. I'm not going to let him hurt me again, Violet, so let's nip any starry-eyed matchmaking ideas you have in the bud right now."

"What did he do to you?" I asked.

"He wouldn't marry me."

My eyes widened. "Did you ask him?"

"In so many words."

"What was his reason for saying no?"

"His wife."

"What!" Had they been having an extramarital affair?

"I should clarify—she was his 'ex' wife by that time."

"What about his ex-wife made him say no? Were they reconciling?"

"No. That's what really burned. He told me he didn't know if he'd ever be able to settle down again after the hell she'd put him through."

"How long had they been divorced when you asked him?" I asked.

"Six months, but they were still fighting over things then, including custody of his kid."

Reid was a dad? Wow! I would have pegged him for the child-free, good-time firefighter with a string of hot women lined up on his doorstep just waiting to check out his hose.

"So, that's why you were gun-shy with the art gallery owner who was just coming off a divorce."

She nodded.

"Reid refused your proposal and then what? You two went your separate ways?"

"Not quite. He refused me and then I let him share my bed for three more months before I wised up and kicked him out of my life for good."

"I always assumed you didn't want to get married."

"No, I was waiting for the right guy to come along. But now I'm happy with how things turned out. I just wouldn't mind a black sports car in my drive every now and then to take the edge off."

"Can you honestly tell me that you have no feelings left for Reid?"

"No, I can't honestly tell you that, which is why I'm not going to give him the slightest chance of getting anywhere near my heart again. He's addictive as all get out, and breaking that habit stung like hell last time."

Layne ran into the kitchen, his cheeks all pink, his eyes practically glowing with excitement. "Aunt Zoe, you have to come see this show on Vikings."

"Vikings? Oh, man, I love those big, hairy, burly guys," she said, winking at me.

"Come on," Layne said. "They're showing how they'd use the skulls of their enemies to drink with."

"Cool." She squeezed my forearm. "Thanks for listening, kiddo."

I covered her hand and squeezed back. "Anytime you feel like talking about cars, I'm all ears."

Layne tugged on her other hand. "Can we watch *The 13th Warrior* when this is over?"

She followed after him. "Let's see, Antonio Banderas, Vladimir Kulich, and Omar Sharif all in one film? I think that sounds absolutely wonderful for tonight."

My cell phone buzzed in my sweat jacket pocket. I checked the screen, which was actually working at the moment.

Doc had sent a text: *Working late. Staying in Rapid City tonight. Want to see you tomorrow. Preferably without clothing.*

Speaking of black sport cars … I typed back: *Clothing stays on until you answer one question. Got a minute?*

Got five, he replied.

I hit the Call button and stepped outside on the back porch, closing the door behind me. The half-moon lit the back yard in pale silver tones.

"Hey, tiger," he answered.

"Pulling an all-nighter?" My sweat jacket did little to offset the cold mountain air. I hunched my shoulders to keep warm.

"This client inherited a nightmare," Doc said. "We're talking boxes full of statements and receipts in the attic with no clear explanation as to what's what. I'm going to put in another four hours or so, and then crash and finish up in the morning."

"Hmmm. Sounds sexy. Wish I could be there."

"If you were here, it would be sexy, but I wouldn't get any work done. So, what's your one question?" he asked.

"It may actually be more than one."

"Whatever it takes to get you naked."

Ahhh, true romance. "How well do you know the librarians at the Deadwood library?" He'd spent enough time there that I figured he should have their kids' and grandkids' names memorized by now.

"I know some basic information and a few financial details, why?"

I'd forgotten that one of the librarians was also one of his clients. "Are any of them into ghosts, medium-ship, or something else having to do with the occult?"

"Not that I've noticed."

"Any funky tattoos or jewelry?"

"The one lady who wears jewelry usually has on something that has pearls on it, but no pentagram, lockets, or goats-morphing-into-pigs accessories."

"Ugh," I said, shivering. "Don't remind me of Lila and her freaky tattoo."

"What's this all about?" Doc asked.

"I was thinking about Prudence's last demand."

"Remind me what she said."

"To bring her 'the librarian,'" I told him. "Do you know any of the Lead librarians at all?"

"Enough to say the same—none of them show any outward signs of interest in the paranormal world. But that doesn't mean they aren't."

"Right. One of them could be hiding something." Or maybe Prudence didn't mean an actual *librarian*. I paced across the porch and back. "Is there any secret test I could use to tell if someone is a medium?"

His full-bodied laughter warmed my chills. "No, Violet, not that I know of."

"Damn. How does one go about asking that kind of question without appearing to be off her rocker?"

"One doesn't, that's how. Give me time to finish down here and catch up with a few other clients tomorrow and then we'll put our heads together."

I nodded to nobody in the darkness. "Fine but when do we get to put our bodies together again?"

"Keep it up, Violet. You're going to make it hard to work."

"Well, it does work best when it's hard, although I'm willing to work with it when it's soft. It's just not as much fun."

"Night, Boots," he said, chuckling. "Sleep tight."

I'd rather sleep nightmare-free. I hung up and leaned against the wall next to the door, staring out across the heavily shadowed yard. A cloud that had been covering the moon moved on, the shadows becoming more defined.

Something moved in the semi-darkness near the back of Aunt Zoe's glass workshop, something low to the ground.

My breath caught. What in the hell was that?

My imagination raced to answer, picturing something crawling toward me—an albino with a barbed hook, a zombie with blood-covered jaws, a killer with a burlap sack over his head. I wanted to look away, but my eyes downright refused.

Get inside!

I fumbled behind me for the doorknob, finally catching hold of it, and stumbled inside. Locking the door behind me, I shut off the kitchen light. Then I put my ear to the crack, listening for the sound of footfalls, breathing, moaning, scratching, anything.

I heard nothing.

My breath rattled in and out of my throat.

I pulled the curtain back an inch and peeked out the back door.

I saw nothing, only shadows.

Maybe I'd imagined the whole thing. All of these ghosts and zombies were starting to mess with my head.

I kept watching. The shadows grew thicker as another thin cloud filtered the moonlight. When the cloud moved on, the shadows grew more defined again.

Then I saw it move again, this time on the other side of the workshop, near the door. I pressed my nose against the glass, squinting. Blood rushed in my ears.

Something grabbed my arm. "Mom, what—"

I screamed.

Addy screamed back at me as my knees gave out and I slid to the floor.

Harvey came busting into the kitchen and hit the lights. "What the hell is going on out here?"

I blinked up at his grizzled face. "I saw something out by Aunt Zoe's workshop."

He grabbed a frying pan off the rack and a flashlight from the cupboard over the fridge next to the liquor. Yanking open the back door, he stormed out into the night.

"Harvey, wait!" I scrambled to my feet and peered out after him through a crack in the door.

"Well, I'll be a son of a gun," he said, standing on the bottom porch step. "You did see something."

I tucked Addy behind me. "What is it?"

He disappeared into the yard, returning a moment later with Elvis tucked under his arm. A big grin hung on his cheeks. "Looks like an attack of the killer chicken."

I closed my eyes and rested my head back against the wall. Christ, I was losing it. What happened to the good ol' days a couple of months ago when a shadow was just a shadow, nothing more?

"You okay, Mom?" Addy asked, touching my forehead with her cool palm, checking my temperature.

"No. I'm definitely, one hundred percent NOT okay." I opened the cupboard above the fridge and grabbed the half-empty bottle of tequila.

Chapter Twenty-One

Sunday, September 9th

The world had turned on its side.

No, wait, it was just me. I lifted my head off my pillow long enough to groan and let it fall back down.

What was wrong with me?

My gaze darted around the room, landing on the bottle of tequila on my nightstand. Make that the three-quarters-empty bottle of tequila.

Oh, my God, what had I done?

Then I remembered—that damned chicken clucking around in the shadows, scaring the crap out of me. I'd taken the bottle of tequila to my room to calm my nerves, worrying about how to keep my kids safe in a world with creepy ghosts, killer albinos, and body-dumping zombies. After a few swigs too many, followed by some texts to Doc and someone else I couldn't remember—maybe Natalie—I'd passed out.

I groaned. Nice irony. So much for being a great protector. Good thing Harvey and his shotgun were practically living here now.

I pushed myself up to a sitting position, sat there for several seconds while the room spun and rippled, and then stumbled to the bathroom where I hugged the toilet for a bit. Brushing my teeth had me bending over the toilet again, so I settled for a swish of minty mouthwash and then slid my shoulder against the wall for support all of the way back to my bedroom.

A look at the clock made me groan again. Dang, I needed to get into the office. I had some paperwork to do, Jeff Wymond's and Cooper's places to show to some new clients, my boyfriend's ex-girlfriend to call, and one frustrating Abe Lincoln doppelganger to track down.

But my bed looked so soft.

As if on cue, a small chicken feather, more like a tuft of down, floated in from who knew where, landing gently on my quilt.

Just five more minutes, I thought as I fell face-first onto the bed. Make it ten, I told my internal alarm keeper …

… I blinked awake, the soundtrack of screams and evil laughter and pain-laden moans that had been playing in my head stopped in an instant, leaving my ears throbbing.

I sat up, swallowed another bout of nausea, and then glanced at the clock.

"Oh, crap," I whispered, blinking at the number eleven. My internal alarm keeper was fired! I needed to dive into a phone booth and turn into Superwoman, because I had a client showing up at my desk at noon. I stood up and immediately sat back down.

Okay, maybe I should call first and then hurry second.

I grabbed my cell phone from the nightstand. Five voicemails waited for me, four of them from Mona, one from Doc.

Damn, damn, damn!

I called Mona's number and got her voicemail. "Hi, Mona. I'm sorry I didn't call in sooner, but I was … uh … ill this morning. Give me a call back when you have a moment. I'll be there soon; I just need to shower first."

Forty-five minutes and two ibuprofen later, I dropped my purse on my desk and practiced smiling at the empty chairs across from me. It felt stiff on my face, but doable.

"Blondie!" Ray's voice boomed behind me, inspiring a bolt of pain to ricochet through my skull, leaving me cringing. "So nice of you to grace us with your presence today."

Mona had passed me in the parking lot on the way to meet a client for lunch, leaving the office empty at the moment except for Ray and me. I didn't even try to hold my tongue. "Kiss off, jackass."

Chuckling, he dropped into his chair and kicked his Tony Lamas onto his desk. "You know, Blondie, you and I haven't really had the chance to talk about that night at Mudder Brothers, have we?"

His cologne burned the back of my throat. Ray gave Stetson cologne a bad rap. Someone from the manufacturer should sue him for sullying their reputation.

"What's to talk about?" Besides, of course, my suspicions that Ray was running some kind of contraband for the late George Mudder under Cooper's supervision—although crates loaded with bottles of mead didn't really seem like contraband.

"Unless you want to discuss how I saved your bacon," I said, referring to when I'd found him tied bare-assed naked to an autopsy table. "Yet you refuse to acknowledge that fact and show me the respect I deserve for saving you from a possible live dissection demonstration."

"Respect you deserve?" he scoffed. "For what? You left me strapped down and you ran away screaming."

"First of all, I wasn't screaming." Well, not aloud anyway. "Second, I left you strapped down because we had company, remember?" As in a huge albino with a barbed hook in his coat pocket who wasn't there to sell me Tupperware. "If I hadn't come along, you'd be just another file in Cooper's caseload."

"If you hadn't started nosing into what we were up to in the first place, I wouldn't have even been on that autopsy table."

I glared at his sneer. "So, it's my fault they figured out you were a nark?"

"Yes."

"How can you possibly blame your inadequacies as an undercover informant on me?"

"Because you distracted me."

"What?"

"I knew you were spying on me, trying to find something you could exploit to fuck with my job."

Well, he had me there. I had wanted to kick his I'm-the-king-of-Deadwood arrogant ass right off the mountain. But he'd have to twist my arm for me to own up to that right now.

"Christ, Ray. You're such a narcissist that you can't even take ownership for your own screw up." I dug through my purse for a tube of lip gloss, trying to act like I was bored with our conversation. "What were you doing running contraband for George Mudder anyway?"

"My actions are still none of your business."

Cooper must have schooled him on that response. "Don't tell me you were doing it for the good of the community …" I continued as if he hadn't parroted my favorite detective, pulling the lip gloss from my bag. Then a thought struck me. "Unless this was some kind of community service you had to do after getting caught breaking the law."

His eyes narrowed, his mouth wrinkling into an ugly scowl.

"That's it! You screwed up somewhere along the line and Cooper busted you." I rubbed my lips together. "The question is, was the screw up from some illegal dealings with George Mudder, like laundering money or running drugs? Did Cooper give you the chance to be a snitch and take down some bad guys?"

"You've been watching too much TV."

"Yeah? Then why is your eye twitching?" I asked.

"Good try, Blondie."

"No, seriously, your eye is twitching." Undoubtedly because I was hitting the mark.

He touched the corner of his eye.

Pulling a small makeup mirror from my desk, I checked my lip gloss. "I'm beginning to wonder if I was wrong about what I told Detective Cooper."

"About what?"

"You and Jane."

"What about us?" His voice sounded downright snarly.

I placed the mirror back in my drawer and shut it, and then faced him. "That she had sex with you out of desperation."

His feet hit the floor with a *thud*. He leaned forward, his nostrils flared. "You shut your mouth now, little girl, before I shut it for you."

Oh, plucked a raw nerve there, did I? I extended my claws and strummed it again. "Now I'm beginning to wonder if she'd caught onto George's and your game. Maybe someone threatened to kill her if she didn't have sex with you." I highly doubted Jane had been blackmailed into sex, but I couldn't resist adding more insult while injuring Ray's big, fat ego.

His fists clenched, his face darkening to a ruddy shade.

I grabbed my stapler in case he lunged. "There were certainly plenty of empty liquor bottles in her office the next morning. For the life of me, I haven't been able to think of a reason she would allow you anywhere near her even if she was drunk as hell," that was the honest truth, "but blackmail makes complete sense."

I purposely kept quiet about Jane's admission that she was lonely, and how she'd given it up to Ray because of her momentary need to feel attractive and wanted again.

"I said shut your fucking mouth, you little cunt."

"Ah, there's the Ray I know and love."

He pushed to his feet, all bristle and hate.

"What happened, Ray? Did she get caught up in your mess and wind up at the bottom of the Open Cut because of it?"

Was there an albino or two mixed up in this?

He took a step toward me. "I should wring your scrawny ne—"

The bell over the front door jingled.

"Lucky girl, Blondie," he said through clenched teeth. "Saved by the bell."

He turned, plastering a big schmoozing smile on his over-tanned face. "Howdy, folks. If you're looking for your dream house, you've come to the right place."

Back off, dickhead.

I waved my new clients over to the chairs opposite my desk, and then squeezed my trembling hands together in my lap. "It's good to see you both again. Would you like some coffee or tea?"

Or a house in Central City with a brand-spanking new garage roof?

* * *

My day had started off with my hugging the toilet and ended with my spanking the chicken.

Well, I never actually made contact with Elvis's butt, since she outran me when I chased her out of my bedroom and down the stairs. But the intention was there after finding her yet again roosting in my closet.

The doorbell rang as I hit the bottom step. "I'll get it," I yelled to Aunt Zoe, who was still clanging around in the kitchen long after supper was over. I figured tonight's ringer had to be Harvey. He'd left a message with Layne before I got home saying he'd be over later this evening after his hot date.

"So, did you get to second base?" I asked as I opened the door.

Cooper stared back at me through the screen door. "I don't believe that's any of your business, Parker," he answered.

My neck warmed. "I thought you were your uncle."

"You keep up on my uncle's sex life, do you?"

"No, your uncle won't shut up about his sex life. I don't have much choice without earplugs."

"Are you going to let me inside?" he asked.

"I don't know. Are you going to arrest me?"

"No, I've done that once this week. I don't want the thrill of it to get old too fast."

"Funny man. I'm beginning to understand why your shirts are full of bullet holes. Why have you decided to grace my front porch with your presence this evening, Detective?"

"I'm not going to talk to you through a screen door."

"Fine." I grabbed my sweat jacket off the coat tree next to the door and stepped outside, closing the door behind me. "So, what have I done now?"

"What were you doing at the Lead library today?"

My mouth fell open. How did he know I was there? I hadn't even told Doc earlier on the phone about my visit to Lead's library, which just so happened to sit conveniently next to the opera house. "Are you having me followed?"

"No, one of the guys from the station was in there visiting his wife who volunteers as an assistant librarian."

"His wife is an assistant librarian?" Hmmmm.

Cooper gave a nod.

My head filled with questions, which I kept to myself. Was she the "librarian" Prudence wanted me to bring to her? If so, why? Was she into the occult like Lila and Millie had been? And if that were the case, could her husband have sneaked her into the evidence room while I was in jail and allowed her to plant that note in my purse?

Okay, so that sounded borderline nutty, but so did a ghost ordering me to bring her a librarian as if she were ordering tiramisu for dessert. My logical brain had left the building after Doc had started being used like a karaoke microphone.

"My reason for hanging out in the library is none of your business." I repeated his favorite line back to him.

His shoulders and jaw stiffened in one grunt. "Excuse me?"

I stood solid under the intensity of his squint. "You heard me."

For a moment, I wondered if I should have grabbed Layne's boxing gloves before joining Cooper on the porch, because it certainly looked like we might come to blows.

"You're right," he said, surprising me. He squeezed the bridge of his nose above the swollen area, grimacing. Then he dropped his hand and when he looked at me, all of the rough ridges and sharp angles on his face had softened. "But here's the deal, Parker. Over the last few months, I've had citizens getting murdered and others going missing, some finding body parts hanging in trees, and some telling me bizarre stories about albinos and zombies."

Shivering in the cool night air, I found myself wishing I'd had no part in the farce. "Did you ever figure out whose foot that was?" I asked, referring to the severed foot Layne had found back in July, hanging from a tree with a sprig of mistletoe stapled to the toe.

"Not yet, but I have a few theories."

"What are they?"

"Not your business," he answered. "Anyway, more often than not, you're connected to these events, one way or another. Or—" he held up his hand when I started to object. "Or you seem to have information about things that you shouldn't, and I don't understand how you know what you know, but you do."

Behind him, a black racy Jaguar with dark tinted windows pulled into Miss Geary's drive. Her visitor honked twice and the garage door opened for the sports car to rumble inside. I tried to peek around Cooper to see who had taken Harvey's place enjoying Miss Geary's sweet tarts, but Cooper stepped into my line of sight, making me focus on him.

"Tonight I came here to find out why you were at the library today, because the off-duty officer who saw you said that while you pretended to be reading a magazine, you were staring at his wife and the other librarian more than seemed normal. This leads me to think you have yet again stumbled onto some piece of information. Something I need to know regarding one of the many open case files sitting on my desk that the chief of police keeps breathing down my neck to solve."

I doubted that my "Prudence" situation would help him out. In fact, I could see it as yet another reason for him to want to throw me in jail, so I kept my mouth shut about her and said, "My reason for being in the library has nothing to do with any of your cases. I didn't intend to make either of the librarians there uncomfortable, I was just ..." I stumbled, searching for something other than the truth about trying to see any occult-like tattoos or symbolism on their bodies, "... distracted after a bad night."

I could tell by Cooper's pinched mouth that he wasn't buying what I was selling. "If you have any more information on Jane's murder, Violet, I really need you to share it with me."

He'd used my first name. Was he trying to soften me up before he reverted to his sledgehammer approach? "A please would be nice," I said.

"Please." His lips barely moved to let the word through.

"Did it hurt to say that?" I couldn't resist.

"Don't push your luck, Parker."

"If I come across anything, Detective, you'll be the first one I'll call." At his suspicion-filled squint, I added, "I'm serious, Cooper. I'd like Jane's killers to be caught."

He rubbed his jaw, the beard stubble making a rasping sound. A whiff of his cologne or deodorant hovered until a cool breeze replaced it with the usual Black Hills pine scent.

"Good," he said. "Try to stay out of trouble tonight. I need some sleep before I have to rescue you again."

He stepped down off the porch, striding away, leaving me

sputtering.

"Again?" I said to his back. "Was I drugged the first time? Because for the life of me, I can't remember *you* ever rescuing *me*."

At the end of the sidewalk, he looked back. "Keep your nose out of Ray Underhill's business when it comes to the Mudder Brothers case," he ordered, pointing in emphasis.

Ray! That big, orange-faced tattletale!

"You keep your nose out of my life, Cooper!"

I swore to God, if I had to put up with one more over-the-top, domineering, testosterone-filled alpha male, I was going to start conversations with my freaking foot.

Chapter Twenty-Two

Monday, September 10th

Here it was only two o'clock in the afternoon and I'd already been to hell and back again.

It had all started this morning when Addy had woken up on the wrong side of the bed. By that, I meant she had somehow managed to sink down into the space between her bed and the wall, trapped in a cocoon of blankets. Her screams for help had me doing the broad jump from my pillow, pulling my groin muscle in the process. With all of my worries and nightmares about someone coming to hurt my family, I didn't need much help in fearing the worst upon a shriek-filled wakeup.

Tripping over Elvis in the hall and banging my knee on the floor hard enough to leave a big, shiny bruise hadn't helped smooth my ruffled feathers. I'd pulled Addy out of her tomb just in time to hear Layne hollering downstairs, "Fire! Fire!"

Addy and Harvey followed me to the scene, all of us arriving in time to see Layne douse the flames coming out of the microwave with Aunt Zoe's full, gallon-sized tub of flour. In the aftermath, the kitchen looked like a fresh coat of snow had fallen. It was going to take hours of scouring to return everything to its normal finger-smudged sparkle.

I'd managed to refrain from biting Layne's head off by stuffing four chocolate chip cookies in my mouth at once. Only a male would choose to have bacon and cheese flavored popcorn for breakfast. For a smart kid, Layne needed to pay more attention to the damned suggested cooking time.

All of the good times at home had made me five minutes late getting to work and left me smelling like burned bacon popcorn, which oddly enough soothed my boss and had Benjamin licking his lips. There just might be a marketing angle there—rubbing cheddar and bacon on my wrists and neck before taking a male client to see a house.

My good times were short lived, though. The photo shoot had been right up there with being put to the rack. Bright lights, multiple coats of makeup and hairspray, lots of loud coaching from the sidelines by Jerry: "Make your lips more pouty," and "Fluff your hair more," and "Pull your shoulders back further; you need more lift."

Jerry just didn't get that my lift had left town after nursing two babies at the same time. It would take helium-filled implants to make them as perky as Tiffany's.

The final straw from my boneheaded boss was, "Think like Marilyn Monroe. Act like Monroe. BE Monroe." At which point I was so frustrated with the man that I lay down and played dead until I noticed the photographer was taking pictures of me even then. Where had Jerry found the camera-happy monkey? The necrophilia wing of Satan's lair?

Ben had acted suave and cool through it all, charming the photographer, all the while playing 007 to my Mary Goodnight. Even now, here at Calamity Jane's, he and Ray leaned back in their chairs, smirking it up as Jerry showed me how to sway my hips while I walked. He was prepping me for the "Runway for Run-aways" charity event he'd signed me up for as the representative for the office.

Jerry's marketing schemes seemed to have no boundaries. Just my luck, he'd picked me to be his Girl Friday, like one of my favorite films from the 1940s. Only Jerry was no Cary Grant and I didn't have the "lift" or the hips to pull off Rosalind Russell.

"Lead with your right foot, Violet," Jerry said. "Like this."

I tried not to scowl at him. I'd lead with a foot, damn it, right up his yin-yang.

"You see how I shift my hips with each step?" Jerry asked.

"Yeah," I said dryly. "You're really good at this. Maybe you should wear the little red dress and three-inch heels and make your lips pouty."

Ray sucked air between his teeth.

Ben chuckled.

"Now, Violet," Jerry said, walking over to pat me on the shoulder. "I told you on the way back up to Deadwood that I was sorry for stepping out of bounds during the photo shoot."

I fought the urge to smack his hand away. "Yes, you did." I shot a sideways glance at Ben, who winked at me.

007 had come to my rescue on the way back up the mountain by pointing out to Jerry that I needed to be treated like a star player on the team, not a cheerleader put out there to make high kicks in a short skirt.

Ben spoke Jerry-speak fluently. I needed to take a few lessons from him because my cursing and growling and rude gestures prior to Ben stepping in and calling a timeout had earned me only frowns in the rearview mirror from my boss.

My cell phone buzzed on my desk. I looked down and saw Cornelius's name. "Jerry, I need to take this." I grabbed my phone and raced out the front door so I could yell at Cornelius in private.

"Where have you been?" I asked in lieu of a greeting.

"Las Vegas," Cornelius answered.

"What? You're in Vegas?"

"My great grandfather passed away."

Immediately I felt like a big, fat, wart-covered toad. "I'm so sorry, Cornelius."

"Don't be. He was too old. We've been waiting for him to cross over for years. I look forward to contacting him on the other side."

"Oh. Okay, uh … when are you coming back to town?"

"I'm not sure. I'm about to go in for the reading of his will. I'll know more later. I wanted to let you know that the manager of my hotel is holding an envelope for you."

"Is it the extra earnest money?"

"No. It's my grocery list for next week."

"You're kidding, right?" Otherwise, I might need a restraining order put on me to protect his bony ass.

"Yes. But it's not a check. It's a series of clues that will tell you where to find the check."

"Please tell me you're kidding again."

"Of course not. I couldn't leave that much money lying

around."

It was a check, not a pile of cash. "You could have called me to come and get it before you left."

"There wasn't much time."

Yet he had time to devise a treasure hunt. I was going to throttle him when I saw him next and jump up and down on his stupid hat.

"I have to go, Violet. They are calling us into the attorney's office now. Good luck with your hunt."

"Wait!" I said, but it was too late. He was gone.

"Shit," I muttered and returned to Jerry's fashion show. Only he was gone and so was Ben, leaving me alone with Shithead since Mona was out showing homes to new clients who'd come by while I was off playing Marilyn Monroe.

"Trouble in paradise, Blondie?" Ray said, picking his teeth with his pinkie nail.

"Nope. Everything is perfect."

"Really? Then why isn't that hotel deal done yet?"

"Go blow a donkey, Ray." I was in no mood to spar with the jerkoff after the morning I'd had. I grabbed my purse and keys. Besides, I had a treasure hunt to begin. *Ahoy, mateys!*

"You know that Ben will outshine you here in every way." Ray apparently wasn't finished with his attempt to sink my ship o' dreams. "He already has Jerry wrapped around his little finger. It's just a matter of time before the boss man sees what a waste of resources you are to this company and fires your pretty blonde head."

I paused by his desk, imagining jamming that pinkie of his right in his eye. "Ah, Ray, that's so sweet of you to call me pretty. Next thing I know, you'll be sending me flowers and wanting to meet my parents."

"You think you're really something, don't you? But I have bad news for you—you're nothing more than a washed up piece of fool's gold, whereas Ben is the real nugget."

This pissing contest regarding Benjamin the Great was going to get old fast. "What's that make you?" I asked him. "Just a flash in the pan?"

"Oh, no, baby. I'm twenty-four karats of pure sales gold."

Twenty-four karats of pure bullshit was what he was. "No, I'd say you're nothing more than gold-plated lead. You look all shiny from the outside, but being around you too much causes irritability, cramps, and behavioral disorders, which might just lead to death—yours, if you're not careful."

"Is that a threat, Blondie?"

I shrugged. "Are you scared, you poor little baby? Are you going to go running to Detective Cooper again?"

He scowled. "What are you talking about? What's Cooper got to do with this?"

"I'm talking about you ratting to Cooper that I was picking on you about the Mudder Brothers mess."

"I didn't say a damned word to Detective Cooper."

"Right."

"You can believe whatever you want in that marshmallow brain of yours, Blondie, but I didn't invite the law to the table. This is private—just between you and me."

I stared at the weasel's face, looking for a cheek twitch or shifty gaze, something showing he was lying. He glared back, all beady-eyed. Unfortunately, I loathed him too much to stomach staring at him for long.

If he hadn't told Cooper about yesterday's bout with Ray, who had? I'd texted Natalie about it and mentioned it to Doc, but neither of them would have gone to Cooper. Or did Cooper have some kind of sixth sense when it came to my topics of conversation? Maybe he'd planted a recording device somewhere on me—or in my purse while I was at the jail. Hell, if someone could slip an anonymous note in it, Cooper could easily bug it.

"Fine. Just be sure to keep your mouth shut in the future." I hitched my purse further up my shoulder and headed for the back door.

"Or what?" he called after me.

"Or I'll tell Jerry that you are hiding a criminal record with the help of Detective Cooper."

"Those records are sealed."

I turned around and pushed open the back door with my butt. "Are they? Are you sure about that, Ray?"

Without giving him a chance to reply, I walked out the door

and pulled it shut behind me. I slid behind the wheel of the Picklemobile and sat there for a second, decompressing.

Ray had to be lying. The weenie undoubtedly contacted Cooper, probably worried about my finding out what was in those sealed records of his. Damn, I'd love to find out what he did that made him agree to be Cooper's bitch in such a risky operation.

I keyed the old pickup to life.

But I'd have to solve that mystery another day. Right now, it was time to go find a treasure. Maybe I should see if Addy would be willing to trade Elvis for a talking parrot.

* * *

"Treasure hunt, my ass," I grumbled aloud as I drove up the street toward Aunt Zoe's.

I'd just wasted my whole afternoon following breadcrumbs, searching up and down through the laundry room, the basement storage room, the haunted stairwell (which gave me goosebumps even without having a sixth sense), and an amazing number of hidden closets and storage areas in The Old Prospector Hotel. When I'd finally found the stupid envelope Cornelius had left, it'd been empty. EMPTY!!

To fuel my internal inferno, Abe Jr. wasn't answering or returning my calls. I wasn't just a little irritated now, I was ready to coat Cornelius in honey and chain him to a fence in that bear park south of Rapid.

I'd stopped back at the office to grab some information Mona was supposed to leave me and ran into Jerry and Ben back from playing basketball at the Rec Center, smelling like a mix of sweat and cologne. While I pretended to research listings on my computer, I eavesdropped on their back and forth about different college basketball teams stats and who they predicted would make it to the finals this year. It wasn't fair. Ben and Jerry were formed from the same mold. How could I possibly hold my own against Ben? Short of keeping Jerry happy with all of his lame-brained, crappy marketing ideas, I had nothing to offer.

I'd stayed later than usual, wanting to look industrious, hating that I was missing homework time with my kids without knowing if my time was well spent or just a waste and I'd be out of a job soon anyway. I pounded on the steering wheel. Damn Cornelius and Jerry and Ray and Cooper and all the other obtuse, overbearing, pushy males in my life.

The sun was low in the sky by the time I slowed for Aunt Zoe's drive. I frowned at my mother's red Prius in the waning daylight. It hogged the driveway, so I was forced to park on the street behind Harvey's Ford. I blinked at the fluorescent yellow bumper sticker on his tailgate that read, "Wanted: Bow-legged Women Who Like to Go Swimmin'." I didn't remember seeing that on there before.

Trudging up the sidewalk, I hummed the tune that inspired Harvey's bumper sticker. Great. That was just what I needed—to spend the evening singing about swimming between the knees of bow-legged women.

I let the screen door slam behind me, the loud crack momentarily mollifying the urge to lie on the floor and thrash around while screaming my lungs out.

The sound of Aunt Zoe's voice coming from the kitchen reminded me that my mother was visiting. I kicked off my heels and checked my face in the hallway mirror, looking for any signs of insanity. Nope, all clear—no twitches, tics, or bloodshot eyes. Well, clear except for the multiple coatings of hairspray and makeup from today's photo shoot that I still wore under the peppering of dust from my treasure hunting adventure at the old hotel. I swore then and there that if my mother made one comment, good or bad, about my helmet of curls or the spider-leg eyelashes, I was going up to my room and not coming out until she left the premises. Good thing I'd left that bottle of tequila on my nightstand.

Time to put on a show. My mother did not have a clue about anything I'd been going through, and today was not the day to break down and get snot all over her shirt about it. I marched into the kitchen wearing a smile on my face that I hoped gave the message that my life was just peachy-keen. The sight of my sister sitting in my usual spot at the table with a glass of lemonade and a chocolate chip cookie in front of her while chatting with Aunt Zoe stopped me in my tracks. My smile crashed down like an anvil on the head of good old Wile E. Coyote.

Beep beep!

Susan, who I'd not-so-lovingly nicknamed "The Bride of Satan" years ago before she'd really pissed me off, stared back at me with her cold, black heart glittering in her big, doe-like eyes. Where was that mean hunter who'd shot Bambi's mom when I needed him?

"Hello, *big* sis," Susan said, emphasizing the adjective with a smug grin. Built like a gazelle, she loved to remind me how short and stocky I was in comparison. She nibbled on one of Aunt Zoe's chocolate chip cookies, truly in character with the rat she was.

Get out! I wanted to bellow at her. Instead, I asked through gritted teeth, "What are *you* doing here?"

She'd apparently forgotten that I'd drawn a line in the sand and she wasn't allowed on my side of it anymore.

Aunt Zoe frowned from me to Susan and back but said nothing. She pushed to her feet. "I need to go check on some pieces in my workshop."

Smart woman, escaping to take shelter before I'd hit the mushroom-cloud stage. She gave my arm a squeeze of support or warning, I wasn't sure which, and then she smiled at the evil concubine. "It was nice to visit with you, Susan. I hope that new job works out for you."

New job? Yeah, right. Susan went through jobs like they were rolls of toilet paper.

Aunt Zoe closed the back door behind her, leaving me alone with *her*. With no mother, father, or neighborhood police officers around to hold me back, I considered sitting on her skinny ass and squishing wads of Addy's chewing gum in her long, straight, black hair.

Loathing was too nice a word for how I felt about my younger sister. Since we'd been children, she'd operated with the mindset of what's hers was hers, and what's mine was hers to destroy. Her list of crimes against me was so long that she'd topped Santa's naughty list every year since she was four years old. As far as I was concerned, coal was far too good for her.

My mother, on the other hand, still held a soft spot for her baby girl. She refused to see Susan's behavior as devious or malicious, labeling her instead as confused and prescribing "more love than normal" as a fix. I'd prefer to show Susan that love from the distance between Earth and Mars.

Having Susan here in my favorite kitchen, my sanctuary, on a day as shitty as today made me wonder if Aunt Zoe had ever found those shotgun shells she'd been planning to use to shoo Reid out the door.

Without even trying to hide my irritation, I pointed at the car keys on the table next to her cookie. "You should go back down to Mom and Dad's now."

Susan sniffed at me, her expression smooth and serene in the snarling face of my wholehearted hostility. "I'll have you know that Aunt Zoe is my aunt, too, even if we don't share the same DNA."

Susan was my mother's child with another man. When I was three, my parents had been having serious problems with their marriage. So much so that they had separated and my father had moved into an apartment, leaving me and my older brother, Quint, with my mom. Over the next year, my mother dated a few men, some I remembered, some I wished I didn't. One from the latter category ended up fathering a child, only he hadn't wanted to be a dad and had left my mom pregnant and alone.

When my father had found out, he had brought Mom flowers and suggested they work out their differences. They had, and he had stepped in to take the daddy role. Years later Quint had filled me in on all the details since I'd been too young at the time to understand what was happening. Per Mom's order, we all had kept Susan's dad's true identity a secret—until the day my sister pushed me too far. Ever since then, when I wasn't throwing knives at her pictures, I was stabbing myself with guilt for blowing Dad's cover.

Since Aunt Zoe was my father's sister, Susan had distanced herself from Zoe after she had learned the truth about her parentage. I'd be the first to admit that I couldn't have been happier about that. Aunt Zoe was *my* favorite aunt, and this chasm between her and Susan gave me a haven free of Susan's malicious ploys.

"Fine," I conceded, "Aunt Zoe is your aunt, too. What are you doing up here?"

"I wanted to see my niece and nephew."

The mother bear in me stood up on her hind legs. "Why?"

"I miss them."

Liar. Susan only cared about Susan. Usually, any time spent around my kids was solely for the purpose of benefitting her in some way—like that time she shoplifted two pairs of expensive panties by stuffing them in Addy's winter coat pockets and sweet talking the security guard while Addy skipped right by.

"What's your angle?" I prodded.

"Honestly, big sis, you are so unattractive when you sneer like that. And you really should see someone about straightening that bird's nest on your head. I have a girl down in Rapid who could probably help you."

After my day of fun and games, my tolerance for Susan disintegrated in a heartbeat.

"Go home," I ordered.

Susan leaned back in the chair, one of her over-plucked eyebrows arching. "I don't get all of this hostility you're harboring. I'm the one who should be full of rage still, but do you see me treating you so rudely?"

Oh, that was rich. I leaned closer, whispering, "Have you forgotten what you did with the father of my children? Because I certainly *never* will."

"Jesus, Violet. You still can't see that I did you a favor? Rex wasn't father material. The man hasn't ever paid you a single penny of support."

That was because he'd signed a paper giving up all rights to both kids after they were born, but I wasn't going to go down that road with the bitch from hell.

"If you would have just let me have him," she continued, "I could have made sure all of you were taken care of until the kids became adults. But no, you had to go and scare him away."

Wow, and here all of these years I'd figured she'd screwed Rex just to hurt me. Turned out she was being altruistic. Silly me for being upset about my sister seducing the guy of my college dreams and father of my children out from under me.

"Get out now," I repeated, hearing a scuffling noise behind me. I glanced back and caught Harvey peeking around the corner. He gave me a finger-sign that showed he had my back; or he was making fun of my eyelashes again, I wasn't sure.

Susan took her time standing up. She handed her nibbled cookie to me. "From the looks of it, you like these quite a bit. You can finish it for me."

I thought about giving her a chocolate chip cookie enema with it, but I'd had enough dealings with assholes today.

"So," she pulled on her leather coat, "Do you have any new boyfriends to tell me about?"

Rage blazed throughout my body. I was surprised steam didn't blast out from every orifice in my head. If the whore even stepped one foot near Doc … ·

"Get the fuck out of this house, Susan. Right now."

"Chill, big sis. I'm just trying to make friendly conversation. When I get home and tell Mom how you're treating me she's going to be so disappointed in you."

Mom was often disappointed in me, especially when it came to Susan, so no hardship there. "Well, why don't you run back down the hill and tattle on me."

That reminded me of Ray tattling. Maybe I should introduce Susan to the rat bastard. Did I hate Ray that much, though? Maybe.

"I'll leave after I say goodbye to the kids."

"Make it quick." I followed on her heels to the living room where both kids were immersed in cartoons. Harvey was missing in action.

Susan kissed both of my kids on the forehead. "I'll see you both again soon."

Not if I had anything to say about it. I needed to find someone who could put some kind of spells around the house that would make Susan break into hives every time she stepped through the door.

She paused to smirk down at me at the front door. "What's with the makeup, big sis? You think you're Marilyn Monroe or something?"

I shoved her out the screen door into the semi-darkness.

"Hey!" she yelled.

I slammed the door in her face and leaned my forehead against it. "And stay out," I said, leaving the porch light off to inspire her to seek her next breath somewhere else better lit.

That was it. I'd managed to endure a visit from Susan without it breaking out into another epic battle. I deserved some kind of plaque to hang on the wall.

Damn. What a stinking rotten day from hell. At least it was over and I could hole up until the sun came out and I got a chance to start over again.

I heard her walking down the porch steps and stole a look through the window to make sure she didn't try to sneak around to the back door in the dark. Susan dawdled getting into her car. With the help of Miss Geary's halogen porch light, I could see Susan staring across the street at the black Jaguar sitting inside the open door of Miss Geary's garage.

"Woo-wee," Harvey said from behind me. He watched out the window, too. "That woman is meaner than a buck-toothed wolverine. Kind of sexy, though, I'll give her that, with those long legs—"

"Harvey," I warned.

"But a first-rate bitch."

"That's better."

"Your aunt told me once that you weren't too keen on her. After meetin' her, I think I see why."

"We have a history," I said.

Damn the bitch for coming around my children. Now I was going to have to deal with a bunch of "Why don't you like Aunt Susan?" questions for a day or two.

"Good riddance to her," Harvey said as she drove off. "Doc should have Cooper keep an eye on her, too. She's the kind that'll turn on you faster than a cross-eyed rattler."

"Undoubtedly." I had callouses from years of her fangs digging in when I least expected. Why couldn't she just move to … Wait a second. "What did you say? Doc should have Cooper keep an eye on her, *too?*"

"Yeah. That one can't be trusted."

"Why would you say 'too'?"

Harvey grimaced. "Ah, well …" He licked his lips.

A lump of ice formed in my chest. "Harvey, did Doc tell Cooper to follow me?" Was that why Cooper seemed to be on top of my every move lately? He was getting inside information from my boyfriend?

Harvey stroked his beard, his eyes not meeting mine. "You're twistin' this up all wrong, girl. It's not like that."

"That son of a bitch," I whispered, the pain of betrayal knocking the wind out of me.

I'd trusted Doc with almost every secret I had about the Mudder Brothers, Prudence, Cornelius, and more. How could he go behind my back to the one man in town who was constantly standing in my way, badgering me, threatening to throw me in jail—hell, throwing me in jail? My knees nearly buckled from anger.

"Violet," Harvey took my arm. "I can tell by the way your face is getting all buggered up that you are makin' a mess of this in that head of yours."

I leaned against the wall for support. "How could he do this to me? Why would he?"

"He's worried about you and lookin' for ways to help keep you safe."

"So he sicced Cooper on me? A pit bull with rabies would have been gentler." I tugged my arm free, slipped into my tennis shoes, and yanked open the front door. "I need you to keep an eye on the kids for me for a bit, please."

"Where are you going?" Harvey yelled after me as I crashed down the porch steps into the post-dusk shadows.

"Doc's house. We need to get a few things straight."

Chapter Twenty-Three

The brisk walk to Doc's house in the almost-dark gave me time to throw some punches in the air, practice a few half-assed karate kicks, and curse at the moon several times before facing him. I debated on calling ahead, but I knew Doc would hear the difference in my tone and I didn't want to give him any head start on escaping over the state line.

By the time I reached the sidewalk leading up to his house, the anger, frustration, and heartache that had been all tangled up in my gut had loosened enough that breathing no longer hurt. But after the day I'd had, smoke still puffed out from my nostrils with each breath. Not even the cool, fresh air could dampen the embers still burning inside of me.

Doc's place looked all shut up for the night from the front, the living and dining room curtains closed but for a sliver. I climbed the porch steps and knocked anyway. If he wasn't home, I'd have to hoof it back home and track him down in the Picklemobile.

For a moment as I stood there in the silence waiting to see any sign of life, I wondered if I should have taken the time to shower, scrub the goop from my hair and face, and calm down a bit more before standing on Doc's threshold. At the least it might have been wiser to wait until the lightning stopped crackling around my head.

Then the porch light came on, the door opened, and it was too late.

Doc did a double take at the sight of me. "Violet? What are you wearing?"

The reminder of my morning spent dancing to Jerry's tune fired the embers in my belly. I shoved past Doc and waited in the brightly lit foyer until he'd shut the door before going into attack mode.

"Did you tell Cooper to keep an eye on me?"

Doc leaned back against the door, his gaze searching mine. "Not exactly."

That was not the answer I wanted to hear. I clutched my stomach and clung to what little calm I had left after my day full of slap-downs. It was that or beat on his chest while crying, *Why? Why? Why?*

He continued to watch me in silence, his expression guarded.

"Define 'not exactly,'" I ordered.

"I told him I was worried about your safety and suggested that having someone at the ready to help you might be a wise precaution, especially when I'm not in town."

That made me feel like I needed a freaking babysitter. "Did you tell Cooper I was at the Lead library yesterday?" I asked.

"No. I didn't know you went there."

"Would you have told him if you had known?"

"That depends."

"On what?"

"If I thought you might sneak over to the opera house and end up in some kind of trouble."

Ah ha! There it was. Doc was just as susceptible as Cooper and Jerry to that dominant male gene that came with a complimentary wooden club and a vocabulary filled with grunts.

"Well, doesn't that just beat all," I said. "My boyfriend is working with the cops to keep me corralled."

He jammed his hands in his pockets. "Your point of view is skewed by your resentment of Cooper's authority."

Resentment? He didn't know the half of it. "How could you, Doc? Of all of the people to go to behind my back, you chose the one man in town who is just looking for a reason to lock me up."

"That's not true."

"Bullshit! You already had to spring me once." A snippet of memory played of that day when Doc went back into the police station while I waited in the parking lot. I poked him in the chest, fighting the urge to pummel him. "Is that when you struck the deal with Cooper? Right after you got me out of jail?"

He grabbed my finger. "Violet, calm down."

"Or have you been in cahoots since the poker game?" I tugged my finger free. "Oh, my God, were you part of the reason I ended up behind bars? Was that some elaborate scheme you two came up with to make me think you were on my side so I'd tell you even more about Helen Tarragon and Jane? So I'd take you completely into my confidence?"

I knew my conspiracy theory was far-fetched and I sounded borderline hysterical, but I had thought I was walking on solid ground when it came to Doc. Suddenly, everything felt slippery underfoot with fissures spreading and water seeping up.

His jaw ticked. "Violet, there is no side in this. Cooper is not out to get you. You've made him into a villain in your head, but he's trying to help you."

"Help me? By riding my ass constantly? By threatening to take me to jail every other day? By dragging me into his office and berating me on how I'm fucking up his cases? You call that helping me?" I threw up my hands. "I can't …" I swallowed, trying to loosen the knot of emotion constricting my vocal cords. "I can't believe you went to him, Doc. That you betrayed me like this."

"I didn't betray you," he enunciated between gritted teeth. "I was trying to protect you."

"Next time just get me a guard dog." It might eat Elvis, killing two birds with one stone.

His dark gaze drilled mine. "You joke and make smartass comments about all of this shit happening to you, but you don't understand what you're getting into here."

"And you do?"

"Yes." Then he growled. "Well, not entirely," he admitted and raked his fingers through his hair. "But I witnessed firsthand what happened to Prudence and the young prostitute's ghost in The Old Prospector Hotel. Something tells me their deaths are somehow connected to you or something you've stumbled onto and I can't always be close at hand. I needed help protecting you."

"I never asked you to protect me." If I'd wanted a bodyguard, I'd have Harvey and Bessie at my side day in and out.

Wait! Was that why Harvey kept spending the night at Aunt Zoe's? Did Doc put him up to that, too?

"It's unspoken in a relationship."

"Right, you Tarzan, me Jane. But maybe I like to swing through the jungle on my own, have you thought of that?"

Doc's jaw tightened, his lips flattening.

"I can handle myself just fine," I said.

"Really?"

"Yeah. I've been doing it for a long time."

"So when that albino was chasing you in Mudder Brothers basement, you had that all under control and didn't need me to step in and get thrown through drywall while trying to buy you time to escape?"

Okay, when he put it that way, no, but I lifted my chin, pride at the helm. "I got rid of him, didn't I? Just like when I took Wolfgang out of the equation."

"And then almost burned to death."

"I was working on an escape plan when you found me." Dangling from an upstairs window would not have been my most graceful exit, but I would have lived, broken leg or not.

He squinted down at me. "I see now that I've been under the delusion that you needed me."

I did need him but not as my babysitter. I needed him to love me, which was something I could never say aloud because it sounded so damned pathetic.

"Hold on a second," I said. "So all of this time, you've been with me *only* because you thought I needed you?"

He scoffed. "Violet, you're not even being rational right now."

While part of me knew he was right, I kept pushing, all of the frustrations from my day pouring out, barreling straight at him. "And here I thought you were sticking around because you actually enjoyed my company."

"I do enjoy your company, especially the five minutes with you that I'm granted here and there when you're not busy with all of your other obligations."

I read between the lines. "I see. You like me but not all of the 'baggage' that comes with me."

He cursed under his breath. "You're putting words in my mouth."

"Well, someone needs to."

"Meaning?"

"You don't talk to me."

"I call you every damned night."

"For phone sex." As soon as I said it, the rational side of my brain winced.

What was I doing? I sounded like some needy female begging for scraps of affection. God, I should leave before this ended with me clinging to his calf, begging for him to tell me that he loved me.

"Stop right there, Violet." He pushed away from the door, taking a step toward me. "You're the one keeping me at arm's length, determining when it's useful for me to be part of your life and for how long."

"What are you talking about?"

"You have Harvey stay at your house every night, but all I get is a damned phone call."

"You think that's my idea?" Maybe Doc hadn't put Harvey up to it after all.

My phone rang in my pocket. Speaking of phones. Thinking of my kids, I checked it and could make out Cornelius's name through the black lines. Really? Now? Great timing, Abe Jr., I thought, and sent him to voicemail, stuffing the phone back in my pocket.

"What about Jeff Wymonds?" Doc asked.

"What about him?"

"You let him play 'daddy' with your children."

"That's different," I said. Our kids were friends, and I was just trying to sell his house.

"Why? Because he has experience with fatherhood and I don't?"

I blinked, unsure exactly what Doc seemed to be hinting at here and not wanting to misread him on this front. "You don't want to be a father."

"Says who?"

Says the way he acted skittish whenever my kids were

around. "You're a thirty-seven-year-old bachelor."

"Thirty-nine."

No way. I had more gray hair than he did. "Okay, thirty-nine. If you'd really wanted children, I'd think there'd be a little Doc Jr. or two running around by now."

"Maybe I haven't found the right woman."

Was he even looking for the right woman? Because Tiffany's skinny ass sure didn't scream "mother" material, and I was doing an excellent job of messing up my own kids' lives. Maybe his right-woman radar needed a new battery.

My phone started ringing again. "Damn it." I pulled it out of my pocket and glared at the screen—Cornelius again. *Now* he finally wanted to talk to me enough to keep calling?

Doc grabbed my hand and looked at the phone. "Take his call."

"I'll get back with him when we're finished here."

"As far as I'm concerned, we're done."

I stared up into his hard squint. Did he mean "done" done? Or just done for now? Because as much as I hated him going to Cooper, I wasn't ready to throw in the towel on whatever was going on between Doc and me.

"Let yourself out," he said and stormed past me heading for the kitchen.

My knees wobbled. Shit, that sounded more like done-done.

"Hello?" I answered the phone.

"Violet," Cornelius said around static. "I need you …" He cut out.

I pressed the phone harder to my ear. "Cornelius, are you there?"

"… help me. I'm stuck under …"

Damned this crappy-ass phone! I smacked it on my leg twice. "Cornelius, I couldn't hear all of that. Where are you stuck?"

"I said I'm … pool in the …"

"You're stuck in a pool?" If he was drunk-dialing me from Vegas while whooping it up in celebration from some huge inheritance, I was going to drive down there and kick his ass all of the way back up here.

"No, under the pool … house."

Under the pool … "Did you say the opera house? Are you here in town?" How in the hell did he get back here so fast? And what was he doing up at the opera house?

"Yes!" he answered loud and clear, making me jerk the phone away. When I put it back to my ear, I heard, "… need you to come down and …" he went quiet again.

That was it. Tomorrow, I'd be driving down to Rapid and buying a new freaking phone. "Cornelius? I think I lost you."

"… got stuck down here. Need your help getting …"

"I don't understand. You need me to come pick you up there?" Where was his rental car?

"… just hurry. Oh, and I have your money in my …"

The line went quiet.

I waited several seconds. "Cornelius?"

Still nothing.

I gave up and hung up, stuffing the worthless piece of shit in my pocket. Now I had to go up to Lead and get Abe Jr. out of a pickle. Guess that sounded like a job for the Picklemobile. He'd better have been talking about that damned earnest money he'd stiffed me on earlier.

"Cooper is trying to protect you, Violet," Doc said from behind me.

I turned and found him leaning against the archway between the dining room and kitchen, an open bottle of beer in his hand.

"Protect me from what? He doesn't believe in albinos or ghosts or anything other than bad guys he can actually see and handcuff. He's useless on the ethereal front and you know it."

"He doesn't want what happened to Jane to happen to you." Doc took a swig of beer. "Neither do I."

Why? Cooper was protecting another citizen, but why did Doc care? Couldn't he say one little line that showed this was about more than being some kind of protector? That he was falling in love with me just a tiny bit? That I wasn't out here walking on this tight rope with no net below all alone?

"I appreciate your concern, Doc. But I'm not some little woman who needs a man to stand guard over her."

I hadn't back in the first grade when I punched Georgie

Hopper in the nose for pinching my butt, and I didn't now, even with an albino on the loose.

"I never thought you were."

"Then why did you go to Cooper?"

"Because I don't think you know what's out there, what you'll be up against before this is all over. You may need all of the help you can get, including Cooper."

I hoped he was wrong, but the cold certainty in his voice gave me the chills.

Doc bounced the bottle of beer against his thigh. "And because Cooper told me something about Jane that made me want to join Harvey on your couch every night."

I'd rather Doc joined me in my bed. "What?"

"When they found her, she was in pieces."

I grimaced, holding the back of my hand up to my lips. "From the impact?"

"No. According to the coroner in Rapid City where the remains were sent, Jane was torn to pieces before they stuffed her in a bag and tossed her into the pit."

Oh, my God! The bloody hook. Nausea boiled up my throat.

My phone started ringing again, giving me a distraction that I clung to right then.

"I have to go help Cornelius," I whispered.

"Of course you do. You always jump for your clients. Maybe I should buy another house so I can have you at my beck and call, too."

"That's not fair."

He pointed his beer bottle at me. "Neither is you coming here to chew me out for wanting to keep you safe. Goodnight, Violet." He turned his back on me and walked back into the kitchen.

My phone stopped ringing.

I hesitated on the threshold. While I still wanted to thump Doc for going to Cooper, I could see his point. Maybe I should follow him back to his kitchen and explain to him how shitty my day had been. I could apologize for taking it out on him, say and do whatever I needed to in order to make his eyes go all liquid chocolate for me again. Harvey would watch my kids for the night if I asked.

I took a step toward the kitchen.

My phone rang again, reminding me of my other obligation. *Damn it!*

Fine. First, rescue Cornelius, get that earnest money, and return him to his suite in The Old Prospector Hotel. Then come back here and try to work through Doc's and my differences of opinion, preferably while naked.

If Doc would let me in the front door again.

* * *

I raced home, shucked my pink monstrosity of a dress for a pair of jeans and T-shirt, and lied to Harvey. I told him that Doc and I were "fine and dandy." I couldn't face his all-seeing blue eyes right then.

Then I grabbed the keys and said I needed to go for a ride to get my day's frustrations out, asking if he'd keep an eye on my kids for a couple more hours. He told me he'd already ordered pizza and suggested I use old Bessie and a fence lined with soup cans to take the edge off. Feeling borderline manic, I didn't think holding a loaded firearm in my hands would lead to any happy endings but thanked him for his offer.

I grabbed a travel mug full of cold coffee to keep me going until I could score some dinner and headed out the door. The Picklemobile and I both chugged all of the way up the hill to Lead. For a few seconds, I thought about driving right on through Lead and heading west, toward Wyoming and all of its wide openness. As cowardly as running away from my troubles was, the appeal of punching the gas and not looking back beckoned.

I tried to peel off one of my fake eyelashes as I drove, but it was really stuck. Come on! Had the photographer's makeup girl used superglue?

Cornelius's black rental car was parked behind the opera house in the little lot where I'd been manhandled and handcuffed by Cooper a few days ago. I pulled in next to it and cut the engine.

When I touched the hood of Cornelius's car, it was lukewarm. What the hell? If he had his car here, why did he need me? I tried to recall what he'd said on the phone, but I'd been a little too busy doing a bang-up job annihilating my relationship with Doc right then to focus. Then I remembered something Cornelius had said about "under the pool."

Looking over at the glass doors I'd used when trying to escape from Cooper, I chewed on my lower lip. The lights were on inside the opera house. Was Peter Tarragon there?

Judging from the cars filling the lot behind the building and lining the curbs, I didn't need a Magic 8 Ball to answer that question. The more important question was what were the chances of running into the asshole?

I pulled out my phone to check the time—almost nine. How long until rehearsal wrapped up for the night? Maybe I should wait out here until everyone left and see if Cornelius came out with the cast.

Or I could just send him a text. Duh, Violet.

I'm parked next to your rental. Where are you? I hit Send and waited.

The sound of an approaching car sent me scurrying into the shadows, hiding behind the Picklemobile as a police cruiser passed. I sneaked a peek after it, watching the cop car roll up Siever Street and take a left onto Main.

Whew! That was close. I didn't need to end this Monday from hell with a trip to jail. Jerry would slap me with the remaining four fouls all at once, and now that we'd had a fight, Doc probably wouldn't take my one phone call.

I checked my phone. Still no reply from Cornelius, damn it. What had happened to his incessant ringing from earlier?

My focus returned to the opera house. Did I go into the building and risk running into Tarragon, or stay outside in the cold and wait for Cornelius to come out?

The choice was a no-brainer. I climbed back into the Picklemobile and closed the door, locking it. I just wished I'd brought a warmer coat.

The waiting began. I turned the key and tuned in to an oldies

AM radio station, singing along with Smokey Robinson and the Miracles about teary-eyed clowns. I sent Natalie a couple of texts, telling her about my photo shoot and visit from Susan. Then I played several games of solitaire, but the black lines on the screen kept making me lose. Then I noticed how low my battery was and pocketed it. Flopping across the bench seat, I stared up at the moon through the front windshield and tried to figure out what I should do about my job, my kids, Doc, and Natalie.

Twenty minutes later, having sung along with Neil Diamond, Linda Ronstadt, and Dolly Parton (twice), I still had no answers and was shivering.

Fall nights in the Black Hills required a bit more than a hoodie. Had I known I'd be playing "stakeout" tonight, I'd have come prepared. I also wouldn't have chugged down all of that coffee on the way up here. The ticklish pain in my bladder had almost reached the squirming level.

I sat up just as another police car turned onto Siever Street, heading down the hill toward me. I slid down in the seat, peering out as it turned left onto Julius Street and then right onto Main, where it disappeared from view. Damn, was the Picklemobile bugged?

Checking the opera house glass doors again for any signs of life, I groaned when I found it the same—lit up and empty. My bladder wasn't going to hold on much longer. I slid behind the wheel. "Sorry, Cornelius, but I'll be right back."

I turned the key.

The old girl whined and clicked, but that was it.

"Not funny," I said, and tried again.

This time, it just clicked.

I turned on the dome light. It flickered, dim, barely lighting the cab.

Shit. I'd killed the battery.

Pulling out the keys, I pushed open the door and gingerly stepped down. Standing in the cold air made my bladder even more obnoxious about its needs. The shadows in front of the pickup beckoned. Maybe I could just ... but I looked back at the glass doors. There was a nice, warm bathroom a minute away.

"Screw it," I muttered and stiff-legged it as fast as I could without risking a dam-burst across Julius Street toward the opera house. With my luck today, the doors would be locked and I'd have to go in the alley, which was when another cop car would drive by and shine his light on me. Could they throw you in jail for peeing in public? I wondered how Jerry would spin that.

The right glass door opened with barely a tug. I'd have jumped for joy if my bladder weren't the size of a watermelon. I rushed down the long, empty hallway, crossed over the concrete-covered pool, and climbed the six steps leading out of the old pool area. One of the double doors that bisected the long hallway stood propped open. I passed through, raced by the supply room Helen had dragged me into, and skidded to a stop in front of the set of restrooms.

Jackpot! I tried the women's bathroom, but the door was locked. The men's bathroom was, too. Damn. Figured. Fine, I'd use the bathroom on the next level up, the one where I'd first heard Helen Tarragon's sobs. I continued down the hall to the stairs I'd come down last time I was here.

I could hear the sound of distant voices, both high and low, along with some pounding noises, as I climbed the stairs. But I didn't come across a single soul—alive or undead, thank God. Either would have probably resulted in a trail of dribbles all the way back out to the Picklemobile.

As I reached the top step, I realized I'd gotten turned around in the old building. When I'd made my way to that bathroom before, I'd gone via the opera house lobby. This particular stairwell dumped me out at the art gallery located in the front of the building looking out at Main Street. Frickety frack!

Stopping to cross my legs for a moment, I debated my options—go back downstairs and pee in the alley, or head up the next flight of stairs and see if I could find a bathroom up there. Fingers crossed that my post-children bladder would hold on a bit longer, I climbed up the next set of stairs.

At the top was a wood door with a glass window. I peered through the glass, recognizing the old library from the tour Cornelius and I had taken last week. Back before the big fire in the early eighties, this was where the Lead library had been housed. Now the books and librarians were all next door.

The room was lit thanks to the hallway light shining through the open door across the way. If memory served me right, there was a unisex bathroom in that hallway.

I tried the old library door handle, surprised to find it unlocked. What were the chances? A janitor must be around somewhere, or the room was left unlocked during rehearsal.

Skirting the old librarian's desk, I charged into the hall. The bathroom was right where I'd remembered it.

Sweet porcelain gods! I'd made it.

I grabbed the door handle and pulled. The door didn't budge.

"You've got to be fucking kidding me!" I cried and kicked the door, the effort almost making me pee my pants.

I leaned against the door, goosebumps now coating my skin from the pain. The whirring of the elevator gave me a start, but I had to pee so badly now I didn't care if someone caught me up here.

The elevator ...

The bathroom Helen had been crying in was right next to the elevator one floor below me, I was almost positive. I rushed over and hit the elevator down button, glancing at the set of stairs next to it. I didn't think my bladder could handle another set of stairs without letting loose. The elevator doors slid open seconds later. I scurried inside and hit the first floor button. The "L" button below it was lit up. Someone else was playing elevator tag with me.

My eyeballs were drowning by the time the bell dinged for the first floor. I dashed out the door, made a sharp right, and scurried down the hall to the women's restroom. The door swung open with ease and I could have sworn angels from heaven sang out. I hit the lights and flew into the first stall. I barely got my jeans down before my bladder gave way.

"That was close," I whispered, closing my eyes in relief.

One long sigh and many, many seconds later, I was standing again, buttoning my jeans, when the bathroom door creaked open. Without thinking, I climbed up on the toilet seat and squatted down so my feet wouldn't be visible.

In the gap under the door, I caught a glimpse of white as

someone passed by. At the same time, a strange mewling hum reached my ears. Then I heard a stall latch clatter into place.

What in the heck? Was someone crying?

The main bathroom door banged open, smacking into the tiles next to my stall wall. I barely managed to stifle my gasp of surprise.

A short shriek came from the other stall's occupant.

"Where are you, my little pretty?" asked a high-pitched voice that sounded almost child-like.

Clack, clack, clack … A pair of black boots with steel-spiked heels passed in front of my stall. They looked like something my sister would wear when man-hunting for one of my boyfriends.

The scrape of something metallic along the stall doors made the hairs on my arms stand up.

"Please," a woman cried out, her voice squeaky with fear. It had to be the woman in white who'd come in first. "Please don't hurt me."

I knew that voice. My brain scrambled to make the connection.

Clack.

Scrape.

Clack.

Scrape.

"I won't tell a soul, I swear," the first woman said.

Then I knew with cold certainty and my heart thumped in my ears. It was Helen Tarragon.

Chapter Twenty-Four

Shit.

Why this bathroom? Why now? What was I? Some kind of psychic magnet for damsels in distress? I should have peed in the damned alley.

What was I going to do? My gaze darted around the stall—a roll of toilet paper and a little plastic trash can for tampons and sanitary pads. That was it. I had no weapons, no way of helping Helen short of throwing Harvey's smiley-face keychain and my phone at whoever had chased her in here.

My phone!

Tugging it free of my jacket pocket, I pushed the wake-up button and stared down at my screen. The battery showed a thin red sliver, and the reception was down to just one bar.

Double shit.

The scraping and clacking stopped at the same time. "Of course you won't tell," Miss Spikey Heels said. I frowned at the ceiling. How did I know that voice? "Because I'm going to take that knife from you and cut out your tongue. Then I'll slice the rest of you apart piece by piece as you watch."

I froze. Was she serious?

The mewling started up again.

Hands trembling now, I opened my phone's address book, scrolling down. My finger hesitated over *Doc.* Right above it was *Detective Cooper.* If what Doc said was true and Cooper really wanted to help, he'd better get his ass over here pronto.

I tapped Cooper's name and typed: *Need help ASAP!! Helen in trouble!!!!*

After I'd hit Send, I realized he had no clue where we were. I added: *Girls bathroom main floor Opera H—*

My shoe slipped off the side of the toilet rim. I caught

myself without making a sound, but my phone slipped from my grip. I watched in horror as it splashed right into the toilet, the screen with my text for Cooper on it going black as it sank.

Silence came from the other side of the stall door.

I winced. *Way to go, numb-nuts.*

Clack, clack, clack. The boots came into view under my door. "Come out, come out whoever you are," she said in a sing-song voice.

I had a brief déjà vu of playing a deadly game of hide-and-seek with Wolfgang while his house sizzled and crackled with flames.

Now what? Short of keeling over dead, which sounded tempting for a split-second, there was no escaping whoever was on the other side of the door. I climbed down off the toilet seat and unlocked the door. Using it as a shield, I poked my head out.

My jaw fell open. "Caly?"

The pixie was covered in spikes—from her white-blonde pokey hair to her heels, including a dog collar, wrist bands, and a belt that she had wrapped around her knuckles. For a moment, I wondered if I'd gotten mixed up in some kind of kooky sexual fetish, hide-and-seek game Helen and Caly liked to play. But then I remembered Caly's threat about cutting Helen to pieces and confusion mixed with fear to create an uncomfortable flutter in my chest.

"Well, well, well," Caly practically purred. "If it isn't Cornelius's little friend."

Little? I hadn't been "little" since I got knocked up with twins, and compared to Caly, even in her big girl heels, I was an Amazonian queen.

The handicapped stall door behind the sprite-turned-dominatrix swung open without a sound. My favorite zombie bride crept out, her index finger held to her lips. In a glance, I noticed her veil was missing and her makeup looked smudged. If this were some role-playing farce, Peter was going to be pissed when he saw her.

I focused back on Caly, going along with Helen the zombie because she was less spikey. "Listen, I won't hold you two up. I just needed to—"

Caly reached out and pinched my lips shut.

Funny, I hadn't noticed her long, sharpened fingernails before. Did Cornelius know she had this sadistic streak? Maybe that was one of the things he liked about her.

In my peripheral vision, I saw Helen pull something from behind her. Something thin and—oh, my God, it was a knife!

Surely, it was a prop. It had to be a prop, right? This was what Caly had been threatening to use moments ago. It must be part of their game—

Before I could finish my thought, Helen swooped in with a battle cry and planted the knife into Caly's left shoulder blade.

I stared into Caly's face, waiting for it to contort in agony, for screams of pain to follow. But the only movement was her lips twisting upward in a grin that would have scared the piss out of me if I'd had any left.

"That was a really foolish thing to do, Helen," Caly said and let go of my lips.

How did ... How could ... *What was going on?!!*

This had to be part of the zombie wedding musical play. They must have come up here to practice a scene. That had to be what this was. I just happened to get caught in the middle of it ... so they were improvising.

Helen stumbled backwards, her eyes widening as Caly took a step toward her.

Clack.

I saw the knife lodged in Caly's back. It looked real, but there was no blood around the blade. Dang, the special effects for this play were going to kick ass.

Caly cackled. *Clack clack.*

Helen spun around and tried to escape into the end stall. Caly's hand snaked out and snared her by the hair, yanking her back out.

Grabbing onto the stall door, Helen struggled for freedom. The terror on her face looked so real that I stepped free of my door-shield and reached for her.

Helen craned her neck in my direction. Her eyes were extra wide, fear rimming them. "Run!"

My feet stayed glued to the tiles as shock overrode my

instinct to flee.

Caly grabbed Helen around the neck and lifted her completely off the floor, as if she were nothing more than a Chihuahua.

My gaze sped from Helen's dangling toes and the torn, blood-splattered hem of her zombie wedding dress up to her face. Her skin was ashen, her mouth gaping at me, her eyes bulging.

Holy shit! How did a pixie lift a full-sized woman clear off the floor like that?

"Put her down!" I shouted and took another step toward her.

"No," Caly smiled at me over her shoulder. "Not until I'm finished. Then it's your turn."

Tears ran down Helen's cheeks. She struggled, clawing at Caly's grip. The whites of her eyes were red, her gaze darting frantically before landing on me again. *Run!* she croaked then reached down and jammed her thumb into Caly's eye.

Screaming, Caly whipped Helen into the closed stall door hard enough to break it clean off its hinges.

My adrenaline kicked into overdrive and I flew out of the bathroom.

The door across from the elevator was locked.

The elevator! No, it would take too long. I raced past the stairs that led up and sprinted to the door at the end of the hall. It would take me to the opera house lobby.

A loud crash and the sound of glass breaking rang out from the bathroom.

I slammed into the door to the lobby. It didn't budge.

Fuck!

Behind me, the elevator dinged, the doors opening. What the …? I didn't remember pressing any buttons.

I waited to see if someone stepped out. When nobody did, I raced back and inside, punching the button for the next floor down several times. "Come on, close!" I cried.

A thud came from the hallway, sounding like the bathroom door slamming open. I jammed the door-close button again and again.

Clack, clack, clack, clack.

Oh, Jesus, why couldn't I have been wrong?

"Close, close, close, close ..." I whispered the order to the elevator as I backed into the corner.

Clack, clack, clack.

The doors started to shut. Something big and white flew in, crashing into the wall next to me.

I screamed as the doors closed, shutting me in with Helen Tarragon, who stared up at me with one sightless red-rimmed eye. A long, wide splinter of mirrored glass stuck out of her other. Blood oozed out her eye socket and dripped onto the elevator floor, its coppery scent wafting up to me. I started to retch at the same time as I gasped for air.

Panic screeched in my head, but something compelled me to tear loose a strip of satin from Helen's hem. I wrapped it around my palm and fingers, protecting them.

The elevator dinged, announcing my arrival on the ground floor. With no time to spare, I squinted and reached down with my satin covered fingers, grabbing the broken piece of mirror. It pulled free of Helen's eye socket. The squishy-slurping sound nearly made me throw up all over her blood-covered dress. Trying not to think about what I was doing, I wiped the blade of glass off on her dress and held it out in front of me as the elevator doors slid open.

I stumbled into the dark basement hallway, discombobulated by what I'd just witnessed. Someone had shut off the overhead lights, damn it. Which way was the Picklemobile?

A commotion of *clacks* and *thuds* came from the stairwell to my left.

I turned right, away from Caly. Staggering into a run with my arms out in front of me in the darkness, I smacked into the double doors. With a quick tug, I opened one. The floor and walls in the covered pool section of the hall were lit in an orange glow from the outside streetlights that shone through the glass exit doors. I pulled the door shut behind me and leapt all six steps at once, racing past an open doorway on my left. I was halfway to the exit when I remembered the dead battery in the Picklemobile and slid to a stop.

Something slammed into the double doors behind me at the top of the pool room stairs, rattling them in their frame. My heart nearly shot out through my nose.

Christ! Had she knocked herself out?

The doors shook again. Damn, no such luck.

I raced into the open doorway and closed the door behind me. I felt for a lock, found one on the knob, locked the door, and leaned my head against the cool wood.

My breath came in shallow bursts. As my eyes adjusted to the darkness, I noticed a red light over my head. I looked up at an Exit sign, blinking away tears I hadn't realized had escaped. I closed my eyes and the image of Helen Tarragon's blood-covered face appeared, so I opened them again.

Why? Why would Caly ... how could she ...

The door knob moved in my hand. I gasped and stepped

back.

Something banged outside in the hall.

What the hell was that? Not like a gunshot, more like a battering ram.

Bang!

Then it hit me—Caly was trying to bust through the double doors. Had I somehow managed to lock them? And if Caly was still behind those doors, who was turning the door knob? One of the cast members?

I looked down at the blade of glass in my hand. It wasn't going to be enough. I needed a freaking baseball bat—better yet, Cooper's gun. Or some help.

Where in the hell was Cornelius? He needed to tame his crazy-ass girlfriend. I gasped. Oh, no, what if Caly had killed Cornelius, too. Had he been trapped by her when he called me for help?

Bang!

God, that tiny bitch was relentless. Surely somebody in the play had to hear that, even clear up in the theatre. Where in the hell was everyone?

I needed somewhere to hide before she huffed and puffed and blew down all of the doors between us.

On a long table to my right, I could just make out a bunch of clubs scattered around, some long, some short. A club would do some damage. Or not, I thought, remembering Helen's knife attempt.

As I reached for one of the clubs, my brain caught up with my eyes. I reeled back, covering my mouth. That was no club. It was an arm!

My gaze swooped over the rest of the table, my knees nearly giving way at the sight of too many body parts to count—legs, more arms, a stack of hands, and several heads. "Holy fuck," I whispered.

Bang!

This time, the bang sounded different, more hollow. A crashing noise followed.

Had she just busted through ...

Bang!

She rammed the single oak door left between us. I jerked in surprise, bumping the table of body parts. The arm closest to me rolled onto its side. A price tag hung off the sleeve.

A price tag. I nudged the arm, which rolled back too easily to be flesh and bone.

It was fake. Jesus, it was all fake.

The play! Zombie pieces. Of course.

Bang!

I stepped back, my legs feeling like they were weighted down with bricks. How long would the door hold under Caly's blows?

I had to hide or I was going to end up like Helen. I ignored the voice in my head that reminded me Helen had been trying to hide when she'd joined me in the bathroom.

There were stacks of boxes two and three high, sitting on pallets on the other side of the table. Through a trail between the boxes, I saw a railing. I made my way to it and found a set of stairs leading down into the shadows.

As my foot hit the bottom step, I hesitated at the closed door in front of me. I put my hand on it—cold steel. I'd like to see Caly kick through this sucker.

What was on the other side? Could it be any worse than the crazed pixie coming to kill me? I reached into my pocket, comforted by the shard of glass.

Bang!

Something clattered to the floor above me. A piece of the jamb?

I was out of time. Tugging the heavy steel door open enough to slip through, I stared into total blackness. If Cornelius and I made it out of this mess alive, I was going to beat the living daylights out of him for luring me to this blasted place tonight.

As I pulled the door quietly closed behind me, another *bang* followed by a loud crack of splintering wood.

I felt along the cold steel for a lock or deadbolt, but there was no lock on this door.

Damn. Now what? I couldn't just stand here by the door waiting for Caly to come through it. Holding my hands out in front of me, I took several steps into the darkness. The cool, dry air was still around me, no airflow at all, smelling of musty concrete.

I felt my way along with my feet. Keeping one hand in front of me, I moved my left hand out to my side, feeling for a wall. If I touched anything fleshy at all, my brain was going to burst from an overload of panic.

My fingers brushed over something soft, cottony. I reached over with both hands and touched the edge of what felt like a sheet. I made a left turn and followed the sheet, which seemed to be hanging from the ceiling. The sheet ended perpendicular to a concrete wall, then another sheet was there. I felt my way along the second one, not brave enough to reach behind it.

Ahead on my right, a light flashed. I stopped and stared into the darkness, wondering if I were seeing things. Extreme stress had been known to inspire UFO sightings. After my elevator trip with Helen, I wouldn't be surprised to see a full-scale alien bumbling around down here.

The white light flashed again, in the shape of a big circle, leaving an imprint on my eyes. I felt my way closer along the wall of sheets until I was sure I stood across from where the light had flashed.

Someone sneezed in the dark. It wasn't me. Did killer aliens have allergies?

I tiptoed toward the direction of the sneeze.

The light flashed again, this time right in front of me, from a big hole in the concrete wall. My shoe hit something. Metal clanged onto the floor before I could catch it.

The light went out.

For several seconds the only sound was breathing—mine and that coming through the hole.

"Whoever's out there, are you alive or dead?" said a familiar voice from the other side.

I held onto the rough wall to keep from crumpling in relief. "Cornelius," I whispered, "I can't believe I found you."

"Violet," he said, turning on his light. He looked out at me. "What took you so long to get here? What day is it?"

I resisted the urge to scramble up the wall and smack him upside the noggin. "Shine your light through the hole."

He stuck his phone through, the light from the screen

helping me find the stool and right it.

I crawled up on it, peering through the circle at him. "What are you doing down here?"

"Getting my hat back. That little tyrant hid it from me the last time I came down to make contact."

"What little tyrant?" Was he talking about his psycho girlfriend?

"The ghost of the boy."

Oh, yeah, I'd forgotten about that ghost after all the hubbub with Prudence. So this was what Cornelius had meant by "under the pool." That still didn't explain why he was on the other side of a hole in the wall. "But why are you in there?"

"The little shit tossed my hat in here, so I crawled through to get it. But when I tried to get back out, the stool on this side broke."

My jaw tightened. "Are you telling me I'm standing in a sub-basement of the opera house while a sadistic bitch covered in spikes hunts me down all because of a stupid-ass hat?"

"By definition, I'm not sure this is structurally considered a sub-basement."

As soon as Caly came busting through that door, I'd be feeding Cornelius to her first.

"And I'll have you know, Violet, this hat has been in my family for generations."

If Cooper didn't come to save the day, it was going to be the end of the line for Cornelius and me. He could stuff that in his damned hat.

Wait a second. He had a cell phone. "Give me your phone," I said.

"It's not holding a signal long enough to call anyone."

"How'd you call me?"

"I had two bars for a while. Now it's down to one that comes and goes." He stood on his toes, leaning closer, and whispered, "I think that boy is affecting the electromagnetic waves."

I didn't care about the damned ghost at the moment. I had more actual worries about tyrants who still had flesh. "So this hole is the only way out for you?"

"There's a door at the other end of this crawlspace," he said, "but it's locked from the other side."

"Shit."

"I've had time to consider several possible escape plans while you took your time getting here."

Silly me, I shouldn't have stopped to pee and watch Helen get killed. "It's one hole in one wall," I said dryly. "How many escape possibilities can there be?"

"You'd be surprised. Now push that stool through the hole to me."

I stepped down and lifted the stool. It got stuck partway through the hole, the legs flaring a little too wide at the bottom.

"Buggers," he said. "Why don't you run upstairs and see if there is a skinnier stool somewhere."

"No."

"Why not?"

"Someone up there is trying to kill me."

He was quiet for a moment then said, "I don't get the joke."

"There is no joke."

He shined his phone through the stool legs at my face, as if it were his third eye. "Is there an unhappy ghost up there?" he asked.

"Probably," I said, thinking of Helen. "But I'm talking about your girlfriend."

"My girl—"

The metal door I'd entered through crashed open.

I grabbed Cornelius's phone to hide the light, my pulse returning to warp speed. She'd found me.

"Here, kitty, kitty," Caly called, I could see her flashlight beam swinging around.

Clack, clack, clack.

Where I'd turned left along the line of sheets in the darkness, she walked straight, seeming to pass through a wall.

I made a very quiet "shhh" sound to Cornelius then moved over to the line of sheets, making my way toward the door. If I could just get back upstairs while Caly was down here looking for me, I could run up the street to the police station and get help.

From my vantage point, I could see glimpses of Caly's

flashlight beam through what looked like a large rectangle cut out of the wall.

I tiptoed closer to the steel door, listening to the sound of her heels clacking around on the other side of the wall.

"Come out and play, my little kitten," she called in a young girl voice, hitting a nine-point-nine on my heebie-jeebie scale.

I slinked along the sheets. With just two to go to reach the stairs, I heard footfalls coming down the steps.

Cooper! For once, I felt like hugging him instead of kicking him in the shin.

"Where is she?" Dominick Masterson said as he stepped through the door holding a lantern-style flashlight.

The sight of the up-and-coming mayor of Lead shocked me so much that I couldn't breathe enough to squeak. I sank back behind a sheet, into what looked like a concrete shower stall. His lantern cast soft light through the white sheet, which had a skull and crossbones spray painted on it, along with several bloody handprints and the word *Beware*.

Nice. As if I needed a visual reminder of how far up shit creek I was at the moment.

"She's down here somewhere," Caly called out from the other side of the wall. "I can smell her fear."

Smell my fear? Who talked like that?

"Why are you using a light?" Dominick asked her.

"These contacts you insist I wear interfere with my vision."

The light coming through the sheet dimmed as he walked straight past my stall and moved to join Caly.

I glanced out from behind the sheet. His shoulders filled the rectangle opening. Maybe I could slip out behind him without anyone noticing.

"We need to find her immediately," Dominick said, "before we have an even bigger fiasco than the one from your last tantrum."

Bigger fiasco? I hesitated, still hiding behind the sheet. Bigger than what?

"There will be no problem this time. Trust me." Caly's cold, hard tone gave me the willies. How could someone so tiny have so much strength? She must be part ant or spider.

"What do you call what I just found in the elevator?" Dominick asked. "You would have destroyed all I've worked to build if anyone else had found it here."

"Poor, poor Masterson," Caly said his name funny, dragging out that last *S* like a snake hiss. "Shackled by your need to feel civilized."

"Do not talk that way to me, fool."

"You are the fool. You demand obedience without any reward and then complain when I take what I deserve." She sighed in an overly dramatic way. "In the old days, you used to let me have more fun."

"Times have changed. We need to change as well."

Caly scoffed. "They are all beneath us, and you know it. They should be our pets. I'll start by making this one mine, as soon as I find her."

"No." His tone left no room for discussion.

"Why not? She's seen too much, just like the other two."

What other two? Helen and … Jane? Had Jane witnessed something after play rehearsals? Had Helen, too? Is that why they were both dead?

"You should have left Jane for me," he said.

For him to kill?

"And Helen, too," he added. "I could have changed their minds."

"Now there is no need to bother with either. I disposed of both."

Caly had killed Jane. Cooper's case board had had it wrong. So had I.

"You're too messy," Dominick said.

"Fine. Let me have this pet and I won't spill a drop."

"No."

"It's that or death," Caly said.

I carefully pulled the chunk of mirror from my pocket, gripping it in my satin-wrapped palm. I wasn't going to be anyone's "pet," nor was I going down without a fight. God, I wished I had listened to Harvey and brought Bessie along with me tonight.

"You've wreaked havoc in *my* territory, usurping my

authority," Dominick said, his voice tight with what sounded like anger. "I decide the measures, not you."

"Your solution with the first did not go well. Your peers whisper behind your back. They laugh about the blatant rejection from the Duzarx."

I'd have to ask Harvey if he knew anyone named *Duzarx*. If I lived long enough to ask, that was. I stole a look through the gap between the sheet and wall, able to see the black outline of Dominick's profile, nothing more.

"You know nothing of my peers," he said. "You're a mere beast of burden. A—" he said something that came across as a mixture of a hiss and a growl. The hair on the back of my neck rose at the sound of it.

A cry of rage came from the other side of the wall. Caly flew at Dominick, her flashlight shoved in his face. "I do not belong to you anymore!"

"You will always be mine, Calypso."

"Do not call me by that name," she said through gritted teeth.

"You will heel to me, or you will suffer the consequences."

She tsked him. "So trite. Your control is fading. Can you feel it slipping away? Soon, *you* will belong to *me*, and I have such special plans for you."

What in the hell were they talking about? Something told me this wasn't some torrid affair gone sour. It had my muscles tense, agitated—ready to pounce.

Cornelius.

Crap! I was supposed to be getting some help, not standing here with my ear pressed against the sheet. Easing out from my hiding spot, I inched toward the door. I had just grabbed the door when a clattering sound rang out from down near Cornelius. A muffled thud followed.

I winced. Oh, no! What part of "shh" didn't he understand?

Caly giggled in that creepy, tear-the-legs-off-spiders-for-fun tone. "There's my little kitten now."

I barely made it back into my shower stall before their lights came closer. I cringed back into the corner, afraid she'd see my shoes—or smell me. Her heels clacked as she passed.

The light grew dimmer. Sticking my head out from behind the sheet, I watched them approach the hole in the wall. I looked to my right. The escape path was wide open, beckoning. It was now or never. I slipped out, tiptoeing toward freedom.

"Oh, look," Caly said, her voice full of mirth. "It's my favorite stick-insect. I think I'll keep him, too."

I stopped, silently cursing at the ceiling. Why couldn't Cornelius have stayed quiet?

Screw it! It was his fault I was here. I'd be damned if I were going to get sliced to pieces because he had to have his damned hat. I had two kids depending on me to come home tonight and tuck them into bed. I pushed the door open wide enough to squeeze through.

"Caly?" I heard Cornelius say as I stuck my foot through the opening. "You're so pointy tonight. Are those real?"

I hesitated, straddling the threshold. As much as I wanted to run far and fast, I couldn't leave him. Not after what I'd witnessed happen to Helen. Maybe I could try to stall Caly long enough for Cooper to get here.

What if Cooper wasn't coming?

I squashed that thought and pulled my leg back into the darkness. Instead of returning to my favorite stall, I moved through the dark rectangle cut out of the wall where Dominick had stood moments before.

It was pitch black inside. I risked lighting Cornelius's phone screen for a second and got a picture in my mind of where I was standing—inside of the pool. To my left, the ground sloped upward. A *3 Foot* sign had been painted on the far wall.

The pool had been split in half lengthwise by a supporting wall that held up the new metal floor joists for the concrete overhead. Another narrow rectangular doorway led to the other half. I rushed through that doorway and shined my light inside, frowning at what looked like a bunch of bales of straw partially covered by a tarp to my right in the deep end. To my left were more boxes stacked on pallets.

"Hey, what are you doing?" I heard Cornelius say in a garbled voice. "What is wrong with you? Ouch! Oh, my God! Stop!"

That was my cue. "Here Caly, Caly!" I called out.

Silence followed. Then I heard Caly say, "Stay with him."

I ducked behind several uncovered bales of straw near the entrance and waited, mirror shard at the ready.

Clack, clack, clack, clack. She didn't even try to keep quiet as she stalked.

I took a deep breath. A calming numbness spread throughout my limbs. Okay, all I had to do was keep hidden a bit longer, give Cooper and his men a little more time to find us. Just one more round of hide and seek.

I heard Caly step into the first section of the pool and stop, her flashlight beam swinging around. "You want to play, do you?" she said. "That's good. I like that in a pet."

She stepped more slowly now, moving around, and then her *clacks* drew near. "Where are you hiding, my curly-haired kitten?"

The room grew brighter around me. I could hear her breathing. I peeked out. She had her back to me, her flashlight on the stack of boxes. Something nudged me forward. Before I realized what I was doing, I stepped up on a bale and lunged at her back.

She spun while I was mid-air, her lips pulling back in a hiss. I tackled her and we slammed to the floor, her body taking the brunt of my weight. The flashlight spun away. She shoved me off, throwing me into the straw like I was some waif. I popped right back up with the mirror shard in my hand at the ready. She rushed me, her claws slashing. I ducked a little too late, feeling fingernails scratch across my cheek as I spun away.

"Come here, you bitch," she said and attacked, catching a handful of my hair and yanking me toward her. Her hand latched onto my throat, lifting me up off my toes. The pain made my eyes water.

I'd seen this act before and didn't like the way it ended. I gripped the piece of glass in my hand and swung, burying it in her forearm.

She screeched and let me drop, clutching her arm, shrieking in pain.

Surprised at Caly's reaction, I scrambled to my feet as Dominick dragged Cornelius into the room by the collar.

How could a piece of glass make her scream when Helen shoving a knife in Caly's shoulder hadn't even made her wince?

Caly held her arm in front of her. Her eyes widened as her wrist turned black, and then her hand and elbow, the blackness spreading outward from the blade. I watched in shock as her fingers shriveled and then turned to ash and swirled away.

Dominick flung Cornelius aside and grabbed Caly's bicep above the shard and the blackness, his face wrinkled in concentration, his eyes closed.

The blackness creeping up Caly's arm stopped, but her forearm had already turned to ash; the chunk of glass fell to the floor shattering upon impact.

Caly's shrieking stopped. In the silence, my gaze lifted to her face. As I stared, her lips pulled back and her face stretched, elongating, her nose sinking inward, her nostrils growing wider. Her forehead pushed out, becoming bulbous, her lower jaw protruding.

I couldn't look away; I couldn't move. I could only watch, my lungs locked in terror.

She raised her remaining hand and rushed at me, her long teeth snapping.

I raised my arm to shield myself, but at the last second something jerked Caly back, as if she'd reached the end of her chain.

Dominick held her by the back of the neck like a kitten. Then he lifted her off the floor, as she had done with Helen. She thrashed and hissed, clawing the air, squealing. One of her spiked heels almost slashed my shoulder in the bedlam.

"Be still," Dominick ordered, but Caly only thrashed harder, growing more feral, like a wild cat. "Be still or I will send you back."

Caly stopped suddenly. Then she looked over her shoulder at her captor. "To hell with you," she said and brought her heel around, catching Dominick in the stomach.

He dropped her, but she scarcely hit the ground. With a hiss, she flew from the room, the steel door crashing in her wake.

In the silence, I looked over to where Cornelius lay on the ground, his eyes wide, his jaw dangling. His gaze connected with mine. "Well," he said, "that was a bit alarming."

Dominick's hand locked onto my arm, his touch so hot it practically burned my skin. My stomach roiled instantly, convulsing. I struggled as he tugged me toward him.

"Hold still, Violet," he said. "I'm not going to hurt you."

I didn't believe him, but his grip wasn't allowing me to go anywhere so I obeyed, fighting a bout of nausea that made my knees want to buckle.

He took my satin-covered hand and unwrapped it. He gouged the center of my palm with his thumbnail, slicing my skin.

"Ow!" I yanked my arm, but he held me tight, staring down at my palm and then sniffed it.

When he looked up, his eyes were all black, no white showing at all.

I gasped.

In a blink, his eyes returned to normal. He let my hand drop, his expression grim. "Now it's in your hands."

What was in my hand? What had he done to me?

Before I could ask, the sound of a single gunshot echoed down the stairwell.

Dominick glanced in the direction of the stairs, then took off in a blur toward the shallow end of the pool. There was a loud *BOOM*, then the crash of stone on stone. When the dust cleared, a gaping hole in the concrete marked his exit.

I gaped, pointing at the hole Dominick had made. "He just busted through that concrete wall like it was made of graham crackers."

"Yeah," Cornelius stood. He brushed off his pants, moving over next to me. "I hadn't thought to try that escape route."

Flashlights hit us, blinding me.

"Here we are again, Parker," Detective Cooper said from the other side of the light. "I have another dead body, multiple incidences of property damage, and what appears to be a hole from a bomb blast in the side of a goddamned historic building. I can't wait to hear your explanation for this mess."

Chapter Twenty-Five

I'd run clean out of logical explanations. All that remained were bizarre descriptions that sounded wacky to my own ears, and Cooper was having none of it. No surprise there.

"You expect me to believe any of that?" the detective asked, glaring at me, his hands on his hips.

I sat on the edge of the theatre stage in the opera house, lights glaring down from over my head. Cooper had moved me and Cornelius into the theatre for questioning, getting us out of the way of his investigation team.

"Knowing you," I said to Cooper, "not at all, except for the part about my having to pee. But I'm telling you the truth." Well, I'd left out a few details about Caly and Dominick that were too messed-up sounding to say aloud. "That's what happened."

Cooper threw up his arms, obviously frustrated, and walked away, trailing a string of muttered curses. He crossed over the boarded up musician's pit to where Cornelius sat in the third row of theatre seats, one of his arms wrapped in a bandage. He was talking to a female zombie, who turned out to be an undercover police officer. Where had she been when Helen needed help? Not in the first floor bathroom, that much was sure.

I looked over at Doc, who leaned back against the stage to my right, not touching me but never leaving my side. He'd been right behind Cooper when they'd found us in the pool. But after a couple of sniffs, he'd paled and held onto the wall marked DEEP for support while taking several *deep* breaths, which I'd found ironic and begun to giggle—hysterically, with tears running down my cheeks. After Cooper hauled me over to join Doc against the wall and ordered me to take several deep breaths of my own, I calmed down and got control of myself.

Claiming he'd been fighting a bout of the flu lately, Doc had then disappeared up the stairs to wait in the props room for us. My guess was his flu symptoms were caused by Cornelius's ghost-boy, who must have been hanging out with us enjoying all of the good times and excitement.

As for my giggling fit, that was a no brainer. I could still feel the manic tremors in the back of my throat, just waiting for me to open the flood gates again.

"I'm trying to be honest with Cooper," I told Doc. "But he's not the most receptive person when it comes to this kind of stuff."

His gaze remained fixed on Cooper, who was now talking to the female officer. "You left out a few bits," Doc said, not really accusing me, more like stating facts.

Doc could read me too well. Unfortunately, when it came to reading him, I'd have more luck deciphering hieroglyphs. I had yet to figure out whether his reason for our lack of physical contact since he'd joined Cooper, Cornelius, and me down in the pool had to do with Cooper and his team milling around, the fight we'd had, or something else.

"I skipped only the parts I don't understand," I said, waggling my fingers at Cooper when he squinted in my direction.

Doc didn't say anything for a handful of seconds. "Are you okay?" he asked, still not looking at me, not touching.

I rubbed my arms, missing his warmth. "I think so. I could use a drink, though." And something to eat. After all of the blood and violence I'd witnessed tonight, I suddenly had a craving for a thick, juicy burger. How deranged was that? There was probably a psychological label for wanting to eat meat after spending time in an elevator with a dead woman dressed as a zombie bride.

"I can get you some water," Doc offered.

"No, it's going to have to be something stronger."

Cooper strode back toward us, his face rife with creases showing his frustration and anger. "Did the paramedics give her the 'all clear'?" he asked Doc.

"Yep. Only scrapes and bruises this time."

"I'm sitting right here, Detective," I said, waving my hand in front of his steely gaze. "Fully conscious and able to speak for myself."

He turned to me, looking like he might sink his teeth into my hand and rip it off, so I sat on it. "Any bites, Parker?"

I frowned. What? Had I said that last thought aloud? "Bites?"

"Yeah, your buddy over there has a nice chunk taken out of his arm. It'll leave an interesting scar."

Caly had bitten him? What the hell? That must have been why I'd heard Cornelius cry out in pain right before I called Caly's name.

"No, she didn't bite me," I answered.

"She just lifted you off the floor and strangled you," he said in a dry voice.

I nodded.

"In the same manner that she strangled Helen Tarragon," he continued, same tone, same pinched smirk.

I nodded again. I'd gone over these details twice already. Maybe I'd get Cooper a hearing aid for Christmas this year.

"And just to confirm," Cooper continued, "we're talking about a five-foot-tall, slender, young girl who probably weighs around one hundred pounds coated in mud?"

I raised an eyebrow. "Do you often weigh your women while they are coated in mud, Detective Cooper?"

"Just answer the damned question, Parker."

"Caly's older than you think," I said, thinking about her conversation with Dominick that I hadn't fully relayed to Cooper. "And she probably weighs more like one-oh-five," especially with all of those metal spikes added in. "Oh, and don't forget her very high heels." I sure wouldn't forget her clacking around in them anytime soon.

Cooper's nostrils flared, looking all bullish. Uh oh, *el toro* alert. I leaned toward Doc, keeping my focus on the detective in case he started pawing the ground. "You didn't happen to see a red cape, fancy jacket, and a matador hat down in the prop room, did you?"

"Get her out of my sight," Cooper told Doc through a clenched jaw. "But don't take her too far. I'm not done with her tonight."

"That makes two of us," Doc said and held out a hand to help me down. "We'll be at my place."

He was willing to touch me now all of a sudden? Why? And what did he mean with that "two of us" comment? If he was breaking up with me after the day I'd had, I just might go grab one of those zombie arms from the prop room and beat him with it.

I took his hand, needing his touch more than his help. After Cooper strode off, I said, "What about my kids?"

"Harvey and your aunt are taking care of them. I called while you were giving your story to Cooper the second time and let them know you were fine, but would probably be detained for quite a while."

I looked over at Cornelius, who gave me a call-me gesture. I nodded, and then remembered that my cell phone was waterlogged and sealed in an evidence bag. I wondered who had had to fish it out of the toilet that I'd not gotten around to flushing after peeing. I'd have picked Cooper for the job.

As Doc led me toward the theatre exit at the back of the huge room, Abe Jr. waved goodbye, his bandaged arm a stark reminder of Caly's venom. Further up the aisle, Peter Tarragon stared straight ahead as we passed, his expression dazed, shell-shocked. He was either putting on a great performance for the cops, or he still sort of liked his wife in the end.

I held tight to Doc's hand all the way to the parking lot, moored to him while flashbacks of Caly's deeds kept replaying in my brain, rocking my calm.

The ride to Doc's place was quiet, filled only by the growl of his Camaro's eight cylinders. I stared blindly into the darkness, still trying to comprehend the shitstorm I'd gone through, trying to figure out the meaning behind Dominick's words and Caly's threats.

He pulled into the detached garage and killed the engine, shutting the garage door with the push of a button. In the silence, we sat there for several seconds just breathing, lit by the overhead light.

I looked out through the windshield. "You don't have any pinup girl posters on the walls in here."

"I'm waiting for your Calamity Jane Realty ads to come out."

I'd forgotten all about Jerry and that stupid photo shoot. Groaning, I covered my face, noticing one of my eyelashes had fallen off sometime during the evening's shenanigans. I flipped down the visor, grimaced at the creepy clown look I had going on thanks to the makeup streaking down my face, and peeled off the remaining eyelash—the glue had loosened thanks to tears, sweat, and Caly.

"What did Dominick Masterson say to you before he made his grand exit?" Doc asked, watching me wipe my makeup off with my jacket sleeve.

"Something about it being all in my hands now."

"That was it?"

"Well, before he said that, he cut me with his thumbnail and then sniffed my palm." I held out my palm with the square bandage on it—my only injury besides the small slash on my face thanks to Caly's fingernail and a few bruises on my neck where she'd tried to strangle me. "Dominick stared at my wounded hand for a moment, and when he looked up I could swear his eyes were all black and eerie looking. Then he blinked and they were back to normal."

"And this is the same hand you used when you stabbed Caly's arm—the arm that shriveled and turned to ash?"

"Yeah." I mirrored his frown. "There was a bit more to their conversation than I shared with Cooper."

"I figured that. You hungry?"

"Starving."

"Harvey told me you didn't get a chance to eat earlier." He shoved open his door. "Come inside, I'll cook you a steak."

Right then and there, I knew it as sure as I knew the sun would rise yet another day over Deadwood—I'd fallen totally, head-over-heels, gob-smack in love with Doc. There'd be no walking away from this relationship if it crashed and burned. He'd ruined me for life. I didn't even give a flippin' shit anymore that he'd gone to Cooper behind my back.

And in that moment, I understood exactly why Aunt Zoe refused to open the door to her home and heart even an inch for Reid to slip back through. She couldn't handle the pain of loving and losing him twice in one lifetime.

The feelings flooding through me made my heart shake, rattle, and roll with both excitement and dread. Falling in love was a sure-fire ticket to the Isle of Temporary Insanity, and I already had frequent flyer miles from too many trips there and back, especially since moving to town.

Doc waited for me by the door, and then walked beside me without touching again. What was going on? Was he pissed at me or not? He held the front door open for me. I resisted the urge to poke him in the ribs for messing with my head and followed him into his kitchen, dropping onto the barstool he pulled out for me.

"Okay," he said, sliding a cold beer in front of me, and then grabbing a cast iron skillet from a hook next to his stove. "I'll cook, you talk. This time, give me the real story—the full one, not the abridged version."

So I did, starting with the moment I'd walked out his door after our fight until the moment he'd joined me in that dark, empty pool. I told him every detail I could remember about Helen, about Caly and Dominick, and what was said about Jane. I ended with how Cornelius had fit into the evening's events.

Doc listened with a periodic head nod or frown. I finished as he set a plate with the thick cut of steaming steak in front of me. I leaned down and breathed in the heavenly smell of cooked meat, groaning with the first bite.

I swallowed and followed it with a gulp of cold beer. "Outrunning a bitch from hell makes a girl hungry."

His grin made the corners of his eyes crinkle. "I think you had help."

"Cornelius did distract her." And screwed up my initial getaway plan. I took another bite of steak.

"I'm not talking about Cornelius. Don't you think it's a little odd how that elevator just showed up when you said you didn't push the button?"

I nodded, chewing.

"And what about those double doors that you were able to open but Caly had to break through? And the door knob that turned after you locked it, but Caly wasn't there yet?"

"I still can't believe someone so petite could tear both doors from their hinges. She must have had cans of spinach stuffed in her bra."

"She also splintered the oak door to the props room," he reminded me.

"I'll never forget the way she threw Helen like she was nothing more than a rag doll."

"My point is that I think someone was leading you away from Caly, helping you escape from her."

I pointed my fork at him. "You had to leave the pool because of a ghost, didn't you?"

"Yes, a boy."

Cornelius's troublemaker? "Did he drown in the pool way back when it was actually filled with water?"

"No, he suffocated. Based on what I could tell from the outfit worn by the nurse who tried to help him, he was a casualty from the 1918 Spanish Influenza epidemic. They'd shut down the theatre that fall due to the rapid spread of the disease and started using the building as a makeshift hospital."

"You think he may have been helping me get away from Caly?"

"Yeah, I do."

"Why? Why help me and not Helen?"

"Maybe he had been trying to help Helen and then you showed up and he had to choose."

"Is it normal for a ghost to be able to lock doors and push elevator buttons?" I thought about Cornelius claiming the boy ghost had taken his hat and hidden it in that crawlspace.

Doc shrugged, taking a drink from my beer. "What part of ghosts existing is normal?"

I guessed that for Doc, ghosts were as normal as cornflakes and milk. "In your experience, then, how many other ghosts have you come across who could physically move things?"

"Only a couple."

"Is this little boy as strong as Prudence?"

"No. It's one thing to use psychokinesis to move things or turn locks; it's a whole other level to inhabit another person, speak through them, and maintain control of the helm so to speak while suppressing them at the same time."

I swallowed. "Do you think the boy knew about Caly all along?"

"Are you even chewing that steak?"

"It's a blend of inhaling and chewing, smartass." I took another bite.

"Maybe he knew," Doc answered my previous question. "Maybe he saw Caly kill Jane."

"Is there any way you can go inside him and find out?"

He pushed away from the counter, crossing his arms. "No. Communicating with the dead is not as easy as they make out on TV. At least not for any mediums I've ever come across."

I absorbed that as I ate. "Do you think ghosts can talk to each other?"

"I don't know. Maybe you should ask your friend Cornelius about that. He's the official ghost whisperer."

The doorbell rang.

"Cooper," I said and snarled in the direction of the front door.

"Down, tiger," Doc said with a chuckle and went down the hall to open the door.

While he was gone, I picked up the T-bone and tore the bits of meat from the bone I couldn't get with my fork.

"Real classy, Parker," Cooper said, striding into the kitchen. "Especially with that makeup job." He turned to Doc, who followed on the detective's heels. "Where did you find her? On the set of *The Planet of the Apes*?"

I could always count on Cooper to point out that I looked like shit after a day spent wrestling alligators and psychotic bitches from hell. I patted my curls and plucked out a piece of straw mixed in the mess.

"I had to choose between Zira or Violet," Doc said, winking at me. "Violet won—she has better hair."

I dropped the T-bone on the plate and wiped my mouth on the napkin Doc held out. "Wasn't Zira a chimpanzee?"

"And a doctor," Cooper supplied. "I'd have picked the smart one."

Flashing the detective my greasy middle finger, I carried my plate over to the sink. "Can we hurry up and get this over with? I want to wash this whole mess off in the shower and then bury my head under a pillow for a few hours."

Whose shower and pillow was still up in the air, but my vote was for Doc's if he'd share with me.

Cooper stole my barstool. "Sure. Walk me through your actions again, from the moment you pulled into the parking lot until I found you in the pool."

"We've gone through this twice already."

"Third time's a charm." He pulled out the notepad he'd been scribbling in earlier when I'd given him my statements and clicked his pen.

When I finished, he wrote one last scribble and closed his notepad, stuffing it back in his pocket. "We found the knife," he told me.

"You mean the one Helen had in the bathroom?"

He nodded.

"Was it a prop?"

"No. But there wasn't any blood on it."

I could have sworn Helen buried it in Caly's shoulder. "Maybe Caly wiped it clean after pulling it out."

"Maybe. We're checking the sink area thoroughly for blood splatters—the toilets, too. We also dusted the handle for prints and sent them off for analysis." He stood. "What I can't make sense of is you claiming Caly was stabbed with this knife and she didn't react to it at all. Yet when you stuck her with a piece of broken mirror, Caly's arm did the shrivel-and-blow away routine that your pal Cornelius confirmed."

"Weird, huh?" I didn't know what else to say. I couldn't make sense of it either.

"This so-called weird stuff seems to happen to you a lot these days, especially when it involves sharp objects."

"It's only happened twice." I suddenly put two and two together. My eyes widening, I looked at Doc. Caly had white-blonde hair. She'd complained about her contacts to Dominick. "Holy shit," I whispered. "Caly is an albino."

Of course, it made sense now. Her arm had disintegrated just like the big nasty albino I'd stabbed at Mudder Brothers; and she'd left the same barbed hook at the bottom of The Open Cut next to Jane's body.

"Great, another disappearing albino case for me to solve," Cooper said, his face one big scowl. "You know, your little incidents are starting to sound like Scooby Doo episodes."

Maybe so, but I had a tingling feeling at the back of my neck that this was a "to be continued …" episode. That albino I'd stabbed at Mudder Brothers had totally disappeared, but Caly had only lost an arm, and I doubted she'd forget who had been the source of that lost appendage. Just the thought of what her vengeance would be like had my heart flapping like a chicken being chased through a fox's den.

Cooper's jacket rang. He pulled his cell phone out of his pocket and grimaced at the screen, then up at me. "As much fun as I'm having here, I need to go."

"So soon?" I said. "Darn, I was just going to get out the poker chips."

He looked at Doc. "You should invest heavily in duct-tape for that mouth of hers." Then he pointed at me. "Don't be leaving town, Parker. We're far from finished."

"And here I thought it was just a summer fling," I muttered.

"I'll call you tomorrow. I strongly suggest you answer the phone when it rings."

My phone would most likely be in the Deadwood Police Department's evidence room by then. "Sure thing, Detective."

Without another threat, he left. Doc followed him. I heard the deadbolt click.

When Doc came back, I was sticking my plate in the dishwasher. I closed the door and turned around. He leaned against the pantry door, his hands shoved deep in the pockets of his faded blue jeans. His dark brown thermal shirt matched his hair and eyes … eyes that held me captive with an intensity that was almost tangible. All signs of his earlier mirth were absent.

I searched for something to say to break the tension that had returned and bridge the distance between us. "Dominick was able to stop Caly from burning up entirely."

Doc dipped his chin once. "Yeah."

"He's not the same as the albinos."

"Nope."

I chewed on my lip. "I'm in more trouble, huh?"

"Probably. But you're safe for now."

"How do you know?"

"Because Caly and Dominick ran. It will take time for them to work out what happened, what went wrong. Just like it will for Cooper."

"And us," I added.

He shrugged. Evidence of some internal struggle lined his face and showed in his hunched shoulder, ribboning the muscles in his forearms.

I sighed quietly, wanting to kick down this invisible wall he'd erected between us. "What's going on, Doc?"

"I don't know, but it sounds to me like Deadwood and Lead have a much bigger problem than a few temperamental ghosts rattling chains in attics."

Right, but I wasn't talking about that mess. I had a different priority at the moment, one much less paranormal. "I'm talking about what's going on with us."

He shrugged. "You tell me."

That was a nice, ambiguous answer, damn it. He was going to make me take the first step. Fine. I took three, closing the distance between us, but didn't touch him, not yet. "I wasn't completely honest when I came over earlier tonight."

"About what?"

"About not needing you and your protection."

"You don't need me, Violet. You said so yourself earlier and then proved it tonight when you took on Caly."

"Is that what all of this not-touching-me business is about tonight? You're keeping your distance because of something I said earlier during our argument? Or are you so pissed at me still that you can't even stand to touch me?"

"I'm not mad."

"What then?"

He hesitated. I got the feeling he was weighing his words in his head. "Violet, you're a strong, independent woman who doesn't *need* anyone. You've made that clear through words and actions."

I winced at how that sounded, apprehensive about what he would say next.

He rubbed the back of his neck. "But I can't stop this need I have to protect you."

"Oh." That wasn't so bad.

"I was trying to give you some space tonight and not do what I really wanted to do."

"Which was?"

"Throw you over my shoulder, haul you back here, and lock you in my bedroom to keep you safe."

I chuckled, relieved. "Holding my hand would have been nice. Even better—a hug, or several."

"Duly noted."

Taking another step, I closed the gap between us. "You know, I have many different kinds of needs." I placed my hands on his chest, feeling his heart under my palm, waiting for a couple of beats to see if he'd pull away. When he didn't, I added. "And right now, I *really* need you."

His eyes darkened, the heat in his gaze encouraging me. "What kind of need are we talking about here?"

I dragged my nails down his shirt, letting them bump over the textured thermal. "I need you to help me in the shower."

"The shower?"

"That soap gets soooo slippery."

One eyebrow rose slightly. "Is that right?"

"Oh, yeah."

Sliding my fingers back up over his broad shoulders, I circled my arms around his neck. I smiled at him, trying to look flirty and sexy, but with my makeup and hair such a mess, I probably looked just this side of deranged. I locked my fingers behind his neck and willed him to look past my scary face to the real me—well, the real me when I had combed hair and not-so-garish makeup.

I stood on my tiptoes and kissed the underside of his jaw, trailing my lips along the scratchy stubble down to his collar bone, which I bit through the fabric. "And when we're done in the shower, I need you to take me to bed. Your bed."

When he didn't move a muscle in response, I pressed against

him, checking to see if my seduction attempts were having any affect at all.

"I know what you're doing, Boots," Doc said, grabbing me by the hips and pulling me even closer.

That was more like it. "What am I doing?"

"Distracting me."

"Maybe I'm distracting *me*. I had a rotten day, one that I'd like to forget about for a while." I pulled his mouth down to mine and ran the tip of my tongue over his lower lip, then sucked on it lightly, dipping into his mouth for a lick … or three. "If you think you're up to the task."

His fingers delved into the hair at the back of my head, holding me still as he took his time kissing me back. His touch was so soft and smooth, unlike the rest of his body. He savored one kiss at a time, his breath quickening with each. My body ached and throbbed for so much more.

"Christ, Violet," he said against my mouth. "You smell like steak and taste like beer." One of his hands slid down to my breast. "It's intoxicating."

"I want to smell like you." I rubbed my palm over his stomach, heading south. "And taste like sex. Take my clothes off, Doc."

He stopped my hand. "Not here. There's something I've wanted to see since you stripped in front of me at your aunt's house." He pulled me up the narrow set of dark stairs that led from the kitchen up to his bedroom. He didn't stop until he'd locked us in his master bathroom. "You sure you want to do this?" he asked, leaning back against the door.

I took off my shirt and threw it at him. He caught it, his gaze sliding to my chest.

"What's next?" I asked.

He pointed at my shoes and socks. When I stood there barefoot in front of him, he said, "More," while still clutching my shirt.

Unbuttoning my jeans, I shimmied them down over my hips. Seeds of insecurity started to grow. I crossed my arms over my pale pink lace bra and white satin underwear, covering as much of my post-pregnancy stomach as possible.

"Don't," he ordered. "Let me see all of you."

I obeyed, uncrossing my arms, unsure what to do with my hands.

"Damn," he said. His gaze ate me up, making heated promises, inciting me to do whatever he said so long as it ended with him touching me.

"Don't move," he said and slid past me to the shower, turning on the tap, checking the water temperature. Then he dropped my shirt on the counter and took my hand, leading me to the tub's edge. He drew back the shower curtain. "Get in."

I frowned, hesitating. "My underwear will get all wet."

He grabbed me and hauled me against him, jeans rubbing my thighs. His mouth covered mine, his palm trailing down the side of my breast, his thumb brushing over my nipple through my bra. He traced the outline of my hip and then his hand slid inside the waist of my panties. As his tongue flicked mine, his fingers brushed over me, exploring.

He pulled back slightly, his mouth moving to my ear. "They already are wet, Boots," he whispered. Then he pulled away long before I was ready for him to and stepped back, pointing at the tub. "Get in."

I stepped gingerly, my legs feeling wobbly all of a sudden, and held onto the bar on the long wall of the tub. "You're not going to turn into Norman Bates on me, right?" When he just stared at me, I added, "Or Prudence again?"

"Cute. Get under the water," he ordered. "All the way," he added when I took my time about it.

I reached down and cranked up the heat of the spray, and then closed my eyes and stepped in, letting the water rinse away today's frustrations. I tipped my chin up, pushing my hair back, washing away what was left of the clown makeup.

"Turn around," he said from behind me, where I knew he stood watching through the curtain opening.

Rubbing the water from my eyes, I faced him, the spray hitting the back of my head and cascading down my shoulders.

His face was taut with a mix of what looked like pain and pleasure. I looked down. My bra and underwear clung to my skin, transparent.

Oh, now I got it.

And now I'd get him.

Reaching down, I traced my breast through the wet cloth, imagining his hands on me, touching and pinching like I'd like him to. I glanced up at him from under my eyelashes and bit my lip at the lust darkening his cheeks. His eyes were locked on my hands, his mouth open. I grabbed the soap and started lathering through my bra.

He gasped, bending forward a bit like I'd punched him in the gut.

I moved the soap lower, circling my stomach and continuing south over my satin panties and down over my thighs and knees. I dragged the soap back up between my thighs and purposely let it slip from my fingers as I reached the apex. It clunked in the tub bottom and slid down by the drain.

Doc got all choked up, coughing and gasping a couple of times like he'd swallowed his tongue.

"See what I mean," I told Doc when he caught his breath. I leaned back to let the water cascade down over my breasts and stomach. "It's just soooo slippery."

He grunted. Tearing the curtain open, he shut off the water, and then threw me over his shoulder.

"Wait!" I said, slapping his butt through his jeans. "I need to finish rinsing off."

"We'll do that later." He tossed me onto his bed.

I landed on my back and pushed up on my elbows. "I'm getting your bed all wet."

"Yep." He tore off his shirt and shoved down his jeans and briefs.

I stared unabashedly and reached to push down my underwear.

"Oh, no you don't," he caught my hand, then snagged the other and held them over my head with one of his, lying next to me on the bed. "I'm not done yet."

His fingers circled down over my breast, first one and then the other. He leaned down and blew on the wet lace, making me shiver and harden. He looked up at me. "So damned hot."

Then his fingers continued down over my stomach, the front

of my underwear, and my thigh, hovering over my kneecap, following my path with the soap. I arched up, wanting so much more. "Doc, please."

"Patience, Boots."

My eyelids dropped, anticipation for where he'd touch next had me burning from the inside out. "Hurry up."

His hand slid to the inside of my knee, swirling slowly up my inner thigh. I opened wider to him, tipping my head back, closing my eyes.

The brush of his knuckles over my underwear nearly sent me over the edge. I tried to move closer to his hand, but he held me in place with his lock on my wrists.

He brushed again through the wet fabric.

I moaned and writhed.

"Tell me what you need, Violet," he whispered in my ear then sucked on my earlobe, grazing it with his teeth.

His fingers stroked once. Just once. It took my breath away.

I was beyond primed and he knew it. "You know what I need."

His fingers ran along the inside of the elastic edge, feathering along the tender, sensitive skin. "Say it."

"I'm going to make you pay for this, Doc."

"That's not it." His fingertips strummed over the outside of my underwear. "You know what I want to hear."

"I want you inside of me now," I said, ending it with a growl.

"I like that better, but it's still not what I want to hear."

He leaned down and bit me through the front of my bra, then sucked where he bit, his fingers still teasing, tickling, staying just out of reach.

Game over. I licked my lips. "Doc."

He looked up at me with one raised brow. The bead of sweat on his upper lip gave away his own internal struggle. "What, Violet?"

I love you, I thought, and opened my mouth, hesitating.

He watched my lips. "Say it."

"I need you," I said, chickening out.

Letting go of my wrists, his hand cupped my jaw. "I need you, too." His mouth covered mine, his body rolling on top of me.

I wrapped my legs around his waist, pushing against him, squeezing him tightly as I rubbed along his length.

"Violet," he said between kisses. "I want to taste you."

"Later." Scrambling half out of my panties, I reached down and grabbed him, positioning him, and then used my ankles to pull him close, helping him slam into me. The friction alone made me arch off the bed. "Yes!" I gasped.

He slid out and shoved all of the way in again. And again. That was all it took. The shudders started deep inside, and wrung me out from limb to limb.

Doc kept moving through it all, whispering in my ear about how much he needed me; how much he loved watching me while he was inside of me.

When I finally stilled, I looked up at him, my heart in my eyes. I couldn't help it.

He stared down at me for a moment, slowing, his dark gaze locked onto mine.

"Violet," he whispered, and picked up the pace, moving faster, pushing harder until he froze several strokes later, his arms covered with goosebumps as a deep groan crawled up from his chest. Then he collapsed on me and rolled us to the side so I wasn't trapped under him.

We lay there in silence for a bit, his face buried in my neck, my hand stroking his back. Something had changed between us. Maybe it was just me, but that had been different, more potent. Sex with Doc was always thrilling, but this time it had knocked me for a loop. My brain was still stumbling around, uncertain which way was up or down.

Doc moved, shifting closer, not leaving me yet. "Violet?" He kissed my neck, making me smile at the shadowy ceiling.

"Yes?"

"You taste like soap."

I laughed. "That's your fault. You didn't let me finish rinsing off."

He lifted his head, his eyes still dark with passion. "I didn't expect you to get all soapy."

"What did you expect?"

"I just wanted to see you standing there all wet in your underwear."

"I improvised."

"You did more than that." He leaned down and kissed my lips, teasing my tongue with his. When I teased back, I felt him begin to stir inside of me.

"You inspire me," I told him.

He ran his finger down my cheek, tenderly skimming Caly's scratch. "And you scare the hell out of me."

"That's kind of hard on my self-confidence."

He chuckled. "I'm talking about what almost happened to you at the opera house. When Cooper called, telling me you'd texted and might be in danger, asking if I had a clue where to find you, *that* scared the hell out of me."

"I dropped my phone in the toilet before I could tell him where I was."

Tipping my chin toward him, he squinted at me. "I know you don't think you need any protection, but could you do me a favor and just let me try to keep you safe anyway? It will help keep me sane."

"That depends."

"On what?"

"You need to do something for me."

"Not talk to Cooper?" he asked.

I thought about that for a moment, weighing what had happened tonight and whether Cooper could help find Caly, who I suspected was going to want revenge if I really did destroy her arm. She didn't seem like the forgive-and-forget type.

"No, I think I see your point with Cooper. Not that I'm thrilled about spending any more time in his company." I grabbed Doc's hand and kissed his knuckles. They smelled soapy. "I want you to start coming over a couple of times a week for dinner with my family."

"Your whole family?"

I nodded. "And Harvey."

"As your *friend?*"

"No. As my boyfriend."

"Your kids?"

"They'll know the truth."

He nodded, all furrowed brow. Then a grin split his face. "You mean about how I like to watch their mom take a shower?"

Chuckling, I grabbed him by the hips and pulled him closer, adjusting to accommodate more of him. "You know, I never figured you for a watcher. You seem more like the doer personality."

"Oh, I'm a doer." He extracted himself from me, standing and hauling me up by the arm. I stood on the bed, smiling down at him. "Come on."

"Where are we going?"

"To the shower. You need to finish rinsing off so I don't get soap in my mouth when I *do-'er* again in the shower."

I wrinkled my nose, laughing. "Oh, that was just bad."

"No," he scooped me up, kicking the bathroom door shut behind us. "Bad is how much you're going to want me when I finish rubbing you down with that slippery soap you keep whining about." He lowered my feet to the floor and turned on the water, and then unhooked my bra. "Let's try this again without your clothes on."

I let the bra fall to the floor and tugged him into the shower with me. "Or yours," I said and closed the curtain.

Chapter Twenty-Six

Thursday, September 13th

I woke up drooling. When I pulled my face out of my pillow, I understood why—someone was cooking bacon for breakfast. After hitting the bathroom, I grabbed one thing from my bedroom and headed downstairs to eat and face the music.

Harvey stood at the stove cooking eggs and bacon while wearing the "World's Best Mom" apron the kids had bought me for Christmas last year in hopes that I'd be inspired to try to improve my cooking skills. I'd forgotten that I had brought it up to Deadwood with us. Most of my stuff was packed in boxes and sitting in a storage unit in Rapid until we landed somewhere more permanent.

At the table, Aunt Zoe was eating with two sullen faced children—mine. I'd spilled the beans about Doc being my boyfriend to Addy and Layne last night, and just as I'd feared, it had resulted in a lot of anxious questions and angry accusations. I'd expected all of this from Layne, since it threatened his self-assigned man-of-the-house status, but Addy's explosive reaction had left me gape-mouthed. I thought she'd be pleased. She'd seemed to like Doc from the start. I hadn't counted on her determination to expand our family with a husband, sister, and baby brother all with the last name of Wymonds.

Pasting a smile on my face, I stepped into the kitchen. "Morning," I said, trying to sound chipper.

Layne shoved his chair away from the table. "May I be excused?" he asked Aunt Zoe.

She looked at me, her forehead lined. I nodded to her.

"Sure, kiddo," she said. "Put your plate in the sink."

I tried to ruffle Layne's hair as he passed, but he jerked away from my hand, the little brat. I watched his retreating back, his shoulders stiff.

Why did everything in my life have to be so damned hard? All I wanted was a chance for us to see whether this thing I had going with Doc had long-range potential. At this rate, we'd scare him away by Halloween.

Alrighty then, one down, one to go. I looked back toward the table and ran smack dab into Addy's brown-eyed glare.

"Oh, come on," I said to her. "I've told you all along that I was not going to marry Jeff Wymonds."

Addy stood, her expression pinched and accusing. "You didn't even let him try out."

"Hey, I kissed him once, if you'll remember." Technically, he'd shoved his tongue in my mouth for several seconds, and when he'd finished licking my back molars he'd attempted to woo me with words about his plow and his desire to plant his seeds in my fertile field. It was one of those romantic moments they showed on engagement ring commercials that I'd not forget anytime soon. "Besides, dating me isn't a sport, Adelynn. There are no tryouts."

"I wanted a sister!"

"You have a brother."

She stomped over to me, leading with her chin. "He stinks," she counted off on her fingers, "he won't play dress-up-the-chicken with me, he's afraid of snakes, and he sucker punches me in the gut when you're not looking."

"All boys stink," I told her. "Get used to it." Wait until she hit high school and was surrounded by guys who'd just come from gym class.

"Hey!" Harvey said from where he stood watching us while his eggs burned. "Some of us only stink part of the time."

Addy's eyes got all watery, her upper lip quivering. "Thanks for only thinking about yourself, Mother."

Oof! Talk about sucker punches.

She ran off in tears. I scowled after her. "Addy!"

For almost ten years, I'd focused on their needs. I'd worked my ass off to provide for them, raise them in a safe environment, put food in their mouths. Now, when I finally found a man who treated me nicely and didn't have a prison record—at least not one that I knew of—my kids acted like I was hooking up with that big-nosed child catcher in *Chitty Chitty Bang Bang*.

I heard her tromping up the stairs and yelled out through the archway, "You're welcome! Get your glasses on your face!"

Only thinking of myself? I shook my hands at the ceiling and growled.

"Violet," Aunt Zoe said, coming over to me, enveloping me in a sweet-smelling hug. "You did the right thing. They'll come around, just give them time. They've had you to themselves for all of their lives. The idea of sharing you is probably pretty scary."

I rested my head on Aunt Zoe's shoulder, letting her make it all better just like she always did. "Addy needs to learn that sisters aren't always a blessing."

"I know, honey." She pushed me back and kissed my forehead. "Now, how are you feeling? Back to your old self?"

"I think so." After a full night in Doc's bed and then two days "sick" off of work, I was ready to take up my sword and go slay some more dragons. Or rather albinos in my case. Which reminded me—I held out the book I'd grabbed from my bedroom. "Doc dropped this by last night while you were at the gallery."

He'd been late for a poker game at Cooper's at the time and my kids were glaring at us out the window, having recently found out about his being my boyfriend, so the exchange had been brief. I'd kept the touching to just a quick peck and a wave goodbye.

Aunt Zoe took the demon book that I'd "borrowed" from Lila a month ago in the Carhart house—the one with my buddy Kyrkozz in it. "This is the book you told me about?" she asked.

"Yep. That's it, creepy illustrations and all."

Harvey came over, holding a piece of bacon out for me. He looked over Aunt Zoe's shoulder. "What is that? Latin?"

I nodded, grabbing the bacon and stuffing it in my mouth. The smoked meat incited a noisy riot in my stomach for more. "You make some extra eggs for me?" I asked him.

"Of course. Someone needs to keep you well-fed. With all of

this crazy shit goin' on around here and out at my place, we all need plenty of gumption."

I stole another piece of bacon from a plate next to the stove. "What do you mean out at your place? What's going on out there? Something with your freaky neighbors in Slagton?"

"Maybe. Or someone else. I thought I saw something hair-raisin' last week out behind my ol' barn."

And he was just now telling me this? Something clicked in my brain. "Is that why you've been camping out on Aunt Zoe's couch?"

He grunted in response, looking away.

Holy crap! What had he seen that spooked him out of his own bed? Something worse than that funeral director's head in the old outhouse? "And here I thought you were staying each night to protect me. What did you see?"

"Violet?" Aunt Zoe interrupted us, her nose buried in the book.

"What?"

"Where did you say Lila got this book?"

"I don't know. She didn't say." And she'd fallen on her knife before I'd had a chance to interrogate her further. I wondered if Prudence would know how Lila came to have it.

Aunt Zoe closed the book and ran her fingers over the cover. When she looked up at me, she had the strangest expression, like I had grown a set of antlers and a red, glowing nose.

"Do you know what this book is?" she said more than asked.

"Some kind of book on how to raise demons?"

"Not raise them. It's more of a reference guide."

I lowered the piece of bacon. "Come again?" She'd figured that out in thirty seconds of perusing it?

"It's sort of an encyclopedia mixed with a how-to guide, covering one demon in particular."

Kyrkozz.

"How do you know that by just glancing at it?"

Aunt Zoe scraped her nails down the cover. "I've seen books like it before, only they each have a different cover."

"What do you mean by 'a different cover'? Are you talking

about the color?"

"No, a different skin."

The phone on the kitchen wall rang.

"I got it," Harvey said, reaching for it.

"When you say 'skin,' are you talking about the cover design?" Like a template of sorts?

"No. I mean skin." She reached out and pinched my arm. "Flesh."

I stepped back from her, pointing at the book as if it might grow talons and sharp teeth. "That thing is covered with human flesh?"

She scratched over it again, half of her face scrunched in thought. "I don't think it's human."

What?! I squinted at her. "How do you know that?"

"Like I said, I've seen books like this before, handled them."

My squint narrowed even further. "Who are you and what have you done with my Aunt Zoe?"

"Violet," Harvey said, his voice sounding like it came from far away.

I looked over at him in slow motion.

He held up the phone. "Cooper's on the phone."

Cooper's words echoed in my skull: *When I call, you'd better answer it.*

I took the phone from Harvey. "What?" I said into the mouthpiece.

"Good morning to you, too, Parker. I got the results back on that box of teeth you brought to me. Where did you say you found them?"

"The Carhart house." Which was the same place I'd found the book of flesh in Aunt Zoe's hands. "Why?"

"The lab says they look like human canines, but they aren't. They are wondering if I got them from an archeologist, telling me they need the location of the damned dig site." Even through the phone, I could hear the clipped tone in Cooper's voice. It snapped me out of my stupor.

"And you're mad at me about it?" I asked, my blood pressure shooting skyward.

Criminy, Cooper needed to get laid and mellow out. I spoke

from experience on that one, with an inner head nod to Doc with his very effective hands and mouth. Tiffany must not be doing the job for the tight-assed detective.

"Yes," he said. "Yes, I am. You have made a fucked-up mess in this town, and I'm the one left trying to clean it up and smooth everything over with the bigwigs who are so far up my ass that I can't see straight. So excuse me if I'm a little frustrated with you and your goddamned box of teeth this morning."

He was barking at the wrong dog today. I bared my teeth. "Listen, *Detective*, it's not my fault I have to keep doing *your* freaking job for you. Now is there anything else you need from me?" Like my foot up his ass along with those bigwigs he was whining about?

"Yes."

"What? You need me to solve another murder case for you?"

"Stop fucking up my life, Parker!" he yelled in my ear and hung up on me. The big, fat jerk.

I hung up the phone and flipped it off for good measure.

Harvey laughed. "Damn, girl. I think you just might make that boy blow a gasket yet."

"He started it."

"I'm sure he did, but he's also gettin' reamed daily from the chief of police because there ain't no murderer sittin' in jail after all of these kooky deaths."

I hadn't thought about Cooper as someone at risk of losing his job. I'd walked in those shoes for months and knew the constant stress that came with worries about the unemployment line. "You think his job is on the line?" I asked Harvey.

He shrugged. "He's not the kind to flap his lips about it, but could be. Or the chief will call in that flannel-mouthed, highfalutin' detective from Rapid again, which will really get Cooper all fired up."

As much as Cooper drove me bugshit, I didn't want him to lose his job. There was something about knowing he and his guns were nearby that brought a level of comfort, at least when I wasn't in his crosshairs.

"Violet," Aunt Zoe said. "We need to talk about this book

you found."

I wrinkled my nose at the flesh-covered book, thinking how many times I'd touched it without washing my hands afterward. Did Doc know it was flesh and hadn't told me?

"I don't want to talk about that thing right now. I have to go to work and focus on selling a house or hotel so I don't lose *my* job."

Harvey held out two more pieces of bacon for me. "I'll take the kids to school."

"Thanks," I told him. "We're not done talking about what's going on at your ranch."

He chuckled. "You're starting to sound like Coop now." He turned me around and gave me a shove. "Go get all fancied up and get your ass to work. We'll save the world another day."

When I pulled into the parking lot, Doc's Camaro wasn't there. He'd had to go back to Rapid City for work yesterday. Maybe he'd driven down there again this morning. I'd try calling him later on the new cell phone he'd bought for me while he'd been there. I needed to warn him about Addy and Layne. I had a feeling dinner tonight was *not* going to be all fun and laughs.

Maybe he'd put up with us until Christmas time. I'd always been a sucker for those romance books with mistletoe, red satin lingerie with white fur, and sex in front of a crackling fire.

Doc had a nice fireplace.

I smelled Mona's jasmine perfume as soon as I stepped inside the back door of Calamity Jane Realty. Good! The office could use a solid dose of estrogen today. Much more testosterone and sports chatter and I'd need to grow me a pair of balls to scratch just to fit in.

"Violet," Jerry called out as I passed his office doorway.

I backed up and looked inside. Mona stood over his shoulder, her cheeks seeming a bit flushed. Her peach sweater molded to her nicely, enhancing her figure. I needed to take her shopping with me to help pick out clothes that would make Doc putty in my hands.

"Did you hear about what happened at the opera house up in Lead?" Jerry asked.

I needed to step carefully, uncertain what Cooper had shared and if I'd get another foul for my part in the whole mess. "Yeah. It's too bad."

Mona was watching me closely, her lips pressed together. I avoided eye contact. The woman was too good at seeing through my smoke screens, just like Aunt Zoe.

"Detective Cooper was in here yesterday," Jerry said.

"Oh, yeah?" Crap. Cooper could have told me that this morning. Instead he'd been too busy chewing my ass.

"He told me they had a solid lead on Jane's murderer."

No shit. Did that mean Cooper actually believed my story about Caly being the killer? "Good. Her murderer needs to be found and dealt with."

I was ninety-nine-percent sure I hadn't seen the last of Caly, and I was one hundred percent sure just the sight of her would scare the holy hell out of me.

"Zelda Britton called for you this morning," Mona told me. "I left her number on your desk."

"Thanks." I needed to see if the Brittons were still interested in Wanda's place. The idea of having a reunion with Prudence made me all fidgety inside, but the need to make money and keep my job left me little choice. However, I wasn't touching anyone under any circumstances while under that roof.

"Your friend, Doc Nyce, stopped by earlier, too." Mona winked at me. "He left you something on your desk."

"Cool," I said, figuring he'd forgotten some attachment for my fancy new phone. "Did you have anything else to tell me, Jerry?"

"Yeah. Get out there and sell that hotel. Oh, and close my door behind you."

"Will do, coach," I said, holding my hand up for an air high-five. With his arms at his sides, Jerry just frowned at me, so I shut him and Mona in his office and headed for my desk, feeling like I'd won the Idiot-of-the-Day award.

I dropped my purse on the floor next to my desk with a sigh. So much for being one of the boys this morning. Lucky for me, selling the hotel was once again a possibility after yesterday's call from Tiffany. Her client had agreed to the extension, so she'd met me at the hotel in the afternoon to collect Cornelius's check and sign off on the extension.

I glanced at Ray and Benjamin's empty chairs. Where were they? Off making a multimillion dollar sale to some big name actor who was looking for a summer log mansion to use as a "cabin"?

A small black box tied with a purple ribbon sat on my desktop. It was too big for a ring, more like a bracelet box. What had Doc given me? I untied the ribbon and pulled off the lid, laughing aloud when I saw the fancy-wrapped soap in the bottom. I picked it up and sniffed. It smelled like chocolate and peanut butter. Yum.

A card was in the bottom of the box. I picked it up and read:

> *Boots,*
> *Look what I found—edible soap. Feeling dirty?*
> *My bed's too dry without you.*
> *Doc*

I pocketed the card and put the soap back in the box while my heart picked petals from a daisy, playing the he-loves-me game.

My desk phone rang. I picked it up. "Calamity Jane Realty, this is Violet."

"Hi, Violet, it's Zelda Britton."

"Zelda, I was just going to give you a call. We've been playing phone tag lately."

"I'm sorry about that. I've been at a librarian's conference for the last week and haven't had much of a chance to talk to Zeke about the house until yesterday."

"Librarian's conference?" I fell into my chair.

"Yeah, it was a blast. There were lots of great workshops with some of my favorite authors, and the parties each night rocked. We librarians aren't as prim and proper as most people think."

Librarian! It all clicked in place. Prudence wanted me to bring her "the librarian." Zelda had been in the Carhart house when it was up for sale the first time.

I tuned back in as Zelda said something about Zeke's uncle passing away. "I'm sorry," I said, wondering how to switch from a family member's death to selling her a house.

"Thanks. He was a wonderful man. That's why I'm calling. He left Zeke some money, and we've decided we're still *very* interested in the Carhart house."

"In spite of its history?" I asked, wanting to be totally on the level with Zelda, whose friendly smile and kind eyes I'd liked right out of the gate.

"Even more so with its history. I think I told you that I'm really into ghosts, didn't I?"

Good, because I had one who I suspected was asking for Zelda specifically. "You may have mentioned it," I said. "When can you two come to town and take a look at the place again?"

"We were thinking about driving up there next week."

"Perfect. Let's get something on the calendar."

Five minutes later, I hung up and gnawed on my knuckles. Was taking Zelda to Prudence a good idea? What did Prudence want with the librarian? What if Prudence hurt her? Could a ghost inflict pain? I'd have to ask Doc what he thought, see if he wanted to be around when I took Zelda there.

The bell over the front door dinged. I looked up and did a double take. Natalie limped toward me, wearing a *Deadwood Rocks* long-sleeve T-shirt and blue jeans, her cast gone. In one hand, she held my other purple cowboy boot. She looked as stunning as ever with her long brown hair curling around her face. Her eyes gave away nothing, her cards held close to her vest.

I stood, feeling my heart beating in my fingertips.

When she stopped in front of my desk, I opened my mouth to beg her not to beat me up with my own boot, but she held up her hand, silencing me.

"You should have told me from the start, Violet."

My eyes watered. "I know. I'm so sorry, Nat. I was such a dipshit."

She nodded once. I wasn't sure if that was an acceptance of my apology or acknowledgment that I was indeed a dipshit. "You haven't texted me for a few days."

So she was getting my texts. The knot in my chest loosened, freed by a thread of hope. "I dropped my phone in a toilet Monday night."

"I heard. I also heard you had some more fun with an albino."

Who told her that? Only Doc, Cooper, Aunt Zoe, and I knew that I thought Caly was an albino. Oh, wait, Harvey knew. He must have talked to her.

"Are you okay?" she asked.

"Mostly." I wasn't sure I'd ever be *okay* again, not after all of the bizarre crap I'd experienced since moving to Deadwood.

"Good, because I still love your crazy ass and don't want to see you hurt." She gave me a crooked smile. "And as pissed as I was that after all of these years you didn't trust in my love for you enough to come clean about Doc right away, I need you in my world."

As pissed as I was … Did that mean she wasn't pissed anymore? "I've missed you so much, Natalie," I whispered, blinking away tears. "I'm really sorry."

"Enough with the sorry shit. You're forgiven, but I reserve the right to punch you in the arm a few times just for the hell of it."

"Deal."

"And at the risk of sounding super corny, let me add that no man will ever come between us, Violet Lynn Parker. Not after all we've been through over the last three decades."

"I love you, Nat."

Her smile widened. "All right, that's enough of this soap opera shit. Now, are you and Doc still …" she let it trail off.

I grimaced, not wanting to hurt her, but there'd be no more hiding Doc from her, from anyone … well, except for Tiffany, at least until Cornelius owned that damned hotel. I didn't want any jealousy about my sleeping with her ex-boyfriend to screw up the sale. "Yes," I told Natalie. "We're still together."

Her lips pursed. "You haven't pushed him away yet. Interesting."

Natalie knew my history with men and my tendency to slam on the brakes as soon as I passed the third date mark. Maybe that was why Doc had lasted so long, we had yet to have a real date.

"Doc doesn't budge very easily."

"I noticed that about him. So, are we talking about a long-term 'wowing' between the sheets for you here or is this the real thing?"

I glanced around to make sure Mona and Jerry weren't behind me before whispering, "I think I've fallen in love with him." Actually, there was no thinking about it. I loved him, and it scared the holy hell out of me.

Her eyebrows lifted. "No shit?"

"No shit."

"That's good. I'm glad things are going well for you in the man department, because I have something to tell you related to another member of the male sex that is going to fuck up your day."

Cooper! My gut clenched. Now what? Was he going to come drag me off to jail again?

"Guess who I just saw up at the Piggly Wiggly?" Natalie asked.

Zeb the zombie? "I don't know, who?"

She held up my other purple boot and let it go. It clunked onto my desktop. "Rex Conner."

I gasped, the wind knocked out of me. I clutched the edge of my desk. "No!"

She pulled out her phone and held it in front of my face, showing me his picture on the screen as proof. "In the stinking, rotten flesh."

My blood boiled at the sight of Addy and Layne's father, still as tall, blond, and handsome as ever. "What's that son of a bitch doing here?"

"I don't know." She snarled down at Rex's picture. "But I'm betting it has something to do with the results of his sperm donation ten years ago."

"God damn it!" I dropped into my chair. "I'm going to end up in jail again."

"You and me both, babe," Natalie said. "After Cooper pries my fingers from around that piece of shit's neck, maybe you and I can share a cell."

THE END ... for now

Speed Dating with Ann Charles

I asked some of my wonderful friends in my Ann Charles' Purple Door Saloon group on Facebook to come up with questions for me to answer in one sentence for the end of this book—speed-dating style.

Will you be going on a book signing tour following the release of this fourth Deadwood book?
I wish, but no; however, I will be in Deadwood in July 2013 for over a week, bugging my friends there, signing books wherever they'll let me, eating frybread and steak until I burst, and trying to soak up as much of the Black Hills as I can.

Is the Historic Homestake Opera House a real place or a fictional building?
Yes, it's a real operating Opera House in Lead with a wealth of wonderful history and architecture—and rumors of ghostly inhabitants.

How much time do you get to spend in the Black Hills/Deadwood doing research and absorbing the atmosphere each year?
Not nearly enough, but I hope to change that in the future and make some of my Black Hills friends really sick and tired of seeing my face.

Are any of the crazy antics in Violet's life taken from your own life (like with her kids)?
Yes—I'm a sponge for all things wacky in the universe, I'm an A-#1 klutz, I'm a parent of adventurous children, and I thrive on laughter (especially at my own follies). Welcome to my world, aka Violet's Deadwood!

Did you always know you wanted to be a writer?
I actually wanted to race camels when I was younger, which seemed really romantic at the time, but now just sounds hot, dusty, and spit-filled.

How many books are planned for the Deadwood series?
I'm a lousy planner, so my answer is: As many as it takes to tell Violet's story.

Why did you want to become a writer?
It was that or a nuclear physicist, and since complex science makes me sleepy, I picked up a pen.

What would be your dream job if you weren't a writer?
A multimillion dollar winning professional lotto player.

Your books make me laugh aloud while reading—do you laugh while writing/creating your books as much as we do while reading them?
What? You're laughing? These are supposed to be dark, serious dramas laced with sadness and melancholy. (Yes, I do laugh, wince, cringe, giggle, steam, and grumble along with Violet and crew; and if I don't, then I need to work harder on the scene because it's too "flat.")

Do you have a real-life Harvey in your life?
I have a few, both young and old, and I love the crusty buggers to pieces for each blush and giggle they inspire. (I also hide out in locker rooms and eavesdrop on old men's conversations with a notepad in hand. Ha! Kidding, of course ... maybe.)

Do you have a sibling that drives you crazy in rage as Violet's sister does?
My brother Chuck, who draws my illustrations and cover art, has been nothing but trouble since he "allowed" my parents to put my crib in his room when he was four years old—I'm still in therapy thanks to him. Ha ha!

Have you ever been thrown in jail for causing trouble?
That depends—are we being recorded and are my parents going to read this?

What is your favorite of all Harvey's hilarious quotes?
Picking just one of Harvey's quotes is as hard as choosing just one dessert from a buffet filled with all of my very favorite sweets—fruit pies, tarts, chocolate-covered everything,

doughnuts galore, ice cream, MoonPies ... yummmm. What was the question again?

How did you get into writing "Psychic Mystery" genre fiction?

It's Violet's fault—I thought we were just going to tell a fun cozy mystery, but she keeps getting her nose into trouble.

How do you stay grounded and so humble after all of the high praise, accolades, fame, and fortune?

Every morning I wake up, stumble into the bathroom, and look in the mirror—enough said.

What is your favorite place to go in the Black Hills (specifically, not just Deadwood)?

Pilot Knob off State Route 385 (on the way to Mount Rushmore)—great viewpoint to sit and look out over the hills for hours where I've recorded lots of funny family memories.

Have you ever seen or "experienced" a ghost?

No, dang it, and I really want to, but I'm a total "dud" like Violet.

Do you still love writing as much now as you did when you started?

I love it even more, because my fingers and brain have become drinking pals and actually get along now when forced to work together (in the past, there was a lot of fighting and name-calling going on, which was very stressful for all of us, especially my shoulders, who were always cinched up from being stuck in the middle).

After developing your basic characters, how do you go about developing their personalities to make them more real?

Wait a second—do you mean to tell me these people aren't real? (I don't have a great answer for this—I just walk up to the character, look them over, and let them start talking, so I'm either a good listener or I have a growing multiple personality disorder.)

What was your inspiration on the first and last names of every character in all of your books?

The answer to this is going to require more than a speed date—I'm going to need you to buy me drinks, appetizers, something grilled and covered in BBQ sauce, and several desserts.

Did you model Cooper on someone you know?

I would tell you, but Cooper just informed me that the answer is "police business," and if I open my big mouth, he'll throw my sorry butt in jail.

About the Author

Ann Charles is an award-winning author who writes romantic mysteries that are splashed with humor and whatever else she feels like throwing into the mix. When she is not dabbling in fiction, arm-wrestling with her children, attempting to seduce her husband, or arguing with her sassy cat, she is daydreaming of lounging poolside at a fancy resort with a blended margarita in one hand and a great book in the other.

Connect with Me Online

Facebook (Personal Page):
http://www.facebook.com/ann.charles.author

Facebook (Author Page):
http://www.facebook.com/pages/Ann-Charles/37302789804?ref=share

Twitter (as Ann W. Charles): http://twitter.com/AnnWCharles

Ann Charles Website:
http://www.anncharles.com

16936774R00232

Printed in Great Britain
by Amazon